THE WORLD'S CLASSICS

A DAY IN THE COUNTRY
AND OTHER STORIES

GUY DE MAUPASSANT was born near Dieppe in 1850 of cultured, middle-class parents. To school, he preferred the holidays which he spent swimming and fishing at Etretat, one of the newly fashionable Channel resorts. He enrolled as a law student in 1869, but the Franco-Prussian War of 1870 ruined the family finances and he was reduced to earning his living as a minor civil servant in Paris. To relieve the boredom and to work off his excess energies, he rowed and swam at Argenteuil and Bezons (favourite haunts too of Impressionist painters), where he enjoyed masculine pursuits and feminine company, sometimes to excess. Flaubert, a childhood friend of his mother, encouraged his literary ambitions and helped shape not only the exactness of his style but also his pessimistic view of life. It was Flaubert who introduced him to Parisian literary life then dominated by the new 'Naturalist' movement led by Zola. The publication in 1880 of *Boule de Suif* in *Les Soirées de Médan*, a collection of stories about the War of 1870, made Maupassant famous. Lionized by fashionable society and courted by newspaper editors, he wrote prolifically and was soon France's best-selling author after Zola. In the decade which followed, he wrote nearly 300 stories, 200 newspaper articles, 6 novels, and 3 travel books. He earned vast sums of money and spent it all—on yachts and houses which symbolized his success, on travel, on his mother, and on his brother Hervé, who died insane in 1889. By this time, his own health was beginning to break down. On New Year's Day 1892, he attempted suicide and was removed to a clinic, suffering from the syphilitic paresis which had driven him mad. He died on July 6 1893, at the age of forty-two.

DAVID COWARD is Senior Lecturer in French at the University of Leeds. He has published numerous articles and studies on the culture and literature of France and reviews regularly for the *Times Literary Supplement*. With Peter Coltman, he has twice won the Educational Television Association's Premier Award and is currently writing a history of French literature. His translation of *La Dame aux Camélias* is also available in the World's Classics.

THE WORLD'S CLASSICS

GUY DE MAUPASSANT

A Day in the Country
and Other Stories

Translated with an Introduction by
DAVID COWARD

Oxford New York
OXFORD UNIVERSITY PRESS

Oxford University Press, Walton Street, Oxford OX2 6DP
Oxford New York Toronto
Delhi Bombay Calcutta Madras Karachi
Petaling Jaya Singapore Hong Kong Tokyo
Nairobi Dar es Salaam Cape Town
Melbourne Auckland

and associated companies in
Berlin Ibadan

Oxford is a trade mark of Oxford University Press

Translation, Introduction, Select Bibliography, Chronology of Maupassant,
Explanatory Notes, Appendix
© David Coward 1990

First published as a World's Classics paperback 1990
Reprinted 1990

British Library Cataloguing in Publication Data

Maupassant, Guy de, 1850–1893
A day in the country and other stories.—(World's
classics)
I. Title
843'.8 [F]

ISBN 0-19-282642-5

Library of Congress Cataloguing in Publication Data

Maupassant, Guy de, 1850–1893
A day in the country and other stories/Guy de Maupassant;
translated with an introduction by David Coward.
p. cm.—(The World's classics)
Bibliography: p.
I. Maupassant, Guy de, 1850–1893—Translations, English.
I. Coward, David.   II. Series.
843'.8—dc20   PQ2349.A4E5 1990   89-34216

ISBN 0-19-282642-5

Printed in Great Britain by
BPCC Hazell Books Ltd
Aylesbury, Bucks

CONTENTS

INTRODUCTION

Guy de Maupassant is one of the world's great storytellers. Curiously enough, this is not as grand a claim as might appear, for the short story, while admitted to be extremely difficult to manage successfully, has long been regarded as somehow second-rate, not least because it is generally felt to suffer from Cleverness. Perhaps it requires too much control, so that the reader feels manipulated, and because many short stories depend so much on irony or sudden reversals, they may seem over-contrived—like a joke which, once told, loses its tension. The artistically successful novel sweeps the reader up into a world which is recognizable and convincing, comes alive and spreads its tentacles the further we read. But the short story simply invites us to peer into a ready-made world where actions seem to be determined less by the organic evolution of character and situation than by the author's eagerness to show us to the exit as quickly as possible. Perhaps the major defect of the short story is that it is short. It is a song rather than a symphony.

Maupassant's standing has always been injured by considerations of this sort. During his lifetime he was the most popular author in France after Zola. Yet by the Great War his star had waned, weakened by the dwindling vogue for the short story and the brighter light shed by Freud, the introspective, self-analytical mood spread by Proust, and a host of compulsive practitioners of the novel which was already turning into the major form of literary expression of the twentieth century. Neither did he adopt a high profile in the aesthetic arguments of his day, nor did he express a cogent philosophy, and both omissions have harmed his name amongst the French who not only treasure all forms of abstraction, but indeed insist upon it in their great men. Furthermore Maupassant liked money and first published his work not in dignified books, but in newspapers and not always reputable magazines. There was, too, the difficulty that the variety of his subject matter created several

Maupassants in the public mind. His comic, often ribald tales of country life placed him within the long but not very honourable tradition of French bawdy. The stories set in high society maintained his reputation as a somewhat old-fashioned libertine, while those dealing with Ministry drudges cast him as the not very sympathetic observer of inadequate people, and not as funny at it as Courteline. There was also the disreputable Maupassant who wrote about prostitutes, and the Maupassant who painted a curious picture of the Franco-Prussian War when, he seems to imply, the only serious resistance was put up by a handful of tarts such as Irma, the heroine of *Bed 29*, and grim old peasants such as Old Milon. Finally, there was the Maupassant who made the skin creep with horror stories which, well done though they might be, appealed to the sensations rather than to the mind. Much more highly regarded in Great Britain and the United States than in his native land, Maupassant has nevertheless never quite gone out of fashion in France where, however, his literary reputation is still very much a matter for discussion.

Yet even if account is taken of the limitations of the short story as a form, no one should seriously doubt that Maupassant was far more than a literary blacksmith but a very considerable writer indeed. His command of form was unerring and his style spans the whole range of expression from the crude and brawny to the subtle and poetic. A few words are enough to sketch a character, and a few sensual lines or a brightly visual image suffice to establish an atmosphere: if Balzac spent words like a sailor, Maupassant measures them with the exactness and economy of a chemist filling a prescription. Moreover, there emerges from his work a single, consistent vision of the human condition which is as honest as it is lucid. Not much more could be asked of an art that is perfect.

He was born in 1850 at Fécamp in the Normandy which served as a setting for many of his stories. He remained very close to his mother, a cultured, well-read woman, who was, however, unpredictable and demanding and an instance of the *grande hystérique*, a type well known to contemporary medicine. Maupassant was educated at a variety of schools where he made a name for himself as an intelligent but wayward pupil given to practical jokes. His parents separated in 1863, and for most of his life he regarded his father as a spendthrift and womanizer who had betrayed his wife. He looked forward to the holidays which he spent with his mother at the newly fashionable Normandy resort of Etretat where he boated and swam. During the summer of 1868 he rescued a drowning man who turned out to be Swinburne, who invited him to lunch (which consisted of roast monkey) and allowed him to look through his collection of drawings and macabre objects. Maupassant was particularly struck by a wizened, severed human hand which he later bought and used as a paperweight.

That autumn he was sent to the Lycée Corneille in Rouen to complete his studies. He had already met Flaubert, a childhood friend of his mother, and now he became close to Louis Bouilhet, the city librarian and an intimate of Flaubert, who read his first poetic effusions and discussed literature with him until July 1869 when he died suddenly. A few weeks later, Maupassant was awarded his *baccalauréat* ('*mention passable*') and on the strength of it he enrolled as a law student in Paris in 1869.

He loved being a student but was less enthusiastic about his studies which were interrupted in July 1870 when France declared war on Germany. Little knowing that the war was to end within months in a humiliating defeat for the French, he was mobilized and sent to Le Havre where he served as a stores clerk. His regiment was forced to retreat to Paris before the Prussian advance and, though he did not see action, he was nearly captured. Like many of his contemporaries he felt the humiliation of defeat bitterly, and blamed the weakness of the French command and the complacency of the middle classes; the arrogance and cruelty of the Prussian invaders appalled him and his war-stories give an honourable place to the plucky patriotism of the lower classes who alone resisted the enemy.

The war ruined the Maupassants' tobacco business and

along with it the family fortunes and Guy's studies. Between 1872 and 1880 Maupassant was himself one of those low-grade civil servants who figure so pathetically in stories such as *Strolling* or *Family Life*. He found the work stultifying and badly paid, and was frequently very miserable. However, there were compensations. He returned to see his mother at Etretat whenever he could and spent Sundays rowing on the river around Argenteuil and Bezons where he drank too much and chased girls (and very probably caught the syphilis which was eventually to kill him). He enjoyed raucous male company and physical exertion and, like the narrator of *Out on the River*, later regarded those times as the happiest of his life.

Each day he worked, none too diligently, until six, and then spent the evening writing. Bouilhet's influence remained strong and directed him to poetry, though he also tried his hand at plays. But by 1873 he was thinking of writing a series of river sketches in the manner of Alphonse Daudet, and it was probably these that he showed to Flaubert to whom, from 1874, he grew increasingly close. From Flaubert, who was a hard man to please, he learned the virtues of a simple, exact style and the lesson of self-effacement. Maupassant always tried to avoid what he regarded as the romantic elements in Flaubert's work, but he shared his belief in the greatness of Art and his general pessimism and cynical view of life.

In 1875 he published his first story—a tale of horror which featured a withered hand—and managed to sell a few poems. But it was through Flaubert that he was drawn into the literary life of Paris where, by 1877, he was associating too with the new Naturalists, led by Zola. And it was under Zola's banner that *Boule de Suif* was published in 1880 in a collection of tales devoted to the Franco-Prussian War. More than the public acclaim which followed, Maupassant valued the praise lavished on his contribution by Flaubert who, dying suddenly in May 1880, did not live to see his protégé's phenomenal success.

Approached by newspaper editors eager to use his new fame to boost their circulation, Maupassant now began turning out large numbers of articles and stories. His choice of subject and treatment varied according to the newspaper or magazine which paid him. For *Gil Blas*, which was frivolous and 'Parisian', he wrote broad farces and stories about sex. Tales for *Le Gaulois* needed to be more sober in form and psychology. His articles dealt with literary, social, and occasionally political subjects (he was a strong opponent of France's colonial policies), but were written quickly and were rarely deeply researched. As a journalist, he was an acute social observer with a jaundiced eye for the vulgarity of his age, but he was also very professional. An anecdote used to lighten a serious article might be developed and offered to another newspaper as a story which, from 1881 onwards, would subsequently appear in volume form. In this way Maupassant ensured that he derived the maximum financial return for his considerable labours.

For he liked money for the freedom and status it gave him. He acquired a succession of boats which symbolized his success, and bought houses on the Normandy coast and on the Rivieria where he lived in style. He travelled to North Africa and Italy to collect material for commissioned newspaper articles. But his constant movement was not dictated solely by professional commitments or even by the need to escape the social and literary life of Paris. From his late 20s onwards he experienced a variety of distressing ailments, including ferocious migraines, digestive disorders, and eye problems. To relieve the symptoms he travelled, but he also resorted increasingly to the use of drugs, some prescribed and others less orthodox and addictive, such as laudanum and ether. He also became interested in the work done by Charcot at the La Salpêtrière hospital in Paris on patients suffering from mental illness. Though a physical and robust man, Maupassant had always had a fascination for the macabre and for hallucinatory states which went somewhat beyond the curiosity of a writer, for as time passed he felt less and less in control of himself.

With literary success came an introduction to high society. Detaching himself from the Zola circle, he was lionized by the financial world of the Faubourg Saint-

Honoré rather than by the aristocratic circles of Saint Germain-des-Prés. Courted by the rich and famous, he continued to exploit his attractiveness to women, remaining, in his private life, eternally and, towards the end of the 1880s, almost pathologically discreet. Admired by women, he was also envied and resented for his success. Frank Harris, who knew everybody, wrote:

His appearance did not suggest talent: he was hardly middle height but markedly strong and handsome; the forehead square and rather high; the nose well cut and almost Grecian; the chin firm without being hard; the eyes well-set and in colour a greyish-blue; his hair and thick moustache were very dark and he wore besides a little spot of hair on his underlip. His manners were excellent, but at first he seemed reserved and unwilling to talk about himself or his achievements . . .

At one time he told me he was a Norman and had a love of sea-faring; at another he confessed that his family came from Lorraine and his name was evidently derived from *mauvais passant*. Now and then he would say that he only wrote books to get money to go yachting, and almost in the same breath he would tell how Flaubert corrected his first poems and stories and really taught him how to write, though manifestly he owed little to any teaching. Towards the end [of his life] he had been so courted by princes that he took on a tincture of snobbism, and, it is said, wore the crown of a marquis inside his hat, though he had no shadow of a right to it, or indeed to the noble *de* which he always used. But at bottom, like most Frenchmen, he cared little for titles and constantly preached the nobility and necessity of work and of the daily task; in fact, he admired only the aristocracy of genius and the achievements of artists and men of science. (*My Life and Loves*, vol. ii, ch. 20)

Applying himself to 'the daily task' between 1880 and 1891, he wrote about 300 short stories, 200 articles, six novels, two plays, and three travel books. His facility was alarming. In 1882, for example, in addition to forty-three substantial newspaper articles and work on his first novel, *Une Vie*, he published two or three tales each month until September and then wrote seven in October, eight in November, and another seven in December. In December 1891 he estimated his total sales in ten years at 373,000 copies, though if newspaper and magazine publication is borne in mind, his readership was even greater than this implies. He was outsold only by the phenomenally success-ful Zola. He realized that he was turning into a 'whole-saler of words', yet the quality of his work rarely suffered from the tremendous pace which he had set himself.

He drove himself hard because, like all artists, he was an obsessive. But he had grown accustomed to an expensive lifestyle and, furthermore, he accepted financial respons-ibility for his mother and for his younger brother Hervé, an unstable and unemployable failure whom he had set up as a horticulturalist near Antibes. By 1889, having become a danger to himself and others, Hervé was admitted to an asylum near Lyons where he died, 'absolutely mad, without a glimmer of reason', in November of that year.

Friends who met Maupassant at this time said he was 'lean', 'fit', 'cheerful', and 'talkative'. But all was far from well. As early as 1885, according to his manservant, he suffered strange memory lapses and persistent eye troubles which sometimes prevented him from working, and he began seeing his 'double' sitting at his desk. To quieten his symptoms, he hunted and sailed and travelled. In August 1886 he came to England. After a quick tour of Oxford, he returned to London where he lingered over the macabre exhibits at Madame Tussaud's, met Henry James, and quickly fled the rain and cold of an English summer.

By 1887 he was writing fewer short stories, partly because newspaper editors were finding difficulty paying the large fees he now commanded but mainly because he hoped to be taken seriously as a novelist. His best novel, *Pierre et Jean* (1888), a brooding 'psychological' study, was prefaced by an essay on the novel (Henry James thought the novel 'faultless' but the literary musings 'slightly common') in which he defined his approach to writing as a search for truth expressed as precisely and as self-effacingly as Flaubert had taught. But self-effacement was not merely an artistic objective; it was the principle by which he now organized his life. He refused to respond to even the most anodyne requests for information about himself and guarded his private life jealously. When, in 1890, the publisher

Charpentier used a group etching of the authors for a new edition of the collective *Soirées de Médan*, he protested furiously: 'Does anyone have any right to draw, exhibit, and sell a man's portrait without his knowledge and against his wishes?' His long-standing interest in 'doubles' and 'reflected images' (which runs from his second published story, *Le Docteur Héraclius Gloss*, to *Le Horla* and beyond) was spilling over into reality.

The desire for privacy and his dislike of personal publicity were, of course, quite reasonable. But his growing irritability, expressed in a taste for litigation (he sued noisy neighbours, for instance), boded ill for the future. In November 1890 he attended the unveiling of a monument to Flaubert in Rouen. Those who knew him were struck by his altered appearance. Daudet noticed his agate eyes which 'took light in but let none out', while Hérédia recalled that Maupassant spoke openly of melancholia, of his memory lapses and periods of temporary blindness which might last up to an hour. In March 1891 Dr Déjérine, the fourteenth doctor he had consulted since 1889, diagnosed neurasthenia and recommended rest, exercise, and cold baths. But he continued to work and his behaviour became erratic. He grew reclusive and secretive and by December 1891 was living in terror. He saw a ghost; he believed a fish bone had lodged in his lungs; he was convinced that his brain was being dissolved by salt. On the night of 1 January 1892 he cut his own throat but was discovered and removed to the Paris clinic of Dr Blanche at Passy. There he suffered the final stage of paresis (progressive paralysis) which was syphilitic in origin. He heard messages from Flaubert and Hervé. He believed that the morphine administered to him made holes in his brain and that his urine was made of diamonds. Goncourt, who visited him, concluded that he had ceased to be human and had become an animal. He lived on in this state for eighteen months before dying on 6 July 1893, a month before his 43rd birthday.

Maupassant's appalling end was a complete and horribly ironic vindication of his deeply pessimistic view of human existence. He never claimed to have a systematic philosophy. He drew on the rationalism of the Enlightenment and the scientific positivism of his own age, but he warmed only to ideas which were consistent with his temperament. His conclusions amounted to an anarchic brand of defiant conservatism. As George Hainsworth put it, his ideas 'recalled Flaubert on "l'éternel néant de tout" and the vanity of action, Schopenhauer on life as a battle-ground and a place of torment, Darwin and the scientists on a mechanistic universe dominated by the play of blind forces'. He found no evidence to support belief in the existence of a good and merciful God, and viewed the world as an environment designed for the efficient but relentless per-petuation of life. Man is no more than a function of forces operating on a cosmic scale, and human thought is a chemical or electrical process enabling us to live, eat, and reproduce. Maupassant admired the generous and creative impulses of the human spirit, but saw that spirit everywhere defeated by baser instincts. Clothes, dentistry, books, cities, and ideas, all the paraphernalia of civilized living, may cushion and even temporarily suspend the awareness of the slavery of appetite, but can never disguise the fact that nature calls us to order. Human beings are animals and the Ideal is constantly at the mercy of the beast that crouches in all of us. We are rats forced to perform in some vast and ignoble experiment.

Of course, nature decks our chains with flowers, and Maupassant never lost his lyrical appreciation of the beauty of the countryside. But moonlight on water or the rustle of spring are no more than the bait which nature uses to enfold us in her coils. Just as the fragrances of flowers attract pollinating insects, so the lazy heat of noon makes Rose, the farm girl, ready for love, and the nightingale conspires against Henriette in *A Day in the Country*. The knowledge that love is not the best part of us but the most insidious of nature's snares led Maupassant to despair. When he looked back to his carefree rowing days, he saw them for what they were: participation in a compulsory ritual which denies free-will and turns us into the pre-programmed playthings of universal drives. All the things which commonly pass for the charm of life—love, friendship, happiness—are so many illusions which nature allows us to compensate for the iron grip in which we are held. And in this infernal merry-go-round, women are the most pernicious of nature's weapons: they are temptresses, the vessels of the eternal cycle of reproduction, the enemy of male energy and creativity. Lord Chesterfield remarked that 'women are but children of a larger growth': Maupassant would have regarded such a view as absurdly liberal and indulgent.

Sometimes acceptance of the plenitude and beauty of nature blocked his despair. He was also prepared to concede that the man of independent judgement who keeps an open mind and sees life for what it is may rise above the forces which control his destiny. The philosopher, the scientist, and the artist create truths which defeat time and rob nature of her secrets. Yet he found little to comfort him. Man is not merely the victim of nature but her instrument, for in our misery we make others miserable. Human beings are rapacious, egotistical, demanding, cruel, and unfeeling, and Maupassant saw in them neither good nor the potential for good. And if man is spiritually vile, he is also physically repulsive, a temporary agglomeration of meat and juices which will rot and leave nothing behind. We are born in the bloody entrails of our mothers and we end in a mess of putrefaction.

If men are disgusting and women nauseating, society can be nothing but sham, betrayal, and exploitation. Maupassant had an idealistic sense of justice, but he viewed politics with distaste. The introduction of universal male suffrage had given France the corrupt, pompous, and stupid leaders she so richly deserved: 'Once upon a time, a man who could do nothing became a photographer; nowadays he becomes a member of parliament.' The public was a mindless herd which did what it was told, and democracy promised nothing less than the rule of vulgarity. Popular education, for instance, had merely released popular stupidity and enabled even larger numbers of imbeciles to say half-baked things. He regarded the Eiffel Tower as an appropriately tasteless monument to 'egalitarian' cant and nationalistic humbug: patriotism, he said, was 'the egg of war'. Society was run by bombastic and incompetent shams who attempted the ludicrous task of directing the collective destiny and thwarted the men of talent and vision at every turn. Like Voltaire's, Maupassant's preference was for enlightened despotism and a society of intelligent and civilized men which he called the 'intellectual aristocracy'.

Though he felt his disgust with the world deeply, it was a considered attitude which was normally overlaid by simpler, warmer, more spontaneous reactions. He had a highly developed comic appreciation of human conduct and laughed readily, if rather cruelly, at the flies struggling in the unavoidable spider's web. But he also showed fellow-feeling, and sometimes genuine compassion, for those who were the victims of fate, society, or other people: Mademoiselle Pearl or the *curé* of *The Christening* are presented delicately and with genuine sympathy and under-standing. And though he put patriotism high on the list of the causes of war, he clearly admired the patriotism of Old Milon and the courage of Irma who accounted for more Prussians than the fine Captain Epivent. He might despise the common herd, but he was not without compassion for the weak, or for women, such as Clochette who sacrifices herself for love, or Rosalie Prudent who kills her babies because she is too poor to keep them. If Maupassant never alienated the large popular audience which he professed to despise, it was because his savage irony reduced readers of all kinds to a sense of helplessness as they ponder such intensely real glimpses of life's wretchedness.

Yet this gap between the bleak mood of his fatalism and the spontaneous warmth of many of his reactions reveals a dualism in Maupassant's character which he forced himself to explore. If most of nature's drives were clear to see, not all were exposed to the light of day, and those which remained hidden filled him not with disgust but with fear and horror. He had a natural fascination with the macabre, as instanced in his reaction to the Swinburne hand, but even in his earliest stories he shows a strange tension between our conscious desires and dark, mysterious, irresistible forces inside us. If the narrator of *Out on the River* overrides his baser self, 'Beau Signoles', who wants to fight his duel in *A Coward*, is prevented from doing so by a power stronger than his will. In *Le Horla* this inner force not only gains the upper hand but emerges as a superior being having a separate existence. The psychological motivation behind such stories (to which *The Little Roque Girl* may be added) belongs less to the field of observation and behaviour than to the exploration of those neuroses which nascent psychoanalytical science was beginning to explore. In this sense, *Le Horla* may be set alongside Stevenson's *The Strange Case of Dr Jekyll and Mr Hyde* (1886), its almost exact contemporary, which anticipated the notion of the 'split personality'. But the intensity with which Maupassant handles such ideas separates him from Stevenson and other writers of horror stories who merely seek to thrill with the sensational and the supernatural. Maupassant communicates a sense of danger made more horrible by the fact that the threat comes from the darker side of the character's own personality, so that he feels that in some obscure but increasingly real and terrifying way he is himself what he fears most. When a man ceases to know who he is and loses confidence in his own will, he becomes mad. Maupassant's finest stories do not merely thrill: they disturb. Other short-story writers might control their material better: few convey the sense of menace and horror more completely.

In a sense, Maupassant's general handling of human psychology derives less from observation of habit and gesture and eccentric motivation than from his feeling that all actions are Pavlovian reactions to natural stimuli. He does not explain why Madame Oreille in *The Umbrella* is careful with money; he simply shows us how she acts. But the fact that he usually deals with obsessive characters hoist on their own compulsions does not mean that his understanding of psychology is superficial. On the contrary, the fact that his characters are eternally at the mercy of circumstances or of their own temperaments is precisely what creates the powerful sense of inevitability which hovers over his tales. The form of the short story, with its sudden illuminations and ironic twists, tends to stress the inescapable predicament, and there is little doubt that Maupassant was attracted to it for this reason. His stories vary considerably in length; some are strongly plotted and others, such as *Strolling*, hardly plotted at all; and the mood runs from the brooding of the horror tales to private tragedy or broad farce, as in *Our Spot*, and satire, as in *A Coup d'État*, via comic dramas such as *Family Life* or *Riding Out* which, though they amuse, usually involve a death or a humiliation and regularly leave us feeling not so much entertained as distinctly ill at ease. For even when he is in playful mood, Maupassant seems to relish making us feel uncomfortable. He rarely points up moral lessons but walks away from the end of a story leaving us to decide whether Madame Loisel, in *The Necklace*, is the victim of fate or of her own pride. He treats honesty and courage with sympathy, but always shows honesty abused and courage defeated. Occasionally he allows a happy ending, but not before Simon or Rose, the farm-girl, have suffered long and hard. They are the fortunate ones, for his stories are so many chronicles of missed opportunities and broken lives engineered by the inhumanity of man and the ruthless demands of nature, which, like some poisonous flower, fills Maupassant's world with treacherous poetry.

His answer to the nastiness of life was thus to show it at work and reveal its absurdity. But the remedy ran the risk of being no more comforting than the ill it sought to cure. For Maupassant goes beyond laughter into acid cynicism and even sadism. When he was a boy he was known as a practical joker. Even at the height of his fame he was fond of releasing mice in the presence of ladies, whom he would scare by describing the swollen corpses of suicides regularly fished out of the river by the police. In a sense, his aim as a story-teller was to put spiders down the neck of his reader, to make us jump, to teach us a lesson, to jolt us out of our complacency. Locked in the grim, bleak, gloomy world of his pessimism, he sought to spread the truth as he saw it: life is not just an empty farce but an extremely bad joke. Maupassant's perfect stories are the celebration of a fine contempt.

SELECT BIBLIOGRAPHY

There are a number of complete collections of Maupassant's tales, but the most comprehensive and the most fully annotated is Louis Forestier's edition of the *Contes et nouvelles* (Bibliothèque de la Pléiade, Gallimard, 1974, 2 vols.).

Among the French critics, Pierre Cogny's *Maupassant, l'homme sans dieu* (Brussels, 1968) is probably still the most balanced and accessible general introduction to his ideas and manner.

Critical biographies in English by Francis Steegmuller (*Maupassant: a Lion in the Path*, New York, 1949; reprinted London, Collins, 1950, and Macmillan, 1972), Paul Ignotus (*The Paradox of Maupassant*, University of London Press, 1967), and Michael Lerner (*Maupassant*, Allen and Unwin, 1975) are all helpful.

The most useful critical studies of the stories are Edward Sullivan's *Maupassant: the short stories* (Arnold, 1972, Studies in French Literature, 7) and Albert H. Wallace's *Maupassant* (Twayne, New York, 1974). On Maupassant's style, George Hainsworth's 'Pattern and Symbol: style in the work of Maupassant' (in *French Studies*, 1951, pp. 1–17) is invaluable. On the vexed issue of Maupassant's patriotism and attitude to war, see Rachel Killick's excellent 'Mock heroics? Narrative strategy in a Maupassant War Story' (in *Modern Language Review*, April 1987, pp. 313–26).

For Maupassant's place in the history of the short story, the following may be consulted with profit: Sean O'Faolin, *The Short Story* (London, 1948); Ian Reid, *The Short Story* (Methuen, 1977, The Critical Idiom, 37); Valerie Shaw, *The Short Story: a critical introduction* (Longman, 1983).

A CHRONOLOGY OF
GUY DE MAUPASSANT

1850   5 August: Birth of Guy de Maupassant, probably at Fécamp. His mother, Laure de Poittevin, a childhood friend of Flaubert, was cultured but highly-strung. His father's family, vaguely ennobled in the eighteenth century, hailed from Lorraine. Gustave de Maupassant was worldly and lazy, and Guy later held him largely responsible for the failure of his parents' marriage.

1856   Birth of Hervé de Maupassant.

1859–60   Maupassant lives with his father in Paris where he attends the Lycée Impérial Napoléon.

1863   Separation of Gustave and Laure formalized. Guy and Hervé live at Etretat with Laure.

1863–7   Maupassant attends a Catholic boarding-school at Yvetot. His teachers consider him able and industrious but finally expel him for indiscipline and for writing 'obscene' verses.

1867   Laure moves to Rouen and sends both her sons to the Institution Leroy-Petit.

1868   Summer: The English poet Swinburne gets into difficulties while swimming at Etretat. Maupassant rescues him and is twice invited to lunch at the 'Chateau Dolmancé', where he is lastingly impressed by the macabre and 'perverse' preoccupations of the Sadean Swinburne.
Autumn: Becomes a boarder at the Lycée Corneille at Rouen. Meets Louis Bouilhet (b. 1821), the city's librarian and friend of Flaubert, who encourages his literary ambitions.

1869   18 July: Death of Bouilhet.
27 July: Maupassant passes his *baccalauréat* examinations (*'mention passable'*).
October: Enrols as a law student in Paris, where he lives with his father.

1870   15 July: France declares war on Germany. Maupassant is mobilized and sent to Le Havre where he serves as a quartermasters' clerk.

1870   1 September: Fall of Sedan.
        27 October: Surrender at Metz.
        December: Prussian forces occupy Normandy and Mau-
        passant retreats with his regiment to Paris, narrowly
        escaping capture.

1871   18 January: Maupassant is stationed at Rouen when the
        Armistice is signed and sees nothing of the siege of Paris
        (March) or the Commune (May).
        November: Demobilized. War having ruined the family
        business, he is unable to continue his studies.

1872   20 March: Becomes an unsalaried minor civil servant. He
        has no money and complains of loneliness.

1873   1 February: Secures a permanent appointment at 1,600
        francs a year at the Admiralty, where he remains until
        1878, when he transfers to the Ministry of Education. In
        the summer of 1880, he is granted successive periods of
        leave until 11 January 1882, when, confident at last of
        being able to live by his pen, he ceases to be a
        government employee.
        To relieve the boredom of his life, he spends weekends
        boating and chasing girls, and continues writing poems,
        plays, and prose, but without success.

1874   Begins a lasting friendship with Flaubert, his friend and
        literary mentor.

1875   Publication of La Main d'écorché, his first published
        short story.

1876   Becomes part of the new 'Naturalist' coterie headed by
        Zola.

1877   August: Leave of absence granted by the Ministry
        for a health visit to Switzerland. Though fit and robust,
        he is bothered by eye trouble, stomach-pains, and
        headaches.

1878   Though he manages to sell a few poems and stories,
        Maupassant's literary ambitions are far from realized.

1879   19 February: Histoire du vieux temps, a verse comedy,
        performed in Paris. It is well received by the critics.

1880   14 February: Maupassant accused of publishing an
        obscene poem. Flaubert writes a letter in his defence.
        16 April: Publication of Les Soirées de Médan, a collection
        of stories about the Franco-Prussian War, by 'Zola's

young men'. Maupassant's contribution, *Boule de Suif*, is admired by Flaubert and hailed as a masterpiece.

8 May: Death of Flaubert.

Summer: Maupassant begins writing articles and stories for newspapers. He resorts to ether, first as a pain-killer, and later experiments with its hallucinatory effects.

1881   Divides his time between Paris, Normandy, the Midi. He begins his travels—to North Africa and Italy—to research commissioned newspaper articles. Publication of *La Maison Tellier*, the first of some thirty collections of stories.

1882   Begins to be lionized by high society and embarks on a number of discreet love affairs.

1883   January–February: Maupassant buys *La Louisette*, a small yacht, the first of a number of boats which symbolize his success.

25 February–6 April: serialization of *Une Vie*, the first of his six novels, which brings him international recognition.

19 March: Dr Landholt relates Maupassant's symptoms to syphilis.

1884   Shares his time between Cannes, Etretat, and Paris. Publication of *Sur l'eau*, the first of his three travel books.

1885   6 April–30 May: *Bel-Ami*, one of his most popular novels, serialized in *Gil Blas*.

Takes an increasingly personal interest in mental illnesses, as exemplified by the work of the neurologist Charcot. Maupassant's valet, Tassart, becomes aware of his master's occasionally disturbed states.

1886   19 January: Marriage of Hervé who is set up by Guy as a horticulturalist at Antibes.

August: Brief visit to England where Maupassant meets Henry James.

1887   Summer: Maupassant writes to *Le Temps* protesting at proposals to construct Eiffel's planned tower which he regards as a triumph of modern vulgarity.

Autumn: Having broken with *Le Gaulois* in 1885, Maupassant severs his connection with *Gil Blas*, which can no longer afford to pay the rates he now commands. His income rises from 40,000 francs in 1885 to 120,000 by 1888.

1888   July: Is treated for his worsening physical and mental symptoms at Aix-les-Bains.
        October–March: Further travels to North Africa.

1889   August: Hervé's behaviour becomes erratic and he enters an asylum. His condition continues to deteriorate into madness.
        13 November: Death of Hervé.
        December: Maupassant threatens noisy neighbours with legal action.

1890   30 May: Maupassant quarrels with his publisher over the use of his portrait for advertising purposes.
        23 November: Inauguration of a monument to Flaubert at Rouen. Although he looks well, his friends are privately shocked at his condition.

1891   4 March: First performance of *Musotte* after a difficult period of rehearsal during which Maupassant upsets the director and the actors.
        Summer: Still working hard against medical advice, he embarks on health cures in the South of France. His condition worsens.

1892   1–2 January: Maupassant unsuccessfully attempts suicide and is transferred to the clinic of Dr Blanche at Passy, where he is diagnosed as suffering from syphilitic paresis. There is no medical record of his decline.

1893   6 July: Death of Maupassant, a month before his forty-third birthday.
        8 July: Zola delivers the oration at his funeral.

1897   24 October: Unveiling of a bust of Maupassant in the Parc Monceau in Paris.

1900   June: Monument to Maupassant erected at Rouen.

A Day in the Country
and Other Stories

Out on the River

LAST summer I rented a small country house on the banks of the Seine several leagues downstream from Paris and each evening I travelled down to spend the night there. A few days after settling in, I got to know one of my neighbours who was maybe 30 or 40 and far and away the oddest man I ever clapped eyes on. He was not just a practised hand with boats, he was mad about them, and was always near the water or on it or in it. He must have been born in a boat and he'll die in a boat.

One evening as we were strolling quietly along the banks of the Seine, I asked this chap to tell me some tales of his nautical life. He perked up at once, a change came over him, and he started talking fifteen to the dozen, waxing almost lyrical. He had one great passion in him, an all-consuming irresistible passion: the river.*

Oh yes! (he said) I've a good few memories of that old river you see rolling along there. People like you from city streets have no conception of what the river's like. But just listen to the way a fisherman says the word. For him, a river is something mysterious, deep, and unknown, a place of mirages and ghostly visions where some nights you see things that don't exist, hear sounds you've never heard before, and you shake in your boots as though you were walking through a cemetery. Come to that, a river is the most sinister cemetery there is: a graveyard where the dead don't have graves.

To a fisherman, dry land is confined and circumscribed, but on dark moonless nights the river has no limits. Sailors don't feel the same way about the sea. True enough, the sea can often be merciless and full of spite, but it shrieks and howls and at least the open sea plays fair. But a river is silent and treacherous. It never roars and thunders but just slips quietly on its way, and that never-ending flow of water gliding smoothly along is to me more frightening than any mountainous ocean waves.

People with too much imagination say that the depths of the sea hide vast blue lands where drowned men roam among great fish through strange forests and caves of crystal. The river bottom is just black and full of mud where bodies rot. Yet it can be beautiful when it shines at daybreak and laps quietly at its murmuring reedy banks.

Talking of the ocean, a poet* once said:

> The foaming waves play host to sombre tales;
> O Angry billows, feared by mothers who pray,
> You tell those tales with each tide rise
> And this no less explains those awful cries
> Which roar as beaching rollers surge at end of day.

Well, I believe that stories whispered by quiet-voiced slender reeds are even more sinister than the sombre tales told by the waves' roar.

But since you've asked to hear some of the things I remember, I'll tell you about something odd that happened to me here about ten years ago.

In those days, I had a room—as I still do—in Madame Lafon's house, and one of my best friends, Louis Bernet, who, now he's a member of the Privy Council, has given up boating and all the spit and polish and larking about that go with it, had found somewhere to stay in the village of C . . . a couple of leagues downstream. We used to have dinner together every day, sometimes at his place, sometimes at mine.

One evening, I was going home alone, feeling pretty tired, having a hard time making headway in my big boat, a sea-going twelve-footer with a drop-keel which I always took out at night. I stopped for a moment to get my wind back just off that spit of reeds over there, a couple of hundred metres below the railway bridge. It was a marvellous night. The moon was bright, the river gleamed, and the air was still and warm. It was so peaceful that I was tempted. I said to myself that nothing could be finer than to smoke a pipe in such a spot. The thought was father to the deed. I got my anchor and dropped it overboard.

With the pull of the current, the boat went the length of the mooring chain and then stopped. I made myself as comfortable as I could on my sheepskin coat in the stern. It was quiet, dead quiet, except that now and then I seemed to catch a faint, almost inaudible sound of water lapping the bank, and I saw the tallest clumps of reeds turn into startling shapes which at times appeared to sway and wave.

The river was utterly peaceful but I felt apprehensive sitting there surrounded by the extraordinary silence. All the marshy creatures, the frogs and toads which sing at night, were hushed. Then, just to my right, a frog croaked. I jumped. It stopped. Hearing nothing more, I decided to smoke my pipe to give myself something to do. Now I'm second to none at getting a pipe going, but I'm damned if I could make it draw. With my second puff, I started to feel sick and gave up. I began humming a little tune but couldn't stand the sound of my own voice. So I settled down in the bottom of the boat and watched the sky. I lay there quietly for some time, but after a while the rocking of the boat made me feel uneasy. I had this sensation that it was yawing wildly, swinging into one bank and then the other; then I felt that some invisible hand or unseen force was gently pulling it down to the bottom then heaving it out of the water before letting it down again. I was being tossed about as though I'd been caught in a storm. I heard noises all round me. I sat up in a hurry. The water was shining and everywhere was calm.

I came to the conclusion that my nerves must be a bit on edge and decided to clear off. I pulled on the chain; the boat surged forward but I felt some resistance. I pulled harder but the anchor wouldn't come free. It must have fouled something on the bottom and I just couldn't shift it. I started hauling on it again, but it was no good. Seizing the oars, I turned the boat round and moved upstream to change the position of the anchor. It was still no use: it was good and fast. I lost my temper and shook the chain in a rage. It wouldn't budge. I sat down disconsolately and began reflecting on my position. There was no way I could break the chain or slip it off the boat, for it was heavy and bolted to a block of wood on the prow that was thicker than my arm; but since the weather continued very fine, I imagined it wouldn't be long before I met up with some fisherman or other who would come to the rescue. The whole business had calmed my nerves and now I managed a smoke of my pipe. I had a bottle of rum with me, drank a couple of glasses, and then laughed as I saw that my predicament was really rather funny. It was very warm and if the worst came to the worst I'd be able to spend the night under the stars without coming to much harm.

All at once, something thudded faintly against the side of the boat. I jumped and broke out all over in a cold sweat. The sound had probably been caused by a piece of timber floating down on the current, but it was enough to set my nerves oddly on edge once more. I took hold of the chain and arched my back in a desperate attempt to haul it up. But the anchor held fast. I sat down again, exhausted.

Meanwhile, the river had become wreathed in a very thick, white mist which hung very low over the water so that when I stood up I couldn't see the river or my feet or my boat, and all I could make out were the top of the reeds and, beyond them, the plain stretching away all pale in the moonlight with great black smudges reaching up to the sky here and there where clumps of Italian poplars grew. I was so to speak swathed up to my middle in a cotton sheet of singular whiteness, and I began imagining the most fantastic things. I thought that someone was trying to clamber into the boat which I could no longer see, and that beneath the opaque mist the river teemed with strange creatures swimming round and round me. I was horribly uneasy, my head felt as though it had been clamped in a vice, and my heart beat so fast I thought I'd choke. I got a bit flustered then and considered swimming to the bank, but the very idea made me shake in my shoes. I could see myself getting lost, floundering about in the thick mist, getting entangled in the unavoidable reeds and rushes half-dead with fear, not knowing where the bank was, not being able to find my boat again, and I seemed to sense that there'd be something trying to pull me down to the bottom of the inky water.

Anyway, since I'd have had to swim upstream for at least five hundred metres before finding a spot free of reeds and rushes where I could scramble ashore, I had one chance in ten of navigating my way through the fog and making it without drowning, good swimmer though I was.

I tried to talk some sense into myself. I felt my will was telling me not to be afraid, but there was something else at work other than my will, and that something else was scared. I wondered what I had to be frightened of. My courageous self jeered at my cowardly self and never more clearly than at that moment did I understand the struggle that goes on between the two opposing forces that lie within us, one wanting, the other resisting, with each taking turns to win the battle.

My idiotic, inexplicable fears went on growing until they turned into terror. I stood there absolutely still, eyes staring and ears cocked, waiting. What was I expecting? I had absolutely no idea, but I was certain it would be something horrible. I do believe that if a fish had taken it into its head to jump out of the water, as they often do, it would have been more than enough to make me fall down in a heap unconscious.

Yet in the end, by making a supreme effort, I managed to reclaim most of my wits which were on the point of turning completely. I reached for the rum-bottle again and took a few good swigs.

Then I got an idea and began yelling as loud as I could to all the points of the compass. When my throat finally seized up, I listened. In the distance, a dog barked.

I took another drink and then stretched out full length in the bottom of the boat. I stayed like that for perhaps an hour, maybe two, not sleeping and not closing my eyes and with nightmares zooming all around me. I didn't dare stand up and yet oh! how I longed to! I kept putting it off from one minute to the next. I kept saying: 'On your feet!' but I was too afraid to move a muscle. In the end, taking every care not to make the slightest sound, as though my very life depended on it, I sat up and looked over the side.

I was dazzled by the most marvellous, the most astounding spectacle anybody could ever possibly expect to see. It was the weirdest sight—like something out of a fairy-tale, or one of those wonders that travellers just back from far-off lands prattle on about while you listen and don't really believe.

The mist which had been clinging to the surface of the water two hours before had lifted slowly and collected all along the banks. Leaving the river quite clear, it had formed into an unbroken ridge which stretched along each side to a height of six or seven metres and shone in the moonlight as blindingly brilliant as a snowscape. As a result, all I could see was the river streaked with fire between two white mountains. And high up, above my head, full and looming, a huge shining moon hung in a milky, blue-washed sky.

All the creatures of pond and marsh were now awake. The frogs were making a tremendous row and against it, throbbing away to right and left, I could make out the squat, unvarying, melancholy croaking which the brass-voiced toads blare at the stars. Oddly enough, I wasn't afraid any more. I was sitting right in the middle of such extraordinary scenic splendour that the weirdest things could have happened and left me cold.

How long it lasted I couldn't say, because in the end I dozed off. When I opened my eyes again, the moon had set and the sky was overcast. The water lapped lugubriously, the wind had got up, it was cold and very dark.

I drank what was left of the rum, then sat shivering, listening to the swish of the reeds and the ominous sound of the river. I peered around but could not make out my boat or even my hands, even when I held them up in front of my face.

Gradually, however, the blackness thinned. Suddenly I thought I sensed a shadow gliding just by me. I gave a cry and a voice answered: it was a fisherman. I called him, he rowed across, and I explained what had happened. He pulled alongside and we both heaved on the chain. The anchor would not shift. Day was breaking, grim, grey, rainy, and bitterly cold, the sort of day that brings sorrow and grief. Then I spotted another boat and we hailed it. The man at the oars joined forces with us and only then, little by little, did the anchor give. It came up slowly, very slowly, weighed down by something very heavy. Finally, we made out a black bulky mass which we manhandled into my boat.

It was the body of an old woman. There was a large stone tied around her neck.

Simon's Dad

IT had just finished striking noon. The school doors opened and the children emerged in a rush, jostling and pushing each other to be first out. But instead of dispersing quickly and going home for their dinners as they did every day, they stopped a little way off, formed into groups, and started whispering. For that morning, Simon, the Blanchot woman's boy, was in school for the first time.

They had all heard about the Blanchot woman at home. People were friendly to her face, but when the mothers got together they talked about her with a hint of patronizing scorn which their children had caught without understanding the reasons for it.

They did not know Simon at all as he never went out, nor did he roam the village streets or river banks with them. As a result, they did not like him very much. And it was with a certain glee and considerable amazement that they had greeted and subsequently repeated something which had been said by a lad of 14 or 15 who, judging by the artful way he winked, seemed to know all about it:

'That Simon. . . . He's got no dad.'

At last the Blanchot woman's boy appeared at the school entrance.

He was 7 or 8. He was a little pale, looked shy, awkward even.

He was about to go home to his mother when the groups of his classmates, still whispering and staring at him with the spiteful, cruel eyes of children who are planning some mischief, slowly gathered round him until he was completely surrounded. He stood in their midst, surprised and rather at a loss, not understanding what they were about to do to him. But the lad who had spread the tale, flushed with his previous success, asked him: 'What they call yer?'

He answered: 'Simon.'

'Simon what?' the lad said.

The boy, feeling confused, repeated: 'Simon.'

The lad bawled at him: 'You gotter be called Simon something. . . . Simon by itself isn't a proper name.'

Near to tears, the boy replied a third time: 'My name's Simon.'

The other boys started to laugh. Triumphantly, the bigger lad shouted: 'See! I told you he got no dad.'

The children fell silent. They were struck dumb by this extraordinary, impossible, monstrous thing: a boy without a father. They looked on him as a phenomenon, a being outside nature, and they became aware of a growing sense of the hitherto inexplicable contempt with which their mothers regarded the Blanchot woman.

Simon, who felt his legs might give way at any moment, leaned against a tree for support. He stood there as though crushed by some irreparable disaster. He tried to explain. But he could not think of an answer to the horrible accusation that he had no father. In the end, deathly pale, he shouted words that came into his head: 'I got a dad. I have.'

'Where is he, then?' the lad demanded.

Simon held his tongue; he did not know where. The others laughed excitedly. They were farmers' sons who lived close to the beasts of the field, and they felt the cruel urge which drives farmyard hens to turn on whichever of them is hurt and kill it. Suddenly Simon noticed a small boy who lived near him, a widow's son he was used to seeing going about alone with his mother, just as he himself did.

'You haven't got a dad neither.'

'Oh yes I have,' said the boy.

'Where is he?' asked Simon.

Drawing himself up to his full height, the boy replied proudly: 'Dead. He's in the cemetery.'

A murmur of approval ran through the gang, as though the fact of having a dead father in the cemetery increased one lad's standing and demolished this other boy who did not have a father at all. These horrible children, whose own fathers were mostly vicious men, drunks, thieves, and wife-beaters, jostled and pushed forward as though they, who were born in wedlock, wanted to squeeze the breath out of this boy who was illegitimate and an outsider.

One of them, pressed right up against Simon, poked his tongue out spitefully and chanted: 'You ain't got no fa—ther! You ain't got no fa—ther!'

Simon grabbed him by the hair with both hands and started kicking him on the shins and bit his cheek savagely. There was a tremendous scuffle. The two were eventually pulled apart and Simon, in the middle of the ring formed by cheering boys, was hit, had his clothes torn, and was beaten and kicked to the ground. As he got up, wiping the dust off his little smock with a mechanical gesture of his hand, somebody shouted: 'Go and tell your dad!'

He felt something snap inside; his heart sank. They were stronger than he was, they had thumped him hard and he had no answer to give them. For he sensed that it was true that he had no father. Proudly, he tried for a few seconds to hold back the tears at the back of his throat. Then he choked and did not so much weep as wail in a rush of great, shuddering sobs.

At this, howls of glee rose from the ranks of his enemies and naturally, like savage tribesmen wildly jubilating, they joined hands and started dancing round him chanting: 'You ain't got no fa—ther! You ain't got no fa—ther!'

All at once Simon stopped sobbing. He was overcome by rage. There were stones on the ground at his feet. He picked them up and threw them at his tormentors as hard as he could. He got two or three of them and they ran off bawling. He looked so fearsome that panic spread among the rest. Cowards at heart, as crowds always are when one solitary man stands up to them, they broke up and fled.

Left alone, the little fatherless boy ran off towards the fields. Something he remembered had come back to him and had shaped a great resolve in his mind. He would drown himself in the river.

What he remembered was that, the week before, some poor devil who begged for his bread had thrown himself into the water because he had no money left. Simon had been there when they had fished the body out. The poor man had seemed to him no more pathetic, dirty, and ugly than most. Simon had been struck because he looked so tranquil with his pale cheeks, his long dripping beard, and his staring eyes which looked so peaceful. Around him, people said: 'He's dead.' Someone added: 'He's happy now.' And Simon too wanted to drown himself because he had no father just as the poor man had no money.

He reached the bank and watched the water flowing by. A few darting fish played in the clear current and now and then gave little leaps as they snapped up flies hovering on the surface. As he watched them he stopped crying, for their antics intrigued him greatly. But from time to time, just as lulls in a storm suddenly turn into great gusts of wind which blow branches off trees and race clear away to the horizon, one thought kept coming back to him like a shooting pain: 'I'm going to drown myself because I got no dad.'

It was a grand, very hot day. The mellow sun warmed the grass. The water shone like a mirror. And for minutes on end Simon experienced the bliss and the torpor which follow tears, and he felt an overpowering urge to fall asleep where he was, on the grass, in the heat.

A small green frog hopped over his feet. He tried to catch it but it escaped. He pursued it but missed three times in a row. At last he grabbed it by the very tips of its back legs and laughed to see the antics the creature made to escape. It drew itself back onto its powerful hindquarters and then, like a spring suddenly released, jerked them straight as a pair of stiff rods. And all the while, its eyes perfectly round and ringed with circles of gold, it beat the air with its front legs which waved like hands. It reminded him of those toys made of narrow wooden slats nailed together like tongs which, with a similar action, put little painted soldiers through their drill. This made him think of his home and his mother and, feeling very sad, he started crying again. His arms and legs began to shake. He knelt down and recited his prayers as he always did before he went to sleep. But he could not finish them, for the sobs came so fast, so convulsively that they quite overwhelmed him. They drove every thought from his mind. He stopped noticing his surroundings. He was too busy crying.

Suddenly, a heavy hand was laid on his shoulder and a deep voice asked him: 'What's gone and put you in this state, then, lad?'

Simon turned round. A tall workman with a beard and black curly hair was looking at him with a kindly expression on his face. With tears in his eyes and a catch in his throat, he replied: 'They hit me . . . 'cos . . . I . . . I . . . got . . . no dad.'

'That can't be right,' the man said with a smile, 'everybody's got a dad.'

Convulsed by his distress, the boy laboured on: 'I ain't . . . I ain't got one.'

At this, the workman looked serious. He had recognized the boy: he was the Blanchot woman's. And though he was new to the district, he had some idea of what had happened.

'Never mind, lad,' he said, 'buck up. Come with me and we'll go home to your ma. We'll see about getting you a dad.'

They set off, the big man holding the small boy by the hand. He smiled again, for he was not sorry to have a chance to see this Blanchot creature who was, or so people said, one of the prettiest women roundabout. There was even a thought in the back of his mind, perhaps, that a girl who had made one slip might very well make another.

They reached a small, very neat, white house.

'This is it,' the boy said. And he shouted: 'Mam!'

A woman appeared and the workman suddenly stopped smiling, for he could see at a glance that there would be no fun and games with this tall, pale girl who stood grimly at her door as though intent on preventing any man entering the house where she had already been betrayed by one of his kind. Intimidated, he held his cap in his hand and stammered: 'Hello, missis. I brought your little lad home. He'd got hisself lost down by the river.'

But Simon flung his arms around his mother's neck and, starting to cry again, said: 'No I din't. I wanted to drown myself 'cos the other kids hit me. . . . They hit me . . . 'cos I got no dad!'

The young woman's cheeks turned scarlet and, with a sick feeling in the pit of her stomach, she clutched the boy roughly to her while sudden tears ran down her cheeks. The man, wincing inwardly, looked on, not knowing how to get away. But all at once Simon ran to him and said: 'If you like, you can be my dad.'

There was a dead silence. Not speaking and tormented by shame, the Blanchot woman leaned against the wall with both hands pressed to her heart. When the man said nothing, the boy went on: 'If you don't want to, I'll go back down and drown myself.'

The workman decided to take it all as a joke and said with a laugh: 'All right, then. Righty-oh!'

'What do they call you?' the boy asked, 'so's I can tell the other kids when they want to know what your name is.'

'Philippe,' the man said.

For a moment Simon said nothing, so that he could get the name fixed in his mind, then he held out his arms, much relieved, and cried: 'That's all right, then. You're my dad now, Philippe.'

The workman picked him up, kissed him quickly on both cheeks, and then hurried away as quickly as his legs would carry him.

Next morning, when the boy reached school, he was greeted by spiteful laughter. And when school was over and the other lads wanted to have some more fun with him, Simon flung these words at their heads rather as he might have thrown stones: 'My dad's called Philippe!'

Shouts of glee rose on all sides: 'Philippe who? . . . Philippe what? . . . Philippe's a funny name. . . . Where'd yer find this Philippe, then?'

Simon did not answer them. Unshakeably sure of himself now, he stared them out, prepared to be beaten to a jelly rather than run away. The schoolmaster rescued him and he went home to his mother.

During the next three months, Philippe, the tall workman, often passed near to the Blanchot woman's house and sometimes plucked up enough courage to speak to her if he saw her chatting at her window. She always replied politely, but remained solemn-faced, never exchanged a laugh with him, and never allowed him in. Even so, since he was a shade conceited, as all men are, he imagined that when she spoke to him her cheeks were often pinker than usual.

But a dented reputation is not easily mended and remains so fragile a thing that for all the Blanchot woman's touchy reserve, people roundabout began to talk.

Simon had become very fond of his new father and went for walks with him almost every evening when the day's work was finished. He attended school assiduously and strode through the ranks of the other children with his head high, never answering them back.

But one day, the lad who had been the first to persecute him said: 'You're a liar! You haven't got no dad called Philippe.'

'How d'you mean?' asked Simon, with a sinking heart.

The lad rubbed his hands and went on: ''Cos if you really had one, he'd be your mam's husband.'

The logic of this dismayed Simon, but he replied: 'I don't care what you say, he's still my dad.'

'P'raps he is an' all,' said the lad with a sneer, 'but he ain't a proper dad.'

The Blanchot woman's boy bent his head and walked down to old Loizon's forge, where Philippe worked, to think things over.

The forge was virtually submerged under the trees. Inside, it was dark and the only light came from the great, glowing bursts of red released by the monstrous furnace which illuminated five bare-armed smiths who made a deafening din as they beat their anvils. They stood there in the flames like demons, their eyes fixed on the red-hot metal which they hammered mercilessly; and their ponderous thoughts rose and fell as they swung their hammers.

Simon entered without being noticed, tiptoed up to his friend, and pulled him by the sleeve. The man turned round. The other men all stopped working and, not wanting to miss anything, stood and watched. Then in the unaccustomed silence, Simon's small, piping voice was heard:

'Philippe, Madame Michaud's son said just now as how you're not my proper dad.'

'And why not?' the workman asked.

The child replied in all innocence: ' 'Cos you ain't me mam's husband.'

No one laughed. Philippe remained as he was, his head pressed against the back of his big hands resting on the handle of the hammer which stood upended on his anvil. He was thinking. His four mates watched him and, dwarfed by these giants, Simon waited anxiously. Then one of the smiths, voicing what everyone was thinking, said to Philippe: 'That Blanchot girl's all right, you know, a fine lass. She's got grit and is pretty steady considering the trouble she's had. She'd make a good wife for some decent man.'

'Aye, that's true,' said the other three.

The smith continued: 'Was it the lassie's fault if she slipped up? She was promised marriage and I can think of more than one woman walking about very respectable today who once acted no different.'

'True enough,' chorused the three men.

He went on: 'The poor girl's slaved hard to raise the boy on her own, and how much she's grieved all this time when she's never gone anywhere except to church, only the good Lord knows.'

'True again,' the others said.

In the silence, the only sound came from the bellows which fanned the furnace fire. Philippe suddenly bent down and said to Simon: 'Go home and tell your mam I'll be coming round to speak to her tonight.'

Then, guiding the boy by the shoulders, he led him outside.

He went back to his work and, with one accord, five hammers struck five anvils simultaneously. They went on striking until it was night, strong, powerful, joyful, like hammers well pleased with their work. But just as a cathedral tenor bell dominates the Sunday morning peal of the rest of the bells, so Philippe's hammer, rising above the clangour of the others, rang out time after time with his deafening strokes. And the man, with eyes blazing, went on swinging his hammer with a will in a shower of sparks.

The sky was full of stars when he knocked at the door of the little white house. He was wearing his Sunday jacket and a clean shirt and he had trimmed his beard. The young woman appeared at the door looking slightly ruffled and said: 'It's not right you coming here after it's dark, you know.'

He tried to answer, stammered, and stood in embarrassed silence before her.

'I thought you understood', she went on, 'that I can't afford to have people talking about me any more.'

All of a sudden, he burst out: 'That wouldn't matter a hang', he said, 'if you'd marry me!'

There was no reply, but inside the darkened room he thought he heard the noise of a body collapsing onto the floor. He ran in. Simon, who was in bed, made out the sound of a kiss and a few words whispered by his mother. Then he suddenly felt himself being lifted up in the hands of his friend who held him up in his powerful arms and cried:

'You can tell those kids at school that your dad is Philippe Remy, the blacksmith. Tell 'em he'll tear the ears off anybody that tries messing about with you.'

The next day, when the classroom was full and lessons were about to start, little Simon stood up. His face was pale and his lips trembled: 'My dad', he said distinctly, 'is Philippe Remy the blacksmith and he promised to tear the ears off anybody that tries messing about with me.'

This time no one laughed, for everyone knew Philippe Remy the blacksmith. He was a real dad, the sort anybody could be proud of.

Family Life

THE Neuilly tram had just gone past the stop at La Porte Maillot and was clanking along the long avenue that leads down to the Seine. The little engine pulling the passenger coach hooted warnings to whatever lay in its path, spitting out steam and puffing in exactly the way people gasp for breath when they run. Its scurrying pistons made a noise like iron legs marching. The oppressive heat late that summer lay heavily on the road which, though there was no wind, sent up stifling, burning, opaque, chalky white clouds of dust which coated sweaty skins, got into eyes, and found its way into lungs. People came out and stood on their doorsteps for a breath of air.

The windows of the tram were down and their curtains flapped wildly as the vehicle bowled along. Only a few people sat inside (for on hot days like this most preferred sitting on top or standing on the platform). There were fat women in peculiar clothes, the sort of middle-class suburban ladies who make up for the natural distinction they lack by standing on their dignity at all the wrong moments. There were office-worn gents with yellow faces, bent backs, and one shoulder set slightly higher than the other from spending hours hunched over desks. And their sad, anxious faces spoke volumes about their domestic troubles, neverending money worries, and all those old hopes which had been dashed for good; for they all belonged to the army of poor threadbare drudges who just about make ends meet in some dismal plasterboard house with a flowerbed for a garden in the rubbish-and-slag-heap belt on the outskirts of Paris.

Just by the tram door, a short fat man with a bloated face and a paunch resting on his outspread legs, dressed entirely in black and wearing in his buttonhole a ribbon which bore witness to official recognition of public service, stood chatting to a tall, thin, unkempt man wearing a very dirty white cotton suit and an old panama hat. The former spoke slowly and so hesitantly that at moments he appeared to stutter: he was Monsieur Caravan, a head clerk at the Admiralty. The other, a former ship's doctor who had served in the merchant navy, had ended up in a practice just on the great road junction at Courbevoie where he belaboured the local population with the hazy medical knowledge he had salvaged from a life of adventure. His name was Chenet and he insisted that people address him as 'doctor'. There was some talk about his private life.

Monsieur Caravan had always lived the regular life of a bureaucrat. For thirty years he had turned up at his office each morning, always going the same way and always meeting the same men at the same time and in the same places as they too went to their place of employment. And every evening he returned home the same way, again meeting up with the same faces which he had seen grow older.

Each day, after buying his cheap newspaper on the corner of the Faubourg Saint-Honoré, he bought his usual couple of bread rolls and crept into the Admiralty building like a criminal giving himself up. He hurried to his office, riddled with worry and living in fear of being reprimanded for making some mistake or other.

Nothing had ever happened to upset the regular pattern of his life, for nothing ever concerned him much beyond what went on at the office—who had got promoted and who might get a raise. Whether he was at the Admiralty or at home—for he had married a colleague's daughter who had not brought him a penny's dowry—he never talked about anything but the office. His mind, atrophied by the stultifying work he did day in day out, was incapable of conceiving any hopes or dreams other than those connected with the Admiralty. But there was one source of bitterness which always prevented him from being content with his lot as a clerk: the matter of the promotion of ships' quarter-masters—'tinsmiths' as they were called on account of the silver braid of their rank—to the posts of Deputy Chief Clerk and Chief Clerk. Every evening over dinner he argued in the strongest terms to his wife, who shared his loathing, that it was wholly and utterly iniquitous to squander employment in Paris on men who were supposed to sail the seas.

He was old now and had never been aware of how his life had gone on ticking away, for the office had been an unbroken continuation of school, and the masters he had once trembled before had now been replaced by his superiors who terrified him. Entering the offices of these petty despots made him quail, and his permanent state of fear had left him with an awkward way of introducing himself, a deferential manner, and a kind of nervous stammer.

He knew Paris no better than a blind man who is led each day by his dog to his pitch in the same doorway. And if he read about events and scandals in his cheap rag, they were to his way of thinking just fanciful stories made up willy-nilly for the amusement of people who worked in offices. A man of routine habits, a conservative without party affiliations but an opponent of anything *new-fangled*, he always skimmed the political news which in any case his paper distorted in favour of some cause it was paid to support. And as he made his way up the Champs-Elysées each evening, he observed the seething crowd of pedestrians and the surging stream of horse-drawn vehicles rather like some rootless traveller traversing foreign fields.

Having just this year put in his statutory thirty years' service, he had, in the New Year list, been awarded the Cross of the Legion of Honour which in the various Defence departments is given a reward for the long and dismal drudgery—called 'loyal service'—of sad, plodding men who spend their lives festooned in red tape. This unexpected honour gave him a new and exalted idea of his abilities and had completely altered his ways. Henceforth he abandoned coloured trousers and jackets with stripes or checks and went in for black breeches and long frock-coats where his Legion of Honour ribbon showed up to better advantage. He shaved each morning, cleaned his fingernails more carefully, changed his underclothes every other day out of a sense of propriety and proper respect for the national Order of which he was now a member, and overnight became another Caravan, freshly scrubbed, regal, and gracious.

At home, he brought 'my gong' into whatever was being said. He was filled with such pride that he could not bear to see ribbons of any kind in other people's buttonholes. He became especially angry when he happened upon foreign medals 'which ought not to be allowed to be worn in France', and he particularly resented Doctor Chenet whom he met every evening on the tram sporting some white, blue, orange, or green decoration or other.

The two men's conversation between the Arc de Triomphe and Neuilly was always the same. And that day, as on other days before it, they discussed various local grievances which both of them found shocking, especially since the Mayor of Neuilly was once again dragging his heels. Then, as inevitably happens in conversations with doctors, Caravan came round to the state of his health, hoping in this way to pick up a few free tips or even, if he played his cards right and took care not to show his hand, to wangle some specific medical advice. For he had been worried about his mother for some time. She had been having frequent and prolonged fainting fits and, though she was 90, refused to have anything to do with doctors.

Her great age affected Caravan who was always saying to Doctor Chenet: 'Do you see many that live as long?' And he would rub his hands happily, not because he particularly wanted his mother to live forever but because the inordinate length of her life was a promise of what lay in store for him.

He went on: 'Oh! They're a long-lived lot in my family. Take me, for instance: I'm pretty sure that barring accidents I'll live to a ripe old age.'

The ship's doctor gave him a pitying look; he glanced briefly at his companion's bright-red face and blubbery neck, the paunch sagging between his two fat, flaccid legs, and the apoplectic corpulence typical of the ageing, flabby clerk. He raised the greyish Panama from his head with one hand and said with a sneer: 'I wouldn't be so sure of that, if

I were you. Your mother's the skinny type but you're a bladder of lard.' Perturbed, Caravan fell silent.

But the tram was now pulling up at their stop. The two men got out and Chenet offered to pay for a round of vermouths at the Globe café just over the street where they were both regular customers. The proprietor was a friend and he held out a limp hand which they shook across the bottles on the counter. Then they went and sat with the domino players who had been there since noon. Cordial greetings were exchanged, including the inevitable 'What's new?' after which the players went back to their game. When in due course the two men bade them good night, they held out their hands without looking up. Then each went home for dinner.

Caravan lived just off the Courbevoie road junction in a small three-storied house, the ground floor of which was occupied by a barber's shop.

Two bedrooms, a dining-room, and a kitchen, where much-mended chairs circulated from one room to the next as and when they were needed, constituted the entire apartment which Madame Caravan spent all her time dusting and polishing while her daughter Marie-Louise, aged 10, and her son Philippe, who was 9, ran wild in the streets and played in the gutters with all the awful children in the area.

Caravan had brought his mother to live on the top floor, a woman so mean that she was famous for it in the neighbourhood, and so thin that people said that when the Good Lord made her he had used her own parsimonious principles to do it with. She was permanently bad-tempered and not a day of her life went by without dreadful quarrels and outbursts of rage. From her window she screamed abuse at neighbours as they stood on their doorsteps, at women hawking their wares, at men sweeping the street, and at the children who, to pay her back, followed her at a safe distance when she went out, shouting: 'Miserable ole bag!'

A little Norman maid, who was incredibly scatterbrained, did the household chores and slept on the same floor as the old woman, in case of accidents.

When Caravan got home, his wife, who was terminally house-proud, had a piece of flannel in her hand and was shining up the few mahogany chairs dotted around the sparsely furnished rooms. On her hands she always wore cotton gloves and on her head a bonnet which teemed with multi-coloured ribbons and was forever slipping down over one ear, and every time she was taken in the act of waxing, brushing, polishing, or washing, she would always say: 'I'm not a rich woman, I keep everything simple, but cleanliness is my luxury and it's every bit as good as the other sort.'

Endowed with a stubborn practical sense, she was her husband's guide in all things. Every evening at dinner and again later when they were in bed, they talked at length about what went on at the office and, though she was twenty years his junior, he confided in her as though she were his confessor and followed her advice in all matters.

She had never been pretty and now she was ugly, squat, and scrawny. Her lack of dress-sense had always successfully smothered her few feminine charms, which ought really to have stood out under decently tailored clothes cut to proper advantage. Her skirts constantly swivelled on her hips and with an unconscious mannerism which verged on the compulsive, she scratched herself all the time, everywhere, paying no heed to whoever might be present. The only self-ornamentation she allowed herself was the maelstrom of jumbled silk ribbons on the pretentious hats which it was her custom to wear in the house.

The moment she saw her husband, she stood up and, kissing his whiskered cheeks, said: 'Did you remember to call in at Potin's, dear?' (This was about an errand he had promised to do.) But he collapsed in a heap onto a chair. He had forgotten again. That made the fourth time. 'I'm fated,' he said, 'fated, that's what I am. I can spend all day thinking about it and then by the evening, it goes clean out of my head!' But since he seemed genuinely sorry, she consoled him: 'It's all right. You'll remember tomorrow. Anything new at the office?'

'I should say: another tinsmith's been appointed Deputy Chief Clerk.'

She looked grave: 'Which office?'

'External purchases.'

She became angry: 'So he'll get Ramon's job. I had my eye on that for you. And what's going to happen to Ramon? Will he retire?'

He stammered: 'He's to retire.'

She became furious and her hat lurched towards one shoulder: 'Well, that's it, then, as far as that set-up is concerned. No good hoping for anything there. And what's this new quartermaster called?'

'Bonassot.'

She took down the Navy List which she always kept ready to hand and looked through the pages. 'Bonassot. Toulon. Born in 1851. Made cadet in 1871 and Quartermaster second class 1875. Has he been to sea?'

The question made Caravan perk up. He began to laugh. His paunch shook. 'As often as Balin, his superior.' And with an even louder laugh, he added an old joke which everyone in the Admiralty thought was a scream: 'You can't send chaps like that on a pleasure-cruise a couple of miles down the Seine to inspect the naval station at the Point-du-Jour: they'd be seasick before they got there!'

But she remained grave as though she had not heard. Then, slowly scratching her chin, she murmured: 'What about trying to get a member of parliament on our side? When the Chamber gets to know all about what's going on, the Minister won't last two minutes . . .'

A great burst of shouting on the stairs cut her short. Marie-Louise and Philippe-Auguste, coming back from playing in the street, were hitting and kicking each other as they climbed each step. Their mother leaped on them furiously and grabbing one in each hand bundled them into the apartment, giving them both a good shaking.

When they saw their father they made a dash for him. He kissed them long and tenderly and then, sitting down, took them on his knee and started chatting to them.

Philippe-Auguste was an ugly child, with uncombed hair and dirt all over him, and the face of a cretin. Marie-Louise looked like her mother, talked like her, repeated the words she used, and even imitated her gestures. She too said: 'Anything new at the office?' He answered cheerfully: 'Your friend Ramon, who comes and has his dinner with us once a month, well, he'll be leaving us, pet. There'll be a new Deputy Chief Clerk taking over from him.' She looked up at her father and commiserated as any forward child might: 'So that's somebody else who's jumped over your head.'

He stopped laughing and did not answer. Then, changing the subject, he said to his wife who was now cleaning windows: 'All well upstairs with mother?'

Madame Caravan stopped her polishing, turned, straightened her bonnet which had fallen right down the back of her neck, and replied with quivering lips:

'Your mother! Don't talk to me about your mother! She landed me right in it! This afternoon, would you believe, Madame Lebaudin, the barber's wife, came up to ask if I'd lend her a packet of starch. I was out and your mother sent her packing and called her a "beggar". I gave the old girl what for. She pretended not to hear like she always does when anybody tells her what's what, but she's no more deaf than I am. It's all bunkum, is that. And if you want proof, she went straight back up to her room without saying a word.'

Caravan, not knowing what to say, was still saying nothing when the little maid rushed in to say that dinner was ready. To let his mother know, he fetched the broom-handle which was kept hidden in a corner and knocked three times on the ceiling. Then they went into the dining-room and the younger Madame Caravan ladled out the soup while they waited for the old lady. She did not come and the soup got cold. In the end they started eating slowly. When the soup dishes were empty, they waited a little longer. Madame Caravan, furious, blamed her husband: 'She does it on purpose, I tell you. And you always side with her.' Flummoxed and feeling caught in the crossfire, he sent Marie-Louise to fetch grandma and sat without moving, his eyes lowered, while his wife fumed and tapped the stem of her wineglass with the end of her knife.

Suddenly the door opened and the little girl reappeared

gasping for breath and looking white as a sheet. She blurted out: 'Grandma's fallen on the floor!'

Caravan leaped to his feet and, throwing his napkin onto the table, dashed up the stairs which reverberated beneath his heavy, hurrying tread while his wife, detecting one of her mother-in-law's nasty tricks, followed more slowly, shrugging her shoulders scornfully.

The old lady was stretched out on the floor face down in the middle of her bedroom, and when her son turned her over she just lay there without moving, wizened, her skin sallow, shrivelled like tanned leather, eyes closed and teeth clenched, and her thin body already stiff all over.

Caravan was on his knees at her side groaning: 'Mother! Oh poor mother!' But the other Madame Caravan peered at her briefly, then declared: 'Nonsense! She's had another fainting fit, that's all. She's done it on purpose to stop us having our dinner, you mark my words.'

They lifted the body onto the bed and removed all the old lady's clothes. Then Caravan, his wife, and the maid all started rubbing and massaging. In spite of their efforts she did not come round. So they sent Rosalie for 'Doctor' Chenet. He lived in a house overlooking the river out Suresnes way. It was a fair distance and a long wait. He came in the end. He took a good look at the old lady, prodded her here and there, and listened through his stethoscope. Then he said: 'It's all over.'

Caravan collapsed onto the body, buffeted by fast-flowing sobs. He showered his mother's rigid face with kisses so uncontrollable and so copious that large tears fell like drops of water onto her dead features.

The younger Madame Caravan's sorrowing heart broke quite satisfactorily and, standing behind her husband, she made little wailing noises and rubbed her eyes stubbornly.

Caravan, his face swollen, his thin hair in disarray, and looking very ugly in his genuine grief, got up suddenly: 'But. . . . Are you sure, doctor. . . . Are you quite sure . . .?' The ship's doctor took a few quick steps forward and, handling the corpse with professional ease, like a salesman demonstrating his wares, said: 'Here, man, take a look at the eye.' He pulled back one eyelid and the old woman stared out from under his finger, exactly as she used to, though the pupil was perhaps slightly distended. The sight pierced Caravan to the heart and a thrill of horror struck him to the bone. Monsieur Chenet took hold of the stiffened arm, forced the fingers open, and said angrily as though dealing with someone who had questioned his judgement: 'Look at the hand here. I never make mistakes, so you can just set your mind at rest.'

Caravan, bellowing almost, again collapsed sprawling onto the bed. Meanwhile his wife, still snivelling, did the necessary. She drew up the night table, spread a cloth over it, and set out four candles which she then lit, reached down a palm cross which had been stuck behind the mirror above the mantelpiece, and placed it in a dish which she filled with tap water since there was no holy water in the house. But after thinking a moment, she added a pinch of salt, imagining no doubt that this would amount to a form of consecration.

When she had finished arranging the emblems and symbols which it is meet to set out in the presence of Death, she remained standing where she was. The ship's doctor, who had been helping her to marshall her things, whispered to her: 'We've got to get Caravan away.' She nodded in agreement and, going up to her husband who was still on his knees sobbing, she raised him by one arm while Monsieur Chenet took him by the other.

They sat him down on a chair and his wife kissed him on the forehead and talked to him firmly. The ship's doctor backed her up with arguments and offered a counsel of steadfastness and courage and resignation and all those attitudes which are impossible to adopt in moments of great stress. Then they both took him by the arm again and led him away.

He went on blubbing like an overgrown child and hiccupped uncontrollably; he sagged, his arms dangled, his legs were like jelly. He went down the stairs not knowing what he was doing, putting one foot mechanically in front of the other.

They deposited him on a chair, the one he always

occupied at the dinner table, in front of his almost empty plate where his spoon still sat in the remains of the soup. There he remained becalmed, staring at his wineglass and so dazed that he stayed as he was without a single thought in his head.

Madame Caravan was talking to the doctor in a corner: she was enquiring about the formalities and asking for information about practical matters. Eventually Monsieur Chenet, who seemed to be hanging around for some reason, reached for his hat and, mentioning that he had not yet had his dinner, set about saying his goodbyes before leaving. She exclaimed: 'You don't mean to say you haven't eaten? But you must stay, Doctor, you must! I'm afraid you'll have to have what we've got, as I'm sure you will appreciate that we shan't be eating much.'

He refused and made an excuse. But she insisted: 'But you must stay, really you must. At times like these, one is only too glad to have one's friends around one. And perhaps you'll be able to get my hubby to perk up a bit. He's going to have to pull himself together.'

With a bow, the doctor put down his hat and said: 'In that case, I shall of course stay.'

She gave instructions to Rosalie who scarcely knew whether she was coming or going, and then sat down at the table, 'to go through the motions,' she said, 'and to keep the good doctor company.'

They helped themselves to the soup which was now cold. Monsieur Chenet asked for a second plateful. Then a tureen of dressed tripe appeared, exuding a strong smell of onions. Madame Caravan thought she might manage just a little. 'First-rate,' said the doctor. With a smile, she said: 'Charmed', and then turned to her husband: 'Won't you have a little, Alfred dear? Just so as you've got something in your stomach? Don't forget, you've got a long night ahead of you.'

He held out his plate submissively. He would have put himself to bed just as meekly if he had been told to, for he obeyed without protest and without thinking. And he began eating.

The doctor, helping himself, raided the tureen three times while Madame Caravan from time to time speared a small mouthful on the end of her fork and swallowed it with a kind of studied preoccupation.

When a salad-bowl full of macaroni was set before them, the doctor murmured: 'By Jove! That looks good!' This time Madame Caravan served everyone. She even piled up the plates of her children who had been playing with their food. Left to themselves, they had been drinking unwatered wine and had already started kicking each other under the table.

Monsieur Chenet reminded everyone that Rossini had been extremely fond of this Italian dish. Then a thought suddenly struck him: 'I say! It rhymes! You could start up a poem with it:

> The famous composer Rossini
> Was a man who adored macaroni . . .'

No one listened. Madame Caravan, suddenly pensive, was turning over the likely outcome of events in her mind. Meanwhile, her husband was rolling bits of bread into little balls which he dropped onto the tablecloth, then stared at them vacantly. His throat burned with an unquenchable thirst, and he kept taking gulps from his brimming wineglass. Unhinged by shock and grief, his mind was beginning to wander and he felt as though it were reeling now that the sudden numbing effects of the digestive processes had got laboriously under way.

All this while the doctor was drinking like a fish and becoming noticeably drunk. Even Madame Caravan, experiencing the reaction which generally follows shocks to the nervous system, fidgeted, came over rather peculiar, and, although she was drinking nothing but water, began to feel a little light-headed.

Monsieur Chenet had started telling stories about death and dying which he found funny. For in this suburb of Paris, where the population hails mostly from the provinces, it is not unusual to come across the peasant's indifference to the departed, even for dead mothers and fathers, a lack of

respect and an unconscious savagery which are as common
in country areas as they are rare in Paris. 'Listen,' he said,
'last week I got called out to the rue de Puteaux. So I
hurried over. When I got there, I found the patient had
slipped his cable and the whole family was sitting round the
bed quietly polishing off a bottle of anisette they'd bought
the night before because the chap who'd been at death's
door had fancied a drop.' But Madame Caravan was not
listening, for she was still thinking about the 'effects' they
stood to inherit. Caravan's brain had stopped functioning
and was not taking anything in.

Coffee was served. It was very strong and intended to
keep their spirits up. Each cup, laced with cognac, brought a
sudden rush of red to their cheeks and threw the few remaining ideas in their already wandering minds into final disarray.

The good doctor made a sudden grab for the bottle and
poured a stiff tot into everybody's cup 'to wash out the
coffee'. Without saying anything, growing drowsy in the
gentle warmth of their digestions, and overtaken in spite of
themselves by that feeling of animal well-being which comes
from drinking spirits after dinner, they wet their already
damp whistles with the sugary cognac which turned into a
yellowish syrup at the bottom of their cups. The children
had fallen asleep and Rosalie put them to bed.

Mechanically responding to the need to drown his
sorrows which comes upon anyone who is unhappy,
Caravan helped himself to several more glasses of brandy.
His glazed eyes glistened.

The good doctor finally got up to leave and, grasping his
friend by the arm, said: 'Here, you'd better come along with
me. A spot of fresh air will do you a power of good. When
you're feeling down, you must keep on the move.'

Caravan acquiesced meekly, put his hat on his head, and
picked up his cane and they walked off together arm in arm
down towards the Seine under the bright stars.

Swirls of scented air swarmed in the warm night, for in
this season of the year the gardens roundabout were full of
flowers. Their fragrance was muted by day but they seemed
to come alive at the approach of evening and released

perfumes which were caught on the light breezes which played in the shadows.

The wide avenue was deserted and silent and its two rows of gaslights stretched all the way to the Arc de Triomphe. But in the distance Paris rumbled beneath a red-stained mist. There was a kind of constant muffled roar and now and then, far away on the plain beyond, the whistle of a train seemed to call out as it approached under a full head of steam or else sped away across shire and province towards the sea.

The fresh air on the faces of the two men came as a shock, upset the doctor's balance, and intensified the dizzy surges which Caravan had been experiencing ever since dinner. He walked along in a dream, his mind vacant, paralysed, feeling no great throbs of grief, gripped by a kind of emotional numbness which dulled his sufferings and even afforded a measure of relief which was heightened by the perfumes suspended in the warm night air.

When they reached the bridge, they turned right where the breeze from the river blew cool on their faces. The melancholy water flowed sedately past a screen of tall poplars. Stars seemed to float on the water, winking in the pull of the current. The thin white mist hovering over the bank opposite made the air they breathed taste dank and damp. Caravan stopped suddenly, brought up short by the smell of the river which stirred very old memories in his heart.

All at once, he saw his mother again, just as she used to be when he was a boy, on her knees outside the door of their house in far-off Picardy, bending over the heap of clothes at her side which she was washing in the little stream which ran through their garden. He heard the thump of her wooden paddle in the peace and country quiet and the sound of her voice as she shouted: 'Alfred! Fetch me the soap!' And in his nostrils were the same smell of running water, the same mist rising from water-logged earth, the same reek of marshes which had stayed within him, pungent and unforgettable, and which now resurfaced this very evening when his mother had just died.

He stopped, stiff and tense under a renewed onslaught of raging despair. It was as if a sudden flash of light had illuminated the full extent of his loss: chancing upon the wandering breeze had cast him down into the black pit of griefs beyond consolation. His heart felt as though it had been shattered now that he was parted from her forever. His life had been cut off short at its middle: the whole of his youth faded, swallowed up in her death. The *old days* were over and done with; all his adolescent memories began to grow faint; there would be no one now to speak to him about those bygone things, about the people he had once known, about himself, about the homely details of his past life. One part of his being had ceased to exist; it was only a matter of time before the rest died too.

Then the endless procession of memories began. He pictured 'his mater', looking much younger, in the thread-bare dresses she had worn for so long that they seemed to be an inseparable part of her; he saw her as she had been in countless forgotten moments: her face was unclear, but here were her gestures, her tone of voice, her ways, her mannerisms, her rages, the lines on her face, the movements of her thin fingers—all the things she used to do and would never do again.

He clutched the doctor's arm and uttered a series of groans. His flaccid legs trembled; his fat, ungainly body was convulsed with sobbing and he stammered: 'Mother! Dear Mother! Poor dear mother!' But his companion, still drunk and with more than half a mind to end the evening in one of his regular secret haunts, gave short shrift to the new outburst of racking grief, sat the clerk down on the grassy river bank, and then promptly left him to it, saying that he had a patient to see.

Caravan went on crying for some considerable time. When he could find no more tears to weep, when all his sufferings had flowed out of him, as it were, he again felt placated, calm, and suddenly at peace.

The moon had risen and the horizon was bathed in its serene light. The tall poplars reared up glinting with silver and the mist hung over the plain like a floating snowfield.

Stars no longer feathered the river which was now a sheet of mother-of-pearl flowing on and on, its surface a-ripple with bright reflections. The air was warm and the breeze was perfumed. The earth stirred gently in its sleep and Caravan drank of the sweetness of the night. He breathed long and deep and became aware that reaching into every part of his body were feelings of coolness and quietude and a surge of consolation that were not of this world.

He fought hard against this flood-tide of well-being and went on repeating 'Mother, poor mother', forcing himself to cry as any decent man ought in the circumstances. But he could not manage it now, for no trace remained of the sadness which had yoked him to thoughts which, only moments before, had made him sob so uncontrollably.

He got to his feet and turned for home, walking slowly, cloaked in the serene indifference of restful nature and with peace in his unwilling heart.

When he reached the bridge, he saw the lights of the last tram which was about to set off and, beyond it, the brightly lit windows of the Globe café.

He felt a sudden urge to tell somebody about the tragedy that had happened, to hear people say they were sorry for him, to make himself interesting. Wearing a doleful countenance, he pushed open the door and walked up to the counter where the proprietor was still ensconced. He was expecting everybody to stop what they were doing, to come over and say, with commiserating hands extended to him: 'Whatever is the matter?' But nobody noticed the devastated expression on his face. He leaned his elbows on the bar and clasping his head in his hands, muttered: 'God, oh God!'

The proprietor gave him a look. 'Not feeling up to the mark, Monsieur Caravan?'

He answered: 'No, nothing like that. Fact is, my mother's just died.'

The proprietor said 'Ah!' with only half a mind, and since a customer at a table at the other end of the room was shouting: 'Give us a beer, will you?' he yelled back in a deafening voice: 'One beer, right away, coming up!' and rushed off to serve him, leaving Caravan crestfallen.

Sitting absorbed and motionless at the same table as before dinner, the same three men were still playing dominoes. Caravan went up to them, looking for sympathy. Since not one of them appeared to notice him, he made up his mind to speak first.

'Since I saw you earlier on, something terrible has happened,' he said.

All three half looked up together while keeping one eye on the dominoes in their hands.

'You don't say.'

'My mother's died.'

One of them muttered: 'Terrible shame!' with the show of concern which people who do not care can always manage very easily. Another, who could not think of anything to say, nodded his head gravely and gave a sad little whistle. The third went back to his game as though he were thinking: 'If that's all, why the fuss?'

Caravan had been expecting them to say something that came, as the phrase goes, 'from the heart'. Seeing the kind of welcome he was getting, he drifted away, feeling very indignant that they should show such calmness when faced with the grief of a friend—though even as he fumed, his grief had so lost its edge that he could hardly feel it. He left.

His wife was waiting up for him in her nightdress, sitting on a low chair at the open window and still thinking about the deceased's effects.

'Get undressed,' she said, 'We'll talk when we're in bed.'

He raised his head and, looking towards the ceiling, said: 'But . . . upstairs . . . there's nobody . . .'

'Oh yes there is, Rosalie's with her. You'll have to go and take over at three o'clock when you've had a bit of a sleep.'

All the same, he kept his combinations on so that he would be ready for any eventuality, tied a scarf around his head, and then joined his wife who had already slipped between the sheets. They lay there side by side for some time. Her mind was busy.

Even at this time of night, her hair was adorned with a bunch of pink ribbons which was tilted over one ear as though doomed to follow the all-conquering habit of every hat she ever wore.

All at once she turned to him and said: 'Do you know if your mother made a will?'

He answered uncertainly, 'Er . . . I . . . I don't think she did. . . . No, I'm pretty sure she didn't.'

Madame Caravan looked her husband straight in the eye and said in a quiet, waspish whisper: 'Well, that's the giddy limit! We've slaved for ten years so she'd be looked after! We took her in and put food on her plate! I can't see your sister would ever have done as much for her and I'd never have either if I'd known the thanks I'd get! It's a stain on her memory, that's what it is! Don't go telling me she paid her way for I won't deny it. But you can't pay for your children's loving care with money. You see them right in your will after you're dead. That's how decent people behave. The way it's turned out, I've had all that work and bother for nothing. Well, I think it's a very shabby carry on.'

Totally at a loss, Caravan kept repeating: 'Please, my dear, don't take on so.'

Eventually she calmed down and said in her normal voice: 'Tomorrow morning, we'll have to let your sister know.'

He gave a start: 'You're right, I never thought. I'll send a telegram first thing.' But she cut him short, like a woman who has thought of everything: 'No, send it between ten and eleven so we've got time to get turned round before she comes. It'll take her two hours at most to get here from Charenton. We'll say you were upset and couldn't think straight. As long as we let her know sometime tomorrow morning, no one can say we didn't do right.'

But Caravan clapped his hand to his head as a thought struck him. In the nervous voice he always used when talking about his chief, the very thought of whom made him quake, he said: 'I'll have to inform the Admiralty too.'

'Why do you have to let them know?' she replied. 'In situations like this, you always have a good excuse for forgetting. Take it from me: don't tell them. Your chief won't be able to say a thing and you'll be landing him in a right pickle.'

'I'll say!' he answered. 'He'll be absolutely furious when he realizes I'm not there. You're right. That's a rich one! And then, when I tell him my mother's dead, he won't have a leg to stand on!' Delighted with the wheeze, he rubbed his hands happily as he thought of the look on his chief's face, while above his head the body of the old woman lay next to the sleeping maid.

Madame Caravan began to look worried, as though she were obsessed by some preoccupation difficult to put into words. In the end, she made up her mind to speak: 'Your mother did give you her clock, didn't she? The one with the girl playing with the cup and ball?'

He made an effort to think and then said: 'Oh yes. She said—mind you, that was a long time ago, when she came here first—she said: "This clock will be yours if you take good care of me." '

Greatly relieved, Madame Caravan brightened: 'Well, in that case, we ought to go and fetch it down. If we just let your sister come, she'll stop us having it.'

He hesitated: 'You really think so?'

She became cross: 'Of course I do! Once it's down here, nobody'll be any the wiser: it's ours. The same thing goes for the chest of drawers in her room, the one with the marble top. She gave that to me one day when she was in a good mood. We can bring it down at the same time.'

Caravan looked as though he could not believe his ears: 'But my dear, that would be taking a great deal upon ourselves.'

She turned on him in a fury: 'Oh really! You'll never change, will you! You'd sit back and let your children die of hunger rather than shape yourself! The minute she said I could have that chest of drawers, it was ours, wasn't it? And if your sister doesn't like it, then she can say so to my face. I don't care tuppence for your sister. So shift yourself and we'll go this minute and fetch the things down that your mother gave us.'

Quaking and routed, he got out of bed and was about to

put his trousers on when she stopped him: 'Don't bother getting dressed, you're all right in your combs. I'm going as I am.' And dressed in their night things, they set off, climbed the stairs without making a sound, opened the door carefully, and stepped into the room where the four candles, which still burned around the dish containing the consecrated palm, seemed to be the sole guardians of the old woman's rigid sleep. For Rosalie, sprawling in her chair, her legs stretched out in front of her, her hands together on her lap, and her head lolling to one side, as motionless as her charge and with her mouth hanging open, was fast asleep and snoring gently.

Caravan took hold of the clock. It was one of those grotesque artefacts turned out in large numbers by craftsmen during the Empire: a young girl in gilt bronze with mixed flowers on her head held a cup in one hand with a ball attached which acted as the pendulum.

'Give me that,' whispered his wife, 'and you take the marble top of the chest of drawers.'

Breathing hard, he did as he was told and with considerable difficulty hoisted the marble top onto one shoulder.

Then they both set off. Caravan had to bend to get through the door, and started down the stairs shakily while his wife walked backwards before him showing a light with one hand and holding the clock under her other arm.

When they were back in their apartment, she heaved an enormous sigh: 'That's the hardest part over,' she said. 'Now let's go and get the rest.'

But the drawers of the chest were full of the old lady's clothes. They would have to be put out of sight somewhere.

Madame Caravan had an idea. 'Go and get the pinewood box from the hall. It's not worth anything so it'll do all right for in here.'

When they had the box, they began moving the contents. One by one, they took out the fancy cuffs, muslin collars, shifts, and hats, all the shabby bits and pieces belonging to the old lady who lay in state just behind them, and arranged them neatly in the pinewood box so that Madame Braux, the deceased's other child who would be arriving the next day, would suspect nothing. When they had finished, they first carried the drawers down, then, each taking one end, the chest itself. They both spent quite a while trying to decide where it would look best. In the end they plumped for their bedroom, at the foot of their bed, between the two windows.

Once the chest of drawers was in place, Madame Caravan filled it with her own things. The clock went on the mantelpiece and they both stared at it to see how it looked. They were immediately delighted with it: 'It goes a treat there,' she said, and he answered: 'A proper treat.' Then they went back to bed. She blew out the candle and soon every one in the house was asleep.

It was broad daylight when Caravan opened his eyes. As he slowly came to, his mind was in a fog. It was a full minute or two before he remembered what had happened. The memory twisted in his heart like a knife. He leaped out of bed feeling deeply affected once more and near to tears.

He raced up the stairs to the room above where Rosalie, still asleep, had not moved since the night before, having made her nap last right through till morning. He sent her about her business, replaced the gutted candles, and then stood over his mother while round and round in his head he rolled those semblances of profound thoughts, those religious and philosophical commonplaces which persons of little brain always repeat when confronted by death.

But his wife called and he went downstairs. She had drawn up a list of things that had to be done that morning and she handed it to him. He was appalled as he read:

1. Register death at Town Hall.
2. See about death certificate.
3. Order coffin.
4. Call in at church.
5. Undertaker.
6. Printer's—order stationery.
7. Go to lawyer's.
8. Telegraph office—let the family know.

In addition, there was a large number of smaller errands. He reached for his hat and went.

By now the news had got out. Neighbours began to arrive and were clamouring to see the body.

In the barber's shop on the ground floor, there was even a nasty scene on this theme between the barber's wife and the barber. It happened while he was shaving a customer. The wife, busily knitting a woollen stocking, muttered: 'That's another one gone, and a tight-fisted old skinflint she was too. They didn't come meaner than what she was. I know I never liked her much but I'd better pop up and have a look at her all the same.'

Her husband snorted as he lathered his customer's chin: 'You don't half get some funny ideas. There's nobody has funny ideas like women. As if it isn't enough for them to make your life a misery when they're alive, they won't even let you alone when they're dead.' But his wife, without dropping a stitch, replied: 'I can't help it. I'm going to have to go. It's been preying on me ever since this morning. If I don't go, I know it'll stay with me till my dying day. But if I can only get a good look at her, you know, get her face clear in my mind, I'll rest easy after.'

The husband, razor in hand, shrugged his shoulders and in a confidential whisper to the man whose cheek he was shaving said: 'I ask you! Women! Where'd they get these ideas from? Gawping at a corpse ain't my idea of fun!' But his wife had heard what he said and, quite unruffled, answered: 'It's the way we are, that's what.' And laying her knitting down on the counter, she climbed up to the first floor.

Two women from next door were there already. They were chatting about what had happened with Madame Caravan who was giving details.

All four went up to the room where the body was laid out. They tiptoed in, sprinkled the sheet with the salt water, knelt, crossed themselves, and mumbled a prayer. Then they stood up and, eyes wide and lips parted, stared for some time at the corpse while the daughter-in-law of the deceased dabbed at her eyes with a handkerchief and manufactured a despairing squawk.

As she turned to leave, she saw Marie-Louise and

Philippe-Auguste just by the door, both in their night clothes, peering in inquisitively. Forgetting her crocodile grief, she hurled herself on them with one hand raised and screamed with rage: 'Clear off, bleedin' little pests!'

Ten minutes later she was back upstairs with another gaggle of neighbours and again waving the palm cross over her mother-in-law and praying and whimpering and doing everything that was expected of her, when she saw that her two children had reappeared and were standing behind her. She cuffed them over the ear for form's sake. But the next time she did not bother. And thereafter, as each new batch of visitors arrived, both brats trailed along behind, dropping to their knees just out of harm's way and imitating everything they saw their mother doing.

By early afternoon the crowd of inquisitive females had dwindled. Soon they stopped coming altogether. Madame Caravan, who had gone back to her apartment, started getting everything ready for the funeral service. The corpse was left to itself.

The window of the upstairs room was open. Through it the torrid heat drifted in on clouds of dust. The flames of the four candles flickered around the motionless body. On the sheet, over the face and the closed eyes, up and down the outstretched hands, small flies crawled and ambled and hurried and scurried restlessly as they inspected the old woman and bided their time which would soon come.

Meanwhile Marie-Louise and Philippe-Auguste had gone off again to play in the avenue. They were almost immediately surrounded by friends, notably by little girls who are generally wider-awake and have a keener nose for the mysteries of life. They asked questions like grown-ups.

'Is your granny dead, then?'

'Yeah, she died las' night.'

'Wot do dead people look like?'

Marie-Louise explained, telling them all about the candles, the palm cross, and her granny's face. All the children became exceedingly curious and they asked if they could go up and see the body too.

Marie-Louise organized the first visit there and then—

five girls and two boys, the oldest and boldest. She made them take their shoes off in case somebody heard them: the gang crept into the house and scampered smartly upstairs like an army of mice. When they got inside the room, the little girl, behaving just like her mother, took charge of the proceedings. Po-faced, she showed her friends where to stand, then knelt, crossed herself, moved her lips silently, sprinkled salt water on the bed. When the children stepped forward, thrilled and fascinated, to view the face and hands, she suddenly began to pretend to sob and hid her eyes in her little hankie. Then quickly wiping away her tears at the thought of the others who were waiting downstairs by the door, she led off her troops at a run and soon brought back another contingent, then a third; for all the awful children from the streets roundabout had turned up to play this new game, including the scruffy urchins who begged on street corners. And for each guided tour she reproduced her mother's affected simperings to perfection.

In the end, however, she wearied of it. The children ran off to play another game somewhere else. The old lady was left alone, completely forgotten now by everyone. Shadows crowded into her room and the flickering flame of the candles cast beams which danced on her wizened, wrinkled face.

At about eight o'clock Caravan climbed the stairs, closed the window, and replaced the candles with new ones. He came and went calmly now, for he was already used to seeing the body as though it had been there for months. He was even able to note that no signs of decomposition were yet visible, and he made a point of mentioning this to his wife as they were sitting down to dinner. She said: 'She always was a tough old stick. She'll keep for a year.'

They drank their soup without speaking. Having been left to themselves all day, the children were worn out and were half-asleep on their chairs. No one felt like talking.

The lamp suddenly dimmed.

Madame Caravan at once turned up the wick, but the lamp gave a hollow wheeze, then a drawn-out gurgle, and the flame went out. No one had remembered to buy any oil!

To run over to the grocer's would have held up the dinner and they looked for the candles. But there were none left except those which were burning upstairs on the bedside table.

Madame Caravan, always a woman of action, sent Marie-Louise up to fetch two of them. They waited for her in the dark.

They distinctly heard the little girl's feet climbing the stairs. There then followed a silence which lasted for several seconds. The next moment Marie-Louise rushed down again. She flung the door open, looking frightened to death and even more frantic than she had been the evening before when she had broken the awful news, and just managed to choke out: 'Papa! Granny's getting dressed!'

Caravan stood up so quickly that he knocked his chair over against the wall. He spluttered: 'What? . . . What did you say?' But Marie-Louise, so overcome that she could hardly speak, simply repeated: 'G . . g . . g . . granny's getting dressed . . . she's coming down!'

He made a wild dash for the stairs. His wife followed in a daze. When he reached the door on the second floor, he stopped, not daring to go in and shaking with fear. What would he see? Madame Caravan was bolder. She turned the knob and went inside.

The room seemed to have grown darker. In the middle of it, a tall, thin figure moved. The old woman was on her feet. Waking from her deep sleep, even before she had fully come round, she had turned on her side and, raising herself on one elbow, had blown out three of the candles which were burning next to the bed on which she had been laid. Then, gathering her strength, she had looked around for her clothes. At first the absence of her chest of drawers had worried her, but she had gone on looking and, finding her things right at the bottom of the pinewood box, had calmly put them on. She had emptied the water out of the dish, poked the palm cross back behind the mirror, and put the chairs back where they belonged, and was ready to go downstairs when she saw her son and her daughter-in-law standing in front of her.

Caravan rushed forward, took her by both hands, and kissed her. There were tears in his eyes. Meanwhile, behind him, his wife kept saying hypocritically: 'It's too good to be true!' But the old lady, showing no emotion and indeed giving no sign that she understood what was happening, stood stiff as a statue, glared at them icily, and simply asked: 'Is the dinner on the table?' Caravan, completely flustered, stammered: 'Yes, mother, we were just waiting for you.' And with unaccustomed attentiveness he took her arm, while the younger Madame Caravan picked up the candle and lit them down stair by stair, walking backwards in front of them just as she had done the night before for her husband as he carried the marble top.

When she got down to the bottom, she almost backed into some people who were coming up. It was the relatives from Charenton, Madame Braux with husband in tow.

The eyes of the wife, a tall, fat woman with a swollen stomach which made her lean back as she walked, almost started from her head, and she seemed ready to make a run for it. Her husband, a socialist who made boots for a living, a small man with hair everywhere, even in his nose, so that he looked like a monkey, remained unmoved and said: 'Hullo, what's this? Been raised from the dead, have we?'

The moment Madame Caravan realized who it was, she began making desperate signs to them. Then, in her normal voice, she said: 'Good gracious! Look who it is! My, my! What a lovely surprise!' But Madame Braux, reeling with the shock, did not understand. She replied in a half-whisper: 'We came when we got your telegram. We thought it was all over.'

Her husband, who was standing behind her, gave her a dig to make her be quiet. With a sly smile which was completely lost in his thick moustache, he said: 'How very kind of you to invite us over. Of course we came at once,' which was an allusion to the fact that for years there had been no love lost between the two couples. Then, just as the old lady was coming down the last few stairs, he stepped forward briskly and brushed her cheeks with the hair which covered his face and shouted into one ear because she was hard of hearing: 'How are we, then, ma? Still keeping hearty, eh?'

Madame Braux, still stunned at seeing her mother alive when she had been expecting to find her dead, did not even dare kiss her. Her bulging stomach almost filled the landing and prevented the others from squeezing past her.

The old lady, uneasy and suspicious, said nothing but stared at all these people standing around her. Her small, hard, beady grey eyes settled on each of her children in turn, brimming with visible thoughts which made them feel uncomfortable. Caravan tried to explain: 'She's been a bit off colour, but she's got over it and she's fine now, just fine, isn't that so, mother?' The old woman started shuffling forward again and replied in her usual quavery voice which now seemed to come from a long way off: 'I only fainted. I could hear every word you said.' There followed an embarrassed silence. They went into the dining-room where they sat down to a hurriedly improvised meal.

Only Monsieur Braux had kept his wits about him. He sat there grinning, with a face that could have belonged to an unpleasant gorilla, making insinuating, double-edged remarks which made everyone else visibly ill at ease.

Oddly enough, the doorbell in the hall kept ringing. Rosalie, quite beside herself, kept coming in to fetch Caravan who kept divesting himself of his serviette and hurrying out. His brother-in-law went so far as to enquire whether this was not his regular day for receiving callers, but he stammered: 'No, no. It's just . . . er . . . deliveries. Just deliveries.' Then a large packet came for him. He opened it without thinking and out spilled the funeral invitations edged in black. He turned bright red, hurriedly resealed the envelope, and stuffed it into his waistcoat.

His mother did not see: she was staring stubbornly at the ball of her clock as it swung to and fro on the mantelpiece. Embarrassment prospered in the icy silence. Then the old woman, turning her wrinkled witch's face towards her daughter, said, with a gleam of spite in her eyes: 'You can bring that little girl of yours here on Monday. I want to see her.' Madame Braux, her face lighting up, cried: 'Of

course, mother,' while the younger Madame Caravan paled
and her legs turned weak with mortification.

In the meantime the two men had slowly struck up a
conversation. For no good reason, they started talking
politics. Braux, defending the principles of revolution and
communism, was jumping up and down in his chair, his
eyes blazing in his hairy face, shouting: 'I tell you property is
theft. . . . The land belongs to everybody. . . . Inherited
wealth is a disgrace and a scandal . . . !' He stopped
abruptly, looking embarrassed, like a man who has just said
something foolish. Then he carried on in a more subdued
voice: 'But this isn't the time to go into all that.'

The door opened and Doctor Chenet appeared. A surge
of panic swept over him but he regained his composure
quickly and, going up to the old lady, cried: 'Well now!
Who do we have here looking fit and well today! I knew it,
you can take it from me! I was only telling myself just this
second as I was coming up the stairs: I bet the old girl's up
and doing.' And patting her gently on the back, he added:
'She's as fit as a fiddle. She'll see us all off, you mark my
words.' He sat down, said yes to the offer of a cup of coffee,
and in next to no time had joined in the discussion which
the two men were having: he sided with Braux, for he had
done his bit during the Paris Commune.

The old lady was feeling tired now and said she wanted to
go on up. Caravan sprang to his feet. She stared him in the
eye and said: 'You can put my chest of drawers and my
clock back upstairs for me. Now.' And he was still
stammering 'Yes, mother' when she took her daughter's
arm and went off with her.

The Caravans remained where they were, aghast, unable
to speak, buried under the appalling calamity, while Braux
rubbed his hands and sipped his coffee. All at once,
Madame Caravan, beside herself with rage, sprang at him
screaming: 'You thief, you scum, you snake in the grass! I
despise you! I could . . . I could . . . oooooh!' She fumed,
but nothing came to mind. He just sat there sniggering and
sipping.

At this point, his wife came back and made angrily for her

sister-in-law. With raucous voices and hands that shook, they stood toe to toe, the one enormous with her stomach jutting out threateningly and the other thin and twitching, and yelled barrowloads of choice insults at each other. Chenet and Braux intervened and the latter, nudging his better half in the back, propelled her out of the room, shouting: 'Get going, you silly cow, that's enough of your noise!'

They were heard on the pavement outside, bickering and squabbling as they went up the street.

Monsieur Chenet said goodbye and left. The Caravans, husband and wife, were left facing each other.

All at once, Monsieur Caravan collapsed onto a chair and broke into a cold sweat. He said: 'What am I going to tell the chief?'

A Farm Girl's Story

I

SINCE the weather was so good, everyone on the farm had eaten more quickly than usual and gone off to the fields.

Rose, the serving girl, was left alone in the huge kitchen where the fire in the hearth was dying under a pan of hot water. From time to time she took some of the water and washed her dishes unhurriedly, pausing now and then to watch two bright squares which, through the window, the sun laid on the long table, and which showed the faults in the glass.

Three very bold hens pecked at crumbs under the chairs. Farmyard smells and the sweet, warm breath of the cowshed drifted through the half-open door. And in the silent, burning noontime, the cocks could be heard crowing.

When she had finished the dishes and wiped the table, tidied the grate and put away the crockery on top of the dresser next to the loudly ticking grandfather clock, she gave a sigh, feeling a little overcome and ill at ease, though she could not have said why. She looked at the blackened clay walls and up at the smoke-brown beams hung with cobwebs, salt herring, and strings of onions: then she sat down, oppressed by the stale emanations which the heat of the day drew from the beaten-earth floor where so many things had dried over so many years. Mingling with them was also the sharp smell of the milk left creaming in the cool of the room next door. She thought she might take up her sewing as she usually did, but she did not feel up to it and went for a breath of air at the door.

There, caressed by the burning light, she felt a sweetness which struck her to the heart, a sense of well-being which coursed through all her limbs.

Outside the door, the dung-heap sent up a thin, steady shimmer of steam. The hens sprawled in it, lying on their sides, scratching for worms with one claw. The cock stood tall and proud among them. He circled them constantly, selecting one and strutting round her while he clucked his throaty summons. The hen stood nonchalantly and received him with an air of unconcern, bending her legs and supporting him on her wings; then she shook her feathers, releasing a cloud of dust before settling back into the heap while he crowed out another triumph. And from all the farmyards, all the other cocks answered as though issuing amorous challenges from farm to farm.

The serving girl watched them mechanically. Then she looked up and was dazzled by the brightness of the apple-blossom nodding like white periwigged heads. Suddenly a young colt, beside itself with high spirits, galloped past her. Twice it raced round the trenches where trees had been planted, before halting abruptly and looking round as though surprised to find itself alone.

She too experienced an urge to run, a need to stir, and at the same time felt a desire to lie down, stretch her arms and legs, and rest in the still, warm air. Closing her eyes, she took a few uncertain steps, overcome by an animal sense of well-being; then very lazily she went to collect the eggs from the hen-house. There were thirteen. She gathered them up and brought them back. When they were safely stowed away in the dresser, the kitchen smells made her feel peculiar once more, and she went out to sit for a while on the grass.

The farmyard, enclosed by trees, seemed asleep. The tall grass, where the yellow dandelions shone like lamps, was a vivid green, the fresh green of spring. At the foot of the apple trees, shadows crowded into circles. The thatched roofs of the farm buildings, high on which grew irises with leaves like sabres, smoked gently as though the dampness of the stables and barns were escaping through the straw.

The girl reached the shed where the carts and traps were kept. Just there, in the bottom of a ditch, was a large green hollow bursting with violets which spread their scent all around, and beyond the slope of the land could be seen open country, a vast plain where crops grew, dotted with clumps of trees and here and there with far-off groups of labourers, small as dolls, and white horses like toys hauling a child's plough driven by a man as tall as your finger.

She fetched a bundle of hay from a barn, tossed it into the hollow, and sat down. But it was uncomfortable. She undid the tie, spread the straw, and lay down on her back with both hands under her head and her legs spread out.

Very slowly she closed her eyes, luxuriating in a delicious drowsiness. She was in fact about to fall asleep when she felt two hands on her breasts. She leaped to her feet. It was Jacques, the farmer's lad, a tall, husky Picard who had been courting her for some time. That day he had been working in the sheepfold and, seeing her lying down in the shade, had crept up on her stealthily, holding his breath, his eyes ablaze. There were wisps of straw in his hair.

He tried to kiss her but she slapped his face, for she was as strong as he was. Slyly he begged for mercy. Then they sat down together and talked amicably. They talked about the weather which was as good as anybody could wish for harvesting, about the year which promised to be a good one, about their master who was a good man, about all the neighbours for miles around, about themselves, the villages they had come from, their young days, their memories, the relatives they had not seen for a long time and might never see again. She was sad when she thought about that and he, with only one idea in his head, rubbed up against her, trembling, overcome by desire. She was saying: ' 'Tis a tidy spell since I saw mother. Why, 'tis a hard thing and no mistake to be parted for so long.' And with a far-off look in her eyes she gazed through space away to the distant north, to the village she had left behind.

Suddenly he seized her round the neck and kissed her again, but she hit him with her fist full in the face so hard that his nose began to bleed. He got up and stood some way off with his head against the trunk of a tree. Then she felt sorry for him and, going up to him, asked: 'Does it hurt much?'

But he began to laugh. No, it was nothing, only she had caught him square on the nose. He murmured: 'Well I'll be . . . !' and looked at her admiringly, filled with renewed

respect and affection, feeling the first stirrings of true love
for so grand, so hearty, so strong a girl.

When the bleeding had stopped he suggested a walk: he
was afraid of what those fists of hers might do if they stayed
as close to each other as they were. But needing no second
bidding, she took his arm exactly as engaged couples do of
an evening when they are out strolling, and said: ' 'Tis not a
very nice thing, Jacques, taking me for granted like you do.'

He protested. What! Take her for granted! Never! He
was in love with her, that was the fact of it.

'So you truly want to wed me?' she said.

He hesitated, then began watching her out of the corner
of his eye as she stared dreamily straight ahead of her. Her
cheeks were red and round, her loose cotton jacket heaved
and swelled over her full breasts, her ripe lips glistened, and
her neck, which was almost bare, was sprinkled with little
pearls of sweat. He felt desire rise in him again and, placing
his lips close to her ear, he whispered: 'Aye, I do and all.' At
this, she threw her arms around his neck and kissed him so
hard that they were both left breathless.

From that moment, love's old story was once more
enacted through them. They snatched kisses in corners.
They arranged moonlit meetings in haystacks. Their legs
were black and blue with all the little kicks they gave each
other under the table with their heavy metal-toed clogs.

Then, little by little, Jacques seemed to grow tired of her.
He avoided her, hardly ever talked to her, and gave up
trying to meet her alone. She was assailed by doubts and a
great sense of sadness; and, after a while, she realized that
she was pregnant.

At first she was dismayed, but then she was filled with
rage which grew stronger with each day that passed because
he was so careful to avoid her that she could never manage
to get him by himself.

In the end, one night, when everyone was asleep, she let
herself out of the farmhouse in her petticoat, made her way
barefoot across the yard, and pushed open the door of the
stable where Jacques slept above his horses in a large loft
full of straw. He pretended to snore when he heard her

coming, but she climbed up to him and, kneeling at his side, shook him until he sat up.

When he was sitting up, asking: 'What are you after?', she said through clenched teeth, trembling with fury: 'I want . . . I want for you to marry me. You promised we would be wed.' He began to laugh and answered: 'Look here, if a chap was to wed all them he'd had a bit of fun with, there'd be no end to all the marrying he'd have to do.' But she grabbed him by the throat, held him down so strongly that he could not break her grip. Keeping her stranglehold on him and bringing her face right up to his, she screamed: 'I'm going to have a baby, do you hear? A baby!' He struggled for breath, almost suffocating. And so they remained without moving or speaking in the dark silence which was broken only by the champing of a horse as it tugged at the hay in its rack and then slowly munched it.

When Jacques realized that she was the stronger, he gasped: 'All right, I'll wed yer, since there's nothing else for it.'

But she no longer believed in his promises. 'There's to be no tarrying,' she said. 'You go tell the priest he's to say the bans.'

'No tarrying,' he answered.

'Swear to God you will!'

He hesitated for a few seconds, then, taking the plunge, said: 'I swear to God.'

She released her hold and left without another word.

A few days went by when she had no opportunity of speaking to him, and as the stable door was now always locked at night, she did not dare make a noise for fear of scandal.

Then one morning, she saw a new farm-hand come in for his dinner. She asked: 'Has Jacques gone away, then?'

'Aye, that he has,' the man said. 'I've got his place.'

She began to shake so much that she was quite unable to lift her saucepan off the fire. And later, when everyone had gone off to work, she went up into her bedroom and cried, burying her face in her pillow so that no one would hear.

During the day she tried to find out what had happened

without arousing suspicion. But so obsessed was she by the thought of her misfortune that she believed everyone she asked was laughing at her spitefully. In the event, she learned nothing save that he had gone far, far away.

II

Then began a period of unremitting torment. She worked like a machine, paying no heed to what she was doing, with only one thought in her head: 'What if they find out!' Her constant preoccupation made her so incapable of thinking clearly that she did not even wonder how to avoid the disgrace she felt was rushing unstoppably towards her, coming closer with each passing day, beyond remedy, and as certain as death itself.

Each morning she got up long before the others and, with stubborn persistence, tried to examine her waist in the small piece of broken mirror she used for doing her hair, wondering anxiously if today was the day when people would notice. And every few minutes during the day, she would stop whatever she was doing and look down to see if her apron was lifting noticeably over her swelling belly.

The months went by. She hardly spoke a word now, and if anyone asked her a question, she seemed not to understand but looked panic-stricken: her eyes were crazed and her hands shook, which made her master say: 'What's up, girl? Your brains have gone all addled.'

In church, she hid behind a pillar and dared not go to confession, for she was afraid of facing the priest whom she believed had superhuman powers enabling him to see into people's consciences. At dinner time, the glances of her fellow workers made her feel faint with fear, and she was forever imagining that she was about to be found out by the cowman, a sly, undersized, precocious lad whose gleaming eyes were always on her.

One morning the postman handed her a letter. She had never received a letter before and was so overcome that she had to sit down. Perhaps it was from him! But not being able to read, she sat anxious and trembling in front of the words on the paper. She put it in her pocket, not daring to reveal her secret to anyone; she constantly stopped what she was doing to stare at the regularly spaced writing which ended in a signature, vaguely hoping that in this way she might suddenly discover what it said. In the end, beside herself with impatience and worry, she went to see the schoolmaster who made her sit down while he read it out:

'My dearest girl, The present favour is to inform you that I am pretty low. Our neighbour, Monsieur Dentu, has written this to say that you are to come home, if you can.

On behalf of your loving mother,
Césaire Dentu, Deputy Mayor.'

Without a word she got up and left. But the minute she was alone, her legs gave way under her and she collapsed by the side of the road; and there she stayed until it was dark.

When she got back, she told the farmer what had happened. He said she could go for as long as she liked and promised to get a temporary girl in to do her work and to take her back when she returned.

Her mother was dying. She died the day the girl arrived. The day after, Rose gave birth to a seven-month baby boy, a distressing little bag of bones, so thin as to make you cringe and apparently eternally in pain, to judge by the tortured way he clenched his poor thin hands which were like a crab's legs. Still, he lived.

She said she was married but could not look after the child herself. So she left him with neighbours who promised to take good care of him. She went back.

But then, in her heart which had been bruised for so long, there rose like a dawning day a new love for the puny little creature she had left so far behind; yet her love became a new pain from which she was never free for an hour, for a minute, because she was separated from him.

Her greatest torture was a wild need to kiss him, to hold him in her arms, to feel the warmth of his little body next to hers. She could not sleep at night; she thought about him every minute of the day; and in the evenings, when she had finished her work, she sat staring at the fire as people do whose minds are far away.

People even started to talk about her and tease her about the young man she was sure to have, asking if he was handsome, if he was tall, if he was rich, and had they fixed a date for the wedding—and the christening? And often she ran off to be by herself to cry, for she felt their questions like so many pinpricks.

To take her mind off the pestering, she set about her work in a rage and, with her mind constantly fixed on her child, looked for ways of earning great sums of money for him. She resolved to work so hard that her master would be forced to raise her wages.

From then on, she put her hand on as many jobs as she could find, persuaded him to get rid of another serving girl who had become unnecessary, since she was working hard enough for two, made the bread, oil, and candles go further, saved on the corn that was given recklessly to the hens, and on the hay for the animals, some of which was being wasted. She was as careful with her master's money as though it were her own and, because she drove a hard bargain, demanded the best prices for the farm's produce, and got the better of the sly peasants who came selling their goods, she was given responsibility for buying and selling, organizing the work of the labourers, and overseeing the stores. And before long she had become indispensable. She kept such a sharp eye on everything that under her management the farm prospered prodigiously. For ten miles around, people talked of 'Farmer Vallin's servant' and the farmer, wherever he went, would say: 'That girl's worth her weight in gold!' However, time passed and her wages remained the same. Her hard work was taken for granted, being the duty of any devoted servant and no more than an expression of loyalty; and with a hint of bitterness, she began to reflect that if the farmer was now banking an extra fifty or a hundred *écus* a month on the strength of her efforts, she was still earning her two hundred and forty francs a year, and not a penny more or less.

She decided to ask her master for an increase in her wages. Three times she approached him and then, when she was face to face with him, talked of other things. She felt uncomfortable asking for money, as though it were a slightly shameful thing to do. Then one day, when the farmer was eating alone in the kitchen, she said, feeling rather embarrassed, that she would like a word in private with him. He looked up in surprise, with both hands on the table, holding his knife in one, with its point in the air, and a piece of bread in the other, and stared at her. She felt confused under his gaze and asked for a week's leave of absence so that she could go home, because she was not well.

He agreed at once; then, a little embarrassed in turn, he added: 'I'll be wanting to have a talk with you when you get back.'

III

Her child was nearly eight months old: she did not recognize him. He had grown pink-cheeked and chubby. He was like a little parcel of live dripping. His fingers, separated by rolls of flesh, waved gently with visible contentment. She flung herself on him as eagerly as an animal pounces on its prey, and kissed him so fiercely that he began to scream with fear. Then she began to cry too because he did not know who she was and because he held out his arms to his foster-mother the moment she appeared.

But the next day he began to get used to her face and laughed when he saw her. She took him out into the country, held his hands and ran about excitedly, and sat him down in the shade of the trees. There, for the first time in her life, though he could not understand what she said, she opened her heart to another human being, told him about her troubles, her work, her worries, cares, and hopes, and wore him out with the strength and intensity of her caresses.

She found endless joy in holding him, in washing and dressing him; she even took pleasure in cleaning up his baby messes, as though such intimate attentions were a confirmation of her motherhood. She watched him, never ceasing to be amazed that he was hers, and whispered to herself over and over as she rocked him in her arms: 'You're my little chick! You're my little chick!'

She sobbed all the way back to the farm and had hardly got in when her master called her into his room. She went, very surprised and very nervous, though she could not have said why.

'Sit down here,' he said.

She sat down and they remained for a while side by side, both feeling embarrassed, their arms dangling awkwardly, not looking at each other, the way country people do.

The farmer, a stout man of 40, twice a widower, cheerful and strong-willed, was visibly uncomfortable, which was unusual for him. In the end he made up his mind and began speaking rather vacantly, stammering a little and with his eyes on the distant fields outside.

'Rose,' he began, 'have you ever thought of settling down?'

She turned pale as death. When she did not answer, he went on: 'You're a grand lass, steady, hard-working, good with money. With a wife like you, a man could do very well for himself.'

She sat without moving, looking frightened, making no attempt to understand, for her thoughts were in a whirl as when great danger threatens. He waited a moment, then went on: 'See here, a farm with no mistress will never amount to much, even with a firm hand like yours at the wheel.' He stopped, not knowing how to go on; and Rose looked at him in a panic, like someone who believes he has come face to face with a murderer and is ready to run at the first movement he makes.

Finally, after letting five minutes tick by, he asked: 'Well, would you be willing?'

Sad-faced, she replied: 'Willing to what, master?'

He said curtly: 'Why, marry me, of course.'

She stood up suddenly, then, as though stricken, collapsed onto her chair where she continued to sit without moving, like someone crushed beneath the weight of a great affliction. In the end, the farmer lost patience: 'Come along, do you want to or not?'

She stared at him wildly; then all at once her eyes filled with tears and in a choking voice she said twice: 'I can't! I can't!'

'Why ever not?' he asked. 'Look here, you're being stupid. I'll give you till tomorrow to think it over.'

And he left her hurriedly, very relieved now that this highly embarrassing business was over and done with, and confident that next morning his servant would accept a proposal which was a godsend for her and a smart move on his part, since marrying her would give him a permanent hold over a woman who in the long run would be worth far more to him than the biggest dowry for miles around.

There were, in any case, no grounds for either of them to think the match unsuitable, for in the country everyone is more or less equal: the master works the land alongside the hired hand who is quite likely to become a master himself sooner or later, while farm girls become mistresses every day without altering their way of life or their habits.

Rose did not go to bed that night. She collapsed onto her mattress and, lacking even the strength to weep, just sat there, completely overcome. She remained inert, with no feeling in her body, her mind in a whirl as though it had been roughed up by one of those tools which carders use for shredding wool. Only for brief moments did she succeed in putting a few frayed thoughts together, and then she was appalled at the very idea of what might happen. Her terror grew, and each time the big clock in the kitchen struck the hours in the silence of the sleeping house, she broke into a cold sweat. Her thoughts became confused, nightmare followed nightmare, her candle went out. Wild fancies took over, uneasy imaginings such as come upon country people who sometimes believe a spell has been cast on them, and they prompted her to run from her troubles as ships run before the storm.

An owl hooted. She shivered, stood up, ran her hands over her face, through her hair, and felt herself all over like a mad thing. Then, as though she were walking in her sleep, she went downstairs. In the yard she crawled on her hands and knees so as not to be seen by any lout who happened to be prowling around, for the waning moon lit the fields brightly. Instead of opening the gate, she climbed over the embankment; then, when she had open country ahead of her, she started walking. She hurried straight on at a springy, rapid trot, and now and then, although she was not conscious of doing so, she cried out shrilly. Her enormous shadow on the ground at her side raced along with her, and now and again some night bird hovered over her head. Dogs in farmyards barked as they heard her pass; one of them jumped a ditch, ran after her, and tried to bite her; but she turned on it and screamed so loud that the animal fled in terror and returned to its kennel where it cowered without making another sound.

Occasionally a family of young hares cavorted in a field, but at the approach of this fury hurrying on like Diana in a rage, the timid creatures disbanded promptly: the leverets and the mother disappeared into a furrow while the father bolted. His leaping shadow, with long ears erect, passed several times in front of the setting moon which was now slipping towards the world's lower depths and lighting the plain with its oblique rays, like an enormous lantern set down on the horizon.

The stars were fading in the damp night sky and a few birds were just beginning to sing: it was nearly day. The girl was panting with exhaustion, and when the sun pierced the purple dawn, she halted.

Her swollen feet refused to carry her any further. But then she noticed a pond, a large pond, full of stagnant water which looked like blood in the ruddy glow of the new day, and, treading gingerly, with one hand over her heart, she limped towards it to dip her legs in its shallows. She sat down on a clump of grass, took off her shoes which were full of grit, removed her stockings, and plunged her bruised calves into the still water where occasional bubbles of air broke the surface.

A soothing coolness rose from her feet and spread all through her. As she sat staring into the depths of the pond, her head suddenly began to spin and she was overcome by a mad urge to throw herself into it. There, her sufferings would be over, over for ever. She did not think of her child now; she wanted peace, complete rest, sleep without end. She got to her feet and, with her arms raised, took two steps forward. The water had reached her thighs and she was about to plunge in further, when she felt a painful stinging around her ankles which made her spring back. She let out a cry of despair, for, from her knees to her toes, long black leeches were sucking the life out of her, swelling visibly as they clung to her flesh. She dared not touch them and screamed with horror. Her desperate shrieks attracted the attention of a peasant some way off who was driving by in his cart. He removed the leeches one by one, put compresses of wild herbs on the wounds, and drove her in his waggon all the way back to the farm where she worked.

She was in bed for two weeks. The first morning she got up, she was sitting outside the front door when her master came from nowhere and stood in front of her. 'Well,' he said, 'it's all settled then, is it?'

For a moment she did not reply, but since he remained standing there, with his staring eyes looking quite through her, she finally mumbled: 'No. I can't.'

At this, he lost his temper: 'Can't! Can't! And why can't you, my girl?'

She started crying again, and repeated: 'I can't!'

He glared and shouted at her angrily: 'You've got yourself somebody else, I suppose, is that it?'

She stammered, trembling with shame: 'Happen I have.'

He turned red as a beetroot and spluttered with rage: 'So at last you admit it, you slut! And who is this scum? Some good-for-nothing with no money, no roof over his head, and nothing to put in his belly? Come on, who is it?' And when she said nothing, he went on: 'So you won't say. . . . Well, I'll tell you who it is. It's Jean Baudu, isn't it?'

She cried out: 'Oh no! It's not him!'

'Well, is it Pierre Martin, then?'

'Not him neither.'

And in desperation, he named all the young men in the district while she denied them all, feeling overwhelmed and dabbing at her eyes with the corner of her blue apron. But with brute obstinacy, he went on probing, scraping away at her heart to dig out her secret, just as a hound will spend all day scratching at a hole to get at the creature he can scent crouching inside. Suddenly he exclaimed:

'I've got it! It's Jacques, the day man I took on a year or two since. They said he was pretty thick with you. They said the pair of you was walking out together.'

Rose could not speak; the blood rushed to her face; her tears ceased suddenly and dried on her cheeks like drops of water on hot metal. She screamed: 'No, it's not him, it's not him!'

'Is that the fact of it?' asked the devious farmer who had got a whiff of the truth.

She replied quickly: 'I swear, I swear . . .'

She tried to think of something to swear by, for she did not dare call up holy things, but he interrupted her: 'But he was always following you around everywhere and couldn't get enough of ogling you when you were serving dinner up. Did you promise to marry him? Did you?'

This time she looked the farmer in the eye: 'No, never, never. I swear by the good Lord that if he was here this minute begging me to wed him, I wouldn't have him.'

She said this with such conviction that the farmer hesitated. Then he went on, as though he were thinking aloud: 'Well, what is it, then? You didn't get into trouble, otherwise people would have known. And since you didn't get into trouble, a girl in your position would never turn her master down on that account. There's got to be something behind it, though.' Choking on her distress, she could not speak.

Again he asked her: 'So you won't?'

With a sigh, she said: 'I can't.'

He turned on his heel and walked away.

She believed she was rid of him and spent the rest of the day more or less at peace, but feeling as battered and worn as if she'd been up since first light and made to take the place of the old white horse which turned the threshing machine. She went to bed as soon as she could, and fell asleep at once.

In the middle of the night she was woken by two hands feeling their way around the bed. She started with fear but immediately recognized the farmer by his voice: 'Don't be afraid, Rose,' he said, ' 'tis only me. I want to have a little chat with you.' At first she felt surprised: then, when he tried to climb into the sheets with her, she understood what he had come for and began to shake violently, feeling alone in the dark, still heavy with sleep, naked, in a bed, beside a man who wanted her. She did not surrender, far from it, but she resisted languidly, forcing herself to struggle against her instinct—invariably stronger in simple souls—and only feebly protected by the weaker will with which such inert, inactive natures as hers are equipped. She turned her face to the wall, then to the room as she tried to escape his mouth which pursued her with kisses, and her body writhed briefly under the bedclothes, weakened by the struggle which wore her down, while he became brutal, drunk with desire. All at once, he yanked the sheets off her. She knew then that could not fight him off any further. Ostrich-like in her shame, she buried her face in her hands and made no further efforts to defend herself.

The farmer stayed until dawn. He returned the next night, and every night thereafter.

They lived as man and wife.

One morning, he said: 'I've had the bans called. We're to be wed next month.'

She said nothing. What could she say? She did not oppose him. What could she do?

IV

She married him. She felt as though she had fallen into a pit with slippery sides from which she would never escape, while over her head, like huge rocks which could crash down on her at any moment, hung troubles of every description. In her mind, her husband was like a man she had robbed who might find her out at any moment. She thought about her child who was the cause of all her troubles, but also the source of all her earthly joys. She went to see him twice a year, and each time came back more unhappy.

With time, however, her fears receded, she became calmer, and she became easier in her mind—though at the back of it a vague dread still lurked.

The years went by and the child was 6. By now she was almost happy, but then her farmer's mood darkened.

For two or three years now he had seemed to be nursing a heavy heart, some secret worry which gnawed at him and preyed increasingly on his mind. He would remain sitting at table long after he had finished eating, with his head in his hands, looking the picture of misery, consumed by his sorrow. He spoke more sharply, even brutally now, as though he had something against her, and there were times when he answered her bad-temperedly, almost angrily.

One day, their neighbour's little boy came for some eggs. She was run off her feet just then, and was being cross with him, when her husband appeared unexpectedly and said in his bad-tempered voice: 'If he was yours, you wouldn't talk to him like that.' She was thunderstruck and stood there dumbly before going indoors with all her fears awakened.

At dinner-time he did not speak to her, avoided her eye, and made her feel that he hated and despised her, that he knew something.

She lost her head. She did not dare to be alone with him after the meal was over and, leaving the house, she ran all the way to church.

Dusk was falling. The narrow nave was quite dark, but she could hear footsteps moving about in the silence, somewhere in the choir, where the sacristan was refilling the tabernacle lamp for the night. Its flickering flame, lost in the vaulted blackness, seemed to Rose like her last hope. Fixing her eyes on it, she fell to her knees.

A chain rattled as the tiny light rose in the air. A moment later, there was the regular sound of clogs on flagstone, then the swish of a dangling rope, and the tinny bell sent the peal of the evening Angelus out into the gathering mist. The man was just leaving when she went up to him.

'Is the priest there?' she asked.

'He might be,' he replied. 'He always has his dinner when the Angelus goes.'

Trembling, she pushed open the presbytery gate.

The priest was just about to sit down to eat. He offered her a chair. 'Yes, I know all about it. Your husband has already had a word with me about what's made you come here.'

The poor woman nearly fainted. The priest went on: 'What do you want, my child?' He spooned up his soup quickly and some dropped onto the belly of his well-filled, greasy cassock.

Rose dared not speak or implore or entreat. She stood up. The priest said: 'Be brave . . .' Then she left.

She walked back to the farm, not knowing what she was doing. The farmer was waiting for her. His labourers had all left while she was out. She collapsed in a heap at his feet and, through a flood of tears, said: 'What is it you got against me?'

He began shouting and swearing at her: 'The fact that I got no kids, that's what! For God's sake, when a man marries a wife, it's not so as they can be by themselves till the end of their days! That's what I got against you! A cow that never calves is no damned good to anybody, and when a man's wife doesn't have kids, she's just as useless.'

Sobbing and spluttering, she repeated over and over again: ''T'ain't my fault! 'T'ain't my fault!'

In the end he calmed down and said: 'I don't say it is. But it's vexatious all the same.'

V

From that day on, she had only one thought: to have a child, another child; and she told everyone what she wanted.

A woman neighbour said there was a way: every evening she should get her husband to drink a glass of water with a pinch of ash in it. The farmer tried it but it did not work.

They told each other: 'Perhaps there's secret ways,' and they made enquiries. They were told of a shepherd who lived twenty-five miles away, and one day Vallin, the farmer, harnessed his gig and drove off to consult him. The shepherd gave him a loaf of bread over which he made some signs. The bread had been baked with herbs and the two of them were to eat a piece at night both before and after their exertions. They got through the whole loaf, to no effect.

The schoolmaster spoke to them of mysteries and of methods of love-making unknown in country districts. They were, he said, infallible. They failed.

The priest recommended a pilgrimage to the shrine of the Precious Blood at Fécamp. Going into the Abbey with the crowds, Rose bowed her head and, joining her prayer to the coarse supplications which flew up from every peasant heart around her, she entreated Him upon whom all were calling to make her fertile once more. But in vain. She came to believe that she had been punished for that first fault, and she was overwhelmed by an immense sadness.

Her sorrows made her grow thin. Her husband too began to look older, 'ate his heart out', people said, and wore himself out with unavailing hopes.

Then war broke out between them. He swore at her and beat her. All day long he picked quarrels and at night, in their bed, breathing hard and full of hate, he shouted insults and obscenities at her.

Finally one night, unable to think up new ways of making her suffer, he ordered her to get up and stand outside by the door in the rain until it was light. When she refused, he seized her by the throat and began to hit her in the face with his fists. She said nothing and did not move. Beside himself, he jumped on her and planted his knees in her stomach. Mad with rage, he then set about knocking her senseless. In a moment of desperate resistance she flung him back against the wall with a furious sweep of her arm, sat up, and, in a voice which was quite changed, hissed: 'I got a kid! I got one already! I had him with Jacques. You remember Jacques. He was going to wed me but he went away.'

Struck speechless, the man remained where he had fallen, as shocked as she was herself. He managed to stammer: 'What did you say? What's that you said?'

She began to sob, and through her gushing tears said falteringly: 'That's why I wouldn't marry you, 'tis the reason why. I couldn't tell you. You'd have thrown me out and left me and my baby without a scrap to eat. You never had children yourself, so you don't know nothing about what it's like. Nothing!'

Over and over, with growing surprise, he repeated dully: 'You got a kiddie? You got a kiddie?'

Through a bout of hiccoughs, she said: 'You forced yourself on me, have you forgotten? I never wanted to wed you.'

He got up, lit a candle, and started walking around the room with his hands behind his back. Prostrated on the bed, she went on crying. Suddenly he stopped in front of her and said: 'So it's all my fault, is it, if we've not had a child together?' She did not answer.

He began his pacing again. Then he stopped a second time and asked: 'How old is he, this kid of yours?'

She murmured: 'He'll be almost 6.'

Again he asked: 'How come you never told me?'

'How could I?', she groaned.

He remained standing quite still. 'Here,' he said, 'get up.'

She got out of bed with difficulty. When she was on her feet, supporting herself against the wall, he suddenly began to laugh as heartily as he used to in happier days. Seeing her look of amazement, he went on: 'Well, we'll go and fetch him here, this kid of yours, seeing as how we got none of our own.'

She felt so panic-stricken that if her strength had not failed her she would certainly have run away. But the farmer was rubbing his hands together and murmuring: 'I been wanting to adopt one, and bingo! here's one ready-made! Ready-made! I been asking the priest to look out an orphan for me.' Still laughing, he kissed his weeping, bewildered wife on both cheeks, and cried in a loud voice, as though she could not hear: 'Come along, mother! Let's go and see if there's any soup left. I could fancy a drop of soup.'

She put her skirt on. They went downstairs. And while she knelt down to relight the fire under the pot, he beamed as he strode round and round the kitchen, repeating: 'Well now, that's bucked me up no end. Though it's me as shouldn't p'raps say it, I'm feeling pleased, pretty pleased.'

A Day in the Country

FOR five months now they had been planning to have lunch somewhere in the country just outside Paris on the birthday of Madame Dufour, whose name was Pétronille. And because they were looking forward to the outing with some impatience, everyone was up early on the big day.

Monsieur Dufour had borrowed the milkman's cart, and took the reins himself. The vehicle had two wheels and was spotless; it had an awning supported by four iron stanchions to which flaps were attached. They were rolled up so that the occupants could see out as they rode along. The flap at the back hung down loosely and fluttered in the wind like a flag. Madame Dufour, seated next to her husband, was radiant in an extraordinary cerise silk dress. Behind them an aged grandma and a young girl sat on separate seats. Just visible was the flaxen hair of a young man who, since there was nothing for him to sit on, had stretched out on the floor, so that only his head could be seen.

After driving up the avenue of the Champs-Elysées and negotiating the fortifications at the Porte Maillot, everyone had started gazing at the passing scene. When they reached the bridge at Neuilly, Monsieur Dufour said: 'Ah! The country—at last!' and his wife, on hearing this signal, went into raptures about nature. At the roundabout at Courbevoie, they had been gripped by astonishment on observing how far away the horizon was. Over there, to the right, was Argenteuil with its spire erect; above and beyond loomed the Sannois hills and the mill at Orgement. On their left, the Marly aqueduct stood out against the clear morning sky, and in the distance they could even see the terrace at Saint-Germain. Meanwhile, straight ahead, at the end of a line of hills, recent excavations marked the new fort at Cormeilles. In the far distance, amazingly far off, beyond the plains and villages, they could make out the dark green of forests.

The sun began to burn their faces; the dust got into their

eyes all the time, and on both sides of the road the land spread out, interminably bare, dirty, and foul-smelling. It looked as though it had been ravaged by leprosy which had even eaten into the houses, for the skeletons of deserted tumbledown buildings, even a number of small villas left unfinished because the builders had not been paid, held out four walls but no roofs. Here and there, tall factory chimneys sprouted from the sterile ground, the only things that grew in these mouldering fields where the spring breezes wafted a scent of oil and slag-heaps mixed with another, even less pleasant odour. Finally they passed over the Seine a second time and, as they crossed the bridge, they were entranced. The river was a blaze of light; mist rose from it, teased up by the sun, and there was sweet content and salutary refreshment to be had now that they could at last breathe a purer air which had not swept up black smoke from the factories or fumes from the sewage-pits. A man passing by told them that the place was called Bezons.

The cart pulled up and Monsieur Dufour began to read out the sign above the door of a cheery tavern: *Poulin's Restaurant, Fish Stews and Whitebait, Assembly Rooms, Shaded Gardens and Swings*.

'Well, Madame Dufour, will this do you? Come on, what's it to be?'

Monsieur Dufour's wife then also read aloud: *Poulin's Restaurant, Fish Stews and Whitebait, Assembly Rooms, Shaded Gardens and Swings*. Then she gave the place a good looking over.

It was a country inn, painted white, and it stood at the side of the road. Through the open door she motioned towards the shiny metal of the bar against which two workmen in their Sunday best were leaning.

Madame Dufour finally made up her mind: 'Yes, this is grand,' she said. '*And* there's a view.' The cart drove into an enormous area behind the inn with tall trees which stretched away as far as the Seine, from which it was separated only by the tow-path.

They got out of the cart. The husband jumped down first, then held out his arms to catch his wife. The

footboard, secured by two iron brackets, was a long way
down, and to reach it Madame Dufour had to show a
glimpse of one leg which, trim to begin with, soon turned
into a cascade of fleshy, drooping thigh. Monsieur Dufour,
already feeling rather bucked at being in the country, gave
her a sharp pinch on the calf, then, taking her in his arms,
set her heavily on the ground, like an enormous parcel. She
patted her silk dress with her hands to shake off the dust
and then stood examining the place that she had come to.

She was about 36 and generously proportioned, a sight to
gladden the eye. She had difficulty breathing for she was
violently constrained by her stays which were too tight: the
pressure exerted by her scaffolding almost squeezed the
wobbling mass of her over-ample bosom up into her double
chin.

Next, the young girl, placing one hand on her father's
shoulder, jumped down lightly by herself. The lad with the
flaxen hair had got down by putting one foot on the wheel
and he helped Monsieur Dufour to unload grandma.

Then the horse was unharnessed and hitched to a tree,
and the cart dropped nose-down with its shafts on the
ground. When the men had taken off their coats, they
washed their hands in a bucket of water and then joined the
ladies who had already settled themselves on the swings.

Mademoiselle Dufour was trying to swing standing up,
by herself, but could not work up sufficient momentum.
She was a pretty girl of 18 or 20, the kind of girl you see in
the street who stings you with a lash of sudden desire,
leaving you vaguely uneasy until nightfall, with senses a-
tingle. Tall, with a small waist and broad hips, she had very
dark skin, very big eyes, and very black hair. Her dress
clearly showed the firm, full curves of her body which were
further accentuated by the thrusts of her back which she
gave in her efforts to gain height. Her outstretched arms held
the ropes above her head, so that with each push she gave
her breasts stood out smoothly. Her hat, blown off by a gust
of wind, had fallen behind her. The swing slowly gathered
speed, and every backward swoop showed her pretty legs as
far as the knee, and into the faces of the two men who

laughed as they watched her, she flung the downdraught of her skirts which was headier than wine fumes.

Sitting on the other swing, Madame Dufour called in a monotonous, unbroken wail: 'Cyprien, come and push me; come and give me a push, Cyprien!' In the end he went over to her and, rolling up his sleeves as though about to start a job of work, managed with considerable difficulty to set his wife in motion.

Clinging to the ropes for dear life, she held her legs straight out in front of her, to avoid stubbing the ground, and surrendered to the swing's exhilarating scythings. Her womanly charms, thus jerked and jolted, shook like jelly on a plate. But as her momentum carried her higher and higher, she became dizzy and frightened. Each time she plunged down, she let out a piercing scream which attracted all the youngsters round about; and some way off, directly in front of her, she dimly saw a sprinking of leering faces variously contorted by laughter.

A serving-girl appeared and they ordered lunch.

'I'll have the Seine whitebait, sauté rabbit, a salad, and dessert,' said Madame Dufour self-importantly. 'Bring us a couple of litres and a bottle of Bordeaux,' said her husband. 'We'll eat out here, on the grass,' added the young girl.

Grandma, who had come over all soft-hearted on seeing the resident cat, had been following it around for ten minutes, vainly cooing the sweetest names at it. Although no doubt inwardly flattered by such attentions, it avoided the old lady's hand without straying far from it and wandered contentedly among the trees, rubbing itself against them with its tail in the air, purring softly with pleasure.

'Coo!' suddenly cried out the young man with the flaxen hair who had gone exploring, 'there's some boats here and they ain't half smashing!' Everyone went to see. In a small wooden shed hung two superb racing skiffs, as elegant and finely wrought as pieces of expensive furniture. They lay side by side, like two tall slim girls, long, narrow, and gleaming, a standing invitation to skim over the water on the fine, soft evenings or clear mornings of summer, to race past banks where flowers bloom and whole trees dip their branches in water trembling with eternally shaking reeds where flashing kingfishers fly up like blue lightning.

The whole family stared at them respectfully: 'Yes, they're smashers, alright,' Monsieur Dufour said several times. And he pointed out their features like an expert. In his time he'd done a spot of rowing, more than a spot, and with a couple of fistfuls (here he mimed his rowing action) he'd not given a toss for anybody. In those days he'd left many an Englishman for dead in races at Joinville; and he made jokes about the word 'rowlocks', the supports on which the oars swivel, saying that rowers, and quite right too, never went out without doing a spot of 'oaring'. He grew heated as he talked and insisted boneheadedly that he would lay odds that with a boat like one of these he could manage fifteen miles an hour without raising a sweat.

'It's ready,' said the serving girl, appearing in the doorway. They rushed off. But in the best spot, which Madame Dufour had already secretly picked out for them to sit at, two young men were already having their lunch. Quite likely they were the owners of the skiffs, for they were wearing rowing clothes.

They were stretched out in deck-chairs, almost lying down. Their faces were tanned dark brown by the sun and their torsos were covered by thin white cotton vests which left their arms bare, arms as muscular as a blacksmith's. They were strong and well-built and, though they put on the heartiness rather, every movement they made betrayed the supple grace of limb which comes with exercise and is a world away from the deforming effects on the working man of strenuous, endlessly repeated labours.

They exchanged a quick smile when they saw the mother, and a look when they saw the girl. 'Let's let them have our place,' said one, 'it'll do for an introduction.' The other got to his feet at once and, holding in his hand a cap which was half red and half black, he chivalrously offered the ladies the only spot in the garden where the sun was not beating down. The offer was accepted with profuse thanks; and to make the occasion more rustic, the family spurned tables and chairs and sat down on the grass.

The two young men moved their plates and glasses a few paces along and resumed eating. Their bare arms, which they displayed constantly, made the girl feel somewhat uncomfortable. She even made a point of turning her head away so as not to see them, while Madame Dufour, rather more boldly and stirred by a feminine curiosity which may have been desire, stared at them the whole time, perhaps regretfully comparing them with the inadequacies which her husband hid under his clothes.

She had collapsed in a cross-legged heap on the grass and fidgeted all the time, saying there were ants running all over her. The presence of two such amiable young men had done nothing to improve Monsieur Dufour's temper, and he tried to get comfortably settled without managing to, while the lad with the flaxen hair ate in silence, like some ghoulish presence.

'It's a lovely day, isn't it?' the fat woman said to one of the oarsmen. She was trying to be pleasant because they had given up their spot.

'Rather,' he replied. 'Do you get out into the country often?'

'Oh, once or twice a year, that's all, for a breath of fresh air. Do you come a lot?'

'I spend every evening out here.'

'Oh! That must be very nice for you!'

'Rather. I should say.'

And he explained how he spent his days, making it sound very romantic, telling it in such a way as to make their shopkeepers' hearts, deprived of greenery and hungry for country walks, thrill with that bovine love of nature which haunts them all year long behind the counters of their shops.

The girl, deeply stirred, looked up at the oarsman. Monsieur Dufour spoke for the first time. 'That's living,' he said. Then he added: 'A bit more rabbit, old girl?'

'No thanks, dear.' She turned again to the young men and, gesturing to their bare arms, she said: 'Don't you ever get cold like that?'

They both began to laugh and appalled the whole family

with tales of how prodigiously they exerted themselves, how they swam in the river without waiting to cool down first, and how they took their boats out at night, in the fog. They beat their chests to give an idea of the sound it made. 'You certainly look fit enough,' said the husband who had stopped mentioning the time when he had left the English for dead.

The girl was now examining them out of the corner of her eye. The lad with the yellow hair took a drink which went down the wrong way and he spluttered uncontrollably all over the cerise silk dress of the wife who lost her temper and sent for some water to wash out the stains.

Meanwhile, it had become terribly hot. The sparkling river seemed to retain the heat and the wine went to their heads.

Monsieur Dufour, rocked by a violent attack of hiccoughs, had unbuttoned his waistcoat and the top of his trousers. His wife, who could not breathe, let out the hooks of her dress one by one. Their apprentice gaily shook his flaxen locks and helped himself to more wine. The grandma, feeling tipsy, held herself very straight and dignified. The girl, however, seemed unaffected; but her eyes seemed to glisten slightly and a pinkish tinge suffused the very dark skin of her cheeks.

The coffee finished them off. They suggested a sing-song and everyone sang in turn while the others clapped wildly. Then with an effort they all stood up and while the two ladies, feeling rather dizzy, got their breath back, the two men, both quite drunk, did exercises. Lumbering and flabby, their faces scarlet, they hung ponderously on the rings quite unable to pull themselves up, while their shirts constantly threatened to part company with their trousers like flags flapping in the breeze.

The oarsmen had launched their skiffs, and now they came back and courteously asked the ladies if they would like a row on the river.

'Would you mind, dear? Do say yes!' said Madame Dufour to her lord and master. He looked at her drunkenly, uncomprehendingly. One of the oarsmen came up to him with two fishing-lines in his hand. At the prospect of catching a gudgeon, every shopkeeper's ideal, his dull eyes lit up and he agreed to everything, after which he went and sat in the shade under the bridge, with his feet dangling above the water, beside the young man with the flaxen hair who promptly fell asleep.

One of the oarsmen gave of himself above the call of duty: he took the mother. 'Race you to the Island!' he shouted as they sped away.

The other boat moved off more slowly. The man at the oars was staring so hard at his passenger that he was unable to think of anything else, for he had been gripped by emotions which robbed him of his strength.

The girl, sitting in the cox's seat, surrendered to the bliss of gliding over water. She felt her mind become blank and her limbs relax and she let herself go, as though overcome by a comprehensive intoxication of her senses. Her face was very flushed and her breath came faster. The giddiness left by the wine, fostered by the torrential heat which fell in streams all around her, made it seem as if all the trees on the bank were waving to her as she passed by. Vague sensual promptings and a quickening of the blood kindled her whole body which had been inflamed by the heat of the day. Moreover, there, on the water, in the middle of the country which had been emptied of human life by the furnace in the sky, she felt uneasy at being so close to this young man who thought her beautiful and kissed her skin with his eyes and whose desire she felt as keenly as the sun.

Because they were powerless to speak, they felt their excitement grow: they looked away, at the surrounding countryside. Finally, he forced himself to ask her name: 'Henriette,' she said, 'Really!' he said. 'My name's Henri.'

The sound of their voices broke the tension. They showed a keen interest in the banks of the river. The other skiff had halted and seemed to be waiting for them. Its skipper shouted: 'We'll see you in the wood. We're going on up as far as Robinson: Madame here is feeling thirsty.' And leaning on his oars, they moved off so quickly that they were soon out of sight.

Meantime, a muffled drone which had been audible for some time now came rushing closer. The whole river seemed to quake as though the subdued roar rose from its depths. 'What's that noise?' she asked. It was the water going over the weir which cuts the river in two at the end of the island. He was in the middle of a long explanation when, through the sound of falling water, they were struck by the song of a bird which seemed to come from far off.

'Listen to that. Nightingales singing in daytime. That means the females as sitting on the nest.'

A nightingale! She had never heard one before and the very idea of listening to one prompted her heart to tender and poetic visions. A nightingale! the very same unseen witness to lovers' trysts which Juliet invoked on her balcony, the music of the gods which accompanies human kisses, the eternal inspiration for all those swooning romances which open up azured ideals to the starved little hearts of love-sick girls. At last she was to hear a nightingale sing.

'Sh! We must be quiet,' her companion said. 'If you like, we'll go ashore and sit in the woods just near where it's perched.'

The skiff seemed to glide along. Trees loomed up on the island, and the bank just there was so low that they could see directly into the depths of the thickets. They halted and tied up the boat. With Henriette leaning on Henri's arm, they walked among the branches. 'Watch your head,' he said. She bent her head and they crept into an inextricable tangle of trailing creepers, leaves, and reeds, a refuge untraceable to anyone who did not know it. With a laugh the young man called it 'his private hideaway'.

Just above their heads, sitting on one of the branches which shaded them, the bird continued to sing. It trilled and it warbled, and it fired off loud, pulsating notes which filled the air and seemed to vanish into the horizon, uncoiling as they sped along the river and taking flight above the plain through the incandescent silence which hung heavy over the landscape.

They did not speak for fear of making the bird fly away.

They were sitting close to each other and slowly Henri's arm stole round Henriette's waist and squeezed her gently. Without anger, she took his bold hand in hers and pushed it away each time he drew her to him, for she did not feel in any way discomfited by his caress: it seemed a completely natural gesture which she should thrust aside just as naturally.

She listened to the bird, lost in ecstasy. She was filled with a vast yearning for happiness. Sudden waves of tenderness swept over her, intuitions of poetical, super-human absolutes, and a softening of heart and nerves so sweet that she wept without knowing why. The young man now held her fast in his arms. She did not try to push him away nor did she think to do so.

The nightingale stopped singing abruptly. A distant voice called: 'Henriette!'

'Don't answer,' he whispered. 'You'll make it fly off.'

She no more thought to answer than to push him away.

They remained as they were for some time. Madame Dufour had sat down somewhere, for now and then they just caught her little shrieks as the other oarsman doubtless set about rummaging her ample person.

The girl was still crying, glowing with the sweetest sensations, feeling her skin hot and all a-tingle with pinpricks which were quite new to her. Henri's head lay on her shoulder. Suddenly he kissed her on the lips. She recoiled furiously and, to get away from him, leaned back on the ground. But he threw himself on her, covering her with his body. He spent an age seeking out the mouth which avoided him, found it, and fastened his own upon it. Then, overwhelmed by powerful desires, she returned his kiss and held him tightly in her arms, all her resistance collapsing as though crushed by some excessively heavy weight.

All around was calm. The bird began singing again. It first emitted three shrill notes which sounded like a love-call, then, after a moment's silence, started to warble slower, softer modulations.

A gentle breeze wafted by, raising a rustle of leaves, and in the thick undergrowth two burning sighs mingled with the song of the nightingale and the faint breathing of the woods.

The bird went into raptures and its call, slowly gathering speed like a house which catches fire or a passion which grows, seemed the accompaniment to a crackle of kisses beneath the tree. The ecstasy of its song turned into a frenzy. It held long, swooning, single notes and burst into wild spasms of melody.

At times it rested briefly, producing no more than two or three subdued trills to which it gave a sudden, shrill climax. Or else it set off on a demented tack, spraying scales, tremors, convulsions as in a wanton song of love which ends in cries of triumph.

At last it fell silent, and to its ears came the sound of a moan so devout that it might have been mistaken for a soul bidding farewell to life. The sound continued for a moment before ending in a great sob.

They were both very pale as they left their bed of greenery. The blue sky seemed to them to have grown dimmer; they did not feel the glare of the burning sun; they were aware of solitude and silence. They walked quickly, side by side, not speaking, not touching, for they seemed to have turned into irreconcilable enemies, as though a sense of loathing had come between their bodies and hatred separated their minds.

Now and then Henriette called: 'Mother!'

A minor earthquake shook a bush. Henri thought he glimpsed a white petticoat being pulled down over a fat leg. Then the large lady, looking a little disconcerted and redder than ever, eyes ashine and bosom heaving like an angry sea, emerged perhaps rather too close to her companion for comfort. Her companion must surely have seen something funny, for his face was creased with sudden gusts of laughter which he was quite unable to control.

Madame Dufour took his arm affectionately and they all returned to the boats. Henri, walking on ahead, with the girl at his side and still not speaking, thought he could make out the sound of a moist, half-smothered kiss.

They returned to Bezons.

Monsieur Dufour, who had sobered up, was waiting impatiently. The young man with the flaxen hair was having a bite to eat in the inn before they left. The cart was harnessed in the yard and grandma, already aboard, was complaining because she was afraid of being overtaken on the plain by night, the roads around Paris being none too safe. Everyone shook hands and the Dufours drove off.

'Cheerio!' shouted the oarsmen.

The reply was a sigh and a tear.

Two months later, walking down the rue des Martyrs, Henri noticed a shopdoor which read: *Dufour: Ironmongers*. He went in.

The fat lady was growing fatter behind her counter. They recognized each other at once and after exchanging courtesies he asked after them all.

'How about Mademoiselle Henriette? How is she?'

'Very well, thank you for enquiring. She's married.'

'Oh! . . .' He felt a pang. Then he added: 'Er . . . Who's the lucky man?'

'That chap who was with us, the young one, you remember. He'll be taking over the shop.'

'I see.'

He was leaving, feeling sad though he could not think why, when Madame Dufour called him back.

'How's your friend?' she asked shyly.

'Oh, he's fine.'

'Give him my very best, won't you. And tell him to pop in any time he's passing . . .' She blushed bright red and added: 'I'd be very pleased to see him, tell him.'

'I won't forget. Goodbye!'

'Not goodbye. Just cheerio!'

The following year, one very hot Sunday, every last detail of his adventure, which he had never forgotten, suddenly came back to him so clear and enticing that he returned by himself to their hideaway in the wood.

When he arrived, he was dumbfounded. She was there, sitting on the grass, looking sad, while at her side her husband, still in his shirtsleeves, was sleeping as conscientiously as a beast of the field.

When she saw Henri she turned so pale that he thought she was going to faint. Then they began to chat naturally, as though nothing had happened between them.

Just as he was beginning to tell her how much he loved the place and how he often came there on a Sunday to get away and think back to times gone by, she looked long and hard into his eyes.

'I think about it every night,' she said.

'Come on, ducks,' said her husband with a yawn. 'Time we was making tracks.'

Marroca

MY dear chap, you asked me to send you an account of my impressions and adventures and especially of my amorous dealings in this land of Africa which I have been eager to see for ages now. How you smiled in anticipation of what you called my dusky conquests, and you pictured me returning towing a tall ebony maiden with a yellow scarf on her head, floating in brightly coloured clothes.

No doubt I shall get round to the Moorish women in due course, and indeed I have seen a number of them who have given me an urge to fish in their dark waters. But for my début, I came across something better, something quite out of the ordinary.

In your last letter, you wrote: 'Tell me how the people of any country manage the business of love, and I shall know that country well enough to be able to write about it, even though I was never there.' I can reveal to you that in this part of the world love is a highly passionate business. Within days of arriving, you feel a sort of quivering zest, a surge, a sudden tensing of desire, a nervous tingling in the fingertips which stimulate the capacity for love and the ability to experience physical sensations to the point of frenzy, from the simple touching of hands to that unmentionable need which drives us to commit so many foolish actions.

Let us be clear about this. I have no idea if what you call true affection and soul-twinning—sentimental idealism or platonism, if you prefer—actually exist under heaven. I rather doubt it. But the other kind of love, sensual love, which has something to be said for it, quite a lot as a matter of fact, is truly awesome in this climate. The heat, the constant searing of the air which makes you feel light-headed, the stifling winds from the south, the broiling tidal waves running in from the open desert just a step away, the oppressive Sirocco fiercer and more withering than flames, the ceaseless incineration of a whole continent scorched to the bedrock by the huge, devouring sun—all inflame the blood, fire the flesh, and turn people into beasts.

But I'm coming to my tale. I won't say anything about the first part of my stay in Algeria. After seeing Bône, Constantine, Biskra, and Sétif, I travelled here to Bougie through the Chabet gorges along an incomparable road which cuts through the middle of the Kabyle forest, teeters along the coast two hundred metres above the sea, and winds among the loops of the high mountains until it comes out at the marvellous Gulf of Bougie which is as splendid as the bays at Naples, Ajaccio, and Douarnenez, the finest I know. Though I would make an exception in my comparison for the unbelievable Bay of Porto on the west coast of Corsica, girt with crimson granite and peopled by those fantastic, blood-red stone giants which are called the 'Calanche' of Piana.

Bougie is visible from far off, very far off, long before you work round the huge bowl in which the still water sleeps. It is built on the steep sides of a very high hill on the top of which sits a wood. It has left a white stain on this green slope and looks for all the world like froth on a waterfall cascading down to the sea.

The moment I set foot in this tiny, entrancing town, I knew I would be staying here for some considerable time. From every point the eye encounters a palpable ring of scalloped, jagged, serrated, outlandish mountain peaks so almost completely perpendicular that the open sea is scarcely visible, while the gulf seems to be a lake. The blue water is a milky blue and admirably clear. The blue sky is a deep blue, as though it had been given two coats of paint, and it spreads its astounding beauty high over the bay. Sky and bay seem to be mirrored in each other, endlessly exchanging their own reflections.

Bougie is the town of ruins *par excellence*. On the quayside, as you arrive, you come across a pile of rubble so imposing that it could have come straight out of an opera. It is the old port of Sarrasine, now buried under ivy. And in the hilly woods around the old city there are ruins everywhere, stretches of Roman walls, remnants of Saracen monuments, and vestiges of Arab buildings.

I took a small Moorish house in the upper part of the town. You are familiar with these types of dwelling which have been described so many times. Having neither exterior doors nor windows, they are lit from the top downwards from an inner courtyard. On the first floor there is a large, cool room where the occupants live by day, and at night they sleep on the roof-terrace.

From the start I adopted the way of life common to all hot countries, which means that I took a siesta after lunch. This is the time of day when Africa suffocates, when breathing is difficult and the streets, plains, and long, dazzling roads are empty, and everyone sleeps, or at least tries to sleep, wearing as few clothes as possible.

In my room with its slender Arab-style columns, I had placed a large downy divan spread with Djebel-Amour rugs. There I would lie dressed more or less like Hassan,* but I could not find rest for I was tortured by continence.

Now there are two kinds of torture in this place which I hope you will never experience: lack of water and lack of a woman. Which is the worse? I couldn't say. In the desert, a man would commit any foul deed for a glass of clean, cool water. On the coast, what would not a man do for a clean, cool girl? For there is no shortage of girls in Africa! On the contrary, they abound in large numbers. But, to continue the image, they are all as pernicious and putrid as the muddy water at the bottom of a Saharan water-hole.

One day, more on edge than usual, I tried to shut my eyes but couldn't. My legs jumped as though something was stinging them from the inside. Spasms of unease made me toss and turn endlessly on my rugs. In the end, unable to stand it any longer, I got up and went out.

It was July and the afternoon was torrid. In the streets, the paving stones were hot enough to bake bread on. My shirt, instantly soaked, clung to my back. And in every quarter of the horizon shimmered a thin white haze: the burning cloud of the Sirocco which seems to strike you like a solid wall of heat.

I walked down to the sea and, skirting the port, began following the shore of the bay where people bathe. The steep mountainside, covered in scrub and strong-smelling aromatic plants, formed a circle around the inlet all along the edge of the water out of which rose large brown rocks.

There was not a soul out of doors. Nothing stirred. No cry of an animal, no bird in flight, no sound, not even of lapping water, so torpid did the sea appear under the sun. But in the searing air, I thought I could just about make out something like the crackling of a fire.

Suddenly, behind one of the rocks which were half in and half out of the silent sea, I sensed a slight movement and, turning round, caught sight of a girl bathing, obviously believing that she was quite alone at this burning hour of day, a tall girl, naked, standing in the water up to her breasts. She had her head turned towards the open sea and bobbed up and down lethargically without seeing me.

She made as surprising a picture as could be imagined: a beautiful woman in water as clear as glass lit by a blinding sky. For she was indeed stupendously beautiful, and tall, and proportioned like a statue.

She turned round, gave a cry, and half-swam, half-walked to her rock which hid her completely.

She could not stay where she was for ever, so I sat down at the water's edge and waited. At this, very slowly she poked out her head which had too much thick black hair carelessly tied back. Her mouth was wide, with lips full and round, she had enormous, brazen eyes and her flesh, lightly tanned by the climate, was like the finest old ivory, hard and mellow, and slightly darkened by the black man's sun.

She shouted to me: 'Go away!' Her voice was full, a little too full-blown even, like the rest of her, and she spoke with a gutteral accent. I did not move. She added: 'You really can't stay there. Show some respect.' The r's rolled round her mouth like chariots. I made no attempt to move. The head disappeared.

Ten minutes went by. Her hair, her forehead, her eyes reappeared slowly and carefully, as when children play hide-and-seek and want to see whoever is hunting for them.

This time she looked furious. She shouted: 'You'll make me take ill. I'm not coming out as long as you're sitting there.' This time I got up and walked away, though I did turn round frequently. When she decided I was far enough away, she emerged from the water, crouching, with her back to me, and vanished into a cleft in the rock over which a skirt was hanging.

I returned the next day. She was swimming there again but was now wearing a full bathing costume. She began to laugh and showed her gleaming teeth.

A week later we were friends. Another week, and we were rather more.

Her name was Marroca, probably her maiden name, and she pronounced it as though it had fifteen r's in it. The daughter of Spanish settlers, she was married to a Frenchman called Pontabèze. Her husband was employed in government service. I never quite discovered exactly what he did. All I know is that he was always very busy and I left it at that.

She changed the time she went for her bathe and began coming to take her siesta in my house each day after I'd finished lunch. And some siesta it was! It did not involve much in the way of rest.

She really was a splendid girl, perhaps a little too instinctive, but gorgeous. Her eyes always seemed to be glinting with passion. There was something ferociously sensual about her half-open mouth, those sharp teeth, and even her smile; and her unusual breasts, long, straight, and pointed like pears made of flesh, and as resilient as though they contained steel springs, lent her body an animal air, turned her into a sort of inferior but magnificent creature made for wild loving, and awakened in me thoughts of those obscene ancient gods who indulged their lascivious loves among grass and leaves.

No woman ever harboured more insatiable desires in her loins. Her reckless sensuality and the vociferous embraces which made her grind her teeth, writhe, and bite, were almost always followed by langours as deep as a little death. Then suddenly she would wake in my arms, ready for more, her throat swollen with loving.

Her mind, by the way, was pretty uncomplicated and a sonorous laugh was about as much as she ever did by way of thinking.

Instinctively proud of her beauty, she could not bring herself to wear even the lightest of veils; and she walked, ran, and pranced about the house with a forthright but quite unconscious lack of decorum. When she was finally sated with love, exhausted by all the groanings and squirmings, she slept a deep and peaceful sleep beside me on the divan, while the stultifying heat brought tiny droplets of sweat to the surface of her bronzed skin and drew from her, from her arms raised above her head and from all her secret recesses, that musky smell which pleases men.

Sometimes, when she came back in the evening when her husband had been called away God knows where, we would lie on the terrace under the barest covering of thin, loose, Oriental fabrics.

When the huge moon that shines bright over tropical lands hung high in the night sky and lit the mountain-rimmed circle of the gulf, we could see that all the other terraces were crowded with what seemed an army of silent shadows which at times stood up, changed places, and lay down again in the languid warmth of the replete sky.

Although these African nights were bright, Marroca stubbornly persisted in wearing nothing at all as she lay under the brilliant rays of the moon. She scarcely gave a thought for all those people who could see us and, in spite of my fears and entreaties, she uttered long, pulsating cries into the night air which made dogs bark in the distance.

One such evening as I lay dozing beneath the wide star-daubed heavens, she came and knelt on my rug and, putting her large, thick lips close to my mouth, said: 'You must come and sleep in my house.'

I did not understand. 'How d'you mean, your house?'

'When my husband goes away. You can come and sleep there instead of him.'

I could not help laughing. 'What on earth for, if you can come here?'

Talking into my mouth, wafting her warm breath into the

back of my throat, making my moustache wet with her
nearness, she went on: 'So that I'll have things to
remember.' And the 'r' of 'remember' rolled as loud as a
torrent over rocks.

I did not get her drift. She slipped her arms around my
neck. 'When you've gone, I'll remember. And when I'm
with my husband, it'll really be like I'm with you.' The r's
seeded her voice with familiar rumbles of thunder.

Moved and rather amused, I murmured: 'You're crazy.
I'd rather stay here.'

Indeed, I have no liking whatsoever for assignations in
the conjugal abode, which are traps which inevitably catch
out the stupid. But she begged and pleaded, even wept, and
promised: 'Trust me, and I'll love you ragged.' The way she
said 'ragged' was like a drum beating the charge.

This fancy of hers seemed so odd to me that I did not try
to explain it. But when I did think about it, I thought I
could detect some deep loathing of her husband or the
secret revenge of a woman who enjoys deceiving the man
she hates, and more, sets out to deceive him under his own
roof, in his home, between his sheets.

I asked: 'Is your husband very unkind to you?'

She looked cross at this: 'Oh no. He's a very good
man.'

'But you don't love him?'

She stared at me, her eyes wide with surprise: 'But I do. I
love him very, very much. But not as much as I love you,
my darrrling.'

I could not make it out and, just as I was trying to guess
what it all meant, she gave me one of those kisses on the
mouth, the power of which she knew full well. Then she
murmured: 'Prrromise you'll come?'

Even so, I remained firm. She at once got dressed and
left.

She went a week without putting in an appearance. On
the ninth day she turned up, paused soberly at the door of
my bedroom, and said: 'Are you coming to sleep in my
house tonight? If you don't, I'll go away and never
rreturrn.'

A week, old man, is a long time, and in Africa that week seemed more like a month. I said: 'Yes!' and opened my arms. She threw herself at me.

When it was dark, she waited for me in a street nearby and showed me the way.

They lived in a small house with a low roof near the dock. First I walked through a kitchen where they took their meals and then stepped into the bedroom which was whitewashed and clean and had photographs of relatives on the walls and paper flowers under glass domes. Marroca seemed beside herself with joy. She jumped up and down and kept saying: 'Here you are, in our house! Here you are, in your house!' And indeed, I behaved exactly as though I were at home.

I admit I was a little uneasy, even slightly anxious. As I stood in those unfamiliar surroundings feeling somewhat reluctant to part company with a certain item of dress without which a man taken by surprise becomes as awkward as he is ridiculous and incapable of action, she snatched it up and carried it off to the next room along with all my other clothes. But I regained my composure and proved it to her with all my strength, and two hours later we were still not quite thinking of sleep, when a sudden violent knocking at the door startled us and a man's voice cried out loudly: 'Marroca! It's me!'

She jumped up: 'It's my husband! Quickly! Hide under the bed!' I started looking frantically for my trousers, but she gave me a push and panted: 'Get under! Go on!' I got down on my stomach and without a word slid under the very bed where I had been doing so well.

She went through to the kitchen. I heard her opening and shutting a cupboard, and then she came back carrying an object I could not see which she banged down somewhere. Since her husband was fast losing patience, she answered in a clear, calm voice: 'I can't find the matches,' and then immediately: 'It's alrright. I've got them. I'm just opening up.' And she opened the door.

The man came in. I could only see his feet. They were

enormous. If the rest of him matched his feet, then he must have been a giant.

I heard kisses, a hand slapping bare flesh, a laugh. Then he said in a Marseilles accent: 'I forget my wallet and had to come back for it. I knew you'd be well away by this time.' He crossed over to the chest of drawers and rummaged at length for whatever he needed. Then, since Marroca had stretched out on the bed as though overcome by tiredness, he came over to her and probably tried caressing her, for with a succession of irritated sentences she riddled him with a rat-tat-tat of angry r's. The feet were so close to me that I had a mad, stupid, inexplicable urge to touch them with my fingertips. I controlled myself.

As he was not getting very far with his plans, he became cross. 'You're not being very nice to me today,' he said. But he decided not to insist. 'So long, girl.' I heard another kiss, then the big feet turned, showed a glimpse of hobnail as they retreated, and crossed into the room next door. Then the street door closed. I was saved!

I eased myself slowly out of my hiding-place, feeling humiliated and cutting a very sorry figure. Meanwhile Marroca, who still had nothing on, danced a jig around me, screaming with laughter and clapping her hands. I collapsed onto a chair. But I jumped up again at once: there was something cold on the seat and since I was wearing no more clothes than my accomplice, the contact startled me. I turned round.

I had just sat down on a small axe of the kind used for splitting wood: it was sharp as a razor. How had it got there? I had not noticed it when I arrived.

When Marroca saw me leap up, she laughed so much that she almost choked. She shrieked and spluttered and held her sides.

I considered her glee misplaced and quite unseemly. We had stupidly gambled with our lives. My blood still ran cold at the thought of it and I was offended by her uproarious laughter.

'What if your husband had seen me?' I asked her.

'There was no danger,' she replied.

'What d'you mean, no danger! That's rich. All he had to do was bend down and he'd have found me.'

She had stopped laughing and merely smiled now as she looked at me with her large, staring eyes where new desires were beginning to form.

'He would never have bent down.'

I went on insistently: 'Oh no? If he'd dropped his hat, he would have gone to pick it up and then . . . with me in a fine state, dressed like this.'

She put her strong, plump arms on my shoulders and, lowering her voice as though she were about to say 'I love you', murmured: 'If he had bent down, he wouldn't have got up again.'

I did not understand what she meant: 'How d'you mean?'

She blinked grimly and reached out with her hand for the chair where I had just sat down: her extended finger, the crease in her cheek, the half-open lips, those sharp teeth, white and savage, all pointed towards the small wood-axe with its keen, gleaming blade.

She went through the motions of picking it up. Then, drawing me very close to her with her left hand and pressing her hip against mine, she mimed the action of an arm as it takes the head off a kneeling man . . .

And that, old man, is how they understand conjugal duty, love, and hospitality in this part of the world.

Country Living

THE two cottages stood side by side at the foot of a hill not far from a small spa town. The two peasant farmers who lived in them worked very hard cultivating the poor soil to rear all the children they had. Each couple had four, and outside each house the whole gang of them played and shrieked from morning till night. The two oldest were 6 and the two youngest about fifteen months. Weddings and then births had occurred at more or less the same times in both houses.

The two mothers were none too sure which of the heaving brood were theirs and which were not, and both fathers were quite incapable of telling them apart. The eight names went round and round in their heads and they were forever getting them mixed up. And when one of them was wanted, the men often shouted three names before getting the right one.

The first of these houses, as you come along the road from the spa, which was Rolleport, was occupied by the Tuvaches who had three girls and a boy. The other was home to the Vallins, who had one girl and three boys.

They all lived on a meagre diet of soup, potatoes, and fresh air. At seven in the morning, at noon, and again at six in the evening, the women called their brood in to feed them, rather as a farmer's boy might gather in the geese. The children were seated in order of age at the wooden kitchen table which shone with fifty years of wear. The mouth of the last in line scarcely came up to the top of the table. In front of them was set a bowl containing bread soaked in the water the potatoes had been boiled in, half a cabbage, and three onions: and they all ate until they were full. The mother pushed food into the youngest herself. A small piece of meat in a stew on Sundays was a treat for one and all, and on that day the father usually lingered over his dinner saying: 'I could get used to having that every day of the week.'

One August afternoon, a horse and trap drew up unexpectedly outside the two cottages, and the young woman who had been driving it herself said to the man sitting next to her: 'Oh Henri, do look at those children. Aren't they pretty, rolling around in the dirt like that!'

The man did not answer, for he was used to these sudden enthusiasms which he felt as a physical hurt and took more or less as a personal reproach.

The young woman went on: 'I must kiss them! Oh, how I'd love to have one of them—that one, the tiny one.' And jumping down from the trap, she ran over to the children, picked up one of the two smallest—the Tuvaches' youngest boy—and lifting him in her arms, planted eager kisses on his dirty cheeks, on his curly, blond, mud-daubed hair, and on his little fists which he waved in his efforts to free himself from attentions which he plainly did not like.

Then she got back into the trap and drove off at a smart trot. But she came back the following week, sat herself down on the ground with them, took the little boy in her arms, stuffed him full of cake and handed sweets to all the others. And she played with them as though she were a little girl herself, while her husband waited patiently in their dainty trap.

She came back again, got to know the parents, and began putting in an appearance daily, her pockets bulging with sweeties and pennies.

Her name was Madame Henri d'Hubières.

When she arrived one morning, her husband got down out of the trap with her. Without stopping to talk to the children, who all knew her well by this time, she walked straight up to one of the farmers' cottages.

The farmer and his wife were busy chopping enough firewood to cook the dinner. They straightened up in surprise, brought out chairs, and then waited. Only then did the young woman begin speaking in a broken, trembling voice:

'You dear people, I have come to see you because . . . because I would very much like . . . I would very much like to . . . to take your little boy away with me.'

Taken completely by surprise and not knowing what to think, the farmer and his wife did not answer.

She paused for breath, then went on: 'We have no children. My husband and I are alone. . . . We'd give him a home. . . . Would you be willing?'

The mother began to have an inkling of what was going on. She asked: 'You be wanting to take our Charlot away with you? Couldn't have that. No indeed.'

At this point, Monsieur d'Hubières intervened: 'My wife has not made herself clear. We would like to adopt him, but he'd be able to come back and see you. If he turns out well, and everything suggests that he will, one day he will inherit everything we own. If we do by some chance have children, he would share equally with them. But if he does not make the most of his opportunities, we will give him the sum of twenty thousand francs when he comes of age, this sum to be deposited as of now in his name with a lawyer. And because we have also been thinking of you, you will receive a hundred francs a month for as long as you live. Do you understand?'

The farmer's wife rose to her feet like a fury: 'You want us to sell you our Charlot? No. Never! It's a thing nobody's got no right asking a mother to do. I won't have it! It'd be sinful and wicked!'

Her husband, looking grave and thoughtful, said nothing. But he indicated his approval of what his wife said by nodding his head all the time she spoke.

It was all too much for Madame d'Hubières who burst into tears and, turning to her husband, stammered in the tear-choked voice of a little girl who always gets her way: 'They don't want to, Henri, they don't want to!'

They made one last attempt: 'Listen. Think about your son's future, about his happiness, about . . .'

Losing patience, the wife interrupted: 'We've heard you out, we've understood, and we've made up our minds. . . . Now just go and don't you ever let me see you round this way again. Never heard the like! The very idea! Wanting to take away a baby just like that!'

As she was leaving, Madame d'Hubières recalled that

there were two little boys and asked, through her tears, and with the persistence of a headstrong, spoilt woman who is not prepared to wait: 'The other little boy isn't yours, is he?'

Monsieur Tuvache answered: 'No. He's next door's. You can go and see them if you like.' And he went back into his house where his wife could be heard complaining indignantly.

The Vallins were sitting round their table, with a plate between them, slowly eating slices of bread thinly spread with rancid butter.

Monsieur d'Hubières restated his proposal to them, but this time he was more subtle, shrewder, and he put honey in his voice.

The man and his wife shook their heads to indicate their unwillingness. But when they learned that they would get a hundred francs a month, they looked at each other, exchanged enquiring glances, and seemed to hesitate.

Torn and uncertain, they did not say anything for some time. In the end, the wife asked her husband: 'Well, what have you got to say?'

He replied sententiously: 'What I say is that it's not to be sneezed at.'

Madame d'Hubières, trembling with anguish, then spoke to them about the future their little boy would have, how happy he would be and how much money he would be able to give them later on.

'This business of the twelve hundred francs,' the man asked, 'it'd be all properly settled by a lawyer?'

'Absolutely,' Monsieur d'Hubières replied. 'It could be all arranged tomorrow.'

The wife, who had been thinking, went on:

'A hundred francs a month, well, it don't compensate us nowhere near for not having our boy around. Give him a couple of years and he'll be old enough to be set to work. We'd need a hundred and twenty.'

Madame d'Hubières was so impatient to finalize matters that she agreed immediately. And since she was anxious to take the child away with her at once, she gave them an extra hundred francs as a present while her husband was drawing up a written agreement. The mayor and a neighbour were hurriedly summoned and willingly witnessed the document.

The young woman, radiant, took the screaming child away as others might bear off a coveted bargain from a shop.

The Tuvaches stood on their doorstep and watched him go, saying nothing, grim-faced, and perhaps regretting that they had said no.

That was the last that was heard of little Jean Vallin. Each month his parents collected their one hundred and twenty francs from the lawyer. They quarrelled with their neighbours, because Madame Tuvache said the most awful things about them and went around other people's houses saying that anyone who sells a child for money must be unnatural, that it was a horrible, disgusting, dirty business. And sometimes she would pick up her little Charlot for all to see and say loudly, as though he could understand: 'I din't sell you, my precious, I din't! I don't go round selling my children. I haven't got a lot of money, but I don't go round selling my children!'

It was the same each day for years and years. Each day coarse jeers were bellowed on one doorstep so that they were heard in the house next door. In the end Madame Tuvache came to believe that she was better than anybody else for miles around because she had refused to sell her little Charlot. And when people talked about her, they said: ' 'Twas a tempting offer, right enough. But she wasn't interested. She done what a good mother oughter.'

She was held up as a model. Little Charlot, who was now almost 18 and had been brought up having this idea constantly repeated to him, also thought he was a cut above his friends because he had not been sold.

The Vallins pottered along quite comfortably on their pension. Which explains why the fury of the Tuvaches, who remained poor, was so implacable.

Their oldest boy went off to do his military service. The second died and Charlot was left alone to work alongside his old father to support his mother and his two younger sisters.

He was getting on for 21 when, one morning, a gleaming carriage pulled up outside the two cottages. A young gentleman, wearing a gold watch-chain, got out and helped down an old lady with white hair. The old lady said to him: 'It's there, dear. The second house.'

He walked straight into the Vallins' hovel as though it were his own.

Old Madame Vallin was washing her aprons. Her husband, now infirm, was dozing by the fire. Both looked up and the young man said:

'Good morning, mother. Good morning, father.'

They both stood up in dismay. Madame Vallin was in such a state that she dropped her soap into the water. She stammered: 'Is that you, son? Is it really you?'

He took her in his arms and kissed her, repeating: 'Hello, mother.' Meanwhile the old man, shaking all over, kept saying in the calm tone of voice which never deserted him: 'Here you are back again, then, Jean,' as though he had seen him only the month before.

When they had got over the shock the parents said they wanted to take their boy out and show him off everywhere. They took him to see the mayor, the deputy mayor, the village priest, and the schoolmaster.

Charlot watched them go from the doorstep of the cottage next door.

That night, at supper, he said to his parents: 'You can't have been right in the head letting the Vallin kid get took away.'

His mother replied stubbornly: 'I'd never have let a child of ours get took.'

His father said nothing.

The son went on: 'I really missed the boat the day I got made a sacrifice of.'

At this, old Tuvache said angrily: 'You're not blaming us for keeping you?'

The young man replied cruelly: 'O' course I blame you. I blame you for being so soft in the head. Parents like you is the reason why children get held back. It'd serve you right if I upped sticks and off.'

The old woman cried into her dinner. She gave little moans as she swallowed each mouthful of soup, half of which she spilled: 'You kill yourself to bring up your kids and what thanks do you get?'

Then the lad said roughly: 'I'd as soon have never been born than be as I am. When I saw him from next door earlier on, it come right home to me. I said to meself: that's what I could have been like now!' He stood up. 'Listen, I think it'd be best if I didn't stay around the place, because I'd only be throwing it in your faces morning noon and night. I'd just make your lives a misery. I'll never forgive you. Never.'

The two old people sat in silence, utterly crushed and in tears. He continued: 'I couldn't stand the thought of that. I'd rather go off and make a fresh start somewhere else.'

He opened the door. Through it came the sound of voices. The Vallins were celebrating with their boy who had come back.

Charlot stamped his feet in rage and, turning to his parents, screamed: 'Know what you are? Stupid, bog-trotting yokels!'

And he vanished into the night.

Riding Out

THEY were poor and just about managed to make do on the husband's meagre salary. Two children had been born to the marriage, and what at first were straitened circumstances had turned into genteel, covert, shameful poverty, the poverty of old, aristocratic families which insist on keeping up their position in society come what may.

Hector de Gribelin had been brought up in the country, in the ancestral seat, by a tutor, an old man in holy orders. His family were not rich, but they got by and managed to maintain appearances.

When he was 20 a situation was found for him and he became a clerk in the Admiralty at an annual salary of fifteen hundred francs. It was a reef on which he had run aground as do any who are not trained at an early age for life's hard struggle, who see existence through a rosy cloud, fail to learn the necessary guile and resilience, or have not when very young acquired special skills or particular abilities or the determination and energy to fight: anyone who has not had a weapon or a tool thrust into his hand.

The first three years he worked in the office were appalling.

He had met up with a number of friends of the family, equally diehard and impoverished, who had grand addresses in the sad streets off the Faubourg Saint-Honoré. He had made a circle of acquaintances.

Strangers to modern ways, meek but proud, his down-at-heel aristocrats had rooms on the upper floors of stagnating houses which were all occupied from top to bottom by tenants with titles, though money was as scarce on the ground floor as under the eaves.

A constant preoccupation with antiquated notions of caste and fears of losing rank haunted these once illustrious families which had been ruined by the intertia of their menfolk. It was in these circles that Hector de Gribelin met and married a girl who was as poor and as well-born as he. They had two children in four years.

For the next four years, hard-pressed by poverty, the only amusements they could afford were walks along the Champs-Elysées on a Sunday and the occasional visit to the theatre once or twice a winter, which they were able to manage only because a colleague passed on complimentary tickets.

But one spring, his superior chose Hector to undertake some additional work, and for it he received a special bonus of three hundred francs.

When he came home with the money, he said to his wife: 'Henriette, my dear, we're going to give ourselves a bit of a treat. We could take the children somewhere nice.'

They talked it over at length and finally decided that they would have lunch in the country.

Hector said: 'We don't do this sort of thing every day of the week, so we'll hire an open coach for you, the children, and the maid, and I'll get a horse from the riding school for me. It'll do me good.'

For the rest of the week, all they talked about was the outing they had planned.

Every evening when he got back from the office, Hector picked up his oldest son, sat him astride his leg, and, rocking him up and down as hard as he could, told him: 'This is how daddy'll be galloping on Sunday when we're riding out.'

All day long, the little boy straddled chairs and rode them round the room shouting: 'I'm like daddy on the gee-gee!'

Even the maid looked wonderingly at her master at the thought of him riding alongside the coach on his horse. At mealtimes she listened to him holding forth about horse-manship and telling tales about his exploits in the old days, on his father's estate. If he did say it himself, he had been properly schooled: put a horse between his legs and he was fearless, quite fearless! Rubbing his hands together, he told his wife several times: 'If they give me a horse that's hard to handle, I'll be only too pleased. You'll be able to see how

well I ride. If you like, we'll come back via the Champs-
Elysées just when people are coming out of the Bois de
Boulogne. We'll be cutting a bit of a dash, and I wouldn't be
at all put out to bump into some of the chaps from the
Ministry. It's the sort of thing that makes the top brass
think better of you.'

When the great day came, the coach and the horse arrived
at the door together. He went down at once to take a look at
his steed. He had had understraps sewn onto his trouser
bottoms. He thwacked his leg with a riding-crop he had
bought the day before.

He lifted and felt the horse's legs one by one, prodded its
neck, flanks, and hocks, probed its back with his fingers,
opened its mouth, examined its teeth, said how old it was,
and, when his family came down, gave a kind of lecturette
on the theory and uses of the horse in general and on this
horse in particular which he pronounced first-rate.

When everyone had been properly seated in the coach he
checked the saddle straps. Then, putting one foot in the
stirrup, he sat heavily on the horse which shied under the
weight and almost unseated its rider.

Unnerved, Hector tried to soothe it: 'Steady, boy,
steady.'

When the mount had regained its calm and the rider his
composure, Hector asked: 'Everybody ready?'

They all replied: 'Yes!'

He gave the order: 'Then away we go!'

The cavalcade moved off.

Every eye was on him. He rode English-style, rising
excessively high in the saddle. He hardly waited to make
contact with it before bouncing up as though launching
himself into space. Several times he looked as though he
would finish up on the horse's neck. He stared straight in
front of him, his face very tense and pale.

His wife, who had one of the children on her knee while
the maid held the other, kept saying: 'Look at daddy! Look
at daddy!'

Excited by the movement of the carriage, the thrill of it
all, and the wind in their faces, the two boys shouted shrilly

until the horse, frightened by their cries, broke into a gallop. While the rider was trying to reign him in, his hat fell to the ground. The coachman had to step down from his seat to pick it up, and as Hector was getting it back from him he called to his wife from a little way off: 'Can't you stop the children shouting like that? You'll make him bolt and me with him.'

With the provisions packed away in the boot of the carriage, they had a picnic lunch in the woods at Le Vésinet.

Although the coachman saw to all three horses, Hector kept getting up and going over to see if his mount needed anything. He stroked its neck and gave it bread and cakes and sugar. He said: 'He's a bit rough when he trots. He even shook me up a bit for the first couple of minutes. But you saw how quickly I got the hang of him: he learned who was master. He'll be as good as gold now.'

They returned via the Champs-Elysées as planned.

The huge concourse swarmed with carriages. And on either side there were so many people strolling that they looked like two long black ribbons stretching from the Arc de Triomphe down to the Place de la Concorde. A burst of sunlight streamed down on the bustling throng and glinted in the varnished coachwork, the steel-studded harness, and the door-handles of the elegant barouches. The crowds of people, carriages, and horses seemed drunk with life and driven by some crazy urge to keep on the move. And at the far end, in the Place de la Concorde, the Obelisk rose up out of a golden haze.

As soon as Hector's horse had passed the Arc de Triomphe it seemed to get a new lease of life. It weaved through the traffic at a fast trot and made for the stables in spite of all its rider's efforts to pacify it.

The coach had been left a long way behind now. When the horse was level with the Palais de l'Industrie, it saw a stretch of turf, veered to the right, and set off at a gallop.

An old woman in an apron was quietly crossing the road. She was right in the path of Hector who was bearing down on her like an express train. Unable to control his mount, he began shouting for all his worth: 'Look out! Get out of the way!'

Perhaps she was deaf, for she carried blissfully on walking until the very last moment. Caught by the chest of the horse which was going flat out, she was bowled over and, three somersaults later, landed ten paces away with her skirts in the air.

There were shouts of: 'Stop him!'

Hector, hanging on for dear life, clung to the horse's mane and yelled: 'Help!' His steed gave a sickening lurch and he shot like a bullet between its ears into the arms of a policeman who had been running towards him.

Within seconds, an angry, vociferous, gesticulating mob had gathered round him. One old gentleman in particular, sporting a large round medal and a large white moustache, seemed quite beside himself: 'Hell's teeth, man! Anybody as inept as you are shouldn't be allowed out! You can't go round killing people in the streets just because you don't know how to handle a horse.'

Then four men appeared carrying the old woman. She seemed to be dead. Her face was yellow, her hat was askew on her head, and she was covered in dust.

'Take her into the chemist's,' the old gent barked. 'We're going straight to the police station.'

Hector was marched off, sandwiched between two policemen. A third led his horse. A crowd walked behind him and suddenly the open coach came into view. His wife leaped out, the maid had hysterics, and the children began to snivel. He explained that he was on his way home, that he had knocked a woman over, that everything was all right. His distracted family drove off.

At the police station matters proceeded quickly. He gave his name, Hector de Gribelin, an official at the Admiralty. But then they had to stand around waiting for news of the injured party. A policeman who had been sent to make enquiries returned saying that she had regained consciousness but was complaining of terrible internal pains. She was a charlady aged 65 and her name was Madame Simon.

When he heard that she was not dead, Hector breathed

again and undertook to meet the cost of her full recovery. Then he hurried back to the chemist's shop.

A crowd had gathered outside the door. The old woman was sitting sprawling in a chair and moaning: her hands were lifeless and her face looked dazed. Two doctors were still examining her. There were no bones broken, but there were fears of internal lesions.

Hector spoke to her: 'Are you in much pain?'

'Ooooh, I'll say.'

'Where does it hurt?'

'It's like a burning I got in me innards.'

A doctor came up to him: 'Are you the person who was responsible for causing the accident?'

'That's right.'

'This woman needs proper medical attention. I know of a clinic which would look after her for six francs a day. Would you like me to arrange it?'

Hector jumped at the offer, thanked him, and went home much relieved.

His weeping wife was waiting for him: he allayed her fears.

'It's nothing. This Madame Simon person is already feeling a great deal better and she'll be quite over it in three days. I packed her off to a clinic. There's nothing to worry about.'

Nothing to worry about!

Next day, after leaving the office, he went round to find out how Madame Simon was getting along. He found her imbibing a dish of beef-tea with evident relish.

'Well, how do you feel?' he said.

She replied. 'Just the same, kind of you to ask, I'm sure. Feelin' pretty down. Can't say I'm much better.'

The doctor said it was best to wait a while since there might be complications.

He let three days go by and then went back. The old woman, fresh-complexioned and clear-eyed, began groaning as soon as she saw him: 'Ain't got the strength to move me arms and legs, bless you. Weak as a kitten, I am. Don't s'pose I'll ever get over it, not till the day I die.'

A shiver ran down Hector's back. He asked to see the doctor. The doctor raised his arms hopelessly.

'I'm afraid there's nothing I can do. I can't make it out. Every time we try to lift her, she screams her head off. We can't even move the chair without her making the most awful racket. I must believe what she tells me. Only she knows how she feels. Until I see her walking, I cannot assume that she may be telling lies.'

The old woman sat there listening, without moving and with a crafty look in her eye.

A week went by, then two, then a month. Madame Simon never left her chair. She ate from morning till night, grew fat, chatted happily with the other patients, and seemed accustomed to being immobile as though it were a well-earned rest for fifty years of traipsing up and down flights of stairs, turning mattresses, carrying coal from one floor to the next, sweeping and scrubbing.

A bemused Hector went to see her every day and every day he found her calm and serene and lamenting: 'Can't move me arms or me legs, bless you, jest can't.'

Every evening, Mme de Gribelin, with lead in her heart, would ask: 'How is Madame Simon?'

And each time she asked, he would reply desperately: 'No change. Absolutely no change.'

They dismissed their maid, for her wages were becoming a strain. They cut back even more and the bonus evaporated completely.

Finally Hector summoned four eminent doctors. They stood round the old woman. She let herself be examined, poked, and probed, but kept a beady eye on them all the time.

'We'll have to get her moving,' said one.

'I can't, I tell you,' she said. 'Can't move a blessed thing.'

They took hold of her, stood her on her feet, and dragged her along for a few steps. But she slipped through their hands and fell in a heap on the floor screaming so dreadfully that they sat her down on her chair again with the utmost care.

The opinion they gave was inconclusive, though they did

state that there was no question that the old woman could return to work.

When Hector gave his wife the news, she collapsed onto a chair and said brokenly: 'It would be better if we had her to live here. It would be cheaper.'

He gave a start: 'Here? To live with us? You can't be serious!'

But resigned now to anything that might happen and with tears in her eyes, she replied:

'I'm sorry dear. But it's not my fault! . . .'

A Railway Story

I

THE compartment had been full all the way from Cannes. The passengers chatted amongst themselves, for they were all acquainted. When they reached Tarascon, someone said: 'This is where all those murders were committed.' And they started talking about the mysterious assassin who for two years now had been occasionally treating himself to the life of the odd traveller. Everyone had a theory and everyone said what he thought: the women shivered as they stared into the black night on the other side of the windows, afraid they might see a man's head suddenly framed in the glass of the door. And they all began telling frightening stories about ill-fated encounters, about people travelling aboard express trains who had found themselves alone in a compartment with a madman, or had sat for hours opposite a suspicious character.

Every man there knew a story in which he played a major role, for they had all browbeaten, floored, or throttled some evil-doer in amazing circumstances and always with admirable daring and presence of mind. A doctor, who spent each winter on the south coast, also offered to recount an adventure:

Now I, he said, have never had the opportunity of testing my courage in the kind of tight corners you've been talking about. But I did know a woman, one of my patients, now dead, who had the oddest thing happen to her which was most mysterious and very, very sad.

She was Russian, the Countess Marie Baranow, a lady of the highest rank and an exquisite beauty. You know how beautiful Russian women can be, or at least the way they seem beautiful to our way of thinking: dainty nose, delicate mouth, close-set eyes of an indefinable colour, a sort of bluey-grey, and that cool grace which seems a mite unfeeling! There is something cruel and attractive about them, and they are both distant and yielding, loving and aloof, a mixture which no Frenchman could ever resist. Still, perhaps it's just differences of race and type which make me see all these things in them.

For a number of years, her doctor had been of the opinion that her lungs were seriously affected, and he kept trying to persuade her to go off to the south of France. But she stubbornly refused to leave Saint Petersburg. Anyhow, last autumn, believing that there was little hope left for her, the doctor informed her husband who immediately ordered his wife to leave for Menton.

She boarded the train and travelled alone in her carriage, her retinue occupying a separate compartment. She sat rather dejectedly near the door, watching the fields and villages speed by and feeling very alone and utterly forsaken, for she had no children, very few relations, and a husband who did not love her any more and had sent her off to the other side of the world instead of coming with her, just as a sick servant is packed off to hospital.

Each time they stopped at a station, her servant Ivan came along to ask if his mistress needed anything. He was very much the old retainer, blindly obedient and always ready to carry out whatever orders she gave him.

Night fell. The train was travelling at full speed. She was too restless to sleep. Then she thought she would count the money, in French gold coins, which her husband had given her just before she left. She opened her small money-bag and poured a gleaming river of metal onto her knees.

Suddenly a breath of cold air struck her face. She looked up in surprise. The carriage door had opened. Alarmed, Countess Marie quickly threw a shawl over the money in her lap and waited. Moments went by, then a man appeared. He was bare-headed, nursed an injured hand, and was breathing hard. He wore evening dress. Closing the door behind him, he looked at her with eyes that gleamed, then wrapped a handkerchief around his wrist which was bleeding badly.

The young woman felt faint with fear. It was obvious that

this man had seen her counting her money and had come to rob and kill her.

He continued to stare at her, still gasping for breath, his face twitching, and clearly ready to leap upon her. All at once he said: 'Please! Don't be afraid!'

She did not reply, for she could not open her mouth and was aware that her heart was pounding and her ears buzzing.

He continued: 'I won't harm you.'

Still she did not speak, but a sudden movement which she made brought her knees together and her gold streamed onto the carpet like rainwater pouring off a gutter. The man stared in surprise at the river of metal then bent down to pick it up.

She stood up in a panic and, letting the rest of her money fall to the floor, rushed to the door intending to throw herself out onto the track. But he anticipated what she was about to do, made a dash for her, grabbed her in his arms, and, holding her by the wrists, forced her to sit down: 'Listen. I won't harm you, and to prove it I'll pick up your money and give it all back to you. But unless you help me get across the frontier, it's all up with me, I'm as good as dead. I can't tell you any more. In an hour, we'll be at the last station in Russia; an hour and twenty minutes from now, we'll just be crossing the imperial border. If you do not help me, I am done for. But I haven't killed anyone, stolen anything, or done anything dishonourable. This I swear. I can't tell you any more than that.'

Getting down on his knees, he picked up all the gold, even looking under the seats and scouring the corners where coins might have rolled. Then, when her little leather bag was full again, he held it out to her without another word and went and sat down on the other side of the compartment.

After this, neither of them stirred. She sat motionless and silent, still weak with terror but slowly regaining her composure. For his part, the man did not move a finger but remained completely immobile, sitting bolt upright, with his eyes staring straight ahead and looking as pale as a corpse. From time to time she glanced quickly at him and then away. He was about 30, very handsome, and all the indications were that he was a gentleman.

The train steamed on into the darkness, piercing the night with its shrill whistles, slowing down at times and then picking up again. But suddenly it dropped its speed, whistled three times, and came to a halt.

Ivan appeared at the door to ask for orders.

Countess Marie glanced one last time at her strange companion and then, in a voice that shook, spoke sharply to her servant: 'Ivan, you are to go back to the Count. I shan't be needing you any more.'

Ivan opened his eyes wide in bewilderment. He stammered: 'But . . . mistress . . .'

She went on: 'You won't be coming with me. I've changed my mind. I want you to remain in Russia. Here, take this money. There's enough to get you home. Give me your hat and coat.'

The old man, greatly puzzled, removed his hat and handed over his coat, obeying without question, for he was used to the sudden fancies and irresistible whims of his betters. Then he went away with tears in his eyes.

The train set off again, heading now for the frontier.

Then the Countess said to the man: 'These things are for you. You are Ivan, my servant. I set just one condition on what I am about to do: you will never speak to me, not one word, not to thank me or for any other purpose.'

The stranger gave a slight bow but said not a word.

Soon they stopped again and uniformed officials inspected the train. The Countess showed them her papers and motioning towards the man seated on the far side of the compartment, said: 'That is my servant, Ivan. Here's his passport.'

The train set off once more. The two of them remained alone together all through the night without speaking.

The next morning the train stopped at a German station and the stranger got out. But at the door he paused and said: 'Forgive me if I break my promise. But I have deprived you of your servant and it would be only right if I should take his place. Is there anything that you need?'

She answered him coolly: 'Go and tell my maid I want her.'
He went. He then disappeared.

But thereafter, whenever she left the train and went into station refreshment rooms, she kept noticing him in the distance, watching her. They finally reached Menton.

II

The doctor paused for a few moments and then went on:

One day, I was seeing patients in my surgery when a tall young man came in and said: 'Doctor, I've come to see you because I would like to know how Countess Marie Baranow is. She does not know me, but I am a friend of her husband.'

'There is no hope,' I replied. 'She will never return to Russia.'

The man suddenly started sobbing, then left, staggering like a drunken man.

The same evening, I informed the Countess that a stranger had come to see me asking about her health. She seemed troubled and told me the story which I have just told you. And she added: 'This man, whom I do not know, follows me everywhere like my shadow. I see him every time I go out. He looks at me in the oddest way, but he's never said a word to me.' She thought for a moment before continuing: 'I'll wager he's there outside my house now.'

She rose from her chaise-longue, went over and drew the curtains, and pointed out the man who had called on me who was indeed there, sitting on a bench on the promenade looking up at the house. He saw us, got up, and walked away without turning round once.

From then on, I became an observer of an amazing and distressing phenomenon—the unspoken love of these two people who knew virtually nothing about each other.

He loved her with the devotion of a rescued animal which is grateful and loyal until death. Each day he would come and ask: 'How is she?', for he realized I had guessed the truth. And when he saw her pass by looking weaker and paler each day, he wept in the most dreadful fashion.

And she would say: 'I only ever spoke to him once. Yet I

feel that I have known that strange man for twenty years.'

And when they happened to meet, she always returned his bow with a grave but charming smile. I sensed that she was happy. I felt that she, who was so alone and fully aware that she was dying, was truly happy to be loved in this way, respectfully, steadfastly, exaltedly, poetically, with a devotion which knew no limits. Yet she remained faithful to her extravagant obsession and despairingly went on refusing to meet him or ask his name or speak to him. She said: 'No, no, it would destroy the rare bond between us. We must remain strangers to each other.'

On his side he, too, had a quixotic streak in his character, for he did nothing to get close to her. He was determined to keep to the end the absurd promise never to speak to her which he had made in the railway carriage.

During her long periods of exhaustion, she would often rise from her chaise-longue and pull back her curtain just a little to see if he was there, outside, beneath her windows. And when she had seen him, sitting motionless on his usual bench, she would lie down again with a smile on her lips.

She died one morning, at about ten o'clock. As I was leaving the house he came up to me, his face grief-stricken. He had heard the news already.

'I would like to see her, just for a moment, in your presence,' he said.

I took him by the arm and went back into the house.

When he was standing by the dead woman's bedside, he grasped her hand and kissed it interminably. Then he fled like a mad thing.

The doctor paused once more.

'That', he went on, 'is the strangest tale about railways I know. Still, you've got to admit that folk can be very peculiar indeed.'

A woman said quietly: 'Those two weren't half as mad as you make out. . . . They were . . . They were . . .' But she couldn't go on, because she had started to cry. And since everyone immediately began talking about other things to take her mind off it, we never did find out what she meant.

Old Milon

FOR a month now the wide-faced sun has been launching its burning fire upon the fields. Life blooms dazzlingly beneath the drenching heat: the land is green as far as the eye can see. The sky is blue even to the edge of the horizon. From a distance, the Norman farmhouses dotted over the plain look like small copses enclosed by belts of tall beech trees. But when you get near and you open a worm-eaten gate, you might as well be seeing a giant garden, for all the old apple trees, which are every whit as angular as the peasants, are in bloom. Their old, twisted, gnarled, black trunks, set out in lines next to the farmyard, offer their white and pink domes to the sky. The sweet fragrance of their fullness mingles with the heavier smells of the open cowsheds and the fumes of the fermenting dung-heap where chickens gather.

It is noon. The family is eating in the shade of the pear tree by the door: father, mother, the four children, two serving-girls, and three labourers. They do not talk much. They eat their soup and then the lid comes off a pot containing a ham and potato stew. Now and then, one of the servants gets up and refills the cider jug from the cellar.

The farmer, a well-made man of 40, stares at the front of his house where a vine, still bare of leaves, coils like a snake under the shutters and across the whole length of the wall. Finally he says: 'The old man's vine is starting to bud early this year. P'raps we'll get some fruit off of it.'

The wife also turns round and looks, without saying a word.

The vine was planted at the exact spot where the old man was shot.

It happened during the Franco-Prussian War of 1870. The Prussians had occupied the whole area. General Faidherbe, in command of the Northern Army, was holding them and blocking their advance.

Prussian headquarters had been set up in this farmhouse. The old peasant who owned it, old Pierre Milon, had let them come and settled them in as best he could.

For a month the Prussian forward troops remained in observation positions in the village. The French stayed put, forty kilometres away. Yet every night Prussian troopers disappeared. None of the independent scouts who were sent out on patrol, when they went out in twos or threes that is, ever came back. The next morning they were picked up dead in a field or just by a farmyard or in a ditch. Even their horses lay where they had fallen in the road, their throats cut by a sabre.

All these murders seemed to be carried out by the same men, but no one could find out who they were.

The whole area was subjected to a campaign of terror. Peasants were shot if they were denounced and women were imprisoned; fear was used to extract information from children. But nothing was discovered.

But then one morning old Milon was observed lying in the stables, with a fresh cut down his face.

Two disembowelled Prussian troopers were found three kilometres from the farm. One still had his sword in his hand: there was blood on it. He had fought back and given a good account of himself.

A court martial was hurriedly arranged in the open air, outside the farmhouse, and the old man was hauled before it.

He was 70. He was short, spare, slightly bow-legged, and had large hands like a crab's claws. His scalp was visible through his thin, dull, wispy hair which was as fine as duck-down. Under the tanned, wrinkled skin of his neck large veins stood out; they dipped under his jaw and resurfaced at his temples. He had a reputation locally for being mean and a hard man to deal with.

He was made to stand between four soldiers at the kitchen table which had been dragged outside. Five officers plus the colonel sat facing him.

The colonel began, speaking in French: 'Look here, Milon, we've had no reason to have anything but praise for you the whole time we've been here. You've always been co-operative, even helpful. But now a very serious charge has been brought against you and the court must get to the bottom of it. Now, how did you come by that wound you've got on your face?'

The old man said nothing.

The colonel continued: 'By remaining silent you as good as admit the charge. But I want an answer, do you understand? Now, do you know who killed the two troopers this morning near the wayside cross?'

The old man said very clearly: ' 'Twas I.'

Momentarily taken aback, the colonel said nothing but stared hard at the prisoner. Old Milon stood there, impassive, looking like any simple-minded peasant, with his eyes lowered as though he were talking to the priest. There was only one indication that he was inwardly disturbed: he kept making considerable efforts to swallow the saliva in his mouth, as if his throat were completely blocked.

The old man's family, his son Jean, his daughter-in-law, and his two grandchildren stood ten paces behind him, looking dismayed and very scared.

The colonel went on: 'And do you also know who killed all those scouts from the regiment whom we've been finding every morning for the past month in the fields hereabouts?'

The old man replied with the same animal impassiveness: ' 'Twas I.'

'You mean you killed them all?'

'Every man jack of 'em. Aye. 'Twas I.'

'By yourself?'

'All by meself.'

'Tell me how you did it.'

This time he looked ruffled. Having to talk at such length clearly made him feel uncomfortable. He stammered: 'Couldn't rightly say. I jes' did it as it took me, like.'

The colonel said sternly: 'I warn you that you must tell me everything. So you might as well make up your mind now to make a clean breast of it. How did it start?'

The old man glanced anxiously at his family behind him who were listening attentively. He hesitated a moment longer, then took the plunge:

'I was coming home one night, must have been 'bout ten o'clock. It was the day after you settled in 'ere. You and then these men of yours went and thieved a hunerd an' fifty francs worth of fodder, and a cow, and two head o' sheep. I says to meself: every time they thieve fifty francs off of me, I swear as how I'll make them pay. And there was a sight more things niggling at me that I'll tell you about too. Anyroad, I comes across one of your cavalrymen a'smoking of his pipe in my ditch, just behind my barn. I went and fetched my scythe off of the wall and I come up behind him, so quiet he don't hear a thing. I cut his head off of his body first time, with just the one swing, like a bit of standing corn, afore he could say Jack Robinson. Jes' go and have a look in the pond yonder. You'll find him in there, tied up in a coal sack weighted down with a stone took from by the gate.

'I had it all worked out. I took all his stuff, boots, cap, everything, and I hid the whole lot in the clay kiln in Martin's wood, behind the farmyard.'

The old man stopped. The officers looked at him in amazement. Then the interrogation began again, and this is what they learned.

Once he had carried out his first murder, the old man had been obsessed with one thought: to kill Prussians. He hated them with the cunning, unrelenting hatred of a covetous old peasant who was also a patriot. As he said, he had it all worked out. He waited a few days.

Because he behaved so deferentially to his conquerors and seemed so submissive and co-operative, he was left free to come and go as he pleased. Now, each evening, he watched the despatch riders as they set off. One night he slipped out after hearing the name of the village where the cavalrymen were headed. He had already picked up the few words of German that he needed from his contacts with the soldiers.

He went out of the farmyard, ducked into the wood, and reached the clay kiln. He crawled through the long gallery in the claypit, retrieved the dead man's clothes, and put them on. Then he started prowling through the fields, crouching, using humps and hillocks as cover, listening for the slightest sound and nervous as a poacher.

When he judged it was time, he went back to the road and hid in a clump of bushes. There he waited. Finally, at about midnight, the sound of galloping hooves rang on the beaten earth of the road. He put his ear to the ground to make sure that only one rider was coming, then he got ready.

The trooper was coming at a quick canter, carrying back the dispatches. He approached, keen-eyed and sharp-eared. When he was no more than ten paces away, old Milon dragged himself across the road groaning: '*Hilfe! Hilfe!* Help! Help!' The rider pulled up, recognized an unseated German soldier, assumed that he was injured, got off his horse, approached unsuspectingly, and, just as he bent over his man, took the length of a curved sabre full in the stomach. He collapsed and died instantly, and did no more than twitch with a few final tremors.

The old Norman peasant got to his feet silently rejoicing and then, for his own satisfaction, cut the dead man's throat. Then he dragged him across to the ditch and pushed him in.

The horse stood quietly waiting for its master. Old Milon got into the saddle and galloped off across the plain.

An hour later he spotted two more troopers who were returning to their quarters together. He rode straight at them shouting '*Hilfe! Hilfe!*' The Prussians, recognizing the uniform, let him come, suspecting nothing. The old man rode through them like a cannonball, striking them both down with his sabre and a revolver. Then he slit the throats of the horses, which were German horses. Afterwards he rode unhurriedly back to the kiln and hid the horse at the far end of the dark gallery. He removed the uniform, put on his own rags once more, and went home to bed where he slept until morning.

He did not venture out again for four days, until the investigations were over. But on the fifth day he made another sortie and killed two more soldiers with the same tactics. From then on he operated regularly. Each night he wandered and prowled according to no set plan, slaughtering Prussians wherever he found them, galloping across deserted fields beneath the moon, a Phantom Trooper hunting men. Then, when his work was done, and the roads behind him were strewn with corpses, the old man rode back and hid his horse and his uniform deep in the kiln.

Around noon, going quietly about his business, he took hay and water to his mount in its underground hiding-place, and he fed it well, for he was asking it to perform a great work.

But the previous night one of the men he had attacked had been on the alert and had marked the old man's face with a sabre cut.

Even so, he had killed both of them. He had ridden back as usual, hidden the horse, and put his old clothes on. But just as he reached home he had been overtaken by exhaustion, and though he had dragged himself as far as the stable, he had not been able to get back to the house.

He had been found lying there, covered in blood, on the straw . . .

When he had finished telling his story, he raised his head suddenly and stared defiantly at the Prussian officers.

The colonel pulled on his moustache and asked: 'Have you anything more to say?'

'Not a nobbut. And it's dead reckoning. I killed sixteen, nor one more nor less.'

'You are aware that you will be shot for this?'

'I never asked for mercy.'

'Were you ever a soldier?'

'Aye. I seen action in my time. Anyroad, it was you killed my father as served under the first Napoleon. And then again it was you killed my youngest boy, François, last month, out Evreux way. There was a debt to settle. I settled it. I reckon we're all even now.'

The officers looked at each other.

The old man went on: 'Eight for my father and eight for my boy, I reckon that's even. 'Twasn't me as was looking

for trouble! I never seen you afore! All I know is where
you're from. You come here and then you start ordering me
around as if you owned the place. I took it out on them
others. And I bain't be sorry for it neither.'

The old man straightened his twisted body and crossed
his arms. He looked every inch the unsung hero.

The Prussians talked among themselves in whispers for
some time. One captain, who had also lost a son the
previous month, defended the old prisoner's generosity of
spirit.

Finally the colonel rose to his feet and, approaching old
Milon, spoke to him quietly: 'Look, there is perhaps a way
of saving your neck, and that is to . . .'

But the old man was not listening. With his eyes fixed
unblinkingly on the victorious officer and with the wind
ruffling the stray hairs on his head, he gave a ghastly grin
which twisted the whole of his sabre-slashed face, pushed
out his chest, and with all his force spat full into the
Prussian's face.

As the colonel lifted one arm bewilderedly, the old man
spat into his face a second time.

All the officers were on their feet shouting orders
simultaneously.

Within a minute the old farmer, as impassive as ever, was
put up against a wall and shot while he smiled at Jean, his
oldest boy, at his daughter-in-law, and at the two children,
who all stood watching in horror.

Our Chum Patience

'ANY idea what became of Leremy?'

'He's a captain with the Sixth Dragoons.'

'How about Pinson?'

'He's sub-prefect.'

'And Racollet?'

'Dead.'

We were casting around trying to think of other names which called to mind young faces staring out from beneath gold-braided army-caps. Since the old days, we'd caught up with a few of our old comrades who were now bearded, bald, married, and fathers several times over. Seeing them again so altered sent unpleasant shivers through us, for these encounters showed how short life is, how temporary things are, and that nothing stays the same.

My friend asked: 'What about Patience, portly Patience?'

Firing on all pistons, I let him have it.

If you want to know about him, just lend me a brief ear. About four or five years ago I was in Limoges on a tour of inspection, hanging about, killing time before dinner. Sitting at a table outside the big café in the square where the theatre is, I was feeling pretty bored. Men of trade in twos and threes and fours dropped by for their tot of absinth or vermouth, talked loudly about business—theirs and other people's—laughed uproariously and lowered their voices when they turned to important, confidential matters.

I wondered: 'What on earth can I do after dinner?' I thought how long an evening could be here in this town in the provinces: the slow, grim stroll through unfamiliar streets, the depressing gloom which the solitary traveller feels oozing out of all those passers-by who are complete strangers in every respect, from the provincial cut of their jackets, hats, and trousers to their ways and the local accent, an all-pervading misery which drips from the houses, the shops, the outlandish shapes of the vehicles in the streets, and the generally unaccustomed hubbub, an uneasy sinking of the spirits which prompts you to walk a little quicker as though you were lost in dangerous, cheerless country and makes you want to get back to your hotel, that loathsome hotel, where your room has been pickled in innumerable dubious smells, where you are not entirely sure about the bed, and where there's a hair stuck fast in the dried dust at the bottom of the washbasin.

I was pondering all this as I watched the gas-lamps being lit, feeling more than ever like a distressed castaway now that the shadows were gathering. Whatever was I to do after dinner? I was alone, utterly alone, abandoned, and feeling very sorry for myself.

A fat man came in, sat down at a nearby table, and bellowed in a voice like thunder: 'Waiter! My usual!'

The *my* of the summons exploded like a shot from a cannon. I could tell at once that everything in life was his, indisputably his and not somebody else's; that his character, by God, his name, his appetite, his trousers, his anything, was *his* in the most utter and absolute way—and more so than with any other man. Then he looked round with a self-satisfied air. His glass of bitters arrived and he called out: 'My paper!'

I wondered: 'Now, what does he read?' The name of the newspaper would surely tell me everything about his opinions, his theories, his principles, his hobby-horses, his eccentricities.

The waiter brought him *Le Temps.** This was a surprise. Why *Le Temps*, which is a solemn, dull, high-principled, serious paper? I thought: 'That makes him a sober type, of sound moral character and regular habits, in short a pillar of the middle classes.'

He put his gold-rimmed spectacles on his nose, leaned forward, and, before settling down to read, cast another glance all around him. He noticed me and began glaring in the most insistent and uncomfortable way. It got to the point where I was about to ask him what he was staring at, when he shouted across the room: 'Good God! If it isn't Gontran Lardois!'

I said: 'But it is. You're absolutely right.'

He stood up at once and came towards me with hands outstretched: 'Hello, old man. How are you?'

I sat there highly embarrassed. I didn't know him from Adam. I stammered: 'Well . . . very well. . . . And you?'

He began to laugh: 'I bet you don't recognize me.'

'Not entirely. . . . But there is . . . er . . . something . . .'

He slapped me on the back: 'That's enough of that. I'm Patience, Robert Patience, your old pal, your old chum.'

I recognized him then. Of course! Robert Patience! I'd been at school with him. That was it. I shook the hand he held out to me: 'Fancy! And how've you been keeping?'

'Me? Right as rain.' His grin was a triumphant gloat.

'What brings you to these parts?' he asked.

I explained that I was doing a job for the government audit.

Gesturing towards the ribbon in my buttonhole, he went on: 'I see you've got on, then?'

I answered: 'Oh, I've not done too badly. What about you?'

'Me? I've done very well for myself.'

'What do you do?'

'I'm in business.'

'Make a lot of money?'

'Lots. I'm very rich. Look, why don't you come along tomorrow about noon, 17 Cock Crow Lane, and let me offer you a spot of lunch. It'll give you a chance to see the place I've got.' He seemed to hesitate momentarily before going on: 'Here, you're still the likely lad you used to be in the old days?'

'I should jolly well hope so!'

'Not married, then?'

'No.'

'Good. And are you still fond of fun and spuds?'

I was beginning to find him appallingly vulgar. Nevertheless I answered: 'Rather!'

'And pretty girls?'

'I should say!'

He began to laugh a happy, contented laugh: 'Capital, capital! Here, d'you remember that first stunt we pulled at Bordeaux, when we went for a meal in Roupie's tap-room? Cripes, what a time that was!'

As a matter of fact, I did remember that particular stunt, and the memory of it lifted my mood. Others came to mind, then more again, and we kept saying to each other: 'I say, and what about the time we locked that junior master in old Latoque's cellar!'

And he laughed, thumping the table with his fist, and went on: 'Yes . . . yes . . . oh yes! And do you remember the look on the geography master's face, Monsieur Marin, when we let off a banger in the map of the world just as he was droning on about the Earth's principal volcanoes?'

All at once I said: 'And what about you? Are you married?'

He bellowed: 'Been married ten years, old man, and I've got four children, amazing kids they are. But you'll be seeing them and their mother.'

We had been talking very loudly; diners at tables nearby turned and watched us in surprise.

Suddenly my old friend looked at his watch, a chrono-meter the size of a pumpkin, and exclaimed: 'Blast! It's a shame, but I'm going to have to leave you. I'm not free in the evenings.'

He got up, took both my hands in his, shook them as if he were trying to tear my arms out, and cried: 'See you tomorrow, around noon. It's all arranged.'

I spent the morning working in the offices of the county treasurer. He wanted me to have lunch with him, but I said I had arranged to meet a friend. Since he had to go out anyway, he walked down with me.

'Any idea where Cock Crow Lane is?' I asked him.

'Oh yes,' he replied, 'It's a five minute walk from here. I haven't anything to do: I'll show you the way.'

We set off.

I soon reached the street I was looking for. It was wide,

handsome in its way, and right on the edge of town where the fields began. I studied the houses and found number 17. It was a fairly pretentious sort of place with a garden at the back. The front was decorated with Italianate frescoes and seemed to me a shade vulgar. Goddesses could be observed pouring from tilted urns while clouds masked the secret charms of others. Two stone cupids held up the number.

'This is the house,' I said to the chief county treasurer.

I held out my hand as a preliminary to taking my leave of him. He made an abrupt, rather odd gesture, but said nothing and shook the hand which I offered.

I rang. A maid appeared.

'Is this Monsieur Patience's house?' I asked.

She replied: 'It is, sir . . . Is it Monsieur Patience himself that you wish to speak to?'

'Why, yes.'

The hall was also decorated, with paintings perpetrated by the brush of some local artist. There were a number of views of Paul and Virginie* kissing under palm-trees bathed in pink light. A hideous oriental lantern hung from the ceiling. There were several doors, all hidden by garish curtains.

But what struck me most was the smell—a sickly, sweet-scented smell which reminded me of a mixture of face-powder and damp cellars—an undefinable smell which hung heavily and overpoweringly in the atmosphere, like a Turkish bath where human bodies are kneaded and pummelled. I followed the maid up a marble staircase which featured some kind of imitation oriental carpet. I was shown into a sumptuously appointed drawing-room.

Left alone, I looked about me.

The room was richly furnished, but with the pretentious-ness of a self-made man with bawdy leanings. Engravings dating from the last century, which were actually rather fine, showed women in tall powdered wigs, half-dressed and surprised in interesting postures by amorous suitors. One such lady, stretched out on an enormous dishevelled bed, was dangling one foot at a little dog which was swamped in bedclothes; another was resisting, though not too hard, a lover whose hand had disappeared beneath her skirts. One drawing showed four feet, and the bodies that went with them could just be detected behind a curtain. This huge room, lined with soft divans, was utterly impregnated with the insipid, demoralizing, smell which had struck me earlier. Something suspect oozed out of the walls, the fabrics, the excessive luxury, out of everything.

I crossed over to the window through which I could see trees, to take a look at the garden. It was very large, shady, and superbly maintained. A wide drive wound round a lawn where a fountain scattered water-drops like seeds, then disappeared beneath the massed foliage only to reappear a little further along. Then all of a sudden, right at the far end, three women came into view. They walked slowly, linking arms, wearing long white day gowns trimmed with clouds of lace. Two were blonde and the other was dark. Almost immediately they went back under the trees. I was thunderstruck, entranced by this brief but charming apparition which forced to the surface of my being a whole world of poetry. They had made only the briefest of appearances, in light that was perfect, in a framework of green leaves, at the bottom of this delightful secret garden. But in that one instant, I had seen those beautiful ladies from another century wandering beneath bowers, the same beautiful ladies whose wanton loves were pictured in the voluptuous engravings which hung on the walls. And I thought of that happy, flower-strewn, witty, and melting age when manners were so easy and lips so ready . . .

A loud voice made me jump. Patience had entered the room and, beaming, held out both hands.

He looked me straight in the eye with that artful look people adopt when speaking confidentially of love, and with a wide, sweeping movement of the hand worthy of Napoleon himself, he gestured to his sumptuous drawing-room, his grounds, and the three women who were now visible again in the distance. Then, in a triumphant voice crowing with pride, he said:

'And to think I started out with nothing . . . just the wife and my sister-in-law.'

A Coup d'État

PARIS had just learned of the disaster at Sedan.* The Republic had been proclaimed. The whole of France huffed and puffed at the onset of the madness which lasted until after the Commune. Throughout the length and breadth of the land, grown men played at being soldiers.

Haberdashers had the rank of colonels and the functions of generals; revolvers and daggers were flaunted on large peace-loving paunches wreathed in red sashes; ordinary townspeople-turned-warriors for the duration commanded battalions of loud-mouthed volunteers and swore like troopers to give themselves a suitably martial air.

The simple fact that they were armed and handling service rifles went to the heads of men who otherwise had never previously handled anything more lethal than a pair of weighing-scales, and made them, for no reason at all, terrifying to anyone they encountered. They executed innocent people just to show that they could kill. As they roamed through fields as yet innocent of Prussians, they shot stray dogs, cows gently masticating, and sick horses grazing in meadows. Each man believed that he had been called upon to play a great military role. Cafés in the most out-of-the-way villages, bursting with shopkeepers in uniform, looked like barracks or field-stations.

The town of Canneville had still as yet to receive the appalling news about the army and the capital. But for a month now it had been in a state of extreme turmoil and the opposing parties stood eyeball to eyeball.

The Mayor, the Vicomte de Varnetot, who was small and thin and prematurely aged, a Bourbon legitimist who had lately transferred his loyalties to the Empire, of which he had hopes of preferment, had been confronted by a sudden burst of determined opposition in the person of Doctor Massarel, a large man with a brick-red face, leader of the local Republican Party, worshipful master of the region's masonic lodge, president of the Farmers' Club and the Fireman's Circle, and the man responsible for organizing the rural militia which was to be the salvation of the province.

Within a fortnight he had managed to rally to the defence of their territory no fewer than sixty-three volunteers, all married men with children—canny farmers from the country and shopkeepers from the town—and each morning he drilled them on the square in front of the Town Hall.

Whenever the Mayor happened to turn up at the civic offices, Commandant Massarel, bristling with pistols, sabre in hand, and strutting proudly in front of his squad, ordered them to shout: 'Long live the Nation!' This cry, people noticed, upset the Vicomte who probably interpreted it as a threat, a challenge, and, to boot, an odious reminder no doubt of the Revolution of 1789.

On the morning of 5 September, the doctor, wearing full uniform and with his revolver lying on the table in front of him, was seeing two of his patients, an elderly country couple—the husband had been suffering with varicose veins for seven years but had waited until his wife was in the same state before coming to consult the doctor—when the postman delivered the newspaper.

Monsieur Massarel opened it, turned pale, stood up abruptly, and, raising his arms in a gesture of exultation, began shouting at the top of his voice while the bewildered yeoman and his wife looked on: 'Long live the Republic! Long live the Republic! Long live the Republic!' Then he sat down again just as suddenly, quite faint with emotion.

When the farmer went on: 'It all started when I got like pins and needles all up and down me legs,' Doctor Massarel screamed: 'Not another word! I haven't got time to bother with your stupid legs. The Republic has been declared, the Emperor has been taken prisoner, and France is saved. Long live the Republic!' And, making a dash for the door, he bellowed: 'Céleste! Quickly! Céleste!'

The maid came running, frightened out of her wits. He spoke so fast that he tripped over his words: 'My boots, my sabre, my cartridge belt, and the Spanish dagger you'll find on the table by my bed: hurry!'

The old farmer, making the most of a moment of silence, carried on stubbornly: 'Then I got these sort of lumps on me veins wot gave me gip when I walked.'

Beyond patience, the doctor yelled: 'Don't bother me now, man, for God's sake. If you'd washed your feet a bit more often, you'd never have got yourself into this state.' Grasping him by the collar, he barked at him: 'Don't you realize that we now live in a Republic, you stupid oaf?'

But almost at once his sense of professional propriety brought him back to earth and he shooed out the bewildered couple, repeating: 'Come back tomorrow, come back tomorrow, there's good people. I just don't have time today.'

While he kitted himself out from head to foot, he gave a new series of urgent orders to his maid: 'Run around to Lieutenant Picart's and Sub-Lieutenant Pommel's, and say I want them here immediately. And get Torchebœuf to come too: tell him to bring his drum. Look lively! Sharp about it!'

When Céleste had gone he collected his thoughts, steadying himself to face the difficult situation ahead.

The three men arrived together, in their working clothes. The Commandant, who had been expecting to see them in uniform, was appalled:

'My God! Haven't you heard what's happened? The Emperor has been captured. The Republic has been proclaimed. We must take action. My position is delicate. I'd even go so far as to say dangerous!'

He paused briefly for thought while his subordinates looked on highly alarmed, then went on:

'We must take action. We must not dither. Minutes are as precious as hours at times like this. The key is the speed with which we take decisive action. You, Picart, go and find the padre and order him to ring the church bell to rally the people so that I can let them know what's going on. You, Torchebœuf, take your drum all round the commune as far as the hamlets of La Gerisaie and Salmare and call out the militia: they're to assemble, armed, in the square. You, Pommel, get into uniform at the double, cap and tunic will do. The two of us are going to occupy the Town Hall and order Monsieur de Varnetot to hand over his powers to me. Understood?'

'Yes.'

'Get on with it, then, and quick about it. Pommel, I'll come round to your house with you since we shall be operating together.'

Five minutes later, the Commandant and his subaltern, both armed to the teeth, reached the square just as the diminutive figure of the Vicomte de Varnetot, walking briskly, wearing gaiters as though he were setting out on a hunting expedition, and with his Lefaucheux rifle over his shoulder, emerged from the other street, flanked by his three gamekeepers dressed in green tunics, with knives strapped to their thighs and guns slung across their backs.

While the Doctor halted in astonishment, the four men went into the town hall. The door closed behind them.

'Beaten us to it,' muttered the doctor. 'We'll have to wait for reinforcements. Nothing to be done for the moment.'

Lieutenant Picart turned up: 'The curé said he wouldn't,' he reported. 'He's even gone and shut himself up in the church with the beadle and the churchwarden.' And on the other side of the square, opposite the white, impassive civic hall, the silent black church flaunted its great iron-studded oak door.

Then, as the intrigued townspeople were beginning to poke their heads out of their windows and come out onto their doorsteps, there was a sudden roll on a drum and Torchebœuf came into view, beating out the rapid triple call to arms. He crossed the square at a brisk trot, then disappeared along the road that led away to the fields.

The Commandant drew his sabre and advanced alone until he was about halfway between the two buildings in which the Enemy had barricaded himself. Then, waving his weapon above his head, he shouted as loudly as he could:

'Long live the Republic! Death to traitors!'

Then he turned and walked back to his officers.

The butcher, the baker, and the chemist anxiously put up their shutters and shut their shops. Only the grocer remained open.

Meanwhile the men of the militia were arriving in ones and twos, all dressed differently but each wearing a black cap with red-braid round the peak, a cap being all the corps had by way of uniform. They were armed with their own rusty old guns which had been hanging above kitchen fireplaces for thirty years, and they looked for all the world like a detachment of foresters.

When he had collected thirty or so around him, the Commandant quickly briefed them on recent events. Then, turning to his staff-officers, he said: 'And now we go into action.'

The townspeople were gathering, watching, and chatting among themselves.

The doctor soon had his plan of campaign worked out: 'Lieutenant Picart, you will advance until you are in full view from the windows of the Town Hall and you will order Monsieur de Varnetot, in the name of the Republic, to hand over all civic buildings to me.'

But the Lieutenant, who was a master mason, refused: 'You wasn't born yesterday, was you? Go and get meself shot? Not likely. Them blokes inside don't miss, you know. Do your own dirty work.'

The Commandant turned red in the face. 'I order you! This is insubordination!'

The Lieutenant said mutinously: 'Think I want to go getting me head blown off without knowin' why?'

The town's clever set had gathered in a little knot nearby. They began to laugh. One of them called out: 'Quite right, Picart. It's a bad time for it!'

The doctor muttered: 'Cowards!' And handing his sabre and his revolver to one of his men, he advanced slowly, his eyes fixed on the windows, expecting to see the barrel of a rifle aimed at him at any moment.

When he was within a few paces of the building, the doors at both ends, which gave access to the town's schools, suddenly opened and a flood of small children streamed out, boys on one side and girls on the other, and started playing in the wide, empty square, shouting and shrieking like a flock of geese around the doctor who could not now make himself heard. When the last pupils were outside, both doors closed again.

Most of the children drifted away eventually and the Commandant called out loudly: 'Monsieur de Varnetot!'

A first-floor window opened. Monsieur de Varnetot appeared.

The Commandant began: 'Monsieur, you are aware of the momentous happenings which have lately changed the face of Government. The administration which you represent has ceased to exist. That which I represent has come to power. In this difficult but decisive situation, I am here to ask you, in the name of the new Republic, to place in my hands the authority vested in you by the outgoing power.'

'My dear doctor,' Monsieur de Varnetot replied; '*I* am the Mayor of Canneville, appointed by duly constituted authority, and Mayor of Canneville I shall remain until I have been removed from office and replaced by order of my superiors. As Mayor, I have every right to be in the Town Hall and here I intend to stay. Anyway, just you try getting me out.' And he shut the window.

The Commandant returned to his men. But before reporting to them, he looked Lieutenant Picart up and down: 'Some brave soldier you are! Rabbits aren't as lily-livered as you. You're a disgrace to the army. I'm reducing you to the ranks!'

The Lieutenant answered: 'Fat lot I care.' And he strolled over to the knot of muttering townsfolk.

The doctor hesitated. What was he to do next? Launch an attack? But would his men obey the order? And in any case, did he have the authority to give it?

He had a bright idea.

He hurried over to the telegraph office which faced the Town Hall on the other side of the square. There he sent three telegrams:

To the members of the Republican Government in Paris;

To the new Republican Prefect for the Seine-Inférieure at
Rouen;

To the new Republican Sub-Prefect of Dieppe.

He reported the situation fully, said what danger the
commune was running by being left at the mercy of the
former monarchist Mayor, offered his loyal services, requested orders, and signed his name, taking care to add all
his letters and qualifications. Then he rejoined his company
and, taking ten francs from his pocket, said: 'Here you are,
men, go and get yourselves something to eat and a drink.
Just leave a detachment of ten men here to make sure no one
leaves the Town Hall.'

But ex-Lieutenant Picart, who was chatting with the
watchmaker, overheard him. He began to snigger and
shouted; 'Hang on. If they come out, that would be your
chance to get in. Otherwise, I don't ever see you ever managing to make it inside!'

The doctor did not reply and went off to have his lunch.

In the course of the afternoon he set up posts all round
the commune as though there were a threat of a surprise
attack. On several occasions he walked past the doors of the
Town Hall and the church without seeing anything suspicious; both buildings might have been deserted.

The butcher, the baker, and the chemist re-opened their
shops.

There was a lot of talk in people's houses. If the Emperor
had been captured, there must have been some dirty work
behind it. No one knew exactly which Republic had been
restored.

Night fell.

At about nine o'clock, the doctor, alone and treading
silently, advanced as far as the entrance to the Town Hall,
convinced that his opponent had gone home to bed. Just as
he was shaping up to break down the door with a pickaxe, a
loud voice belonging to one of the gamekeepers suddenly
barked: 'Who goes there?'

Monsieur Massarel beat a hasty retreat.

Day broke with the situation unchanged.

The armed militia still occupied the square. The entire

population had gathered round them, waiting for a solution to be found. People from the surrounding villages kept arriving, to see for themselves.

Then the doctor, realizing that his reputation was at stake, decided to get the whole business over and done with one way or another. He was on the point of deciding on a course of action—he did not know what but it would of course be decisive—when the door of the telegraph office opened and out came the little girl who worked for the woman who ran it, holding two pieces of paper in her hand.

First she made for the Commandant and gave him one of the telegrams. Then, crossing the deserted middle of the square, crushed by all the eyes that were fixed on her, head lowered and walking with small, quick steps, she proceeded to knock timidly at the barricaded building, as though quite unaware that a party of armed men was hidden inside.

The door opened halfway. A man's hand took the paper and the girl walked back again, blushing scarlet and close to tears, aware that the whole locality was staring at her.

The doctor called out in a ringing voice: 'Can I have silence, please!' And when the hoi-polloi had fallen silent, he went on grandly: 'Here is the message which I have this moment received from the Government.' And holding up the telegram, he read it out:

Former mayor removed from office. Please advise promptly. Further instructions follow.

For the Sub-Prefect,
SAPIN, Councillor.'

He had won! His heart thumped with joy. His hands shook. But Picart, his ex-subaltern, shouted out from the group nearby: 'That's all very well. But if the other gang won't come out, a fat lot of good your bit of paper'll do you!'

Monsieur Massarel turned pale. If in fact the others did not come out, then he would have to make a move. It was not only a question of rights now, but of duty.

He looked anxiously towards the Town Hall, hoping to see its doors open and his opponent withdraw. The doors remained closed. What was he to do? The crowd argued amonst themselves and pressed close round the militia. Some were laughing.

The doctor was especially tormented by one thought. If he ordered an attack, he would have to march at the head of his troops. And since confrontation would cease if he were killed, it was at him and him alone that Monsieur de Varnetot and his three gamekeepers would shoot. And they were good shots, very good, as Picart now reminded him once more. But he had in idea and, turning to Pommel, said: 'Go and ask the chemist to lend me a towel and a pole. At the double!'

The Lieutenant hurried off.

He would make a flag of truce, a white one, the sight of which might possibly rejoice the former Mayor's legitimist heart.

Pommel returned with the piece of cloth he had been asked to fetch plus a broomhandle. With some pieces of string they organized a standard which Monsieur Massarel seized with both hands. Then, brandishing it before him, he set out once more for the Town Hall. When he faced the door, he again called out: 'Monsieur de Varnetot?' The door opened suddenly and Monsieur de Varnetot appeared on the threshold accompanied by his three gamekeepers.

Instinctively, the doctor took one step back. Then he saluted his adversary courteously and, choking with emotion, managed to say: 'I am here to inform you of the instructions which I have received.'

Without returning his salute, his high-born enemy replied: 'Sir, I withdraw. But do not think that I do so out of fear or out of deference to the odious government which has usurped power.' And stressing each word separately, he declared: 'I have no wish to appear to serve the Republic, not even for a single day. That is all.'

Quite at a loss for words, Massarel did not answer. Monsieur de Varnetot broke into a quick march and disappeared around one of the corners of the square, still flanked by his escort.

Then the doctor, drunk with pride, walked back to the waiting crowd. The moment he was near enough to be heard, he shouted: 'Hooray! Hooray! The Republic is winning up and down the line!' This brought no reaction whatsoever.

The doctor continued: 'The people are free. You are free and independent. You should be proud!' The inert villagers stared at him. No glory shone in their eyes.

Then he in turn stared at them, appalled by their indifference, and he cast round for something he could say or do which would produce a mighty effect, electrify this sleepy township, and fulfil his mission as champion of a new order.

He was visited by inspiration. Turning to Pommel, he said: 'Lieutenant, go and see if you can find the bust of the former Emperor which is in the Council debating chamber, then bring it here with a chair.'

Pommel soon returned carrying on his right shoulder the plaster bust of Louis-Napoleon and holding in his left hand a chair with a straw seat.

Monsieur Massarel stepped forward to meet him, took the chair, set it on the ground, placed the white bust on it, and, stepping back a few paces, addressed it in a sonorous voice:

'Oh tyrant! How fallen are the mighty, fallen into mud and mire. The dying nation groaned beneath thy foot. Avenging fate has struck thee down. Defeat and shame have jumped onto thy back; thou hast fallen in defeat, a prisoner to the Prussian. But out of the ruins of thy crumbling empire, the Republic rises, young and radiant, picking up thy broken sword . . .'

He waited for the applause. There was no acclamation, no spontaneous burst of clapping. The startled yokels remained silent. Meanwhile the bust, with its waxed moustaches extending beyond the cheeks on both sides, and its head held quite still and combed as immaculately as a barber's model, seemed to be watching Monsieur Massarel with its indelible, mocking, plaster smile.

And so they faced each other, Napoleon on his chair and the doctor standing three paces away. The Commandant was suddenly filled with anger. But what was he to do?

What could he do to rouse the people and carry off public opinion victoriously and definitively? By chance, his hand came to rest on his hip and, under his red sash, he felt the butt of his revolver.

At this moment no inspiration, no words came to him. Instead, he drew out his pistol, took two paces forward, and, at point blank range, blasted the fallen Emperor.

The bullet made a little black hole in the forehead. It might have been a spot and was nothing to speak of. The effect had been missed. Monsieur Massarel fired a second shot, which made another hole, then a third, and, without pausing, loosed off his last three bullets. Louis-Napoleon's forehead flew up in a cloud of white dust, but his eyes, his nose, and the fine points of his moustaches remained intact.

At the end of his patience, the doctor knocked the chair over with a flick of the wrist and, placing one foot in the pose of a conqueror on what remained of the bust, turned to the bewildered crowd bellowing: 'And so perish all traitors!'

But since no display of enthusiasm was as yet forthcoming and the spectators seemed to have been struck dumb with astonishment, the Commandant called to the men of the militia: 'You may return to your homes now, men!' And he himself walked off quickly towards his house, as though he were running away.

As soon as he appeared, his maid said he had patients who had been waiting in the surgery for more than three hours. He hurried along to see. It was the country people with the varicose veins. They had come back and had been stubbornly, patiently sitting there since early morning.

The old farmer immediately carried on with what he had been saying:

'It started when I got like pins and needles all up and down me legs . . .'

The Christening

OUTSIDE the farmhouse door, the men waited in their Sunday best. The May sun shed its clear light over the apple trees in bloom which bulged like huge, white and pink, sweet-smelling bouquets of flowers and threw a canopy of blossom over the entire yard. Around them they showered a continuous snow of small petals which whirled and fluttered as they fell into the tall grass where dandelions burned like flames and poppies showed like drops of blood.

With belly distended and dugs swollen, a sow dozed just by the manure heap while a litter of piglets swarmed around, their tails rolled up like balls of string.

Suddenly, from a long way behind the trees which rose above the farmhouses, the church bell tolled. Its iron voice sent a faint, distant summons up into the joyous skies. Swallows swooped like arrows through the blue space trapped between the tall, still beeches. From time to time a smell of stables wafted by and mingled with the soft, sweet breath of the apple trees.

One of the men standing outside the door turned to face the house and shouted: 'Come on, Mélina, shift yourself. Bell's ringing!'

He was perhaps 30. He was a big farm worker, as yet unbent and unbroken by years spent toiling in the fields. An old man—his father—gnarled as the trunk of an oak, with misshapen hands and crooked legs, declared: 'Trouble with women is they never be ready on time!'

The old man's two other sons started to laugh and one of them turned to the oldest brother who had already shouted once, and said: 'Go in and fetch 'em out, Hippolyte, else they'll still be in there come noon time.'

So the young man went into his house.

A flock of ducks which had halted nearby began quacking and flapping their wings. Then they waddled off slowly towards the pond.

In the open doorway a fat woman appeared holding a two-month-old baby. The white strings of her tall bonnet hung down her back over a red shawl which glowed bright as fire, and the infant, wrapped in white cloths, rested on the woman's swollen belly.

The mother emerged next, a big, strong girl, not quite 18, blooming and smiling and clutching her husband by the arm. The two grandmothers followed, like two withered old apples, visibly worn down and broken and twisted by hard, patiently borne work. One was widowed; she took the arm of the grandfather who had remained by the door, and they set off at the head of the procession immediately after the child and the foster-mother. The rest of the family walked behind them. The youngest were carrying paper bags full of sugared almonds.

In the distance the little bell rang continuously, ready and waiting, summoning the frail child for all it was worth. Little boys climbed onto banks; people appeared at gates; farm-girls set down their two pails of milk and stood between them to watch the christening procession go by.

The foster-mother carried her living burden in triumph, stepping carefully round the puddles in the sunken lanes which ran between tree-lined banks. The old people advanced at a stately pace, shuffling along as well as age and painful joints allowed; the young men felt like dancing and kept an eye out for the girls who stopped to watch them as they passed; the father and mother, serious-faced, walked soberly behind the child who one day would take their place in life and carry on their name in the district, the name of Dentu, which was well known throughout the shire.

They emerged onto the plain and cut across the fields to save themselves the trouble of going the long way round by road.

They could see the church now, with its pointed steeple. A gap was visible just beneath its slate roof where something moved, something which swung briskly forwards and backwards and passed to and fro behind the narrow belfry window. It was the bell which continued to ring out, calling to the newborn child to come and enter the House of the Lord for the very first time.

A dog tagged along behind the procession. They threw sugared almonds to it. It romped excitedly among them.

The church doors were open. The priest, a tall young man with red hair, spare and strong, also a Dentu and in fact uncle to the child and brother to the father, stood waiting at the altar. He proceeded to christen his nephew Prosper-César according to the rites. Prosper-César, who had got a taste of the symbolic salt, began to cry.

When the ceremony was over, the family stood in the porch while the priest removed his surplice. Then they set off again, walking quickly now, spurred on by the thought of dinner. All the children from roundabout followed them, and when handfuls of sweets were thrown in their direction there were furious scuffles, fights, and hair-pullings. The dog threw itself into the scrum in pursuit of the sweets and in spite of being yanked out by its tail, ears, and paws, it burrowed more stubbornly than any of the ragged boys and girls.

The foster-mother, feeling a little weary, said to the priest who was walking by her side: 'How'd it be, Father, you being agreeable that is, if you was to hold your nephew for a spell while I has a bit of a stretch. I got a stitch or near enough.'

The priest took the child. Its dazzling christening robe made a great splash of white against his black cassock. He kissed it, feeling awkward, not knowing how to hold this bundle of thistledown or where to put it. Everyone laughed. One of the grandmothers shouted from some way off: 'Don't it ever grieve you, Father, to think as how you'll never have one of your own like him?'

The priest did not answer. Striding along, he stared intently at the blue-eyed child. He felt an urge to kiss its round cheeks again. When he could contain himself no longer, he lifted the baby, pressed his lips to its face, and held them there.

The father shouted to him: 'Oy, padre! If you wants a kiddie, you only has to arsk!' And they began chaffing and joking as country people do.

As soon as they were settled around the table, gross

peasant high spirits broke over them like a storm. The other two sons were also to be married; their intendeds were there, having turned up just for the christening banquet, and the guests kept making references to future issue promised by their twin unions.

There were vulgar jokes and smutty comments which made the blushing girls snigger and doubled the men up with laughter: they banged on the table with their fists and shouted. The father and the grandfather kept up a stream of ribald pleasantries. The mother smiled. The old women joined in the fun and threw in suggestive remarks of their own.

The priest, who was used to such country jollifications, sat quietly next to the foster-mother and tickled his nephew's mouth with one finger to make him laugh. He seemed astonished by the sight of the child, as though he had never seen one before. He watched him with intense concentration, looking sober and thoughtful, and feeling a tenderness rise within him that he had never known, a strange, keen, and slightly sad tenderness for this fragile little being who was his own brother's son.

Neither hearing nor seeing, he watched the child. He would have liked to sit him on his knee, for he could still feel, warm against his chest and in his heart, the sweet sensation he had experienced as he had carried him back from church just a short while ago. He was deeply moved by this promise of a man to be: it was as though he were contemplating an ineffable mystery to which he had previously given no thought, the solemn, holy mystery of a new soul made flesh, the great mystery of life beginning, of love awakening, of the continuation of the race and the onward march of human kind.

The foster-mother ate heartily, her face red, her eyes shining but hampered by the child who came between her and the table.

The priest said to her: 'Give him to me. I'm not hungry.' He took the child from her. Everything around him faded, then vanished, and he sat with his eyes fixed on the baby's chubby pink face. Slowly the warmth of the little body spread through the swaddling clothes and the material of his cassock to his legs; it permeated his being like a soft, chaste, kindly touch, an exquisite caress which filled his eyes with tears.

The noise made by the others as they ate grew deafening. Distressed by the hullabaloo, the child began to cry.

A voice shouted out: 'Go on, Father, give 'im a little drop of titty!'

The room was rocked by a gale of laughter. But the mother got to her feet, took her son, and bore him off to the next room. She returned a few minutes later saying that he was sleeping quietly in his cot.

The banquet proceeded. From time to time the men and women left the room and went out into the yard; then they returned and sat down again at the table. Meat, vegetables, cider, and wine were stuffed into gullets and made stomachs swell, eyes shine, and wits turn.

Night was falling by the time they got to the coffee. The priest had been gone a long time but no one was surprised by his absence.

Eventually the young mother got up to go and see if her little boy was still asleep. It was dark now. She felt her way into the room, holding her arms in front of her so as not to bump into any of the furniture. But a peculiar sound brought her up short; she turned and hurried out in a panic, sure that she had heard someone moving. She returned to the others, white-faced and trembling, and told them what had happened. All the men jumped up, roaring drunk and dangerous. The father, lamp in hand, led the way.

The priest, kneeling at the side of the cot, was sobbing with his face on the pillow where the child lay sleeping.

Coco

IN the countryside roundabout, the Lucas farm was known as The Grange. No one could have said why. Perhaps the country people linked the word 'Grange' with a notion of wealth and splendour, for it was beyond doubt the largest, the richest, and the best-kept farm for miles around.

The enormous yard, bounded by five rows of magnificent trees intended to protect the compact, delicate apple trees from the strong winds which blew over the plain, was enclosed by long tiled-roofed buildings where hay and grain were stored, handsome cow-byres made of flintstone, stabling for thirty horses, and a farmhouse built of red brick which looked a little like a small country manor. The muck-heaps were well tended, the guard dogs lived in kennels, a tribe of hens wandered through the tall grass.

Each day at noon, fifteen people—masters, hired hands, and serving-girls—gathered round the long kitchen table on which the soup steamed in an enormous earthenware tureen decorated with blue flowers.

All the animals—horses, cows, pigs, and sheep—were sleek, well cared for, and clean. And Farmer Lucas, a tall man now thickening at the waist, did his rounds three times each day, seeing to everything and neglecting nothing.

At the back of one of the stables, out of charity, they kept a very old white horse which the mistress had decided should be cared for until the end of its natural life, because she had raised it, because she had always looked after it, and because it reminded her of times gone by.

A lout of a lad named Isidore Duval, Zidore for short, was put in charge of this old relic. In winter he brought its ration of oats and hay and in summer had to traipse four times a day to the slope where it was kept, to move its tethering peg so that it always had plenty of fresh grass.

The animal was almost lame and had difficulty lifting its heavy legs which were thick at the knee and swollen just above the hoof. Its coat, which was never combed now, looked like white hair, and very long lashes made its eyes look sad.

When Zidore led it to grass, the horse walked so slowly that he had to pull hard on the halter rope. Bent over and breathing hard, the youth swore at it, resenting having to waste his time seeing to a broken-down old nag.

When they saw how much Zidore resented Coco, everyone on the farm was hugely amused and talked to him of nothing but the horse to make him lose his temper. His friends poked fun at him. In the village he got called Coco-Zidore.

The youth fumed until there dawned in him a determination to get even with the horse. He was a thin boy with long legs, very dirty, with a shock of thick, coarse, bristling red hair. He looked stupid and stammered so badly when he spoke that it seemed as though ideas found it impossible to take shape in his sluggish, brutish brain.

For some time now he had been scandalized that Coco should have been kept on, and he grew indignant when he thought how much money was being thrown away on such a useless beast. He believed that once it had stopped working, it was not fair that it should be fed, not right that expensive oats should go on being wasted on a crippled hack. And in spite of Farmer Lucas's orders, he often saved on the old horse's feed, giving it half-measures and economizing on the straw he put down in its stall. In his confused, childish mind, hate grew—rapacious, sly, savage, brutal, underhand, peasant hate.

When summer came round once more, he was obliged to go and *get the horse shifted* on its sloping field. It was a long way. Each morning, feeling angrier and angrier, he set off heavy-footed through the cornfields. The men working the land pulled his leg and shouted: 'Oy! Zidore! Mind you give Coco our very best!'

He never answered; but as he trudged along he would snap off a stick from a hedge and, when he had moved the old horse's tether, would let it start grazing again; then, sneaking up on it, he would slash viciously at its fetlocks. The animal tried to run away to avoid the blows, and it would turn at the end of its rope as though it were trapped inside a circular track. And the youth would continue hitting it frenziedly, running after it in hot pursuit, his teeth clenched with rage.

Then he would turn slowly and walk away without looking back, while the horse's old eyes watched him go, its sides heaving, gasping with the effort of raising a trot. And it did not lower its bony white head to the grass again until it had seen the young peasant's blue smock disappear into the distance.

Since the nights were warm now, Coco was left out permanently in its pasture near the ravine, on the other side of the wood. Only Zidore went to see it.

The boy enjoyed throwing stones at it. He would sit on a hillock ten paces away, stay there half an hour, and from time to time throw a sharp pebble at the horse which stood motionless, fettered before its enemy, watching him unblinkingly and not daring to graze until he had gone.

But in the youth's head, there was always this thought: 'Why go on feeding a horse that did not work?' It seemed to him that the broken-winded nag was stealing the food out of the mouths of other animals, stealing the goods of men and the Good Lord's bounty, and stealing from him too, Zidore, who had to work for his living.

And so, little by little, day by day, the boy reduced the area of grass which he allowed it by shortening its tether.

The horse went without, grew thin and emaciated. Too weak to break the rope, it raised its head towards the wide sweep of gleaming green grass close by which it could smell but not reach.

Then one evening Zidore had an idea: he would simply stop shifting Coco around. He was tired of walking so far to tend a bag of bones.

Still, he went on coming, to enjoy his vengeance. The horse eyed him anxiously. The first day, he did not hit it. He walked round it with his hands in his pockets. He even went so far as to pretend he was about to move it but he put the stake back into its hole, then walked off, feeling very pleased at his cleverness.

When the horse saw him go, it whinnied, calling him back. But the youth started to run, leaving it to itself, quite alone in its glen, firmly tethered, and without a single blade of grass anywhere near its jaws.

Ravenously it tried to get at the lush pasture which it could touch with its muzzle. It knelt, craning its head forward, reaching out with its great drooling lips. But it was hopeless. All through the day, the old animal wore itself out with the useless, terrible struggle. It was consumed by hunger which was made all the keener by the sight of all that green grazing which stretched clear away to the horizon.

The youth did not come back that day. He went roaming in the woods, looking for birds' nests.

He reappeared the following day. Coco was lying down exhausted. When it saw the boy it stood up, expecting to be moved at last.

But the young peasant went nowhere near the mallet which lay in the grass. He came up close, stared at the animal, threw a clod of earth which landed on the white hair of its muzzle, then walked off whistling.

The horse remained standing for as long as the youth remained in sight. Then, realizing that all efforts to reach the grass nearby would be quite useless, it lay down again on its side and closed its eyes.

The next day Zidore did not come.

When, the day after, he went up to the horse which was lying in the same spot, he saw that Coco was dead.

He stood there a while, staring at it, feeling pleased with his handiwork yet at the same time surprised that it was all over so soon. He nudged it with his foot, lifted one of its legs and then let it fall. He sat down on it, and remained sitting there with his eyes on the grass and nothing in his head.

He returned to the farm, but did not report what had happened because he wanted to go on being able to roam around at those times when he would normally be going off to shift the peg.

He went to see it the following day. Crows flew up as he approached. Innumerable flies crawled over the body and buzzed all around.

When he got back he broke the news. The animal had been so old that no one was surprised. The farmer said to two of his hands: 'Take a shovel, lads, and just dig a hole for him where he is.'

The men buried the horse on the spot where it had starved to death.

And the grass grew thick, green and strong on the paltry remains.

A Coward

IN social circles he was known as 'Beau' Signoles. His name was Vicomte Gontran-Joseph de Signoles.

Both his parents were dead and, master of a considerable fortune, he cut a dash, as the expression goes. He was a fine figure of a man and had a definite way with him. He spoke well enough to be thought witty, and possessed a certain natural grace and a proud and noble air. His moustache was jaunty and his eyes were soft and pleasing to women.

He was in great demand in fashionable salons, ladies queued up to waltz with him, and in men he aroused the kind of genial hostility which people of energetic disposition frequently attract. A number of love affairs were laid at his door, of the sort likely to do no harm to the reputation of a man of the world. He was happy and contented and enjoyed total peace of mind. It was known that he was a good swordsman and an even better shot. 'When I do fight,' he would say, 'I shall choose pistols. With pistols, I shall kill my man. You can depend on it.'

Now one evening he had accompanied two young women of his acquaintance, suitably escorted by their husbands, to the theatre. Afterwards he invited them all for an ice at Tortoni's.* They had been inside for a few minutes when he noticed that a man at a nearby table was staring persistently at one of the two ladies. She seemed embarrassed and uneasy and avoided his eye. In the end she said to her husband: 'That man over there is staring at me. I've never seen him before. Do you know him?'

Her husband, who had noticed nothing, looked up and said: 'No. Don't know him from Adam.'

The young woman went on, half amused and half angry: 'It's very embarrassing. That man is preventing me from enjoying my ice cream.'

Her husband shrugged: 'Pay no attention. If I had to sort out all the uncivil people I meet, there'd be no end to it.'

But the Vicomte stood up suddenly. He could not allow a stranger to interfere with the enjoyment of an ice for which he had paid. The insult was directed at him, since it was at his suggestion and at his invitation that his friends had come to the café. It was clearly a matter which concerned him alone.

He went up to the man and said: 'Sir, you are looking at these ladies in a manner which I cannot tolerate. I must ask you to desist.'

'Go to hell!' the man replied.

Through clenched teeth, the Vicomte said: 'Take care, sir, don't make me go too far.'

The man gave a two-word answer, coarse words which rang out from one end of the café to the other and made the heads of all the customers jerk simultaneously as though they were on a spring. Those facing away turned round, the rest looked up. Three waiters spun on their heels like whirling tops. The two ladies behind the counter jumped, then swivelled their whole bodies like a couple of mechanical dolls responding to the same command.

The room went very quiet. Then there was the sharp sound of a blow. The Vicomte had struck his opponent on the cheek. Everyone rose to their feet to come between them. Cards were exchanged.

When the Vicomte got home he strode energetically around his room for several minutes. He was too agitated to think clearly. His head was full of one idea—a Duel— though the idea as yet prompted no particular feelings in him. He had done what he had to do. He had behaved as he should. People would talk about it, say that he was right, and congratulate him. As frequently happens in moments of mental stress, he talked to himself and said several times: 'The man's a perfect brute!'

Then he sat down and began to think. He would have to choose his seconds first thing next morning. Whom should he ask? He tried to decide which of his friends had the coolest heads and the most illustrious names. In the end he settled on the Marquis de la Tour-Noire and Colonel Bourdin. A lord and a soldier. Most suitable. Their names would look well in the papers. Suddenly aware of being thirsty, he drank down three glasses of water. Then he started walking up and down again. He felt tremendously invigorated. If he showed reckless courage and granite determination, laid down stiff, dangerous conditions, and insisted on a real duel, with no holds barred, then his opponent would probably back down and apologize.

He picked up the card which he had taken from his pocket and thrown onto his writing table, and read it again, though he had already glanced at it in the café and looked at it on the way home each time his cab passed a street light. 'Georges Lamil, 51, rue Moncey'. That was all it said.

He studied the letters which formed words which looked mysterious and full of hidden meanings. Georges Lamil! Who was the man? What did he do? Why had he looked at the lady like that? Was it not outrageous that an unknown stranger should be able to waltz in and upset things just because he had taken it into his head to stare insolently at some woman or other? And again the Vicomte said aloud: 'The man's a brute!'

He stood motionless, pensive, his eyes still fixed on the card. A surge of anger welled up in him against the piece of paper he was holding, bitter, hate-filled anger tainted by an odd sense of unease. The whole business was stupid! He picked up an open knife which he found to hand and jabbed it through the printed name, as though he were stabbing someone.

So he was going to have to fight! Would he choose swords or pistols?—for he considered that he was the injured party. With swords, there was less risk to himself; but with pistols he stood a better chance of forcing his opponent to back down. Duels with swords are rarely fatal, for participants are wary enough to stand sufficiently close to each other to prevent thrusts going home too deeply. With pistols, he would be risking his life; but he might equally be able to emerge with honour intact and without having to go up against his man.

Aloud he said: 'Got to be firm. He'll be scared.'

The sound of his own voice startled him and he looked

around. He felt very restless. He drank another glass of water and then began to undress for bed.

When he was in bed, he blew out the lamp and closed his eyes.

'I've got all day tomorrow to see to my affairs,' he thought. 'Let's get a good night's sleep. That way I'll be cool and collected.'

He was very warm in his bedclothes but he could not get to sleep. He twisted and turned, lay on his back for five minutes, tried his left side and then rolled over onto his right.

He was still thirsty. He got up for a drink. Then he thought of something that made him uneasy: 'Will I be scared?'

Why did his heart begin to beat wildly each time his room made one of its familiar sounds? When the clock was about to strike, the faint whirring made by the spring as it tightened made him jump, and afterwards he had to keep his mouth open for several seconds to catch his breath, so tense did he feel.

He tried to think the thing out rationally: 'Will I be afraid?'

No, of course he would not be afraid, because he was resolved to see the thing through and because he was absolutely determined to fight and show no fear. But he felt so profoundly uneasy that he wondered: 'Is it possible to be afraid in spite of oneself?'

Doubt, anxiety, panic flooded over him. If a power stronger than his will were to get the better of him, an overmastering, irresistible force, then what would happen? Yes, what could happen? Of course, he would present himself at the place appointed because he wanted to turn up. But what if he shook? What if he passed out? He thought of his social position, his reputation, his name.

He was seized by an odd compulsion to get up and look at himself in the mirror. He lit a candle. When he saw his face reflected in the polished glass, he barely recognized it. He felt as though he had never seen himself before. His eyes seemed enormous and he was undeniably pale, very pale.

He remained standing in front of the mirror. He put out his tongue as though he were checking up on the state of his health and suddenly a thought came into his head like a bullet: 'This time the day after tomorrow, I could be dead.'

His heart began beating furiously again.

'This time the day after tomorrow, I could be dead. This person standing in front of me, the me I can see in the mirror, will be done for. I'm here, I'm looking at myself, I can feel myself alive. Can it be that in twenty-four hours I shall be laid out on this bed, dead, with my eyes closed, cold, lifeless, no more?'

He turned and looked at his bed and distinctly saw himself lying face upwards in the sheets which he had left only a moment before. He had the sunken face of the dead and the limpness of hands that will never move again.

His bed made him feel afraid and, to avoid seeing it, he went through to his smoke-room. Mechanically he took a cigar, lit it, and resumed his pacing. He was cold. He began to reach for the bell-pull to wake his valet, but with his hand out he paused: 'The fellow will see that I'm scared.'

So he did not ring, and lit a fire himself. His hands were affected by a nervous tremble, and when they touched things they shook a little. His mind wandered; his confused thoughts whirled and darted uncomfortably; his head swam as though he had been drinking. And over and over he asked himself: 'What am I to do? What is to become of me?'

His whole body throbbed and twitched spasmodically. He stood up, went to the window and opened the curtains.

Day—a summer's day—was breaking. The town, the roofs, and the walls were pink under the rosy morning sky. A great flood of soft light, like the caress of the rising sun, engulfed the waking world. And with this burst of light, a sudden surge of blithe, savage hope conquered the Vicomte's soul! Why, he must be mad to let himself be unmanned by fear like this, before anything was settled, before his seconds had spoken to Georges Lamil's, before he even knew if he was to fight at all! He washed and shaved, dressed, and, stepping out confidently, left the house.

As he walked, he kept telling himself: 'I must be resolute, utterly resolute. I must prove that I am not afraid.'

His seconds, the Marquis and the Colonel, agreed to place themselves entirely at his disposal and, after shaking him firmly by the hand, they discussed conditions.

'You wish this to be a serious affair?' asked the Colonel.

'Most serious,' replied the Vicomte.

'Do you insist on pistols?' said the Marquis.

'Yes.'

'Will you give us a free hand to settle the outstanding details?'

In a curt staccato, the Vicomte rattled off: 'Twenty paces, fire on command, weapons to be raised and aimed and not lowered. Exchange of shots to continue until one party is seriously wounded.'

'Splendid conditions,' declared the Colonel in a satisfied voice: 'You shoot well. You have the odds on your side.'

They left the Vicomte, who went home to wait for their return. His agitation, which had been temporarily relieved, now grew by the minute. He felt a kind of permanent trembling or throbbing all down his arms and legs and in his chest. He found it impossible to remain sitting or standing where he was for any length of time. His mouth was almost completely dry and he kept making noises with his tongue as though it were stuck to his palate and he were trying to free it.

He decided to have lunch but could not eat anything. Then he thought that a stiff drink might harden his resolve. So he sent for a small carafe of rum and downed six small glasses in rapid succession. A feeling of warmth burned right through him and was immediately followed by a general numbness of the senses. He thought: 'That's the answer. I'll be fine now.' But an hour later he had emptied the carafe and had become unbearably agitated once more. He felt an insane urge to roll on the ground and scream and bite. Then it was evening.

A ring at the door so stopped his breath that he did not have the strength to get up and greet his seconds. He did not even speak to them, say 'Good evening', or utter a word for fear that the change in his voice would give him away.

The Colonel reported: 'It's all settled according to the conditions you specified. At first your opponent tried to claim the privileges of the injured party, but he backed down pretty smartly and agreed to everything. His seconds are both military men.'

'I'm obliged,' said the Vicomte.

The Marquis went on: 'Forgive us if we don't stay but we've still a good number of matters to attend to. We'll need a good doctor since the contest won't end until one party is seriously wounded—and as you know bullets usually mean business. We'll have to appoint a place which is near to a house where the wounded man may be transferred, if necessary, and so on and so forth. So there's enough to keep us busy for two or three hours.'

'I'm obliged,' said the Vicomte for the second time.

'Are you all right? Feeling calm?' the Colonel asked.

'Yes, quite calm, thank you.'

The two men withdrew.

Conscious once more of being alone, he felt he was going mad. When his valet had lit the lamps, he sat down at his table to write some letters. Taking a fresh sheet of paper, he wrote 'This is my last will and testament . . .' then he stood up abruptly and turned away, feeling quite incapable of putting two ideas together, of making up his mind, of deciding anything.

So he was going to have to fight! There was no way now of avoiding it. What was happening inside him? He wanted to fight: his intention and his resolve were beyond question. Yet however much his mind struggled, however much he stiffened his will, he knew that he would not even have the strength to drag himself to the place where the encounter was to be held. He tried to imagine the fight, how he would behave and how his opponent would conduct himself. From time to time his teeth chattered and made a faint, brittle sound in his mouth. He thought he might read and took down Chateauvillard's duelling code.* Then he wondered: 'Has my opponent been practising regularly on the ranges?

Is he well known? Is he in the rankings? Now, how can I find out?'

He remembered the Baron de Vaux's book on famous crackshots and went right through it. Georges Lamil was not named. But, surely, if he were not skilled with the pistol, would he have agreed so promptly to fight with such a dangerous weapon on such lethal conditions?

He idly opened a pistol case made by Gastinne-Renette which was lying on a small table and took out one of the guns, then stood in the firing position and raised his arm. But he shook all over and the barrel waved about in all directions. Then he said: 'It's no good. I can't fight in this state.'

He looked at the barrel which ended in the small, deep hole which spits death, and he thought about dishonour, the whispers in the clubs, the laughter in the salons, the scorn of women, the comments in the newspapers, and the insults which cowards would throw in his face.

Still staring at the gun, he pulled back the hammer and behind it suddenly saw the cap of a cartridge gleam like a little red flame. The pistol had been left loaded by accident or neglect, a circumstance which prompted an obscure, inexplicable feeling of great happiness.

If he failed to face up to his man in the cool, noble manner which was expected, he would never be able to show his face again. His honour would be tarnished. He would be branded with infamy and expelled from polite society. And he knew, he felt in his bones, that he would never be able to conduct himself with the necessary display of cool daring. Yet he must be courageous, since he wanted to fight! . . . He knew he was brave, because . . .

The thought skimmed his mind but was never completed. Opening his mouth wide, he rammed the barrel of his pistol against the back of his throat and pulled the trigger . . .

When his valet came running, attracted by the detonation, he found him lying dead on his back. The spurting blood had splashed onto the sheet of paper on the table and left a streak of blood to underline these words:

'This is my last will and testament . . .'

The Patron

NEVER in his wildest dreams had he thought that he would ever have done so well for himself! The son of a provincial bailiff, Jean Marin, like so many others before him, had come to the Latin Quarter as a law student. In the various cafés which he had frequented in turn, he had become friendly with a number of loquacious students who talked politics furiously as they drank their beer. He had conceived a great admiration for them and stubbornly followed them from café to café, even paying for their drinks when he had the money.

Then he became a lawyer and took on cases which he regularly lost. One morning, he read in the paper that one of his old friends had just become a member of parliament. Once more, he became as faithful as the proverbial dog, the friend who does the unpleasant jobs and the nasty business, the one who always gets sent for, the one with the feelings which do not have to be considered. But as a result of some party infighting, the member of parliament became a Minister. Six months later, Jean Marin was appointed Privy Councillor.

At first he felt a surge of pride which he could barely contain. He would walk through the streets taking huge delight in showing himself off, as though people could tell what an important position he held simply by looking at him. He always managed to slip a mention of it into even the most trivial conversations he had with shopkeepers he patronized, newspaper-sellers, or even cab-drivers: 'Now, as a Privy Councillor, I . . .'

Next, he felt as a matter of imperious need that it was incumbent upon him, as a result of his dignity, as a requirement laid down by professional necessity, as the expression of his duty as a powerful and generous man, to offer his patronage. He offered his support to everyone on every possible occasion with unquenchable generosity.

Whenever he was out strolling along the boulevards and met up with someone he knew, he approached him delightedly, shook him warmly by the hand, enquired after his health, and then, without prompting, declared: 'You know, I am a Privy Councillor and would be only too glad to be of service. If I can be of help in any way at all, please do not hesitate to call on me. When you have a position like mine, there's a lot that can be done.' And he would go into the nearest café with the friend he had just met and ask for his pen, ink, and a sheet of writing paper—'just the one, waiter; it's for a letter of introduction.'

He wrote many letters of introduction—ten, twenty, fifty a day. He wrote them at the Café Américain, Bignon's, Tortoni's, the Maison Dorée, the Café Riche, the Helder, the Café Anglais, the Napolitain, anywhere and everywhere.* He wrote to every civil servant in the Republic, from justices of the peace to Ministers. And he was a happy, a very happy man.

One morning, just as he was leaving his house for a meeting of the Privy Council, it began to rain. He thought of taking a cab, but did not do so, and instead set off walking through the streets.

The rain became torrential, filling the gutters and flooding the roads. Monsieur Marin was obliged to shelter in a doorway. An old priest with white hair had got there before him. Before becoming a Privy Councillor Monsieur Marin had had little time for the clergy. But now he treated them all with respect, ever since a cardinal had courteously sought his views on a delicate matter. The rain continued to beat down, and to avoid being drenched by the spray the two men were forced to retreat into the concierge's lodge. Monsieur Marin, who still felt the urge to speak and let everyone know who he was, declared: 'What appalling weather!'

The old priest said with a polite nod: 'Oh yes, it's very unpleasant, especially if you're only in Paris for a few days.'

'Ah! So you've come up from the country?'

'That's right. I'm just passing through.'

'In that case, it really is unpleasant if all you have is rain for your few days in the capital. Civil servants like myself, who live here all year round, hardly give it a thought.'

The priest did not reply. He looked out into the street where the rain was easing. And then, quickly making up his mind, he lifted his cassock exactly the way women lift their skirts when walking through puddles.

When Monsieur Marin saw that he was about to make off, he exclaimed: 'You'll get wet through. Wait a few minutes longer and it'll stop.'

The priest paused uncertainly, then said: 'The fact is I'm in rather a hurry. I have an urgent appointment.'

Monsieur Marin looked most anxious: 'But you will be soaked to the skin. May I venture to ask which part of town you are making for?'

The priest seemed to hesitate, then said: 'I'm going towards the Palais Royal.'

'In that case, if you'll allow me, let me offer the protection of my umbrella. I myself am on my way to a meeting of the Privy Council. I am a Privy Councillor.'

The old priest raised his head and looked at him, then declared: 'I am most grateful for your kind offer which I accept with pleasure.'

Monsieur Marin took him by the arm and led him off. He showed him the way, supervised and counselled him: 'Be careful of this gutter. And above all beware of carriage wheels: sometimes they can splash you all over. Watch out for umbrellas coming in the opposite direction. There's nothing more dangerous for the eyes than those spokes. The women especially are a menace. They don't look where they're going and they always poke the points of their sunshades and umbrellas right into your face. And they never get out of anybody's way. They behave as if the whole town belonged to them. Whether you're on the pavement or in the road, they've always got to be first. I take the view myself that they've not been brought up right.' And Monsieur Marin started to laugh.

The priest said nothing. He walked along, slightly bent

over, carefully choosing where he put his feet so as not to get mud on his shoes or his cassock.

Monsieur Marin went on: 'I expect you're in Paris for a short break, then?'

'No. I'm here on business,' the old man replied.

'Oh? And is it important business? May I venture to ask what sort of business? If I can be of any help, I'm entirely at your disposal.'

The priest seemed rather embarrassed. He murmured: 'Oh! It's a small piece of personal business. A little difficulty with . . . with the bishop. You wouldn't be interested. It's a . . . an internal matter.'

Monsieur Marin renewed his offer: 'But it's the Privy Council's job to settle matters of that sort! And since that's the case, please do not hesitate to call on me.'

'It is indeed the case, which is why I'm going to the Privy Council. You are too kind. I have to see Monsieur Lerepère and Monsieur Savon, and perhaps also Monsieur Petitpas.'

Monsieur Marin stopped dead in his tracks. 'But they are friends of mine, my best friends, excellent colleagues, charming men. I shall recommend you to all three, and in the warmest terms. You may count on it.'

The priest thanked him, apologized profusely, and stammered innumerable expressions of thanks.

Monsieur Marin was delighted. 'Oh! You can congratulate yourself that you have had a rare stroke of luck. You'll see, you'll see that thanks to me your business will go like clockwork.'

They reached the Privy Council. Monsieur Marin showed the priest up to his office, offered him a seat, installed him in front of the fire, sat down at his desk, and began writing: 'Dear colleague, Allow me to recommend to you, in the warmest terms, one of the most worthy, deserving, and venerable men of the cloth . . .' He paused and asked: 'What is your name, please?'

'I am the abbé Ceinture.'

Monsieur Marin began writing again: '. . . of the cloth, Monsieur l'abbé Ceinture, who has need of your good offices in a small matter which he will explain to you.

'I am thankful that this occasion has arisen, for it gives me an opportunity to . . .' And he ended with the usual compliments.

After writing the three letters, he handed them to his protégé who went off with inordinate expressions of gratitude.

Monsieur Marin completed his tasks, went home, spent the rest of the day quietly, slept peacefully, woke up feeling pleased with himself, and asked for the newspapers to be brought.

The first one he opened was a radical paper. In it, he read the following:

'Of the Clergy and of Civil Servants.

Recording the misdemeanours of the Clergy is an unending task. A priest, Ceinture by name, convicted of conspiring against the present government, accused of actions so unworthy that we shall not even hint at their nature, furthermore suspected of being a former Jesuit-turned-parish priest, disowned by a bishop for reasons said to be unspeakable, and summoned to Paris to explain his conduct, has found an ardent supporter in a Privy Councillor named Marin who has not balked at furnishing this cassocked criminal with the warmest of letters of introduction addressed to all the Republican civil servants among his fellow Councillors.

'We wish to bring to the attention of the Minister the totally unacceptable conduct of this member of the Privy Council . . .'

Monsieur Marin leaped out of bed, dressed, and hurried round to his fellow Councillor Petitpas who told him: 'My God! You must have been mad to offer your support to an old conspirator like him.'

Monsieur Marin stammered bewilderedly: 'But. . . . Look here. . . . I had the wool pulled over my eyes. . . . He seemed such an upstanding. . . . He took me in. . . . Took advantage in the basest way. Can't you please arrange things so that he gets a long sentence, a very long sentence? I'll write a letter. Tell me what I should write to ensure he gets a long sentence. I'll go and see the Attorney General and the Archbishop of Paris, that's it, the Archbishop . . .' And sitting down suddenly at Monsieur Petitpas's desk, he wrote:

'My Lord Archbishop, I have the honour to bring to your Grace's attention the fact that I have been the victim of the intrigues and lies of a certain abbé Ceinture, who has taken advantage of my good faith.

'Misled by the protestations of this man of the cloth, I . . .'

Then when he had signed and sealed his letter, he turned to his colleague and said:

'Now, old man, let this be a lesson to you: never give your patronage to anyone.'

The Umbrella

MADAME OREILLE was the careful sort. She knew the value of money and had an arsenal of principles concerning its increase. Her maid found it very difficult to make anything on the side, and Monsieur Oreille had the dickens of a job trying to get his spending money out of her. They were quite well off, really, and had no children; but Madame Oreille felt physically ill when she saw her silver coins leave home. It was as though her heart were being torn in two; and each time she was called upon to undertake an expense of any size, however unavoidable, she always slept badly the night before.

Monsieur Oreille was always telling his wife: 'You shouldn't be so close. We never spend what we've got coming in.'

And she would reply: 'You never know what's going to crop up. It's better to be on the safe side.'

She was a tiny woman of 45, alert, lined, neat, and often cross.

Her husband perpetually complained of the privations which she made him endure, some of which he found particularly painful since they wounded his vanity.

He was a head clerk in the Ministry of War where he had remained solely out of deference to his wife, to swell further the underspent household purse.

Now for the last couple of years he had been arriving at the office with the same much-mended umbrella which made all his colleagues laugh. In the end, weary of their jibes, he insisted that Madame Oreille buy him a new one. She found one for eight-and-a-half francs in a department-store sale. The clerks at the office, when they saw the same umbrella sprouting all over Paris by the thousand, made more jokes which caused Monsieur Oreille considerable suffering. The umbrella was a bad buy. Within three months it was quite useless and the hilarity in the Ministry turned into an epidemic. There was even a song about it which rang out from morning to evening through every part of the enormous building.

Irritated beyond measure, Monsieur Oreille ordered his wife to select a new brolly for him, with a silk covering, for twenty francs, and told her he would want to see the bill.

She chose one costing eighteen francs and, scarlet with anger, told her husband as she handed it to him: 'There, that should last you five years at least.'

Monsieur Oreille made a triumphant appearance at the office.

When he got home that evening, his wife looked anxiously at the umbrella and said: 'You're not going to leave it rolled up tight with that elastic strap round it, are you? It'll wear the silk. You're going to have to look after it, because I shan't be buying you any more umbrellas for a while.'

She took it from him, unhooked the ring, and shook out the folds. But she stood there, struck with horror. A round hole, the size of a penny, had appeared in the middle of the umbrella. It was a cigar burn!

She stammered: 'What's the matter with it?'

'Matter? Matter with what?' said her husband without looking.

She almost choked on her anger. She could not speak: 'You . . . you . . . you've burnt a hole . . . in . . . in your . . . umbrella. Have you . . . have you taken . . . have you taken leave of your senses? Do you want to ruin us?'

He turned to her, feeling the colour drain from his face: 'What d'you mean?'

'I mean that you've burnt a hole in your umbrella. Here, see for yourself!' And launching herself as though she were about to hit him, she thrust the small round burn right under his nose.

Confronted with the mutilation, he was aghast and stammered: 'What? Where? . . . What's this? I haven't the foggiest. I'm not responsible, I swear. How should I know how it got into that state?'

She was shouting now: 'I'd bet good money that you've been playing the fool with it at the office, messing about, opening it to show off.'

He replied: 'I did open it once to let them see how smart it was. That's all. That's the honest truth.'

But she was quivering with rage and staged one of those scenes of married life which make hearth and home a more fearsome place for a man of peace than a battlefield bristling with bullets.

She mended the hole with a piece of the silk from the old umbrella, which was a different colour. And, next morning, Monsieur Oreille, in chastened mood, set out grasping his patched-up gamp. He stowed it away in his office cupboard and gave it no further thought, in the way that no further thought is given to a bad memory.

But he had hardly set foot through the door that evening when his wife snatched the umbrella out of his hands, opened it to inspect its condition, and stood choking on the irreparable disaster she found. It was riddled with small holes which were clearly burns, as though someone had tipped the burning ash from a pipe onto it. This time it was ruined, ravaged beyond return.

She just stood there glaring, not saying a word, too outraged for the smallest sound to emerge from her throat. He too examined the extent of the damage and felt bewildered, appalled, dismayed.

They turned and looked at each other. He lowered his eyes. Then he was struck in the face by the tattered umbrella, which she had thrown at him. Then, finding her voice in a flood of fury, she screamed: 'You clown. You stupid clown. You did it on purpose. But I'll make you pay! You'll not get another . . .'

And the same scene was repeated. When the storm blew itself out an hour later, he managed to put his side of the case. He swore he couldn't make head or tail of it; that the thing could only have been done out of spite or because someone wanted to get his own back.

He was saved by a ring at the door. It was a friend who was to dine with them.

Madame Oreille lay the facts of the case before him. Buying another umbrella was definitely out of the question: her husband would not get a new one.

The friend reasoned coolly: 'If that happens, he'll ruin his clothes, and clothes cost a lot more.'

Still furious, the tiny woman replied: 'In that case, he can have a cheap one. I'm not going to buy him a new silk umbrella.'

This was too much for Monsieur Oreille. 'If that's the way it is, I'll hand in my notice! I'm not turning up at the Ministry with a cheap umbrella.'

The friend said: 'Why not get it recovered? It won't cost much.'

At the end of her tether, Madame Oreille spluttered: 'Recovering it will cost at least eight francs. Eight and eighteen makes twenty-six! Twenty-six francs for an umbrella! It's sheer madness! You must be out of your mind!'

The friend, a professional man of very modest means, then had an inspiration: 'Get your insurance to pay. Insurance companies pay up for fire-damage providing that the fire occurred on the property of the insured.'

When she heard this piece of advice Madame Oreille calmed down instantly. Then after a brief consideration, she said to her husband: 'Tomorrow, before going to the Ministry, you will call in at the offices of La Maternelle, report the state of your umbrella, and put in a claim.'

Monsieur Oreille started: 'I'd never have the nerve! Look here, it's only eighteen francs down the drain. We won't die of it.'

Next morning he went off to work carrying a cane. Fortunately it was a fine day.

Alone in the house, Madame Oreille could not reconcile herself to losing her eighteen francs. She had put the umbrella on the dining-room table and walked round and round it without managing to make up her mind.

The thought of the insurance kept coming into her head, but she could not bear the prospect of facing the mocking reactions of the clerks she would have to deal with, for she was shy with other people, blushed at the slightest thing, and was tongue-tied if ever she had to speak to strangers.

However, her regret for the eighteen francs was like a physical ache. She tried to put it out of her mind, but the memory of her loss was like vinegar on a cut finger. What was she to do? The hours slipped by and still she could not make up her mind. Then all at once, like cowards who become foolhardy, she formed her resolve: 'I'll go, and we'll see what happens!'

But first she had to attend to the umbrella so as to make its ruin complete and put her cause beyond doubt. She took a box of matches from the mantelpiece and made a large burn as big as her hand between the spokes; then she carefully rolled what was left of the silk, fastened it with the elastic band, put on her hat and coat, and hurried off to the rue de Rivoli, where the company's offices were situated.

But when she was almost there, she slowed her pace. What was she going to say? How would they answer?

She studied the numbers on the doors. She still had twenty-eight to go. Good. That gave her time to think. She walked more and more slowly. Suddenly she gave a start. Here was the door and on it was written in letters of gold: La Maternelle Fire-Insurance Co. So soon! She paused anxiously for a moment, feeling rather shamefaced, then walked on, turned and came back, walked past the door a second time, and then retraced her steps again.

Finally she said to herself: 'There's no going back now. Best get it over and done with.' Even so, as she went through the doors, she was aware that her heart was racing.

She stepped into an enormous room with booths all round the walls; in each booth a man's head was visible, the rest being hidden by a lattice-work frame.

An employee appeared carrying a sheaf of papers. She halted and asked in a small, shy voice: 'Excuse me, could you tell me where I should go to ask about putting in a claim for fire-damage?'

He replied in a booming voice: 'First floor, turn left. You want Disasters.'

The word make her feel even less assured than before.

She had an urge to run away, to say nothing, to wave goodbye to her eighteen francs. But at the thought of the money her courage revived slightly and she began climbing the stairs, panting and pausing at each step.

On the first floor she saw a door. She knocked. A confident voice shouted: 'Come in!'

She went in and found herself in a large room where three solemn men, each wearing a ribbon recognizing service to the community, stood chatting.

One of them asked: 'Can I help you?'

She did not know what to say and stammered: 'I've . . . I've come . . . about . . . a Disaster.'

The man politely motioned to a chair. 'Please be good enough to take a seat. I'll be with you in a moment.' And turning to the others once more, he went on with his conversation. 'Gentlemen, the Company takes the view that its liability in your case does not exceed four hundred thousand francs. We do not accept your claim for the further hundred thousand which you argue we should pay. In any case, the assessment . . .'

The other two men broke in: 'Very well. We shall let the courts decide. There is little point in prolonging this discussion.' And after a moment of formal leave-taking, they departed.

Oh! If she had dared go with them, she would gladly have done so. She would have dropped everything and fled! But how could she? The man returned and said with a bow: 'In what way can I be of service?'

With some difficulty, she managed to get out: 'I've come about . . . about this.'

The manager looked down in amazement at the object with which he had been presented.

With trembling hands, she tried to undo the elastic fastening. After a few attempts she managed it and suddenly opened the tattered skeleton of the umbrella.

'It looks in a bad way,' said the man sympathetically.

After a moment's hesitation, she said: 'I paid twenty francs for it.'

He looked shocked: 'Really? As much as that?'

'Yes, it was a very good one. I want to report the state it's in.'

'Quite right. I see. But I don't quite understand what I'm supposed to do about it.'

She was seized by a sudden anxiety. Perhaps the company did not pay out on small items and she said: 'But . . . it's been burnt.'

The man did not deny it: 'I can see that.'

She sat with her mouth open, not knowing how to go on. Then suddenly remembering what she had forgotten to say, she blurted out: 'I am Madame Oreille. We are insured with La Maternelle and I've come to make a claim for the damage to this umbrella.' Fearing a categorical refusal, she added hastily: 'I want you to have it recovered. That's all.'

The manager, quite nonplussed, replied: 'But . . . dear lady . . . this is not an umbrella shop. We cannot undertake that type of repair work.'

Madame Oreille felt her composure return to her tiny frame. She was going to have to fight. So fight she would! No longer afraid, she said: 'I simply wish to claim for the cost of repairs. I am quite able to do the work myself.'

The man seemed to be out of his depth: 'I must say that the sum involved is very small. We are never asked to settle claims for such trifling accidents. I am sure that you will appreciate that we cannot possibly pay out for handkerchiefs, gloves, brooms, old shoes, and the host of small items which are daily exposed to damage by fire and smoke.'

Her face turned red as she felt anger flood over her: 'Let me tell you that only last December our chimney caught fire and did at least five hundred francs worth of damage. Monsieur Oreille didn't make a claim against the company then, so it's only right that you should pay out on my umbrella now!'

The manager, detecting a lie, said with a smile: 'But you will admit, dear lady, that it is very odd that Monsieur Oreille should not submit a claim for five hundred francs but is now asking for five or six francs for repairing an umbrella.'

She did not hesitate and replied: 'I'm sorry, but the five

hundred francs was a matter for Monsieur Oreille's budget whereas the eighteen francs comes out of Madame Oreille's budget, and that's not the same thing at all.'

Seeing that he was not going to get rid of her and that he could easily spend the whole day arguing, he resigned himself and asked: 'Then perhaps you would be good enough to explain how the accident happened.'

Scenting victory, she began to tell her story:

'It was like this. In my hall at home I have this brass thing where you put umbrellas and walking-sticks. Well, the other day, as I was coming in, I put this umbrella in it. I should explain that just above it there's a little shelf for putting matches and candles on. I reached out and I took out four matches. I struck one but nothing happened. I struck another. It lit but went out. I tried another and the same thing happened.'

The manager broke in at this point with a little joke: 'I take it they were these new Government matches?'*

But she did not understand and continued: 'They might very well be. Anyway, the fourth one was alright and I lit the candle; then I went into the bedroom to lie down. But a quarter of an hour later, I thought I could smell burning. Now I've always been afraid of fire. Oh! if the house ever burned down, it wouldn't be my fault! Especially since the time I told you about when the chimney caught fire, I've gone about in fear and trembling. I got up, I went out of the bedroom, I searched everywhere, sniffing like one of those hunting dogs, and in the end I found my umbrella on fire. Most likely one of the matches had fallen into it. You can imagine the state I was in . . .'

The manager had decided the line he would follow and asked: 'And what is your assessment of the damage?'

She remained speechless, not daring to name a figure. Then, wishing to show her generosity of soul, she said: 'You have it repaired. I put myself in your hands.'

He refused: 'Out of the question, dear lady. Just tell me how much you are asking.'

'But . . . I should think . . . er . . . I hope you understand that I have no wish to take advantage of your good will . . .

but may I suggest this. I shall take my umbrella to the maker's for him to recover it in good-quality silk, something that will last, and I'll present you with the bill. Would that be acceptable?'

'By all means, dear lady, perfectly acceptable. I will give you an authorization for the cashier who will reimburse you.'

He proffered a card to Madame Oreille who took it, rose, and, expressing her gratitude, left, anxious to get outside in case he should change his mind.

Now, with a light step, she went along the street in search of a suitably high-class umbrella-maker's. When she found one which looked expensive, she entered and said confidently:

'I have an umbrella which I want you to recover in silk, good-quality silk. Use the best you have. Price is no object.'

The Necklace

SHE was one of those pretty, delightful girls who, apparently by some error of Fate, get themselves born the daughters of very minor civil servants. She had no dowry, no expectations, no means of meeting some rich, important man who would understand, love, and marry her. So she went along with a proposal made by a junior clerk in the Ministry of Education.

She dressed simply, being unable to afford anything better, but she was every whit as unhappy as any daughter of good family who has come down in the world. Women have neither rank nor class, and their beauty, grace, and charm do service for birthright and connections. Natural guile, instinctive elegance, and adaptability are what determines their place in the hierarchy, and a girl of no birth to speak of may easily be the equal of any society lady.

She was unhappy all the time, for she felt that she was intended for a life of refinement and luxury. She was made unhappy by the run-down apartment they lived in, the peeling walls, the battered chairs, and the ugly curtains. Now all this, which any other woman of her station might never even have noticed, was torture to her and made her very angry. The spectacle of the young Breton peasant girl who did the household chores stirred sad regrets and impossible fancies. She dreamed of silent antechambers hung with oriental tapestries, lit by tall, bronze candelabras, and of two tall footmen in liveried breeches asleep in the huge armchairs, dozing in the heavy heat of a stove. She dreamed of great drawing-rooms dressed with old silk, filled with fine furniture which showed off trinkets beyond price, and of pretty little parlours, filled with perfumes and just made for intimate talk at five in the afternoon with one's closest friends who would be the most famous and sought-after men of the day whose attentions were much coveted and desired by all women.

When she sat down to dinner at the round table spread with a three-day-old cloth, facing her husband who always lifted the lid of the soup-tureen and declared delightedly: 'Ah! Stew! Splendid! There's nothing I like better than a nice stew . . .', she dreamed of elegant dinners, gleaming silverware, and tapestries which peopled the walls with mythical characters and strange birds in enchanted forests; she dreamed of exquisite dishes served on fabulous china plates, of pretty compliments whispered into willing ears and received with Sphinx-like smiles over the pink flesh of a trout or the wings of a hazel hen.

She had no fine dresses, no jewellery, nothing. And that was all she cared about; she felt that God had made her for such things. She would have given anything to be popular, envied, attractive, and in demand.

She had a friend who was rich, a friend from her convent days, on whom she never called now, for she was always so unhappy afterwards. Sometimes, for days on end, she would weep tears of sorrow, regret, despair, and anguish.

One evening her husband came home looking highly pleased with himself. In his hand he brandished a large envelope.

'Look,' he said, 'I've got something for you.'

She tore the paper flap eagerly and extracted a printed card bearing these words:

'The Minister of Education and Madame Georges Ramponneau request the pleasure of the company of Monsieur and Madame Loisel at the Ministry Buildings on the evening of 18 January.'

Instead of being delighted as her husband had hoped, she tossed the invitation peevishly onto the table and muttered: 'What earthly use is that to me?'

'But, darling, I thought you'd be happy. You never go anywhere and it's an opportunity, a splendid opportunity! I had the dickens of a job getting hold of an invite. Everybody's after them; they're very much in demand and not many are handed out to us clerks. You'll be able to see all the big nobs there.'

She looked at him irritably and said shortly: 'And what am I supposed to wear if I do go?'

He had not thought of that. He blustered: 'What about the dress you wear for the theatre? It looks all right to me . . .' The words died in his throat. He was totally disconcerted and dismayed by the sight of his wife who had begun to cry. Two large tears rolled slowly out of the corners of her eyes and down towards the sides of her mouth.

'What's up?' he stammered. 'What's the matter?'

Making a supreme effort, she controlled her sorrows and, wiping her damp cheeks, replied quite calmly: 'Nothing. It's just that I haven't got anything to wear and consequently I shan't be going to any reception. Give the invite to one of your colleagues with a wife who is better off for clothes than I am.'

He was devastated. He went on: 'Oh come on, Mathilde. Look, what could it cost to get something suitable that would do for other occasions, something fairly simple?'

She thought for a few moments, working out her sums but also wondering how much she could decently ask for without drawing an immediate refusal and pained protests from her husband who was careful with his money. Finally, after some hesitation, she said: 'I can't say precisely, but I daresay I could get by on four hundred francs.'

He turned slightly pale, for he had been setting aside just that amount to buy a gun and finance hunting trips the following summer in the flat landscape around Nanterre with a few friends who went shooting larks there on Sundays. But he said: 'Very well. I'll give you your four hundred francs. But do try and get a decent dress.'

The day of the reception drew near and Madame Loisel appeared sad, worried, anxious. Yet all her clothes were ready. One evening her husband said: 'What's up? You haven't half been acting funny these last few days.'

She replied: 'It vexes me that I haven't got a single piece of jewellery, not one stone, that I can put on. I'll look like a church mouse. I'd almost as soon not go to the reception.'

'Wear a posy,' he said. 'It's all the rage this year. You

could get two or three magnificent roses for ten francs.'

She was not convinced. 'No. . . . There's nothing so humiliating as to look poor when you're with women who are rich.'

But her husband exclaimed: 'You aren't half silly! Look, go and see your friend, Madame Forestier, and ask her to lend you some jewellery. You know her well enough for that.'

She gave a delighted cry: 'You're right! I never thought of that!'

The next day she called on her friend and told her all about her problem. Madame Forestier went over to a mirror-fronted wardrobe, took out a large casket, brought it over, unlocked it, and said to Madame Loisel: 'Choose whatever you like.'

At first she saw bracelets, then a rope of pearls and a Venetian cross made of gold and diamonds admirably fashioned. She tried on the necklaces in the mirror, and could hardly bear to take them off and give them back. She kept asking: 'Have you got anything else?'

'Yes, of course. Just look. I can't say what sort of thing you'll like best.'

All of a sudden, in a black satinwood case, she found a magnificent diamond necklace, and her heart began to beat with immoderate desire. Her hands shook as she picked it up. She fastened it around her throat over her high-necked dress and sat looking at herself in rapture. Then, diffidently, apprehensively, she asked: 'Can you lend me this? Nothing else. Just this.'

'But of course.'

She threw her arms around her friend, kissed her extravagantly, and then ran home, taking her treasure with her.

The day of the reception arrived. Madame Loisel was a success. She was the prettiest woman there, elegant, graceful, radiant, and wonderfully happy. All the men looked at her, enquired who she was, and asked to be introduced. All the cabinet secretaries and under-secretaries wanted to waltz with her. She was even noticed by the Minister himself.

She danced ecstatically, wildly, intoxicated with pleasure, giving no thought to anything else, swept along on her victorious beauty and glorious success, and floating on a cloud of happiness composed of the homage, admiration, and desire she evoked and the kind of complete and utter triumph which is so sweet to a woman's heart.

She left at about four in the morning. Since midnight her husband had been dozing in a small, empty side-room with three other men whose wives were having an enjoyable time.

He helped her on with her coat which he had fetched when it was time to go, a modest, everyday coat, a commonplace coat violently at odds with the elegance of her dress. It brought her down to earth, and she would have preferred to slip away quietly and avoid being noticed by the other women who were being arrayed in rich furs. But Loisel grabbed her by the arm: 'Wait a sec. You'll catch cold outside. I'll go and get a cab.'

But she refused to listen and ran quickly down the stairs. When they were outside in the street, there was no cab in sight. They began looking for one, hailing all the cabbies they saw driving by in the distance.

They walked down to the Seine in desperation, shivering with cold. There, on the embankment, they at last found one of those aged nocturnal hackney cabs which only emerge in Paris after dusk, as if ashamed to parade their poverty in the full light of day. It bore them back to their front door in the rue des Martyrs, and they walked sadly up to their apartment. For her it was all over, while he was thinking that he would have to be at the Ministry at ten.

Standing in front of the mirror, she took off the coat she had been wearing over her shoulders, to get a last look at herself in all her glory. Suddenly she gave a cry. The necklace was no longer round her throat!

Her husband, who was already half undressed, asked: 'What's up?'

She turned to him in a panic: 'I . . . I . . . Madame Forestier's necklace . . . I haven't got it!'

He straightened up as if thunderstruck: 'What? . . .
But . . . You can't have lost it!'

They looked in the pleats of her dress, in the folds of her
coat, and in her pockets. They looked everywhere. They
did not find it.

'Are you sure you still had it when you left the ballroom?'
he asked.

'Yes, I remember fingering it in the entrance hall.'

'But if you'd lost it in the street, we'd have heard it fall.
So it must be in the cab.'

'That's right. That's probably it. Did you get his
number?'

'No. Did you happen to notice it?'

'No.'

They looked at each other in dismay. Finally Loisel got
dressed again. 'I'm going to go back the way we came,' he
said, 'to see if I can find it.' He went out. She remained as
she was, still wearing her evening gown, not having the
strength to go to bed, sitting disconsolately on a chair by the
empty grate, her mind a blank.

Her husband returned at about seven o'clock. He had
found nothing.

He went to the police station, called at newspaper offices
where he advertised a reward, toured the cab companies,
and tried anywhere where the faintest of hopes led him. She
waited for him all day long in the same distracted condition,
thinking of the appalling catastrophe which had befallen
them.

Loisel came back that evening, hollow-cheeked and very
pale. He had not come up with anything.

'Look,' he said, 'you'll have to write to your friend and
say you broke the catch on her necklace and you are getting
it repaired. That'll give us time to work out what we'll have
to do.'

She wrote to his dictation.

A week later they had lost all hope.

Loisel, who had aged five years, said: 'We'll have to start
thinking about replacing the necklace.'

The next day they took the case in which it had come and called on the jeweller whose name was inside. He looked through his order book.

'It wasn't me that sold the actual necklace. I only supplied the case.'

After this, they trailed round jeweller's shops, looking for a necklace just like the other one, trying to remember it, and both ill with worry and anxiety.

In a shop in the Palais Royal they found a diamond collar which they thought was identical to the one they were looking for. It cost forty thousand francs. The jeweller was prepared to let them have it for thirty-six.

They asked him not to sell it for three days. And they got him to agree to take it back for thirty-four thousand if the one that had been lost turned up before the end of February.

Loisel had eighteen thousand francs which his father had left him. He would have to borrow the rest.

He borrowed the money, a thousand francs here, five hundred there, sometimes a hundred and as little as sixty. He signed notes, agreed to pay exorbitant rates of interest, resorted to usurers and the whole tribe of moneylenders. He mortgaged the rest of his life, signed papers without knowing if he would ever be able to honour his commitments, and then, sick with worry about the future, the grim poverty which stood ready to pounce, and the prospect of all the physical privation and mental torture ahead, he went round to the jeweller's to get the new necklace with the thirty-six thousand francs which he put on the counter.

When Madame Loisel took it round, Madame Forestier said in a huff: 'You ought really to have brought it back sooner. I might have needed it.'

She did not open the case, as her friend had feared she might. If she had noticed the substitution, what would she have thought? What would she have said? Would she not have concluded she was a thief?

Then began for Madame Loisel the grindingly horrible life of the very poor. But quickly and heroically, she resigned herself to what she could not alter: their appalling debt would have to be repaid. She was determined to pay. They dismissed the maid. They moved out of their apartment and rented an attic room.

She became used to heavy domestic work and all kinds of ghastly kitchen chores. She washed dishes, wearing down her pink nails on the greasy pots and saucepans. She washed the dirty sheets, shirts, and floorcloths by hand and hung them up to dry on a line; each morning she took the rubbish down to the street and carried the water up, pausing for breath on each landing. And, dressed like any working-class woman, she shopped at the fruiterer's, the grocer's, and the butcher's, with a basket over her arm, haggling, frequently abused and always counting every penny.

Each month they had to settle some accounts, renew others, and bargain for time.

Her husband worked in the evenings doing accounts for a shopkeeper and quite frequently sat up into the early hours doing copying work at five sous a page.

They lived like this for ten years.

By the time ten years had gone by, they had repaid everything, with not a penny outstanding, in spite of the extortionate conditions and including the accumulated interest.

Madame Loisel looked old now. She had turned into the battling, hard, uncouth housewife who rules working-class homes. Her hair was untidy, her skirts were askew, and her hands were red. She spoke in a gruff voice and scrubbed floors on her hands and knees. But sometimes, when her husband had gone to the office, she would sit by the window and think of that evening long ago when she had been so beautiful and so admired.

What might not have happened had she not lost the necklace? Who could tell? Who could possibly tell? Life is so strange, so fickle! How little is needed to make or break us!

One Sunday, needing a break from her heavy working week, she went out for a stroll on the Champs-Elysées.

Suddenly she caught sight of a woman pushing a child in a pram. It was Madame Forestier, still young, still beautiful, and still attractive.

Madame Loisel felt apprehensive. Should she speak to her? Yes, why not? Now that she had paid in full, she would tell her everything. Why not? She went up to her.

'Hello, Jeanne.'

The friend did not recognize her and was taken aback at being addressed so familiarly by a common woman in the street. She stammered: 'But . . . I'm sorry . . . I don't know . . . There's some mistake.'

'No mistake. I'm Mathilde Loisel.'

Her friend gave a cry: 'But my poor Mathilde, how you've changed!'

'Yes, I've been through some hard times since I saw you, very hard times. And it was all on your account.'

'On my account? Whatever do you mean?'

'Do you remember that diamond necklace you lent me to go to the reception at the Ministry?'

'Yes. What about it?'

'Well I lost it.'

'Lost it? But you returned it to me.'

'No, I returned another one just like it. And we've been paying for it these past ten years. You know, it wasn't easy for us. We had nothing. . . . But it's over and done with now, and I'm glad.'

Madame Forestier stopped. 'You mean you bought a diamond necklace to replace mine?'

'Yes. And you never noticed the difference, did you? They were exactly alike.' And she smiled a proud, innocent smile.

Madame Forestier looked very upset and, taking both her hands in hers, said:

'Oh, my poor Mathilde! But it was only an imitation necklace. It couldn't have been worth much more than five hundred francs! . . .'

Strolling

WHEN old Monsieur Leras, a ledger-clerk with Messrs Labuze & Co, stepped out of the shop, he stood for a moment or two, dazzled by the glare of the setting sun. He had been working all day in yellow gaslight at the very back of the shop which gave onto a yard as narrow and as deep as a well. The tiny room where he had spent every day of the last forty years was so gloomy that only between the hours of eleven and three was it possible to keep the lamps unlit.

It was always damp and cold, and the emanations which rose from the pit outside, onto which the window opened, sidled into the dark room, filling it with a musty smell and a stench of sewer.

For forty years Monsieur Leras had entered this prison at eight each morning. He stayed until seven in the evening, stooped over his ledgers, driving his pen with the conscientiousness of the model employee.

He was now earning three thousand francs a year. He had started on fifteen hundred. He had remained a bachelor, his modest means ruling out any thought of marriage. And never having had much, there was little he wanted. Yet now and then, when he was tired of his monotonous, never-ending labour, he would allow himself a pious wish: 'Dear Lord, if I had a private income of five thousand a year, wouldn't I just have a fine time of it!' But since he had never had more than his monthly salary coming in, he had never had a fine time of anything. His life had passed without incident, without excitement, and almost without hope. The capacity to dream, which everyone has in him, had never bloomed within the mediocrity of his ambitions.

He had gone into Messrs Labuze & Co at the age of 21. And he had never come out again.

In 1856 he lost his father, and then his mother in 1859. And ever since, the only thing that had happened was the time he moved house, when his landlord put up the rent.

Each morning, at six sharp, he was catapulted out of bed by his alarm-clock which made a ghastly noise like a chain being unwound. (Twice, however, in 1866 and 1874, the mechanism had gone wrong, though he never discovered why.) He would dress, make his bed, sweep out his room, and brush the dust off his armchair and the top of his chest of drawers. These tasks took him an hour and a half. Then he would leave, buy a roll at Lahure the baker's—he had known eleven different proprietors though the shop had never changed its name—and set off gnawing his roll as he went.

In this way, his entire existence had been led in the narrow, gloomy office where the wallpaper had never been changed. He had gone into it as a young man as assistant to Monsieur Brument whom he hoped to replace. He had replaced Monsieur Brument and now expected nothing more. That harvest of memories which other men gather in the course of their lives, the unexpected incidents, love affairs sweet or tragic, bold journeys—all the chance events of a free life had passed him by.

The days, the weeks, the months, the seasons, the years, had all grown alike. Each day at the same time he got up, went out, arrived at the office, lunched, walked home, had his dinner, and went to bed, with nothing to interrupt the monotonous regularity of identical actions, identical occurrences, and identical thoughts.

There had been a time when he looked into the small round mirror left behind by his predecessor and saw a blond moustache and curly hair. Now, each evening as he left the office, he would stare into the same mirror at his white moustache and balding dome. Forty years had gone by, long, fleeting years, empty as a day of sorrow and all identical, like the hours of a sleepless night! Forty years of which nothing remained, not a memory, not even a grief, of the time since the death of his parents. Nothing.

That day, Monsieur Leras stood in the doorway into the street, dazzled by the glare of the setting sun. And instead of going home, he decided to go for a little stroll before dinner, as was his custom four or five times a year.

He reached the boulevards where the crowds streamed by under the trees which had turned green once more. It was an evening in spring, one of those first warm, soft, unsettling evenings which makes hearts leap with the thrill of being alive.

Monsieur Leras walked along falteringly as old men do, but as he walked there was a sparkle in his eye and he was happy because everyone around him was happy and because the evening was warm. He reached the Champs-Elysées and continued beyond, refreshed by the breath of youth which hung on the breeze.

The whole sky was ablaze, and the Arc de Triomphe loomed massively black against the brilliant backcloth of the horizon, like a giant standing in a huge bonfire. Reaching the monstrous monument, the old ledger-clerk suddenly felt hungry and he chose a cheap restaurant to have dinner.

Outside, on the pavement, he was given sheep's trotter with parsley, a salad, and a dish of asparagus, and Monsieur Leras ate the best dinner he had had in a long time. He washed down his piece of Brie with half a bottle of good Bordeaux. Then he drank a cup of coffee, something which he hardly ever did, and finally took a small glass of liqueur brandy.

When he paid his bill he felt elated, rather merry, and even slightly tipsy. He said to himself: 'It really is a very fine evening. I shall continue my stroll as far as the entrance to the Bois de Boulogne. It'll do me a power of good.'

He set off again. An old tune, which a girl who had once been a neighbour used to sing, started going round and round in his head:

> 'Under the greenwood tree,
> My true love said to me:
> Won't you come, O creature rare,
> To yonder grove and take the air?'

He hummed it endlessly, starting it over and over again. Night had fallen on Paris, a windless night as close as an oven. Monsieur Leras strolled along the Avenue of the Bois de Boulogne and watched the cabs pass by. They advanced with shining eyes, one after another, allowing a glimpse of a couple embracing, the woman wearing a light dress, the man in black.

It was one long procession of young people in love, driven along beneath the burning starry sky. And on they came, in a constant stream. They drove up and down, leaning back in their carriages, silent, clasping each other tightly, lost in the delusion and fever of desire, trembling in anticipation of passion to come. The warm shadows seemed full of whirling, fluttering kisses. A surge of tenderness softened the air and made it more oppressive still. These embracing couples, these young people drunk with the same expectation, the same thought, spread a fever around them. As they passed by, the carriages, full of caresses, gave out subtle, disturbing exhalations.

Monsieur Leras, eventually a little tired of strolling, sat down on a bench to watch the love-laden carriages pass by. Almost at the same time, a woman came up and sat down beside him.

'Hello, darlin',' she said.

He did not reply. She went on: 'Give yourself a good time, dearie. You'll see if I'm not ever so nice.'

'You're making a mistake, my good woman,' he said.

She slipped her arm through his: 'Don't be like that, silly boy. Listen . . .'

But he stood up and walked away with ice in his heart.

A hundred yards further along, another woman accosted him: 'Want to come and sit down by me for a bit, lovey?'

He said: 'How can you stoop to such a business as this?'

She stood and faced him squarely. Her voice was altered, harsh and sharp: 'Well it ain't always because I enjoy it, for God's sake!'

'Then what makes you do it?' he went on mildly.

She growled: 'A girl's got to live, worse luck.' And she went off, humming a little tune.

Monsieur Leras stood there, appalled. Other women passed close by. They called to him. They beckoned.

He felt as though something black and lowering had settled on his head. He sat down on a bench again. The carriages kept rolling on. 'I'd have been better off not coming,' he thought. 'It's knocked me sideways. It's proper unsettled me.' He began to reflect on all the love, true or sold for money, and all the kisses, bought or freely given, which were now filing past him.

Love! He hardly knew what it was. In his life there had been only two or three women and he had known them by chance, providentially: his modest means prevented anything more. And he thought of the life he had led, so different from other people's, a life that had been so dismal, dreary, flat, and empty.

Some people never have any luck. All at once, as though a thick veil had been whisked aside, he clearly saw the wretchedness—the bottomless, monotonous wretchedness—of his existence. The wretchedness which had been, which was, and which was yet to come. His last days indistinguishable from the first, with nothing ahead of him or behind him or around him, nothing in his heart, nothing anywhere.

The line of carriages continued to pass by. As each open cab trotted quickly past, he watched the two silent, embracing passengers inside loom up and vanish. It seemed to him that all mankind was passing him by, drunk with joy and pleasure and happiness while only he looked on, alone, all alone. He would still be alone tomorrow, alone forever: as lonely as it is possible to be.

He stood up, took a few steps, and then, suddenly feeling as exhausted as though he had walked a long way, sat down on the next bench along.

What did he expect? What was he hoping for? Nothing. He reflected how good it must be in old age to come home to the sound of the chatter of little children. Growing old is sweet when you are surrounded by those to whom you have given life, who love you and kiss you and say those nice, silly words which warm the heart and comfort you against all ills. And as he thought of his empty room, the clean, sad little room where no one else ever set foot but him, his whole being was overcome by a wave of anguish. His room seemed even more dismal than his office.

No one ever came; no one ever spoke in it. It was dead, dumb: no echo of a human voice lingered there. It may be that walls retain something of the people who live within them, something of their manner or faces or words. Houses lived in by happy families are more cheerful than the homes of miserable people. His room was devoid of memories, like his life. The thought of returning to that room all alone, of getting into his bed, of repeating the actions and tasks he carried out every evening suddenly appalled him. As though to get further away from his ghastly lodgings, and put off the moment when he must go back there, he got to his feet and, suddenly, chancing upon the first pathway in the Bois, he stepped into a thicket and sat down on the grass . . .

All around him, over his head, everywhere, he could hear a dull, immense, endless rumbling made up of countless different sounds, a muffled, near, far-off roar, an indistinct, gigantic throb of life: the living murmur of Paris, breathing like some colossal creature.

The sun was already high and poured a stream of light onto the Bois de Boulogne. A few carriages were already driving around and the first riders cantered cheerfully by.

One couple sauntered along a deserted pathway. All of a sudden, the young woman looked up and caught sight of something dark among the branches. Surprised and uneasy, she raised her hand and pointed: 'Look there. . . . What's that?' Then, with a cry, she fainted into the arms of her companion who had to set her down on the ground.

The keepers, who were summoned immediately, cut down the body of an old man, hanged by his braces.

The time of death was given as the previous evening. The papers found on the body revealed that the deceased was a ledger-clerk with Messrs Labuze & Co and that his name was Leras.

The cause of death was established as suicide, though there was no indication of motive. Possibly the balance of the mind was disturbed?

Bed 29

WHENEVER Captain Epivent walked down the street, all the women turned their heads. He was every inch the handsome officer of hussars. Accordingly, he was always walking up and down, forever strutting and swaggering, proud and very aware of his legs, his waist, and his moustache. In all these departments, he was splendidly equipped. His moustache, fair and very strong, sprang warlike from his lip in a twist of hair the colour of ripe wheat, fine and carefully rolled, and it hung from either side of his mouth in two strong waxed points which could not have been jauntier. His waist was as slim as if he wore corsets, while above it his gratifyingly manly chest, swelling and convex, expanded tremendously. His thighs were splendid, for they might have belonged to a gymnast or a dancer, and the muscles could be clearly seen rippling under the tightly stretched cloth of his red trousers.

He walked stiff-legged, feet and arms apart, with the lightly rolling gait of a horseman which is admirably suited to showing off the legs and torso and is as irresistible in anyone who wears uniform as it is common in those who do not.

Like many officers, Captain Epivent wore civilian clothes badly. Dressed in grey or black, he looked like nothing so much as a shop-assistant. But in uniform, he was utterly commanding. Moreover, he had a very handsome head: his nose was thin and curved, his eyes were blue and his forehead high. He was rather bald, but never understood why his hair had fallen out.* He consoled himself with the thought that a slightly balding head actually goes quite well with a large moustache.

He held everyone in general in contempt, though he despised some more than others.

To start with, in his book, the middle classes simply did not exist. He regarded them as other people regard animals, and he paid them no more attention than is usually given to sparrows or chickens. In all the world, only army officers counted, though he did not have the same regard for all officers. He only really respected fine figures of men, since the true, the only quality in a soldier was first and last his military bearing. A soldier was a rare dog, devil take him! a hell of a fellow created for making war and love, strong as a horse, tough as they come, a stalwart—that's what a soldier was. He classified the generals commanding the French Army according to their height, their dress, and the grimness of their expressions. To him, Bourbaki* was the greatest fighting man of modern times.

He laughed a good deal at officers of the line who happened to be short and fat and wheezed as they walked. But above all, he felt an invincible distaste, a loathing almost, for the poor specimens who were fresh out of military school—small, weedy men in glasses, clumsy and awkward, who seemed as fitted for wearing uniform, he said, as a rabbit for saying mass. It made his blood boil to think that the Army should tolerate undersized, puny-legged, misbegotten squits who marched like crabs, did not drink, ate little, and appeared to prefer mathematical equations to pretty girls.

Captain Epivent had constant success, triumphs even, with the fair sex.

Whenever he dined with a woman, he took it more or less as read that the evening would end on intimate terms, in the same bed; and if insuperable difficulties made victory impossible, then he was at least certain that battle would be joined again the next day. Comrades of his were not keen on letting him meet their mistresses, and shopkeepers with pretty wives behind their counters knew him, feared him, and hated him wholeheartedly.

When he passed by, such a wife might exchange an involuntary glance with him through the glass of her shop window; one of those glances which say more than tender words, and contain both an appeal and an answer, a desire and a confession. Then her husband, warned by a sort of instinct, would turn round sharply and stare angrily at the proud, stiff-backed figure of the officer. And when the captain, with a smile on his face and pleased with the effect he had produced, had gone his way, the shopkeeper, fiddling nervously with the wares spread out in front of him, would declare: 'Now there's a right one for you! How long do we have to go on feeding all these useless soldiers who go strutting round the streets rattling their ironmongery? Now me, I'd sooner a butcher than a soldier any day. If there's blood on a butcher's apron, then at least it's animal blood; and a butcher is at least good for something; and the knife in his hand isn't intended for killing men. I can't understand for the life of me why these public murderers are allowed to carry weapons of death about in public places. I realize you've got to have them, but at least they should be kept out of sight, and they certainly shouldn't be allowed to go around in fancy dress and red breeches and blue coats. They don't dress the public hangman like a general, do they?' Without replying, his wife would shrug her shoulders imperceptibly, while he, sensing her gesture which he could not see, would exclaim: 'You'd have to be soft in the head to go and watch those silly buggers on parade!'

Furthermore, Captain Epivent's reputation as an all-conquering warrior was firmly established throughout the whole of the French Army.

Now in 1868, his regiment, the 102nd Hussars, was posted to the garrison at Rouen.

He was soon well known in the town. Every evening about five, he appeared on the Cours Boïeldieu on his way to drink a glass of absinth at the Café de la Comédie, though before entering this establishment he made a point of taking a turn along the promenade to show off his legs, his waist, and his moustache.

The town's men of business, who also walked there with their hands behind their backs and their minds full of their business, talking of markets rising and falling, nevertheless gave a glance in his direction and murmured: 'By Jove! Now there's a fine figure of a man!' And when they knew who he was: 'Look, it's Captain Epivent. Say what you like, he's a hell of a fellow!'

When women passed him, they gave a slight movement of the head which was very droll, a sort of maidenly quiver, as though they had come over all weak or felt undressed before him. They lowered their eyes with just the shadow of a smile on their lips, wishing to be thought charming and to receive a glance from him. When he walked with a comrade, the comrade never failed to mutter enviously every time he witnessed the usual goings on: 'Old Epivent's got the luck of the devil!'

Among the town's whores there was a struggle, a race, to see who would get him first. They all turned up at the Cours Boïeldieu at five, the officers' regular time, and in twos they trailed their skirts from one end of the promenade to the other while lieutenants, captains, and commanders, also in twos, trailed their sabres over the pavement before entering the café.

One evening, the beautiful Irma—who was rumoured to be the mistress of Monsieur Templier-Papon, a rich manufacturer—ordered her driver to halt opposite the Café de la Comédie. As she stepped down, she gave every impression that she was about to buy some writing-paper or order some visiting cards from Monsieur Paulard, the engraver, though the whole thing was of course engineered to allow her to pass in front of the officers' table and to give Captain Epivent a look signifying: 'Ready when you are!' which was so transparent that Colonel Prune, who was drinking a glass of green absinth with his Lieutenant-Colonel, was unable to prevent himself muttering: 'That swine's got the luck of the devil!'

What the colonel said was repeated; and the next day Captain Epivent, in full dress uniform, delighted at having such high-level approval, strolled by (and did so again several times) under the windows of the beautiful Irma.

She saw him. She appeared at her window. She smiled.

The same evening he became her lover.

They were seen everywhere together, drew attention to themselves, and compromised each other fully, for they were both proud to be part of such a well publicized intrigue. All over town, people talked of nothing else but the beautiful Irma's affair with her officer. Monsieur Templier-Papon alone remained in ignorance.

Glory shone around the captain and he was forever saying: 'Irma's just been telling me. . . . Irma said last night. . . . Yesterday, when I was having a bite to eat with Irma . . .'

For more than a year, for all Rouen to see, he paraded, displayed, and unfurled their love like a flag captured from the enemy. He felt increased by his conquest, envied, more confident about the future, and nearer to the military cross he coveted, for everyone now had their eyes on him, and high visibility is usually enough to ensure that one is not forgotten.

And then war broke out, and the captain's regiment was among the first to be sent to the front. The leave-taking was extremely painful and lasted the whole night.

His sabre, red trousers, officer's peaked cap, and jacket had been thrown over the back of a chair or were lying on the floor; her dresses, skirts, and silk stockings were scattered about, left lying where they had fallen, intertwined with his uniform, in a desolate heap on the carpet; the room had a blasted look, as though a battle had been fought in it; Irma, frantic and dishevelled, kept desperately throwing her arms around the officer's neck, holding him tight then letting him go, rolling on the floor, upsetting furniture, tearing the fringes and biting the legs of the armchairs, while the captain, distraught but unskilled at finding words of consolation, kept repeating: 'Irma, Irma my sweet. Nothing for it. Got to go.'

Yet with a fingertip, he did wipe away a tear that trembled in the corner of his eye.

They separated as the sun rose. She followed her lover in a carriage as far as the first stage. And at the moment of parting she kissed him in front of almost the whole regiment. This was judged to be very commendable, most dignified, and wholly admirable, and his comrades shook the captain's hand, saying: 'You lucky dog! That girl's got her heart in the right place.'

The incident was seen really as being somehow rather patriotic.

The regiment had a hard time during the campaign. The captain behaved like a hero and was finally awarded his military cross, and then, when the war was over, he returned to the garrison at Rouen.

The moment he got back he asked for news of Irma, but no one could tell him anything definite. According to some, she had had a wild time with the Prussian general staff. Others said that she had gone back to her parents who were farmers near Yvetot. He even sent his batman to the Town Hall to look through the register of deaths. The name of his mistress was not in it.

He felt a deep sorrow of which he made no secret. He even blamed the enemy for his misfortune, attributing the young woman's disappearance to the Prussians who had occupied Rouen, and he declared: 'In the next war, I'll make the swine pay!'

Then one morning, just as he was going in to lunch in the mess, a messenger, an old man wearing overalls and a waxed cap, handed him an envelope. He opened it and read:

> My darling,
>   I am in hospital and am very, very ill. Won't you come and see me? I'd like it so much if you did!
>
> Irma.

The captain turned pale and, stirred by pity, said: 'Oh my God! Poor girl! I'll get along there the minute I've had lunch.' And throughout the meal he told the officers' table how Irma was in hospital and how he'd get her out, he'd be damned if he didn't! The whole thing was again laid at the door of the Hun. She must have been left quite alone, without a penny to her name, dying of poverty, for all her furniture had been plundered. 'Oh! the swine!'

Everyone who heard him felt angry too.

The moment he had slipped his rolled serviette through its wooden ring, he stood up. Collecting his sabre from the hatstand and swelling his chest to make himself look slim, he fastened his sword-belt and set off at a cracking pace for the civilian hospital.

But though he had expected to be allowed in immediately, he was categorically refused permission to enter the building, and was even reduced to having to call on his colonel, to whom he outlined his problem before being given a note for the head man.

After settling the handsome captain in a waiting-room for some time, the hospital's director finally, with a cool, disapproving bow, issued him with a pass.

As he crossed the threshold, he felt uneasy in this place of poverty, suffering, and death. To avoid making a noise, he advanced on tiptoe through the long corridors where there hung a stale, musty smell of sickness and medicines. Only the sound of subdued voices disturbed the silence of the hospital from time to time. Now and then, through an open door, the captain caught a glimpse of a ward, a line of beds where the sheets were raised over the shapes of prone bodies. Women patients who were convalescing sat on chairs at the foot of their cots, all dressed in the same uniform of grey calico and each wearing a mob-cap.

His guide suddenly stopped at the door of one such ward crowded with patients. Above the lintel was a sign, in large letters, which read: 'Syphilitic Ward'. The captain gave a start and then felt his face flush red. A nurse was getting some medicines ready on a small wooden table near the entrance.

'I'll show you,' she said. 'It's bed 29.' And she showed him the way.

She motioned to a bed: 'This is it.'

All that was visible was a heap of bulging bedclothes. Even the patient's head was hidden beneath the covers.

All around, faces peered over sheets and stared at his uniform, pale, surprised faces, women's faces, the faces of women young and old, faces which all looked ugly and vulgar in their regulation bed-jackets.

The captain, holding his sabre in one hand and his officer's hat in the other, and feeling very dismayed, said softly: 'Irma?'

The bed heaved and the face of his mistress appeared. It was so altered, drawn, and thin that he did not recognize her.

She gasped for breath, choking with emotion, but managed to stammer: 'Albert! . . . Albert! . . . It's you. . . . Oh! it's good to see you! . . . So good!' Tears ran down her cheeks.

The nurse brought him a chair: 'Would you like to sit down?'

He sat down and stared at the pale, utterly wretched face of a girl he had left looking so beautiful and alive.

He said: 'What's been the matter with you?'

She replied with a sob: 'You saw. It's written over the door.' And she hid her eyes with the corner of her sheet.

Aghast and shamefaced, he went on: 'But how did you manage to get a dose, old girl?'

She murmured: 'It was those Prussian bastards. They just about damn well had to tie me down. They were the ones who infected me.'

He could think of nothing to say. He went on staring at her, turning his hat in his hands on his knees.

The other patients were looking at him, and he thought he could detect a smell of decay, an odour of rotting flesh and ignominy which ran through the ward full of women who had gone down with this ignoble, ghastly disease.

Meanwhile, she said softly: 'I don't think I'll pull round. The doctor says it's pretty bad.' Then, noticing the military cross pinned on the officer's chest, she exclaimed: 'So you got your gong, then! I'm so pleased! So very pleased! Oh! I'd like it ever so much if I could give you a kiss.'

A pang of fear and disgust made the captain's flesh creep at the thought of kissing her. He wanted to leave, to be outside in the fresh air, not to see her any more. However, he remained where he was, not knowing how to set about getting to his feet or how to say goodbye. He spluttered: 'You didn't get treated, then?'

Irma's eyes flashed momentarily: 'No, I wanted to get my own back, even if it killed me! And I infected them back too, the lot of 'em, as many as I could. As long as they were in Rouen, I didn't do anything about it.'

Awkwardly, but forcing a note of jollity into his voice, he said: 'Quite right too! Well done!'

She grew agitated and her cheeks became flushed: 'I should say! There's more than one swine who'll be dying because of me. I tell you: I paid them back all right.'

He spoke again: 'Well, that's something.' Then he stood up: 'Look, I'm going to have to toddle along. I've got to be at the colonel's for four.'

This upset her visibly: 'So soon? You're going so soon? But you've only just come! . . .'

But he had to get away. He said: 'I came to see you at once, didn't I? I've really got to be at the colonel's for four, can't get out of it . . .'

'Is it still Colonel Prune?' she asked.

'He's still the colonel. He was wounded twice.'

She went on. 'And what about the others? Any get killed?'

'Yes. Saint-Timon, Savagnat, Poli, Sapreval, Robert, De Courson, Pasafil, Caravan, and Poivrin all bought it. Dahel had an arm blown off and Courvoisin had a leg mangled. Paquet lost his right eye.'

She listened eagerly. . . . Then all of a sudden she stammered: 'Go on, give us a kiss before you go. Madame Langlois isn't around.'

Although disgust rushed to his lips, he put his mouth on her pale forehead while she, throwing her arms around him, covered the blue cloth of his tunic with wild kisses.

She went on: 'You will come back? Say you'll come back. Promise you will.'

'I promise.'

'When? Can you come on Thursday?'

'Right-ho. Thursday.'

'Thursday. Two o'clock.'

'Fine. Thursday at two.'

'Promise?'

'I promise.'

'Goodbye, darling.'

'Goodbye.'

He went, embarrassed by the eyes that watched him leave

the ward, bending his huge frame in an attempt to look inconspicuous. When he was in the street, he breathed freely.

That evening, his comrades asked him: 'Well, how's Irma?'

He replied awkwardly: 'Pneumonia. She's in a bad way.'

But a junior lieutenant, sensing something from the way he had answered, made enquiries, and the next day, when the captain walked into the mess, he was greeted with a salvo of laughter and jibes. It was their opportunity at last to get their own back.

It further appeared that Irma had had a stormy affair with the whole of the Prussian general staff, that she had gone riding round the countryside with a colonel of the Blues and with lots of others too, and that in Rouen she had been known as 'the Huns' woman'.

For a week the captain was the butt of the regiment. Through the post he received revealing notes, prescriptions, the names of specialist doctors, and even samples of medicines the nature of which was always written on the packet. And the colonel, duly informed, said grimly: 'Well, the captain's got a wrong un' there. I shall tell him so.'

When twelve days had gone by, he was summoned by another letter from Irma. He tore it up in a fury and did not reply.

A week later she wrote again, saying that she was very ill and wished to say goodbye. He did not answer.

After another few days he received a visit from the hospital almoner. Irma Pavolin was on her death bed and begged him to come.

He did not dare refuse to accompany the almoner, but he walked into the hospital with a heart full of spite and rancour and oozing wounded vanity and humiliation.

He found her very little changed and assumed that she had led him up the garden path.

'What do you want with me?' he said.

'To say goodbye. They say there's not much time.'

He did not believe her. 'You've made me the laughing

stock of the whole regiment, and I'm not putting up with it any more, do you hear?'

'But what did I do?' she asked.

He became angrier when he found no answer to this. 'Don't imagine that I'll be coming back here so that people can have a jolly good laugh at my expense.'

She stared at him with her lacklustre eyes where an angry spark flashed, and she said once more: 'What did I do? Wasn't I good to you? Did I ever ask you for anything? If it hadn't been for you, I would have stayed with Monsieur Templier-Papon and wouldn't be here today. See here, if there's anybody who's got anything to say to me in the way of blame, it certainly isn't you.'

In a voice that shook, he said: 'I don't blame you for anything, but I can't keep coming to see you because the way you behaved with the Hun has made the whole town ashamed.'

She sat up suddenly in her bed: 'The way I behaved with the Hun? But I told you they had to use force! I told you that I didn't go near a doctor, and if I didn't see a doctor it was because I wanted to infect them. If I'd wanted treatment I could have had it, for God's sake! But I wanted to kill them and I killed quite a few!'

He remained standing: 'However it was, it's still shameful,' he said.

For a moment she could not breathe. But then she resumed: 'Tell me, what's shameful about killing myself to exterminate them? You never talked like this when you used to come to see me in the rue Jeanne d'Arc. Shameful, was it! You could never have done what I did, military cross or no military cross! Listen, I've got more right to it than you have, more right, and I killed a damn sight more Prussians than you ever did . . .'*

He stood facing her, aghast and quivering with indignation. 'That's enough! . . . Enough! . . . Will you be quiet! . . . I cannot allow . . . such things . . . to be . . . cheapened.'

But she hardly heard him: 'What did you ever do to the Hun, anyway? Would any of this have happened if you'd prevented them from reaching Rouen in the first place? It was you who were supposed to stop them, wasn't it? I hurt the Hun more than you did, yes, a damn sight more, because I'm going to die while you'll still be parading about preening yourself to catch the eye of the ladies . . .'

Heads had appeared over every bed, and every eye was fixed on the man in uniform who was now stammering: 'Be quiet! . . . Will you be quiet!'

But she would not be quiet. She screamed: 'Oh yes! You're all mouth and trousers! I know you like the back of my hand, and I'm telling you that I hurt the Hun more than you did, 'cos I killed more of them than your whole damned regiment put together, you . . . chicken!'

He went, or rather fled, stretching out his long legs, striding between the two rows of beds where the venereal patients stirred restlessly. In his ears he heard Irma's breathless, piercing voice as it pursued him: 'More, I said, I killed more of 'em than you did, more . . .'

He took the stairs four at a time, ran back to his quarters, and locked his door.

The next day he was informed that she was dead.

The Gamekeeper

AFTER dinner, we got round to telling tales about hunting and hunting accidents.

One of our oldest friends, Monsieur Boniface, a great slaughterer of wildlife and a great drinker of wine, a sturdy, cheerful man with a quick wit, a fund of good sense, and a sceptical, resigned philosophy which he always expressed not in miserable observations about life, but in bitingly funny jokes, suddenly spoke up:

'Here, I know a hunting story, or at least a hunting incident, quite dramatic, rather an odd business altogether. It's not at all the usual sort of hunting story, which is why I've never told it before, because I never thought anyone would find it very entertaining.

'It's not a very nice story, you understand. I mean it doesn't have the sort of appeal that grips or fascinates or gladdens the heart.

'Well, anyhow, this is how it goes.'

At the time it happened I was about 35 and mad about hunting.

In those days I owned a property well off the beaten track near Jumièges. It was surrounded by woodland and was very good rabbit and hare country. I used to go down for just four or five days a year by myself, since it wasn't suitable for taking a friend along.

To keep an eye on the place, I employed a gamekeeper, a retired police constable, a decent enough chap but rather violent, who was very keen on enforcement, hated poachers, and feared nothing. He lived by himself some way out of the village in a small cottage, or rather shack, with two rooms on the ground floor, a kitchen and a larder, and two bedrooms upstairs. One of these, which wasn't much more than a boxroom just big enough to take a bed, a wardrobe, and a chair, was set aside for my use.

Old man Cavalier slept in the other. When I said he lived in the house by himself, I expressed myself badly. He had taken in a nephew of his, a not very nice sort of lad of 14, who used to fetch provisions from the village which was three kilometres away and help the old man with his regular chores.

This lad, who was tall and lanky and slightly crook-backed, had yellow hair so fine that the down of a plucked chicken wasn't in it, and so thin that he looked quite bald. In addition, he had huge feet and massive hands, like a giant's.

He squinted slightly and never looked you in the eye. As far as I was concerned, he was to the human race what malodorous creatures are in the animal world. That young villain was a human polecat or a fox.

He slept in a sort of recess at the top of the stairs that led up to the two first-floor rooms.

But during my short stays at the Lodge—I called the hovel a Lodge—Marius gave up his niche to an old woman from Ecorcheville called Céleste who used to come in and cook for me, for old Cavalier's stews weren't really up to much.

So now you know the characters and the setting. Here's the story.

It was 15 October 1854—a date which I remember and will never forget. I set off from Rouen by horse with my dog Bock, a large Poitou hound with a deep chest and strong jaws who rooted among the briars at the roadside like a Pont-Audemer spaniel. I had hitched a travel bag to my saddle behind me and carried my rifle over my shoulder. It was a cold day, with a strong, unpleasant wind and dark clouds scudding across the sky.

As I rode up the steep bank at Canteleu, I looked out over the wide valley of the Seine through which the river flowed in serpent's coils clear away to the horizon. To the left, the spires and steeples of Rouen rose into the sky and, on the right, my view was impeded by distant wooded hills. I went through the forest of Roumare, walking my horse at times and pressing on at a trot at others, and at about five o'clock I reached the Lodge where old Cavalier and Céleste were waiting for me.

I had been turning up at the same time of year, in the same way, for ten years, and the same mouths always said the same words: 'Good evenin', sir. We all hopes as how your health has been up to the mark.'

Cavalier had hardly changed. He stood firm against the passing years like an old tree. But Céleste, especially these last four years, had become quite unrecognizable.

She had almost snapped in half for, though she still managed to get about well enough, she walked with the upper part of her body bent so far forward that it was near enough at right angles to her legs.

She was a loyal old soul and always seemed on the verge of tears when she saw me. And every time I went away she would say: 'Spare a thought, sir, p'raps 'tis the last time . . .'

The woebegone, frightened farewells of that sad old servant and her desperate resignation in the face of death, which is inevitable and certainly was none too distant for her, always moved me strangely each year.

I dismounted and while Cavalier, after I'd shaken his hand, led my horse away to the low-roofed shed that did as a stable, I went into the kitchen, followed by Céleste. The kitchen doubled as dining-room.

Then my gamekeeper joined us. I saw at once by his face that something was up. He seemed preoccupied, uneasy, worried.

'Well now, Cavalier,' I said, 'things going according to plan?'

He muttered: 'There's some as are and then again some as ain't. And there's a good few as doesn't come up to the mark.'

I asked: 'What's the trouble, Cavalier? Tell me about it.'

But he shook his head: 'Not jes' at the minute, sir. I got no wish to go worryin' you with all my troubles like that the second you get here.'

I tried to insist, but he categorically refused to put me in the picture before dinner. Judging by the face he had on

him, I got the impression that it was something pretty
serious.

At a loss for anything to say to him, I said: 'What about
game? How are we doing this year?'

'Oh aye, there's game all right. You'll find plenty of
game. I gotter nose for it, I have, thank the Lord.' He said
this with such gravity, such pathetic gravity that it was
comic. His large grey moustache looked as if it was about to
drop off his lip.

I suddenly realized that I hadn't seen his nephew about.

'How's Marius? Where is he? Why hasn't he shown his
face?'

My gamekeeper gave a sort of start, turned, and looked
me in the eye. 'Well, sir, I'd just as soon come out with it,
I'd rather. 'Tis on his account that my spirits is lowish.'

'Oh? Well, and where is he?'

'In the stable, sir. I was biding my time till he came out.'

'What's he been up to?'

'Well, sir, it's like this . . .' But he stood there hesitating,
his voice breaking and quavery and his face suddenly
creased with deep wrinkles, an old man's wrinkles. He went
on slowly:

'It were like this. This winter past, I noticed as how
somebody was setting snares down in the woods at Les
Roseraies, but I could never nab the feller that was doing it.
I spent night after night watching out for him. And while I
was down there, blow me if he didn't start setting snares
over Ecorcheville way. I lost weight, I were that furious.
But could I catch the prowler? Could I hell! Anybody would
have thought the swine knew all about every movement I
made and what I was going to do next.

'And then one day, when I were brushing the mud off of
Marius's britches, the ones he wears of a Sunday, I found
forty sous in his pocket. Now where could a lad like him get
hold of money like that?

'I thought it over for a week and a bit, and I noticed as
how he used to go out regular. He'd be just going out when
I was coming in off duty, and that's a fact.

'So I decide to keep a bit of a watch on him, though I

didn't suspect nothing at the time, nothing at all. So one morning, I goes up to bed with him still here, then up I get again quick as a flash and I follows him. And there's nobody can follow a trail like me.

'Anyhow, I catches him at it. That's right, Marius, getting snares on your land, sir. My nephew! And me your gamekeeper!

'I saw red and I very near killed him on the spot, I hit him that hard. Oh, I hit him all right. And I told him that when you got here, he'd get another good hiding from me in the presence of yourself. Got to make an example.

'Well, that's how it is. I lost weight what with worrying about it. You know how it is when somebody vexes you like that. But tell me, sir, what would you have done in my place? The lad's got no mother or father, and I'm all the family he's got. I raised him. I could hardly send him packing, now could I?

'But I told him if he started his tricks again, then that would be the finish. He'd get no more sympathy from me. And that's the size of it. Did I do right, sir?'

I held out my hand to him and said: 'You did well, Cavalier. You are a good man.'

He got to his feet. 'Much obliged, sir. And now I'll go off and fetch him here. He's got to have his hiding. Got to make an example.'

I knew there was no point trying to talk the old man out of something he'd set his mind on. So I let him get on with it. He scurried off to get his ne'er-do-well nephew and brought him back, dragging him by the ear. I was sitting on a straw-bottomed chair with a face as stern as any judge's.

Marius seemed to me as if he'd grown. He was even uglier than the year before, and he had a mean, cunning look to him. And his hands seemed monstrously large.

His uncle pushed him unceremoniously before me and said in his best sergeant-major's voice: 'Tell the master you're sorry.'

The lad said nothing.

Grabbing him and tucking him under one arm, the former police constable lifted him off the ground and started swotting him so hard that I stood up, intending to put a stop to it.

By this time, the boy was bawling: 'Please! Oh please! I promise!'

Cavalier set him back on his feet, and taking him by the shoulders, forced him to his knees: 'Say sorry,' he said.

The lad muttered, with eyes lowered: 'I beg pardon.'

His uncle set him upright and sent him packing with a clout that almost knocked him off his feet. He ran off and I didn't see him again for the rest of the evening.

But old Cavalier seemed as though he'd been struck all of a heap. 'There's bad blood in that one,' he said. And all through dinner, he said over and over: 'Oh, it grieves me, sir. It grieves me more'n I can say.'

I tried to cheer him up, but it was no good.

I went to bed early so that I could be out with my gun at first light. My dog was already asleep on the floor at the foot of my bed when I blew out the candle.

I was woken in the middle of the night by Bock who was barking his head off. I realized at once that my room was full of smoke. I leaped out of bed, lit the candle, ran over to the door, and opened it. Tongues of flame shot in. The house was on fire.

I shut the stout oak door quickly, and after getting into my trousers I let my dog down through the window by means of a rope made of knotted sheets. Then, throwing my clothes, game-bag, and gun out after him, I made my escape the same way.

Then I began shouting at the top of my voice: 'Cavalier! Cavalier! Cavalier!' But I couldn't rouse my gamekeeper who slept as sound as any retired policeman ever did.

Through the lower windows I could see that the whole of the ground floor was a blazing inferno. And I noticed that someone had filled it with straw so that the fire would have something to feed on.

Someone had deliberately set fire to the place!

I started shouting again for all I was worth; 'Cavalier!' Then it struck me that the smoke might have made him pass out. I had an idea. Slipping a couple of cartridges into my gun, I fired one shot at his window.

The six panes exploded into his room in a shower of broken glass. This time the old man heard all right, and he appeared at the window in his nightshirt, looking startled and not quite knowing what to make of the violent glow which lit up the whole of the front of the house.

I shouted up to him: 'The house is on fire. Jump out of the window. Hurry! There's no time to lose!'

Tongues of flame shooting up from the windows below licked the wall, reached up to him, and were about to cut him off. He jumped and landed on his feet as lightly as a cat.

He was just in time. The thatched roof sagged suddenly in the middle just above the staircase which had become a kind of chimney for the fire below. A huge red plume leaped into the air and spread out like the spray of a fountain, scattering a shower of sparks all round the cottage.

Within seconds, the whole thing was a mass of flames.

Cavalier, looking absolutely appalled, asked: 'How ever did it happen?'

I replied: 'Somebody started a fire in the kitchen.'

He muttered: 'Now whoever could have done such a thing?'

Suddenly I saw the whole thing clearly: 'Marius!' I said.

The old man saw it too. He stammered: 'Oh God in heaven! So that's why he never come back.'

Then a horrible thought struck me. 'What about Céleste?' I shouted. 'Where's Céleste?'

He did not answer, but even as we watched the house collapsed, leaving only a solid furnace, incandescent, blood-red, and painful to the eyes, a mighty pyre, and in it the poor old woman could not have been much more than a heap of white-hot cinders, so much carbonized flesh.

We hadn't heard a single scream.

But since the fire was now spreading to the adjoining shed, I suddenly remembered my horse and Cavalier ran off to let it out.

The moment he opened the stable door, a nimble, agile

figure shot between his legs and knocked him over. It was Marius making off as fast as he could go.

The old man was on his feet instantly. He started running in an attempt to catch the wretch, but then realized he'd never manage it. Beside himself with rage and giving way to one of those instant reflex reactions which no one can anticipate or check, he seized my gun which was lying on the ground just where he was standing, took aim, and before I could do a thing to stop him, blazed away without even knowing if the gun was loaded.

One of the cartridges I had slipped into the breech to warn everybody that the house was burning had not been fired. The full force of the blast caught the runaway in the back and he fell face down, covered in blood. He began tearing at the ground with his hands and knees as though he still thought he could get away on all fours, just as a mortally wounded hare does when it sees the hunter approach.

I rushed up to him. The lad was already gasping his last and he died before the blaze finally burnt itself out, without saying a word.

Cavalier, still in his night-shirt and bare-legged, just stood around nearby, not moving and looking dazed.

When people from the village turned up, they led my gamekeeper off. He looked quite mad.

At the trial, I appeared as a witness. I explained everything that had happened without changing any of the details. Cavalier was acquitted. But the same day he disappeared and left the area.

I never saw him again.

And there, gentlemen, you have my hunting story.

The Little Roque Girl

I

THE country postman, Médéric Rompel, whom everyone roundabout called Médéri for short, left the post office at Roüy-le-Tors at his usual time. Striding through the town with the military step of an old soldier, he first cut across the fields at Villaumes before reaching the banks of the Brindille and following its course which led him to the village of Carvelin where his round began.

He walked quickly along the narrow river which sparkled and gurgled and seethed as it raced down its grassy bed under an arch of willows. Great rocks standing in its path were ringed with a collar of water which became a gentleman's tie ending in a knot of froth. Here and there, it dropped in cascades a foot high which, though generally hidden from view, could be heard roaring in subdued anger under the leaves and trailing creepers of the green canopy above. Further downstream, the banks widened and between them appeared a small stretch of water where trout swam among those green fronds which always wave like tresses in quiet streams.

Médéric walked on, seeing nothing and thinking only: 'The first letter is for the Poivrons, then there's one for Monsieur Renardet. So I'll have to go through the wood.'

His blue postman's jacket, nipped in at the waist by a black leather belt, moved at a crisp, steady trot above the bank of green willow. His stick, a stout length of holly, marched at his side and kept pace exactly with his legs.

Proceeding thus, he crossed the Brindille over a bridge made out of a single tree-trunk, the only handrail being a stretch of rope supported by two wooden stakes driven into the bank at either end.

The wood, belonging to Monsieur Renardet, mayor of Carvelin and the biggest landowner in the district, was an extensive grove of enormous, very old trees which rose into the air like columns, and it stretched for a couple of miles along the left bank of the stream which marked the limit of its immense canopy of leaves. Along the water's edge large bushes grew in the warmth of the sun; but inside the wood there was nothing but moss, thick, sweet, soft moss, which released a faint tang of decay and dead timber into the stagnant air.

Médéric slowed his pace, removed his black postman's cap with the red braid round it, and wiped his forehead, for it was already hot in the fields even though it was not yet eight o'clock.

He had just replaced his cap and was striding off again when he noticed a knife, a small child's knife, lying at the foot of a tree. As he stooped to pick it up, he noticed a thimble, and, a couple of paces further on, a needle-box.

When he had picked up these objects, he thought: 'I'll hand 'em over to his honour the mayor', then set off again. But now he kept an eye open, expecting to find more.

All at once he stopped short, as though he had walked into a wooden door. For ten paces in front of him, a child's body, quite naked, lay face upwards on the moss. It was a little girl of perhaps 12. Her arms were wide open, her legs were spread apart, and her face was covered by a handker- chief. A small quantity of blood was spattered on her thighs.

Médéric started forward on tiptoe, as though he were afraid of making a noise or half-sensed some danger. He opened his eyes wide.

He could not fathom it. Was she asleep, perhaps? But then he thought, no one sleeps like that, with no clothes on, at half past seven in the morning among the cool trees. She must be dead, then. And he was at the scene of a crime. As this thought struck him, a cold tingle ran up and down his spine, old soldier though he was. For a murder was such a rare event in the area, the murder of a child especially, that he could hardly believe his eyes. There was no sign of a wound on the body, only the dried blood on the legs. So how had she been killed?

He had halted barely a step or two from her, and, leaning on his stick, he stared down at her. He had seen her before, of course, for he knew everybody in the district. But as he could not see her features, he could not put a name to her. He bent down to remove the handkerchief which hid her face and then stopped, with his hand outstretched, halted by a thought.

Was he within his rights to touch anything to do with the body before the law arrived to examine it? He thought of 'the law' as being a kind of commanding general who misses nothing and attaches as much importance to a stray button as to a knife wound in the stomach. Beneath the handkerchief they might find a crucial clue—and the handkerchief itself was clearly prima facie evidence which might be rendered useless if disturbed by clumsy hands.

So he straightened up and prepared to hurry off to the mayor's. But he was halted in his tracks by a new thought. If the little girl happened to be still alive, he could not leave her lying there. Very carefully he knelt down at a prudent distance and reached out for her foot with his hand. It was cold, icy cold. It had the ghastly coldness which makes dead flesh repulsive and leaves no room for doubt. At the contact, the postman felt his stomach churn, as he put it later, and his mouth went dry. Getting to his feet quickly, he began running through the wood towards the house of Monsieur Renardet.

He moved at the double, his stick tucked under his arm, hands clenched and head craned forward. His leather bag full of letters and newspapers beat time on his ribs as he went.

The mayor's residence was situated at the far end of the wood which served as the mayor's parkland. One side of the house stood with its foot in the Brindille which formed a small pool at this spot.

It was a large, square house, built of grey stone, very old— it had withstood sieges in its time—and it rose to a great tower, twenty metres high, which was built in the water.

From the top of this stronghold, watch had been kept in times gone by over the whole of the surrounding countryside. It was called Renard's Tower though no one knew quite why. This was doubtless the origin of the name Renardet which had been borne by successive lords of a manor which, it was said, had remained in the family for more than two hundred years. For the Renardets were part of that semi-aristocratic middle class which was so strongly represented in the provinces before the Revolution of 1789.

The postman charged into the kitchen where the servants were having breakfast and cried: 'Is the mayor up yet? I got to have a word with his honour, urgent.' Now Médéric was known as a man of consequence and authority, so everyone realized immediately that something serious had happened.

Monsieur Renardet was informed and ordered him to be shown up. The postman, looking pale, breathing hard, and carrying his cap in his hand, found the mayor seated at a long table littered with papers.

He was a tall, heavily built man, fleshy and red-faced, strong as an ox, and, though he could be excessively violent, he was well liked in the locality. Aged about 40 and a widower of six months' standing, he lived on his estate like a country squire. His fiery temper had frequently got him into difficulties from which he was regularly extricated by the magistrates at Roüy-le-Tors, his discreet, indulgent friends. As, for instance, when he threw the driver of the stage from the driving seat for almost running down his pointer Micmac. Or when he broke several ribs of a gamekeeper who had stopped him as he walked with a gun on his arm across a field belonging to a neighbour. Or when, during a routine visit which Monsieur Renardet described as electioneering, he took the sub-prefect by the scruff of the neck and shook him—for opposing the government was a family tradition.

'What's the trouble, Médéric?' the mayor asked.

'I found a little girl dead in your wood.'

Renardet looked up, his face the colour of brick. 'What's that? A little girl?'

'Yes, sir, a little girl with no clothes on, lying on her back, blood everywhere, dead. Dead as a doornail.'

The mayor swore: 'God in heaven! I'll wager it's Roque's girl. I was told she didn't go home to her mother last night. Where did you find her?'

The postman explained where, in detail, and offered to take the mayor to the spot.

But Monsieur Renardet suddenly became brusque: 'That won't be necessary. I shan't be needing you. Go and tell the gamekeeper, the town clerk, and the doctor I want to see them at once, and then carry on with your round. Come on, man, sharp about it. Say they're to meet me in the wood.'

The postman, who was used to taking orders, did as he was told, then left them all to it, furious and bitterly disappointed not to be in on the offical inquiry at the scene of the crime.

In a while, the mayor too left the house. He reached for his large, wide-brimmed, grey felt hat, then paused momentarily at his front door. Before him was a huge expanse of lawn where three great bursts of colour, red, blue, and white, erupted in three enormous circular beds of radiant flowers, one directly in front of the house and the others to either side. Beyond, the first trees of the wood reached towards the sky while, to the left, on the far side of the pool formed by the Brindille, could be seen extensive fields constituting a wide, flat, green meadowland bisected by ditches and banks of willow which looked like monsters—shrivelled dwarfs to be precise—and had been uniformly lopped so that a plume of thin branches waved above each short, thick trunk.

On the right, behind the stables, the coach-houses, and the rest of the outbuildings which belonged to the property, began the thriving village with its population of cattle breeders.

Slowly Renardet walked down the flight of steps in front of his house. Turning left, he reached the water's edge, then proceeded along the bank at a leisurely pace with his hands behind his back. He walked with his head lowered. From time to time he looked around him, watching out for the people he had sent for.

When he got to the trees he stopped, removed his hat, and wiped his brow just as Médéric had done, for the burning July sun was falling on the land like a rain of fire. Then the mayor set off again, halted once more, and retraced his steps. Suddenly he bent down, dipped his handkerchief in the stream gliding by at his feet, and spread it over his head, under his hat. Drops of water ran down his temples, down his ears which still showed scarlet, down his powerful red neck, and then trickled one by one behind the white collar of his shirt.

Since there was as yet no one else in sight, he began stamping his feet and shouting: 'Hello! Hello-o!'

On his right, a voice answered: 'Hello! Hello-o!'

The doctor appeared from beneath the trees. He was small and slightly built, a former army doctor, thought by people roundabout to be a very capable man. He limped, a legacy of an old army wound, and walked with the aid of a stick.

Then the gamekeeper and the town clerk came into view, for they had been told at the same time and had come together. They looked alarmed and approached breathing heavily, walking and running by turns in their hurry and waving their arms so wildly that they seemed to be working as hard with them as with their legs.

Renardet said to the doctor: 'You've heard what all this is about?'

'Yes. Some child Médéric found dead in the woods.'

'That's it. Let's go.'

They set off side by side, the other two bringing up the rear. Their feet made no sound on the moss; their eyes strained at the terrain ahead.

All at once, Doctor Labarbe raised one arm and pointed: 'Over there!'

A good way off, under the trees, something light-coloured was visible. If they had not known what it was, they would never have guessed. It seemed to glow and was so white that it might have been mistaken for washing fallen from a line; for the sun's rays sliding between the branches lit up the pale flesh, casting a wide, oblique shaft across the abdomen. The nearer they drew, the more clearly they made out the body with its shrouded head facing the water and the two arms outstretched as though nailed to a cross.

'I'm damned hot,' the mayor said. And stooping once

more, he again dipped his handkerchief in the Brindille and then put it back on his forehead.

The doctor hurried forward, engrossed in the discovery. The moment he reached the body, he bent down to investigate, but did not touch it. He had put on his pince-nez as though examining some curious object and prowled slowly round it. Without straightening up, he said: 'Raped and murdered, as we shall confirm in just a moment. By the by, the girl was almost a woman, you can see by the thorax.'

The two breasts, already quite well developed, lay flat on the chest, relaxed in death.

The doctor gently removed the handkerchief covering the face which was suddenly revealed: it was black, contorted, with the tongue protruding and the eyes bulging. He went on: 'My God, whoever it was strangled after having his way with her.' He felt the neck: 'Strangled with bare hands, no traces left to speak of, no nail scratches, no finger marks. That's that, then. It's Roque's girl right enough.' He replaced the handkerchief delicately: 'Nothing I can do. She's been dead for twelve hours at least. We'll have to inform the public prosecutor.'

Renardet stood with his hands behind his back, staring at the small body stretched out in the grass. He murmured: 'What a swine! We'd better look for her clothes.'

The doctor was feeling the hands, arms, and legs. He said: 'She'd probably been bathing. They'll be down by the water.'

The mayor gave the order: 'Principe,' (this was the town-clerk) 'go and look for her things along the stream. You, Maxime,' (this was the game-keeper) 'off you go as quick as you can to Roüy-le-Tors and bring me back the examining magistrate and some of his officers. I want them here within the hour. Understand?'

The two men moved off quickly. Renardet said to the doctor: 'What swine round here could have done a thing like this?'

The doctor murmured: 'Who knows? Everybody is capable of doing something like this. Everybody in particular and no one in general. Be that as it may, it was probably some tramp or unemployed labourer. Ever since we've been a Republic, types like that are all you come across on the road.'

Both men were good Bonapartists.

The mayor went on: 'You're right. It can only be a stranger, somebody passing through, a vagrant with no home to go to . . .'

The doctor added, with a hint of a smile: 'And no wife either. He had nothing to eat, no place to sleep, but he managed to fix himself up with the rest. There are plenty of men around who are quite capable of the most horrible crimes in the right circumstances. Do you happen to know when the girl disappeared?' And with the end of his cane, he prodded the corpse's stiffened fingers one by one, pressing on them like the keys of a piano.

'Yes. The mother came and called me out yesterday, about nine last night, because the child hadn't come home for her supper at seven. We were out on the roads calling for her till midnight, but we never thought to try the wood. Anyway, we would have had to wait till it was light to carry out any kind of useful search.'

'Care for a cigar?' said the doctor.

'No thanks. I don't feel much like smoking. It's given me a turn, seeing all this.'

They both stood there looking down on the frail adolescent body lying so white against the dark moss. A large fly with a blue abdomen walked along one thigh, paused at the streak of blood, started advancing again, travelling steadily upwards, advancing over the flank in quick jerky movements, crawled up one breast, climbed down and set off to explore the other, seeking something to guzzle on the dead girl. The two men watched the black dot as it wandered.

The doctor said: 'A pretty sight, a fly on skin. Those eighteenth-century ladies knew a thing or two when they used to stick beauty spots on their faces. Why on earth did they ever stop doing it?'

The mayor, lost in thought, seemed not to hear.

But then he turned round sharply, for a sound had

disturbed him. A woman wearing a bonnet and a blue apron was running towards them through the trees. It was the mother, Roque's wife. As soon as she saw Renardet, she began to scream: 'My little girl, where is she? Where's my little girl?', and so distraught was she that she did not look on the ground. Then all at once she saw her, stopped dead in her tracks, put her hands together, and raised both arms, uttering a shrill, piercing wail like the howl of a wounded beast.

She sprang towards the body, fell to her knees, and lifted, or rather snatched, the handkerchief covering the face. When she saw the ghastly, black, twisted features, she stood up recoiling with shock, then collapsed with her face to the ground, sending horrible, continuous screams into the thick moss. Her tall, spare body shuddered convulsively and heaved under the clothes which clung to it. Her bony ankles and the withered calves encased in coarse blue stockings could be seen quivering dreadfully and with hooked fingers she tore at the earth as though trying to make a hole in which to hide.

Deeply moved, the doctor murmured: 'Poor woman!' Renardet's stomach rumbled oddly and he gave a kind of loud sneeze which exploded in his nose and mouth simultaneously. Drawing his handkerchief from his pocket, he began weeping into it, coughing and sobbing and wiping his nose noisily. He stammered: 'What sort of . . . swine . . . could . . . do such a thing? I'd like to see him go to the guillotine for this . . .'

But Principe reappeared, woebegone and empty-handed. He said apologetically: 'I couldn't find anything, your worship, not a thing anywhere.'

The mayor, quite flustered, answered in a thick, tear-choked voice: 'What couldn't you find?'

'The little girl's things.'

'I see. . . . Well . . . keep looking . . . and make sure you find them . . . or else . . . you'll have me to deal with.'

Knowing better than to argue with the mayor, the man set off again at a hopeless lope, casting as he went a fearful sideways glance at the corpse.

Far-off voices sounded under the trees, a muffled clamour, the noise of an approaching crowd. For as he went on his round, Médéric had spread the news from house to house. The local people, amazed at first, had wagged their tongues on their doorsteps; then they had got together and for a while had jawed and argued and given their opinions about what had happened; and now they had come to see for themselves.

They arrived in groups, vaguely uncertain and worried, fearful of the first shock. When they saw the body they stopped, not daring to proceed further and talking in whispers. Then they grew bolder, advanced a few steps, halted again, took a few steps more, and soon there formed around the dead girl, her mother, the doctor, and the mayor a solid ring, restless and noisy, which was compacted by the insistent shoving of late arrivals. Soon they were almost touching the corpse. One or two even bent down to feel it. The doctor shooed them away. But suddenly rousing himself from his torpor, the mayor became furious and, seizing the doctor's cane, threw himself on these people whose affairs he administered, bawling inarticulately: 'Clear off! . . . Clear off! . . . Ghouls, the lot of you! . . . Clear off!' Instantly the cordon of onlookers widened into a circle two hundred metres across.

Roque's wife had raised herself, turned over until she was sitting, and was now weeping with her hands clasped over her face.

In the crowd, everyone was talking about what had happened; and the eager eyes of boys ransacked the exposed young body. Renardet noticed them and abruptly removing his linen jacket, he threw it over the girl, completely hiding her with his large coat.

The onlookers inched forward again; the wood was filling with people; a continuous rumble of voices rose into the thick foliage of the tall trees.

The mayor, in his shirtsleeves, stood where he was, cane in hand, in a fighting stance. He seemed riled by the inquisitiveness of the people and kept repeating: 'If anybody comes close, I'll knock him down like a dog.'

The peasants were extremely frightened of him; they kept their distance. Doctor Labarbe, who was smoking, sat down beside Roque's wife and talked to her, trying to take her mind off things. The old woman immediately removed her hands from her face and answered with a flood of tear-filled words, venting her grief in garrulity. She told her life story, relating how she had married, how her husband, a cowman, had been gored to death, how she had raised her daughter, how she, a poor widow woman, had eked out a precarious existence with her little girl. Her little girl, her little Louise, was all she had. And now somebody had killed her. Somebody had killed her here, in this wood. She felt a sudden urge to see her again and, dragging herself towards the corpse on hands and knees, lifted one corner of the coat which covered her; then she let it drop and began wailing again. The crowd fell silent, greedily watching every movement she made.

All at once there was a great stir. Voices shouted: 'It's the police!'

Two policemen appeared in the distance, advancing at a fast trot, escorting their captain and a short, red-whiskered gentleman who bounced like a monkey high on a tall white mare. The gamekeeper had in fact found Monsieur Putoin, the examining magistrate, just as he was about to mount his horse prior to setting off on his daily ride, for he believed he cut a dash on a horse, much to the delight of his staff.

He dismounted at the same moment as the captain and shook the hands of the mayor and the doctor while he glanced ferret-eyed at the linen jacket which swelled over the body lying under it.

When he had been put fully in the picture, he ordered the wood to be cleared of people. The policemen broke up the crowd which however regrouped in the meadow where it formed into a tall hedge composed of excited, bobbing heads which ran the length of the Brindille on the opposite bank.

The doctor in turn provided details which Renardet took down in pencil in a notebook. All the facts were duly established, recorded, and discussed, but no further lead emerged. Moreover, Principe had returned having found no trace of the clothes.

The disappearance of the clothes puzzled everyone, and nobody could explain it beyond saying that they must have been stolen. And since they were old and worn and worth hardly anything, even theft was ruled out.

The examining magistrate, the mayor, the captain, and the doctor themselves began searching in pairs, leaving no branch undisturbed along the water's edge.

Renardet said to the judge: 'How on earth is it that the villain hid or removed the clothes and left the body like that, in the open, for anyone to see?'

The judge, a wily, shrewd man, replied: 'Aha! Could it be a trick? The man responsible for this crime was either an animal or a cunning devil. Whichever it was, we'll get him soon.'

The sound of coach wheels made them look round. The deputy public prosecutor, the doctor, and the clerk of the court had arrived. The search was begun again and was conducted amid animated conversation.

Out of the blue, Renardet said: 'I assume you'll all be staying for lunch?'

Everyone accepted with broad smiles, and the examining magistrate, deciding that they had spent quite enough time for one day on the Roque girl, turned and said to the mayor: 'Will it be all right if I have the body transferred to your house? I'm sure you have a room where you can keep it for me until this evening.'

The mayor seemed flustered and stammered: 'Yes, no . . . no. . . . To be honest, I'd rather not have it under my roof . . . because . . . because my servants . . . they . . . they already say there are . . . ghosts in my tower, Renard's Tower. . . . You know how it is. . . . I wouldn't be able to keep a single one of them. . . . No. . . . I'd rather not have it my house.'

The magistrate said with a faint smile: 'Very well. I shall have it taken at once to Roüy, for the autopsy.' And turning to the deputy prosecutor: 'I assume I may use your carriage?'

'But of course.'

Everyone turned back to the corpse. Roque's wife was now sitting by her daughter's side, holding her hand and staring dully and vacantly in front of her.

The two doctors tried to lead her away so that she would not see the girl being removed; but she understood at once what was about to be done and, flinging herself onto the body, hung on with both arms. Lying on top of it, she screamed: 'You'll not have her, she's mine. She's mine now! Somebody's gone and killed her. I want to keep her. You'll not have her!'

All the men, feeling awkward and not knowing what to do, stood around her in a circle. Renardet knelt down to speak to her.

'Listen, Madame Roque, it's got to be done so that we can find out who killed her. Otherwise we'll never know. He's got to be caught so that he can be punished. You'll get her back the minute we've laid hands on him, and that's a promise.'

This explanation blunted the woman's resolve, and with hate waking in her wild eyes she said: 'So they'll get him?'

'Yes. I promise.'

She stood up, having decided to allow these gentlemen to do as they saw fit. But when the captain happened to mutter: 'It's very surprising that we haven't found her clothes', a new idea, something she had not thought of before, entered her peasant head and she asked: 'Where's her things? They belongs to me. I want 'em. What's become of her bits and pieces?'

They explained that the clothes had not been found. Moaning and snivelling, she demanded to have them with desperate obstinacy: 'They belongs to me, I want 'em. Where's her bits and pieces, I got to have 'em!'

The more they tried to calm her, the louder she sobbed and the more stubborn she became. She had stopped asking for the body; now she wanted the clothes, her daughter's clothes, no doubt as much out of the ingrained close-fistedness of the poor for whom a coin can be a fortune as out of maternal love.

And when the small body, wrapped in blankets which had been fetched from Renardet's house, finally vanished into the carriage, the old woman, standing under the trees and supported by the mayor and the captain, wailed: 'I got nothin' left of her, nothin', nothin' left in the world, not even the 'at off 'er 'ead, 'er little 'at. Nothin'. All gone. Not even the little 'at off 'er 'ead.'

The priest had just arrived, a very young priest already running to fat. He undertook to escort Roque's wife and they went off together in the direction of the village. The mother's grief was assuaged by the comfortable words of the cleric who promised her consolations innumerable. But over and over she went on repeating: 'If only I 'ad 'er little 'at!', worrying at this idea which had driven all others from her mind.

From a distance, Renardet shouted to the priest: 'You're having lunch with us, father. In an hour.'

The priest turned his head and answered: 'Delighted, your worship. I'll be there for noon.'

Then everyone turned and made for the house. Through the trees could be seen the grey façade and the high tower rising out of the Brindille.

Lunch lasted an age, and they made a separate meal of the crime. Everyone was agreed on one thing: it had been committed by a tramp who had been passing through just as the girl was bathing.

Afterwards, the magistrates returned to Roüy saying that they would be back early next day. The doctor and the priest set off home while Renardet, after taking a long stroll across the meadows, went back to the wood where he walked around slowly, with his hands behind his back, until nightfall.

He went to bed very early and was still sleeping next morning when the examining magistrate burst into his bedroom. He was rubbing his hands and looking pleased with himself. He said: 'What's all this! Still asleep! Well now, my dear chap, this morning there's been a new development.'

The mayor sat up in bed: 'What's happened?'

'Something rather odd. You remember how the mother went on and on yesterday about having something of her daughter's, especially her little bonnet. Well, when she opened her front door this morning, there on the step were the child's little clogs. This proves that the crime was committed by someone in the locality, someone who felt sorry for her. Furthermore, Médéric the postman has come to me with a thimble, a knife, and a needle-box all belonging to the victim. This means that as the man made off with the clothes to hide them, he dropped these objects which were in a pocket. As far as I'm concerned, I attach considerable importance to the business with the clogs which suggests a measure of ethical awareness in the murderer, a capacity for human feeling. So if you agree, the two of us will run through what is known of the more important people in the locality.'

The mayor had got out of bed. He rang for hot shaving water for his beard and said: 'Of course. But it'll take some time. Why not start at once?'

Monsieur Putoin had sat down straddling his chair, thus persisting, even indoors, with his mania for riding.

Renardet was by now covering his chin with white foam and looking at himself in the mirror. Then he sharpened his razor on the leather strop and went on: 'The most important inhabitant of Carvelin is one Joseph Renardet, the mayor, a rich landowner, a curmudgeon with a temper who thrashes gamekeepers and coachmen . . .'

The examining magistrate guffawed: 'That'll do. Who's next?'

'The second most important person is Monsieur Pelledent, the deputy mayor, who raises cattle, also a rich landowner, a cunning peasant type, very crafty, slippery as they come where money is concerned, but in my view quite incapable of committing such a foul crime.'

Monsieur Putoin said: 'Next . . .'

And so, as he shaved and washed, Renardet went on with his moral review of the entire population of Carvelin. After two hours of talk, their suspicions had fallen on three rather dubious characters: a poacher named Cavalle; a shrimp-

and-trout fisherman called Paquet; and a cowman called Clovis.

II

Investigations continued throughout the whole summer. The murderer was not found. The men who had been arrested on suspicion proved their innocence without difficulty, and the public prosecutor's office was forced to give up the search for the guilty man.

But in a curious way, the murder seemed to have stirred up the whole countryside. At the back of people's minds, there remained a vague fear, a feeling of dark dread, which did not stem just from the fact that it had proved impossible to discover any clue at all, but also—and mainly—from the strange way the clogs had come to be found on Roque's wife's doorstep the next day. The certainty that the murderer had been present when the body was officially examined at the scene of the crime, and that he was probably still living in the village, haunted people's minds, obsessed them, and seemed to hang over the land like an ever-present threat.

Moreover, the wood was now a place which was feared and shunned, and people believed it was haunted. Previously they had used to go for walks there on Sunday afternoons. They had sat on the moss at the foot of the great tall trees, or sauntered along the bank of the river watching for the trout darting under the water weeds. The lads had played bowls and skittles and cork-penny and ball games at certain venues which they had cleared, levelled, and beaten flat; and the girls, in rows of four or five, had strolled by, linking arms, joining their shrill voices together and squawking tender love-songs which grated on the ear and sent wrong notes flying up to disturb the quiet air and set the teeth on edge like a spoonful of vinegar. But nowadays people never ventured beneath the high, thick canopy, as though they still half-expected to find a corpse lying there.

Autumn came. The leaves fell. They fell night and day, dropping and spinning, brisk and light, down the tall trees. The sky began to show through the branches. Sometimes, when a gust of wind blew through the tree-tops, the slow steady rain quickened suddenly into a dully rustling shower that covered the mossy ground with a thick yellow carpet which squelched lightly underfoot. And the almost imperceptible whisper, the incessant, muffled, mournful, floating whisper of the falling leaves was like a lament, and the ever-falling leaves like tears, bitter tears shed by the great sad trees which wept night and day for the passing of the year, for the passing of warmly dawning days and mild twilit evenings, for the passing of baking winds and clear sunny skies, and perhaps too for the crime which they had seen committed within their shadow, for the girl who had been raped and killed at their feet. They wept in the silence of the empty deserted wood, now abandoned and feared, where the tiny soul of the little girl walked alone.

The Brindille, swollen by the storms, yellow and angry, now flowed faster between its dry banks, between its two rows of thin, bare willows.

And then, quite unexpectedly, Renardet resumed his strolls in the wood. Each day, as night fell, he left his house, walked slowly down the flight of steps in front of it, and wandered off among the trees, looking thoughtful, with his hands in his pockets. Steadily he tramped over the damp spongy moss, while a legion of rooks which arrived from miles around to sleep in the high tree-tops, unfurled across the sky like a huge mourning veil flapping in the wind and uttered explosive, baleful cries. Sometimes they settled, peppered the tangled branches with flecks of black against the red, bleeding sky of autumn twilight. Then suddenly they flew off, crowing horribly and once more trailing the long dark wreath of their flight above the wood. Eventually, they perched in the tops of the highest trees and gradually ceased their noise, while the gathering gloom of night commingled their sable plumes with the black of space.

And still Renardet loitered and dawdled at the foot of the trees. When the shadows grew so thick that he could walk no further, he returned home, sank heavily into his armchair by the bright hearth, holding out his wet feet which steamed for a long time in the heat of the flames.

One morning, the news ran through the countryside like wildfire: the mayor was having his wood cut down.

Twenty woodcutters were already hard at work. They had begun on the corner nearest the house and were moving quickly under the master's eye.

First, the loppers and trimmers climbed the trunk.

To begin with, they wrap their arms around it, safely held by a rope harness, then lifting one leg they stab at it powerfully with an iron spike fixed to the sole of their boot. The spike sinks into the wood where it is held fast and the man hoists himself up as if he were climbing a step and then strikes out with the other spike on the other leg on which he supports himself again as he repeats the manoeuvre with the first foot.

With each rising step, he jerks the rope collar which attaches him to the tree one notch higher; at his side dangles his glinting steel axe. He continues climbing steadily, like a parasite attacking a giant, and, with his arms wrapped round the trunk and raking it with his spurs, he ponderously ascends the immense column the better to cut off its head.

When he gets to the lowermost branches, he halts, unhitches the sharp bill-hook hanging at his side, and begins to swing it. He strikes slowly and with method, chopping the limb very close to the trunk, and all at once the branch gives a crack, lurches, sags, tears itself free, and falls, brushing against nearby trees as it comes tumbling down. It crashes to earth with a loud noise of snapping branches, and every twig goes on twitching for some time.

The ground was littered with fallen timber which other men were cutting up, tying it into bundles which they put into piles, while the trees left standing looked like inordinately tall poles or gigantic stump-posts amputated and close-shaven by the sharp steel of the bill-hooks.

And when the trimmer had finished his task, he left the rope harness he had taken with him hanging from the straight, slender apex and climbed down by digging his spikes into the pollarded trunk which the woodcutters now began to attack at the foot with powerful swings of their axes which rang out through the rest of the wood.

When the gash at the base seemed deep enough, several men together, shouting the beat, heaved on the rope fixed to the top, and with a sudden loud crack the steepling column fell to the ground with the dull roar and recoil of a distant field-gun.

The wood grew smaller by the day, losing felled trees as an army loses men.

Renardet hardly went anywhere else now. He stayed there from morning to evening, scarcely moving, with his hands behind his back, watching his wood slowly dying. When a tree fell, he put his foot on it as on a dead body. Then he looked up at the next one to go in a mood of concealed, contained impatience, as though he were expecting something—even hoping for something—at the end of the massacre.

Meanwhile, the spot where Roque's girl had been found was drawing closer and closer. They reached it one evening as twilight fell.

The light was failing, for the sky was overcast, and the workmen were all for stopping and leaving the felling of an enormous beech for the next day. But the master would have none of it, and told them then and there to get on with lopping and cutting down the monster in whose shadow the crime had been committed.

When the trimmer had lopped it bare, as a prison barber shaves a condemned man for the last time, and the woodcutters had weakened the base, five men began hauling on the rope attached to its top.

The tree resisted. Though cut almost half way through, its strong trunk was as rigid as iron. All heaving together in a series of regular backward skips, the men pulled the rope so tight that they almost finished up lying flat on the ground, and, as they pulled, they uttered hoarse cries which punctuated and co-ordinated their efforts.

Two woodcutters stood close to the giant, axes at the ready, like executioners poised to strike again, and Renardet, motionless, with one hand on the bark, waited for the fall, seeming worried and agitated.

One of the men said: 'You're standing too close, your worship, sir. When she goes, you could get hurt.'

He did not answer and did not move back. He looked set to grapple with the beech and hurl it to the ground himself, like a wrestler.

Then, at the base of the tall column of wood, there was a rending sound which seemed to travel all the way up to the top like a spasm of pain; and the tree leaned slightly, ready to fall but still resisting. Excitedly, the men stiffened their arms and pulled even harder; and as the tree, broken now, began to topple, Renardet stepped forward, then stopped, with shoulders hunched to take the irresistible, fatal impact which would crush him into the ground. But the beech, falling not quite true, did no more than graze his back and sent him sprawling on his face five metres away.

The workmen leaped forward to help him up. He had managed to get up onto his knees by himself and looked stunned and wild-eyed as he passed one hand over his brow as though waking from a moment of madness.

When he was on his feet again, the astonished men fired questions at him, for they did not understand what he had done. He replied falteringly that something had come over him, or rather, just for a second, he had gone back to childhood and fancied he had plenty of time to dash under the tree, just as boys run in front of trotting coach-horses, that he had played with danger, or that, for the past week, he had felt a growing urge to try it, for every time he heard a tree give a crack before falling, he wondered if it was possible to run under it without being hit. He agreed it was a stupid idea; but everybody gets these moments of madness and stupid, childish temptations.

He said all this slowly, finding his words with difficulty, in a hollow voice. Then he walked away saying: 'Tomorrow, I'll see you tomorrow.'

When he was back in his room, he sat down at his table, which was brightly lit by his lamp under its shade, and, putting his head in his hands, began to weep.

He went on weeping for a long time, then, wiping his eyes, he raised his head and looked at the clock. It was not yet six o'clock. He thought: 'I've got time before dinner,' and he went over to the door and locked it. Then he sat down again at his table. He pulled out the middle drawer, took out a revolver, and placed it on his papers, in the full glare of the lamp. The gun metal gleamed and threw off reflections like flames. Renardet stared at it for a while with the fuddled eyes of a drunk. Then he stood up and started walking up and down.

He went from one end of the room to the other, stopping from time to time only to resume his pacing immediately. Suddenly he opened his bathroom door, dipped a towel in the water jug, and moistened his forehead, exactly as he had done on the morning of the crime. After this he began pacing up and down again. Each time he passed near his table, the gleaming pistol attracted his eye, making his hand itch. But he kept watching the clock, thinking: 'There's still time.'

Half past six struck. He picked up the gun, twisted his face into a hideous grimace, opened his mouth as wide as it would go, and thrust the barrel inside as though he were trying to swallow it. He remained in this position for some seconds, without moving, his finger on the trigger, then suddenly, shaken by a convulsion of horror, he spat out the gun onto the carpet.

He collapsed into his armchair sobbing: 'I can't do it! I daren't! My God! Oh my God! What do I have to do to have the courage to kill myself?'

There was a knock at the door. He got to his feet in a panic. A servant called 'Dinner is served, sir.' He answered: 'Very well. I shall be down at once.'

He picked up the gun, put it away again in the drawer, and stared at his face in the mirror over the mantelpiece to see if it did not look too ravaged. It was red, as it always was, perhaps a little redder. But that was all. He went downstairs and sat down at table.

He ate slowly, like a man who is in no hurry to finish his meal and has no wish to be left alone with himself. Afterwards he smoked several pipes in the dining-room while the table was cleared. Then he went back to his room.

As soon as he was inside, he looked under the bed, opened all his cupboards, peered into every corner, and searched every piece of furniture. He lit the candles on the mantelpiece and, wheeling around several times, ran his eye over the entire room in an anguish of fear which contorted his features, for he knew that he was about to see, as he did each night, Roque's daughter, the little girl he had raped and strangled.

Every night the loathsome vision returned. It began as a muffled roaring in his ears like the noise of a threshing machine or a distant train rattling over a bridge. He would then start to pant and choke and he had to undo his shirt-button and loosen the belt. He walked about to get his circulation going, tried to read, attempted to sing. But it was no good. In spite of himself, his mind went back to the day of the murder and made him relive each most secret detail and every raging emotion from the first moment to the last second.

As he had got up that morning, the morning of his day of horror, he had experienced a slight dizziness and a touch of migraine which he had put down to the heat and, as a result, he had remained in his room until he was called to lunch. After lunch he had taken a nap, then, in the late afternoon, he had gone out for a breath of the cool, soothing breeze under the trees in his wood.

But as soon as he got outside, the heavy, burning air of the plain sat even more heavily on him. The sun, still high in the sky, poured a stream of blazing light over the frazzled, parched, desiccated earth. No breath of wind stirred the leaves. All the animals, all the birds, even the grasshoppers were silent. Renardet reached the tall trees and began walking across the moss where the Brindille released a little coolness beneath the immense canopy of branches. But he felt ill at ease. He felt as though some unknown, invisible hand had grasped him by the neck. He was not thinking of anything at all—and in any case he did not normally have many notions running around his head. But one nebulous thought had been haunting him for three months: the idea that he might remarry. Living alone made him very unhappy, and his unhappiness was both emotional and physical. For ten years he had been used to feeling that there was a woman by his side, had been accustomed to her presence each moment, to her embraces each day, and he had an overriding but ill-defined need for contact with her, for her punctual touch. Since Madame Renardet's death he had suffered endlessly without knowing quite why, suffered from not feeling her dress brush against his legs morning, noon, and night, and above all from being no longer able to find peace and ease in her arms. His wife had been dead for barely six months and already he was casting round the neighbourhood for some young woman or widow whom he might marry when he was out of mourning.

His soul was pure but it was housed in a robust, masculine body, and carnal images had begun to trouble his sleep and his waking hours. He drove them away; they returned; and at times he would mutter with a smile against himself: 'I'm Saint Anthony* to a T!'

That morning he had been visited by a number of these compulsive fancies, and he had felt a sudden urge to bathe in the Brindille to cool and quench the fires in his blood.

A little further along, he knew of a wide, deep pool where local people sometimes went for a dip in summer. He took himself off there.

Thick willow trees hid the clear standing water where the current nodded and dozed a while before continuing on its way. As he approached, Renardet thought he heard a faint noise, a soft splashing which was not the sound of the stream lapping against the banks. He carefully parted the leaves and looked. A young girl, quite naked, her body showing white through the transparent water which she beat with both hands, was dancing after a fashion and wheeling round and round with delightful movements. She was not a child and she was not yet a woman; she was fully fleshed and fully formed and yet retained a hint of the precocious little girl who has grown up quickly and is almost ripe. Rigid with surprise and anguish, he did not move a muscle, and his breath was almost stopped by an odd, keen feeling of excitement. He remained where he was, his heart pounding as though one of his sensual dreams had turned into reality, as if some disagreeable sprite had conjured up this creature who was disturbing and too young, a peasant Venus rising from the eddies of the stream as the other, the adult Venus, had risen from the waves of the sea.

Suddenly the child emerged from the water and, without seeing him, came towards him in search of her clothes to get dressed. As she drew nearer, treading slowly and carefully to avoid the sharp pebbles, he felt himself impelled towards her by an irresistible force, a bestial urge which set his flesh on fire, threw his mind into turmoil, and made him shake from head to foot.

She stood for a few moments behind the willow which hid him. Then, losing all self-control, he pushed the branches aside, flung himself on her, and grabbed her in both arms. She fell to the ground, too startled to resist, too frightened to call out, and he forced her to submit without being aware of what he was doing.

He woke from his crime as other people wake from a nightmare. The girl began to cry. He said: 'Hush now! Hush! I'll give you money.' But she did not listen. She went on sobbing. He continued: 'Hush now, do you hear! Stop it! Be quiet!' She shrieked and twisted this way and that in her efforts to escape.

The realization that he was lost came upon him suddenly and he seized her by the throat to put an end to the harrowing, horrible screams emerging from her mouth. But she went on flailing at him with the desperate strength of a live thing struggling to escape the clutches of death, and his huge hands closed around her slender neck now swollen with her cries. So furiously did he squeeze that he strangled her probably within seconds, without meaning to kill her, merely to make her keep quiet.

He stood up in horror.

She lay on the ground at his feet, bleeding, her face black. He was about to run away when he felt the working of that mysterious, puzzling instinct which guides all creatures in moments of great danger.

He was about to throw the body into the water. But another impulse directed him towards the clothes which he made into a small bundle. Then he tied the bundle with a piece of string which he had in his pocket and hid it in a deep part of the stream under the trunk of a tree growing on the verge.

Then he walked away quickly, reached the meadow, made a huge detour to ensure that he would be seen by farm-workers who lived a considerable distance from the spot, on the far side of the locality, and returned home for dinner at his usual time, telling his servants exactly where his walk had taken him.

He nevertheless slept well that night. He slept the heavy sleep of the beasts of the field, as men sentenced to death sometimes do. He did not open his eyes until the first glimmering of daylight, and, tormented by the fear that the appalling crime had been discovered, he lay there waiting for the time when he normally woke.

He could not avoid being present for the official investigation. He participated much as a sleepwalker might have done, moving through a daze in which he saw people and things in a kind of dream, passing through clouds of delirium and those feelings of unreality which trouble the mind when great disasters strike.

Only the harrowing wail of Roque's wife touched him to the quick. When he heard it, he almost threw himself at the old woman's knees shouting: 'It was me!' But he restrained himself. Yet during the night, he went and fished out the dead girl's clogs and left them on her mother's doorstep.

As long as the inquiries continued, as long as he went on guiding and misleading the investigations, he remained composed, master of himself, crafty and smiling. With the magistrates he calmly discussed all the conjectures which ran through their heads, differed with their views, and demolished their arguments. He even took a certain bitter, hurtful pleasure at hindering their searches, confusing them, and proving the innocence of persons they suspected.

But from the day the search was abandoned, he gradually became nervy and even more excitable than before, though he mastered his anger. Sudden noises made him leap up with fear; he started at the slightest thing, sometimes jumping almost out of his skin when a fly settled on his forehead. At such times, he was overcome by an overriding need for physical exertion which forced him to go for immense walks and kept him up padding around his room through long nights.

It was not that he was devoured by remorse. His brutal nature did not lend itself to shades of feeling or moral anxiety. A man of energy, of violence even, born for waging war, for ravaging conquered lands and massacring the vanquished, full of the wild instincts of the hunter and the fighter, he was no respecter of human life. Although he deferred to the Church, he believed in neither God nor the Devil and consequently expected neither punishment or reward in the next life for his actions in this. His only belief was in a vague philosophy cobbled together out of the ideas of the Encyclopédistes of the last century; and he viewed religion as a moral sanction for Law, both having been invented by men as a means of regulating social relationships.*

Killing somebody in a duel or in time of war or in a quarrel or by accident or for revenge or even out of bravado, would have seemed to him an amusing, dashing thing to do and would have left no more trace in his mind than taking a potshot at a hare; but he had felt profoundly disturbed by the murder of the girl. Of course, he had committed it under the influence of an irresistible urge, in a kind of sensual storm which had blown his reason away. And in his heart, in his flesh, on his lips, even on his murderer's fingers, he had retained a bestial love of sorts, but also a feeling of the most awful horror for the little girl whom he had surprised and killed so cravenly. His thoughts returned constantly to the terrible scene; and though he attempted to drive the image away and push it out of his mind in terror and disgust, he felt it prowling about inside his head, hovering around him, just waiting for the moment when it would materialize before his very eyes.

From then on, he came to dread the evenings and fear the darkness as it closed about him. He did not yet know why the shadows seemed so frightening, but he feared them instinctively; he sensed that they were inhabited by terrible things. Daylight does not lend itself to terror: objects and people are plain to see; and we encounter there only those things which dare to show themselves in the glare of day. But night, opaque night denser than walls, night, empty and infinite and so black and fathomless that terrifying things reach out and touch us, night when we feel horror stirring, mysteriously prowling—night seemed to him to hide some unknown, imminent, threatening danger. What could it be?

He soon found out. Late one evening when he could not sleep and was sitting up in his armchair, he thought he saw the curtain at his window stir. He waited apprehensively, his heart racing. The curtain stopped moving. Then it suddenly moved again. Or at least he thought it did. He dared not stand up, dared not breathe, though he was a brave man and had fought duels and would have relished any opportunity to disturb burglars in his house.

Had the curtain really moved? he asked himself, fearing that his eyes had tricked him. It had been hardly anything really—a gentle swelling of the cloth, a shiver of hanging folds, but something less than the undulation produced by the wind. Renardet sat there with eyes staring and head craned forward; then suddenly he got to his feet feeling ashamed of his fear, took four steps forward, grasped the curtains in both hands, and flung them back. At first he saw nothing but the window-panes gleaming black as ink. Night, vast and impenetrable, stretched way beyond them to the invisible horizon. He remained where he was, looking into the boundless dark. Then he saw a light, a light which moved; it seemed to be some distance away. He brought his face close to the glass, assuming it was doubtless someone poaching for shrimps in the Brindille, for it was past midnight and the light bobbed and weaved along the water's edge. Not being able to make out more, he cupped his hands round his eyes. Suddenly, the light became clear and bright and he saw the Roque girl lying naked and bloody on the moss.

He recoiled in horror, stumbled over his chair, and fell

backwards onto the floor. He remained there for several minutes with his mind in a whirl, then sat up and began to think. It was a hallucination, that was it! a hallucination brought on by some night prowler walking along the river bank with his lantern. Anyway, was it particularly surprising that the recollection of his crime should occasionally produce visions of the dead girl in his mind?

He got to his feet, drank a glass of water, and sat down again. He thought: 'What'll I do if it comes again?' And it would come again, he was sure of it, he felt it in his bones. For his eyes were drawn to the window which beckoned and called. He turned his chair round so that he could not see it. He picked up a book and tried to read. He thought he heard something stir behind him and swung his chair round suddenly on one leg. The curtain was still swinging. This time it had really moved; he could be in no doubt about it. He leaped up and seized it so savagely that he pulled it to the ground and the rail with it. Greedily he pressed his face to the window. He could see nothing. Outside all was dark, and he breathed again with the relief of a man whose life has just been saved.

He turned and started for his chair. But almost at once he was overtaken by an urge to look out of the window again. Now that the curtain was down, it made a kind of ghostly, enticing, black hole onto the dark countryside. So that he would not succumb to so dangerous a temptation, he undressed, snuffed out his candles, got into bed, and shut his eyes.

He lay on his back, not moving, his skin hot and sticky, waiting for sleep. Suddenly a blinding light flashed across his closed eyes. He opened them, thinking that the house was on fire. It was dark everywhere and he propped himself up on one elbow in an effort to make out the window which still beckoned irresistibly. So hard did he stare that he saw one or two stars shining. He got out of bed, groped his way across the room until he could feel the window panes with his outstretched hands, and leaned his forehead against the glass. There, beneath the trees, the body of the girl glowed like phosphorus, pushing back the shadows around it. Renardet cried out and made a dash for his bed where he remained till morning with his head hidden under the pillow.

From then on, his life became intolerable. He spent his days dreading the nights ahead. And each night the vision came again. The moment he locked his door behind him, he tried to fight it. But it was no use. An irresistible power pulled at him and drove him towards the window as though to summon the ghost, and each time he saw it instantly. At first it lay at the scene of the crime, arms outspread and legs wide open exactly as it had been when the body was discovered. Then the dead girl rose and came towards him, treading carefully, just as she had done when she emerged from the river. She advanced slowly, walking straight ahead over the lawns and the circular beds where the flowers had withered. Then she rose into the air and made directly for Renardet's window. She came towards him as she had done on the day of the crime, towards her murderer. And he recoiled as the apparition drew nearer, retreated to his bed, and collapsed into it, in the full knowledge that the little girl had entered the room and was now standing behind the curtain which would begin to stir at any moment. And until day broke, he continued to watch the curtain unblinkingly, expecting to see his victim emerge from behind it at any moment. But she never did. She remained where she was, hidden by the cloth which occasionally stirred. Grimly clutching his sheets, Renardet squeezed his hands together just as he had squeezed the Roque girl's throat. He heard the hours strike; in the silence he heard the ticking of the pendulum in his clock and the bottomless beating of his heart. Wretch that he was, he suffered as no man had ever suffered before him.

But no sooner did a line of light appear on the ceiling announcing that day was not far off, than he experienced a feeling of deliverance, sensing that he was alone at last, alone in his room. Then he went back to his bed. He slept for a few hours, restless and feverish, often reliving the awful vision of the night in recurring dreams.

Later, when he went down for lunch at midday, he would feel stiff and beaten as though he had over-exerted himself with strenuous exercise. He hardly touched his food, for he was haunted by fear of her whom he would see once more when night came.

He was quite aware that what he saw was not an apparition, that the dead do not return, and that his sick mind, obsessed with a single thought, a single memory, was the sole cause of his torment, the only begetter of visions of the deceased girl who had been brought to life by his mind and summoned by his mind which alone had conveyed her to him and stood her before his very eyes which retained the indelible imprint of her image. But he was equally aware that he would never get over it, never escape the savage persecution of her memory. He resolved to die rather than go on enduring such torture any longer.

He looked for a way of killing himself. He wanted something simple and natural which would not make people suspect suicide. For he cared for his reputation and for the name bequeathed by his forbears. If the true cause of his death were to be suspected, people would think perhaps of the unsolved crime, of the murderer who had never been found, and would soon begin to lay the horrible murder at his door.

A strange notion had entered his head—the idea that he should get himself crushed to death by the very tree at the foot of which he had killed Roque's girl. He made up his mind to have his wood cut down and stage an accident. But the beech refused to break his neck.

On returning home, sunk in the blackest despair, he had picked up his revolver but had not dared use it.

The dinner gong had struck. He had eaten and then returned to his room. He had no idea of what he was going to do. But he had turned coward now that he had survived his first attempt. Then he had been ready, braced, his mind made up, master of his courage and his resolve; but now he felt weak and feared death as much as he feared the dead girl.

He stammered: 'I daren't! I just daren't!', and his glance moved in terror before the gun on his table and the curtain which hid his window. Moreover, he sensed that something horrible would happen the moment his life ended. But what would that something be? That they would meet? She was watching for him, waiting for him, calling to him, and it was because it was her turn to trap him, to draw him into her vengeance and make him take his life, that she appeared to him each night.

He began to cry like a child, repeating over and over: 'I daren't! I daren't do it!' Then, falling to his knees, he stammered: 'My God, my God!' Yet he did not believe in God. But, sure enough, he dared not look towards his window where he knew the apparition lurked nor towards the table where his revolver gleamed.

When he was standing up once more, he said aloud: 'This can't go on! I've got to put a stop to this!' The sound of his voice in the silent room sent a shiver of fear to all parts of his body. But since he could not make up his mind one way or the other, and because he sensed that his finger would go on refusing to press the trigger, he lay down again on his bed and, hiding his head under the bedclothes, began to think.

He would have to find something which would make him die—invent a trick he could play on himself which would leave him no possible opportunity for hesitation, delay, or regret. He envied convicted criminals who are led to the scaffold surrounded by a squad of soldiers. Oh! If only he could ask someone to shoot him! If only he could confess the state of his soul, admit his crime to a loyal friend who would never tell, and persuade him to put an end to his life! But who could he ask to undertake such a terrible service for him? Who? He ran through the people he knew. The doctor? No: he was likely to tell the tale at some future date. All at once, a bizarre thought flashed through his mind. He would write to the examining magistrate, whom he knew intimately, and denounce himself. In his letter he would reveal everything—the crime, the torments he had gone through, his determination to die, his waverings, and the means he had used to bolster his waning courage. He would beg him in the name of their old friendship to destroy the letter the moment he knew that the guilty man had taken the law into his own hands. Renardet could count on the magistrate. He knew him to be sound, discreet, and quite incapable of loose talk. He was one of those men of inflexible moral rectitude which is governed, directed, and regulated by reason alone.

This plan was no sooner formed than a strange feeling of relief surged through him. He felt at peace now. He would write his letter, slowly, then at first light he would go and drop it into the box nailed to the wall of his farm, climb to the top of his tower to watch for the postman to arrive at the magistrate's, and when he saw the postman's blue uniform leave, he would throw himself head first onto the rocks on which the foundations stood. He would make sure that he was first seen by the men who were chopping down his wood. Then he would clamber onto the projecting stone which held the mast for the flag which was always flown on holidays. He would snap the mast with a jerk of his body and plunge down with it. How could anyone suspect it was not an accident? And given his weight and the height of the tower, he would be killed instantly.

He got out of bed at once, sat down at his table, and started writing. He omitted nothing, not a single detail of the crime, or of his life of torment, or of the rackings of his heart, and he ended by saying that he had passed sentence upon himself, that he was about to execute the criminal and requested his friend, his old friend, to see to it that his memory should never be impeached.

He became conscious that it was day just as he was finishing the letter. He closed it, sealed it with wax, wrote the address on it, and then padded downstairs, made quickly for the little white box which was fixed to the wall at one end of the farmhouse, and, after posting the missive which made his hand shake, hurried back, pushed home the bolts on the great door, and climbed his tower to watch for the arrival of the postman who would walk away bearing his death sentence.

He felt calm now, delivered, saved!

A bitingly cold wind drove freezing air into his face. He gulped it in greedily through his open mouth, devouring its icy embrace. The sky was red, red as fire, winter red. The whole plain, white with hoar-frost, sparkled in the first rays of the sun as though it had been dusted with powdered glass. Bareheaded, Renardet stood watching the rolling countryside, meadows to the left, and to the right the village where chimneys were beginning to smoke in readiness for the first meal of the day.

At his feet he could see the Brindille as it flowed around the rocks on which he would be dashed in just a little while. He felt himself come alive again in the beauty of the icy dawn, full of strength and full of life. The light streamed over him, surrounded him, settling on him like hope. He was besieged by countless memories—of other mornings like this, of brisk walks across frost-bound earth which rang beneath his feet, of successful shoots on the banks of meres where the wild ducks doze. All the good things which he loved, the good things in life surfaced in his memory, spurred new desires, awakened all the robust appetites of his energetic, full-blooded body.

And to think that he was about to die! Why? Was he going to kill himself stupidly because he was afraid of the dark? Afraid of nothing at all? He was rich and still young! He must be mad! Occupying his mind, going away, travelling—any of these would be enough to blot it all out. Last night he had not seen the girl at all because his mind had been busy and distracted by other things. Perhaps he would never see her again! She might haunt him in his house, but she would certainly not follow him to other places! The world was big and the future long! Why should he die?

As his gaze wandered over the meadows, he saw a spot of blue on the path which followed the Brindille. It was Médéric on his way to deliver letters from the town and collect those posted in the village.

Renardet started and felt a physical pain coursing through him. He flung himself down the spiral stairs to retrieve his letter. Being seen did not matter now. He ran across the grass with its froth of delicate night ice and reached the letter-box at the corner of the farmhouse at about the same moment as the postman.

The postman had opened the little wooden door and was taking out the few letters which local people had deposited inside.

'Morning, Médéric,' said Renardet.

'Good morning, your worship.'

'Fact is, Médéric, just now I posted a letter I need. I've come out to ask if you'll let me have it back.'

'Can't see why not. Of course you shall have it.'

The postman looked up. He was stunned by the expression on Renardet's face. His cheeks were purple and his eyes were clouded, ringed with black, and somehow sunk deep in his head; his hair was dishevelled, his beard a tangle, and his tie was undone. It was obvious that he had not been to bed.

The postman asked: 'You not feeling well, your worship?'

Renardet, suddenly realizing that his behaviour must appear very strange, went to pieces and began stammering: 'No, no . . . not at all. . . . It's just that I leaped out of bed to ask you for the letter. . . . I was asleep. . . . Do you follow me?'

A vague suspicion flashed through the old soldier's mind. 'What letter?'

'The one you're going to let me have back.'

But now Médéric was not so sure, for the mayor's attitude did not seem at all natural. Perhaps there were secrets in the letter, political secrets. He knew that Renardet was no republican and he was familiar with all the tricks and frauds people get up to at elections. He asked: 'Who is this letter addressed to?'

'To Monsieur Putoin, the examining magistrate. You know: Monsieur Putoin. A friend of mine.'

The postman searched among the letters and found the one he had been asked to return. He began to look it over, turning it round and round in his hands, very confused and terribly anxious in case he did something seriously wrong or made an enemy of the mayor.

Seeing him hesitate, Renardet made as if to grab the letter and snatch it away. The sudden movement convinced Médéric that there was some big mystery behind it all and he decided to do his duty, whatever the cost. He slipped the envelope into his bag and closed it, saying: 'Can't do it, your worship. Not if it was a letter addressed to the police, I couldn't.'

Searing anguish gripped Renardet's heart. He spluttered: 'But you know me! You even know my writing! I tell you I need that letter.'

'I can't.'

'Come now, Médéric. You know I'd never try putting anything across you. I'm telling you I need it!'

'No. I can't.'

A spasm of anger rocked Renardet's violent nature. 'Now you take care, by God! You know I don't play games. I could get a clown like you sacked, and pretty damn quick too! Don't forget I'm the mayor after all, and I'm ordering you, now, to hand over that letter.'

The postman was adamant: 'No, I can't do it, your worship!'

Losing his head, Renardet grabbed him by the arms and tried to take his bag away from him. But the postman shrugged him off and, taking a step back, raised his thick holly staff. Still remaining quite cool, he said: 'You just keep your hands off, your worship, or I'll let you have it. You take care. I'm only doing my duty!'

Sensing that all was lost, Renardet suddenly turned humble and meek and began wheedling like some crying child. 'Be reasonable, won't you? Give me back the letter and I'll see you right, I'll give you money, here, look, I'll give you a hundred francs, all right? A hundred francs.'

The postman turned on his heel and began walking away.

Renardet followed him, gasping and stuttering: 'Médéric, Médéric, listen, I'll give you a thousand francs, you hear? A thousand.'

But the postman walked on without answering. Renardet continued: 'I'll make you a rich man . . . do you hear? I'll give you anything you like. . . . Fifty thousand francs. . . . Fifty thousand francs for the letter. . . . What do you say? . . . You won't take it? . . . A hundred thousand, then . . . all right? . . . a hundred thousand. . . . Do you understand? . . . a hundred thousand . . . a hundred thousand francs.'

The postman turned. His face was hard and his eyes stern: 'That's enough, or else I'll away and tell the police everything you just said.'

Renardet pulled up short. It was all over. His last hope was gone. He turned and fled towards his house, scurrying like a hunted beast.

Médéric halted too and watched his flight in amazement. He saw the mayor go into his house, and then waited, as though something unexpected were bound to happen.

And so it proved, for Renardet's tall figure soon appeared at the top of Renard's Tower. He ran round the parapet like a madman, took hold of the flagpole and shook it furiously but failed to snap it, then suddenly, like a diver taking a header, he threw himself into the void, with both arms stretched out before him.

Médéric ran over to see if he could help. As he crossed the grounds, he saw the woodcutters on their way to work. He called to them and shouted that there had been an accident. At the foot of the wall they found a bloody, broken body with its head crushed by a rock. The Brindille flowed round the rock and on its surface, here at this spot where it formed a wide pool of clear, quiet water, they saw a long, pink, floating skein of mashed brains and blood.

Mademoiselle Pearl

I

I really can't think what got into me that evening, choosing Mademoiselle Pearl to be my queen* like that!

Every year I spend Twelfth Night at the house of my old friend Chantal. My father, whose closest companion he was, always used to take me along with him when I was a little boy. I have kept on going and probably shall continue to do so as long as I live and for as long as there's a Chantal still left alive.

Actually, the Chantals lead a rather peculiar existence. They live in Paris exactly as though they were living at Grasse, Yvetot, or Pont-à-Mousson.

They have this house with a small garden near the Observatoire. They feel as much at home there as though they lived in the provinces. They know nothing about Paris, the real Paris, and are incurious to a degree: they live in a world of their own. From time to time, however, they do go on trips, sometimes venturing quite far. Then Madame Chantal 'stocks up', as they say in the family. This is how they 'stock up'.

Mademoiselle Pearl, who has the keys to the kitchen stores (the linen cupboards are looked after personally by the mistress of the house), gives notice that the sugar is running low, that the jam has all gone, and that there are hardly any coffee beans left in the bag.

Having been alerted to the threat of imminent famine, Madame Chantal then inspects the various remaining supplies, making notes as she does so in a little book. Then, when she has collected a great many numbers and figures, she sits down and does a lot of sums before embarking on endless discussions with Mademoiselle Pearl. They always come to an understanding about the quantities of each item, enough of which will be bought to last three months: sugar, rice, prunes, coffee, jam, tins of peas, beans, and lobster, fish salted and smoked, and so on and so forth.

Next, they decide on a day when they will go and buy it all and set off in a cab with a luggage-rail which takes them to a big grocer's on the other side of the bridges, in the 'new' parts of town.

Madame Chantal and Mademoiselle Pearl go off furtively together, and are back by dinner-time, worn out but still excited and shaken to pieces by the joltings of the cab which has piles of bags and parcels on the roof, like a removal van.

For the Chantals, the 'new' parts of town are made up of the whole area of Paris situated on the other side of the Seine, inhabited by peculiar people who make a great deal of noise, are not to be trusted, pass their days in self-indulgence and their nights in idle amusements, and spend money as though tomorrow will never come. Even so, the young ladies are taken to the theatre from time to time—the Opéra-Comique or the Comédie Française—when there's a play on which has been recommended in the newspaper which Monsieur Chantal reads.

The young ladies are now 19 and 17 respectively. They are good-looking girls, tall and fresh-complexioned, very well brought up, too well really: they are so well brought up that they are as noticeable as two pretty dolls. It would never enter my head to pay the Chantal girls any special attention, let alone make up to them. They are so refined that you can hardly bring yourself to speak. They almost make you feel afraid of being improper if you say 'Hello'.

The father is a charming man, very knowledgeable, very open-minded, very genial, but all he wants is peace, a quiet life, and taking things easy. He has been largely responsible for embalming his family so that he can live as he pleases, in a slough of stagnation. He reads widely, loves talking, and is easily moved. His avoidance of social contact and of the knocks which come with rubbing shoulders with other people has left him with a thin, sensitive, skin—his emotional skin, that is. The least thing brings forth the tears, upsets him, and makes him feel awful.

The Chantals do know people, however, carefully chosen among the neighbours, but not many. They also exchange two or three visits a year with relatives who live a long way off.

I go and dine with them on Assumption Day and Twelfth Night, that's all. I feel it as an obligation, rather as taking communion at Easter is for Catholics.

II

To cut a long story short, this year like other years, I toddled along to dinner with the Chantals on Twelfth Night.

In accordance with custom, I gave warmest greetings to Monsieur Chantal, Madame Chantal, and Mademoiselle Pearl, and I was fulsome towards Louise and Pauline. They asked me all sorts of questions about what was happening in town, about politics, about what the public thought of the Tonkin business,* and about what members of parliament were up to. Madame Chantal—a large woman whose ideas always strike me as being square-shaped, like stones dressed by a mason—was in the habit of concluding any political discussion with the remark: 'As ye sow, so shall ye reap'. Why have I always imagined that Madame Chantal's ideas are square? I've no idea, but everything she says goes into that shape in my mind: a block—a large one—with four symmetrical angles. Other people have ideas which always seem to me to be round and roll along like barrel-hoops. The moment they begin a sentence about something or other, away it goes, out it trundles in ten, twenty, fifty spherical ideas, some big and some small, which I watch as they go bowling along one after the other, clear away to the horizon. Then again, some people have pointed ideas. . . But this is neither here nor there.

We sat down to dinner as we always do and the meal passed off without anything of note being said.

When we got to the pudding, the Twelfth-cake made its appearance. Now every year, Monsieur Chantal was always king. Whether this was the result of permanent good fortune or of some family understanding, I have no idea, but he invariably discovered the lucky charm in his piece of cake and promptly nominated Madame Chantal to be his queen. So I was thunderstruck when I felt in a mouthful of pastry something very hard on which I very nearly broke a tooth. I removed the object gently from my mouth and saw that it was a small china figure, no bigger than a bean. The surprise made me say: 'Oh!' Everyone looked at me and Chantal clapped his hands and cried out: 'It's Gaston! Gaston's It. Long live the king! Long live the king!'

They all took up the refrain: 'Long live the king!' I blushed scarlet, as you often do, for no reason, in slightly silly situations. I was sitting there with eyes down, holding the little china thing between two fingers, trying to laugh and not knowing what to do or say next, when Chantal went on: 'Come on, you've got to choose a queen.'

This floored me. In the space of a single second, a billion thoughts and conjectures went through my mind. Did they want me to pick out one of the Chantal girls? Was it a way of getting me to say which one I preferred? Were the parents giving a bland, subtle, gentle hint in the direction of a possible marriage? The idea of marriage lurks perpetually in houses containing marriageable daughters and assumes many shapes and guises and forms. I was overcome by a horrible fear of compromising myself, and the unbendingly proper, wooden way Louise and Pauline just sat there made me feel extremely shy. To choose one and not the other seemed to me about as difficult as choosing between two drops of water. Furthermore, I was sorely troubled by the fear that I was on the verge of something which could lead me to the altar against my will, in easy steps and by methods as discreet, masked, and quiet as my new-found royalty was trivial.

And then I had an inspiration: I held the symbolic figure out to Mademoiselle Pearl. At first everyone was taken aback, but then probably sensed how delicate and discreet I was being, for they all applauded furiously. They shouted: 'Long live the queen! Long live the queen!'

The poor old girl did not know where to look. She shook, she looked panic-stricken, and she stammered: 'No! . . . Oh no! . . . Not me! . . . Please! . . . Not me. . . . Please . . .'

Then for the first time in my life, I looked at Mademoiselle Pearl and wondered what she was like.

I had grown used to seeing her around the house rather as you see the old tapestry armchairs you've been sitting on since you were very young and have never really noticed. One day, without having the least idea why, perhaps because a bar of sunshine falls across the seat, you suddenly think: 'I say! that's an interesting old piece', and you discover that the wood is hand-carved and that the cloth covering it is rather fine. I had never noticed Mademoiselle Pearl.

I always thought of her as part of the Chantal family, nothing more. But how, exactly? On what footing was she? She was tall and thin and always tried to avoid drawing attention to herself, but she was not insignificant. She was treated in a friendly way, better than a housekeeper but not so well as a relation. I suddenly understood a host of little things which I had never bothered about before. Madame Chantal called her 'Pearl'. The girls said 'Mademoiselle Pearl', and Chantal, slightly more ceremoniously perhaps, just said 'Mademoiselle'.

I began to observe her. How old was she? 40? Yes, 40. She wasn't old but she behaved and dressed older than she was. This thought struck me forcibly. She did her hair and dressed and got herself up in the most ridiculous manner, but for all that she was not herself ridiculous, for there was in her such simple, natural grace, a grace which was masked and carefully hidden. Really, what an odd creature she was! How on earth had I never taken more notice of her? The way she wore her hair was grotesque, in little curls that were really too comical for words; and below her well-preserved Madonna braids was a high, serene brow bisected by two deep lines suggestive of past sorrows, and beneath her brow a pair of blue eyes, big and gentle and so shy, so timid, so humble! Beautiful eyes which had remained innocent and still brimmed with little-girl surprise and youthful excitement, but also told of the sad things they had seen which made them softer but left their calm undisturbed.

Her whole face was delicate and unassuming, the kind of face which loses its glow without ever having been blighted or withered by life's ravages and emotional strains.

Such a pretty mouth! Such pretty teeth! And yet it was as though she dared not smile!

I compared her with Madame Chantal. Mademoiselle Pearl was unquestionably better, a hundred times better: she was altogether finer, nobler, and more dignified.

I was staggered by what I had seen. The champagne was being poured. I held up my glass to my queen and toasted her health with a nicely turned compliment. I could see that she wanted to hide her face in her napkin but when she wet her lips with the clear, light wine, everyone cried: 'The queen drinks! The queen drinks!' And she turned bright red and coughed and spluttered. They all laughed. But I could see very well that everybody in the house was genuinely fond of her.

III

As soon as dinner was over, Chantal took me by the arm. It was time for his cigar—a sacrosanct moment of the day. If he was by himself, he would normally step outside and smoke it in the street. If he had someone to dinner, they would have a game of billiards and he would smoke as he played. That evening, a fire had even been lit in the billiard-room, because of Twelfth Night. My old friend reached for his cue, an extra-slim one which he chalked with great care, and then he said: 'You can break, my buckeroo!'

Although I was 25 he still called me by such names, for he had known me since I was a very small boy.

So I broke. I managed a couple of cannons and missed quite a few more. But the thought of Mademoiselle Pearl was still running around inside my head and I came out with a question: 'Tell me, Monsieur Chantal, is Mademoiselle Pearl any relation?'

He paused in mid-shot, seemed rather startled and stared at me: 'You mean you don't know? You've never heard the story?'

'What story?'

'Didn't your father ever tell you?'

'Never.'

'How odd! How very, very odd! It's quite a tale.'

He paused a moment and then went on: 'If you only knew how strange it is that of all the times you could choose, you should ask me about it on Twelfth Night!'

'Why?'

Why? I'll tell you. It all happened forty-one years ago, forty-one years this very night, at Epiphany. In those days we lived at Roüy-le-Tors. We owned a house on the ramparts. I'll have to tell you about the house first so that you'll be able to follow. Roüy is built on a hill, or rather a hillock, which stands above a great flat expanse of grass and meadow. We had a house there with a hanging garden which stood high in the air on top of the old defensive walls. So the house was in the town and the front door opened onto the street, while the garden looked out over the plain. There was also a way out of the garden into the surrounding countryside, a door at the bottom of a secret flight of steps which led down inside the thick walls, just like the ones you read about in novels. A road ran past this door which was armed with a loud bell, for to save the long hike round, the country people used to bring their produce in that way.

So you get the lie of the land. Now that year, come Twelfth Night, it had been snowing for a week. It was like the end of the world. When we went out on the ramparts to take a look at the plain below, the endless white land, unrelievedly white, hard-frozen, and gleaming as though it had been polished, made a chilling sight. It was as though the good Lord had parcelled up the earth and sent it for store in the granaries of ancient worlds. I tell you, my boy, it was a sorry spectacle.

The whole family was together in those days and we were a numerous tribe: my father and mother, my uncle and aunt, my two brothers, and four girls who were cousins of ours. They were all pretty—I married the youngest of 'em. Of all that crowd, there are only three of us left now: my wife, myself, and a sister-in-law who lives in Marseilles. My God, it's amazing how families just drop away! It gives me the shivers just to think of it. I must have been 15 at the time because I'm 56 now.

Anyway, we were getting ready for Twelfth Night and were all terrifically excited. Everyone was in the drawing-room waiting for dinner when my older brother, Jacques, said: 'There's been a dog howling down on the plain for the last ten minutes. Poor thing must be lost.'

The words were hardly out of his mouth when the bell at the garden door rang. It made a deep, loud clang, like a church bell, and pretty funereal it was too. It sent a shiver through all of us. My father called a servant and told him to go and see what was up. We waited in total silence, thinking of the snow blanketing the land for miles around. When the servant returned, he said he couldn't see anything. The dog was still howling and the sound seemed to be coming from the same spot.

We sat down round the table, feeling slightly uneasy, especially us younger ones. All went smoothly until we got to the roast and then the bell began ringing again. It rang three times, three long, loud peals which made our fingers tingle and stopped our breath short. We sat there, forks poised, looking at each other, straining our ears and struck by a sort of unearthly fear.

In the end, it was my mother who spoke: 'It's very odd that whoever it was should take such a time to come back and ring again. Don't go by yourself, Baptiste. One of the gentlemen will go with you.'

My uncle François stood up. He was a huge man who was proud of his strength and feared nothing. My father said: 'Take a gun. You never know what it might be.' But my uncle just took a stick and went off with the servant.

The rest of us remained where we were, not eating, not talking, but quaking with terror and alarm. Father tried to reassure us: 'You'll see,' he said, 'it'll be a beggar or somebody who's got lost in the snow. The first time he rang no one answered straight away, so he probably had another try at finding his way and then, when he couldn't, he came back to our door.'

My uncle seemed to be away for about an hour. In the end, he came back furious and cursing: 'Nobody there. Must be some blasted practical joker. There's just that damned dog howling out there about a hundred metres from the foot of the wall. If I'd had a gun with me, I'd have shot him. That would have shut him up.'

We returned to our interrupted dinner but everybody felt apprehensive. We all sensed that it was not all over, that something was about to happen, and that sooner or later the bell would ring again.

It rang at the precise moment when the Twelfth-cake was being cut. All the men stood up together. Uncle François, who'd been putting away the champagne, was so beside himself as he announced that he was going to kill the damned thing that both my mother and my aunt grabbed hold of him to stop him. Father had a cool head but was slightly lame (he had walked with a limp ever since he broke a leg when he was thrown by a horse), yet even he said that he wanted to know who it was and that he was going. My brothers, who were 18 and 20, ran to get their guns, and since no one was paying any special attention to me, I bagged an old blunderbuss and got ready to join the expedition.

We moved off at once. Father and Uncle François led the way with Baptiste who carried a lantern. Then came my brothers, Jacques and Paul, and I brought up the rear, in spite of the pleadings of my mother who stayed at the door to the garden with her sister and my four cousins.

More snow had fallen during the past hour and the trees were weighed down with it. The pine trees bent under their heavy, pallid mantle and looked like white pyramids or huge sugar-loaves. Through the grey curtain of tiny swirling flakes we could just about make out the lighter shapes of bushes which stood out palely against the dark. The snow was falling so fast that visibility was no more than ten metres. Still, the lantern lit up the ground in front of us well enough. By the time we started going down the spiral steps inside the ramparts, I was pretty scared. I felt there was somebody coming down behind me who was about to grab me by the shoulders and carry me off. I wanted to turn back, but since this would mean going back through the garden by myself, I did not dare.

I heard the door leading to the plain outside being opened. Then my uncle started swearing again: 'Hell and damnation! He's gone! Just give me one quick sight of his shadow and I'll get the swine!'

It was eerie seeing the plain, or rather feeling it there, because you couldn't see it. All you could see was a never-ending covering of snow—snow overhead and underfoot, in front, to the right, to the left, snow everywhere.

Uncle François went on: 'Hello, there's that dog howling again. I'll show him I can handle a gun. Anyhow, it'll be something done.'

But father, who was a kind-hearted man, said: 'It would be better all round if we went and fetched the wretched animal back here. The poor thing's howling with hunger. It's barking for help. It's calling like a man in distress.'

So we set off through the curtain of white, through the thickly falling, unrelenting snow, through the froth and foam filling the night and the air, whirling, hanging above our heads, swooping down and chilling our flesh as it melted, leaving us smarting as each small white flake landed on bare skin with sudden sharp pricks like little burns.

We sank up to our knees in the soft, cold drifts, and had to lift our legs and step very high to be able to walk at all. As we advanced, the dog's barking became more distinct and much louder. Uncle François shouted: 'There he is!' We all stopped to look, as is only prudent when you come across an enemy at night.

I couldn't make anything out. But then, coming up on the others, I saw it. The dog was a frightening and unreal sight. It was big and black, a long-haired Alsatian with a wolf's head, standing on all fours at the head of the long shaft of light cast on the snow by the lantern. It didn't move. It had stopped barking. It was watching us.

Uncle François said: 'That's odd. He's not coming to meet us and he's not backing away either. I've half a mind to put a shot across his bows.'

But father said firmly: 'No. We're going to have to catch him.'

Then my brother Jacques said: 'But he isn't on his own. There's something else just by him.'

There was indeed something just behind him, a grey shape which we couldn't identify. We moved forward gingerly.

When it saw us coming nearer, the dog sat down on its hindquarters. It didn't look dangerous. On the contrary, it seemed pleased to have succeeded in attracting our attention.

Father went right up to it and stroked it. The dog licked his hands. Then we saw that it was tied to the wheel of a small cart, a sort of closed doll's pram, swathed in three or four woollen blankets. Somebody carefully raised the blankets and when Baptiste brought the lantern right up to the door of the contraption, which looked rather like a nest on wheels, we saw a small child asleep inside.

We were all so staggered that we just stood there speechless. Father recovered first and, being a good-hearted soul with a penchant for the dramatic, he put his hand on the roof of the little carriage and said: 'You may have been abandoned, but we will take you in!' He told my brother Jacques to push our piece of human flotsam home while we followed.

Speaking his thoughts aloud, father went on: 'We have here a love child whose poor mother came and rang my doorbell on this night of Epiphany in memory of the Lord who was once a baby Himself!'

Then he stopped again and at the top of his voice turned through the four quarters of the sky and four times he shouted: 'We shall give him a home!' Then, putting his hand on his brother's arm, he murmured: 'Think what would have happened if you'd shot the dog, François . . .'

Uncle François did not answer, but under cover of the darkness made the sign of the cross, for he was very religious for all his damning and blasting.

The dog had been untied and followed us in.

Believe me, the way we all trooped back to the house was a sight to behold! To start with, we had a lot of trouble getting the little cart up the steps inside the wall. But we managed it and wheeled it right into the hall.

Mother was very funny about it, pleased but flustered. My four small cousins (the youngest was 6) fussed like old hens round a roost. In the end the child, still asleep, was removed from its little carriage. It was a little girl, about six weeks old. Among the blankets she was wrapped in we found ten thousand francs in gold: ten thousand francs! Father later invested the money so that she would have a dowry. So her parents weren't poor people . . . perhaps she was the child of some nobleman and the wife or daughter of one of the town's worthies . . . or then again. . . . We thought of all sorts of conjectures but came up with nothing definite, nothing at all, not a clue. Nobody even recognized the dog. It was new to the area. Even so, the man or woman who had rung our bell three times must have known my parents to have selected them like that.

And that's how Mademoiselle Pearl came to live in the Chantal house when she was just six weeks old.

Actually, we didn't call her Mademoiselle Pearl until much later. At first we had her christened Marie Simonne Claire. The 'Claire' was intended to be used as a surname.

I can tell you that we made a pretty odd sight as we trooped back into the dining-room bearing the baby who was now awake and looking round at the people and the lights with puzzled, uncertain, blue eyes.

We sat down again round the table and the cake was divided up. I was king and, like you just now, I chose Mademoiselle Pearl to be queen. At the time, she had no idea of the honour of it.

Well, the child was adopted and brought up in the family. She grew up. The years passed. She was sweet-natured, good, and obedient. Everybody loved her and would have spoiled her dreadfully if mother had not put a stop to it.

Mother was a person who had a love of order and a proper respect for rank. She was perfectly prepared to treat little Claire just as she treated her own sons, but insisted that the distance which separated us was suitably underlined and the situation made absolutely clear. And so, as soon as the child was of an age to take it all in, she told her the whole story and gave her to understand, in the kindest, even tenderest

way, that for us Chantals she was just an adopted daughter
who had been given a home and that she was, in a word, an
outsider.

Claire surprised us by grasping the situation instinctively,
and with unusual perceptiveness. She succeeded in occupying and keeping the place allotted to her with such tact,
grace, and sweetness that she moved my father almost to
tears.

Even mother was so touched by the warmth of her
gratitude and by the faintly overawed devotion which the
pretty, loving creature showed, that she began calling her
her daughter. Sometimes, when little Claire had done
something good, something thoughtful, mother would hoist
her glasses onto her forehead, a gesture which always meant
that something had moved her, and say: 'Why, the child's a
pearl, a real pearl!' The name stuck and little Claire became,
and always has been for us, Mademoiselle Pearl.

IV

Monsieur Chantal fell silent. He was sitting on the billiard
table, with his legs dangling. With his left hand he was
playing with a billiard ball while with his right he fiddled
with the cloth we called the 'blackboard duster', which was
used for wiping off numbers chalked up on the slate
scoreboard. Slightly flushed, he spoke in a muted whisper,
and what he said was for his own benefit now. Lost in
memories, he gently turned over bygone things and old
happenings which surfaced in his mind, just as you might
stroll through the garden of the house you were brought up
in, where every tree, every path, and every plant—the
prickly holly, the sweet-smelling bays, the yews with the
luscious red berries which squash when you press them with
your fingers—brings some small detail of your past life
rushing back with every step you take, one of those
delightful, momentous trifles which are the very stuff, the
weft, of life itself.

I stood in front of him, leaning with my back to the wall,
with my hands resting on my now useless cue.

After about a minute, he went on; 'My God, she was a

good-looking girl when she was 18 . . . very winning . . . quite perfect. Oh she was pretty, so pretty . . . and good . . . a fine girl . . . utterly charming. . . . Her eyes . . . her eyes were blue . . . clear . . . bright. . . . I've never seen eyes like them, never!'

He fell silent once more. I asked: 'Why did she never marry?'

His answer was directed not at me but at the question posed by the word which had cropped up: 'marry'.

'Why? Why? She never wanted to, that's why. She had a dowry of thirty thousand francs and there were several offers for her hand. But she didn't want to! At the time she seemed rather miserable. That was when I married my cousin Charlotte, now my wife, to whom I had been engaged for six years.'

I looked at Monsieur Chantal and had the impression that I had stepped inside his mind. I felt I had stumbled into one of those cruel, unspectacular dramas which honest, upright, reproachless people can experience; that I had blundered into a nest of unspoken, unexplored feelings, of the kind which have never been openly acknowledged, not even by the people who are their silent, resigned victims. Bold curiosity made me say out of the blue: 'Are you the one who should have married her, Monsieur Chantal?'

He started, looked up at me, and said: 'Me? Marry who?'

'Mademoiselle Pearl.'

'How do you mean?'

'Because you loved her more than you loved your cousin.'

He looked at me. His eyes were strange, staring, and filled with panic. He stammered: 'Loved her? . . . I loved her? . . . How d'you mean? Who told you all this?'

'Nobody had to. It's pretty obvious. And it was because of her that you delayed marrying your cousin and kept her waiting for six years.'

He dropped the billiard ball he'd been holding in his left hand, grabbed the duster with both hands, and, holding it over his face, began to sob into it. The way he wept was quite distressing and made him look rather foolish, for he cried like a pressed sponge, through his eyes, nose, and mouth at the same time. He coughed, spluttered, and blew his nose in the duster, wiped his eyes with it, sneezed, and then began leaking through all the orifices in his face, to a throaty accompaniment which put me in mind of someone gargling.

I stood there feeling appalled and utterly ashamed of myself. I wanted to run away. I had no idea what to say or do or how to intervene. Then Madame Chantal's voice suddenly echoed up the stairs: 'Are you men going to make your cigars last all night?' I opened the door and shouted: 'Coming, Madame Chantal. We'll be down directly.'

I rushed over to her husband and grabbing him by the elbows, I said: 'Monsieur Chantal, old friend, listen to me. Your wife's calling you. Try and be calm! There's no time to lose. You'll have to go down. You must be calm!'

He stammered: 'Yes . . . all right. . . . I'm coming. . . . Poor girl! . . . I'm coming. . . . Say I'm on my way.'

Putting everything he had into it, he began wiping his face with the rag which for the last two or three years had been used for rubbing out the numbers chalked on the scoreboard. When he was done, his face was half red, half white, his nose, cheeks, and chin were all smudged with chalk, and his eyes were swollen and still brimming with tears.

I took him by both hands and led him off to his bedroom murmuring: 'I'm so sorry, so very sorry, Monsieur Chantal, for upsetting you . . . but . . . I had no idea. . . . I hope . . . I only hope you understand.'

He shook my hand: 'Can't be helped. . . . Sometimes things aren't very easy . . .'

He immersed his face in the wash-basin. When he straightened up, I still did not think he was presentable. But then I had an idea. He was peering anxiously into the mirror. I said: 'Just say you've got a bit of dirt in your eye and you'll be able to cry both your eyes out in front of everybody.'

And he went downstairs rubbing his eyes with his handkerchief. They were all concerned and everybody wanted to get the little bit of dirt, which they couldn't find, out of his eye, and told stories of similar cases when it had been necessary to send for a doctor.

I rejoined Mademoiselle Pearl and, burning with a curiosity which almost hurt, I stood watching her. She must certainly have been very pretty once, with those gentle eyes, so calm, so wide that they looked as if she never closed them the way other people do. She was dressed in slightly silly clothes—her style was distinctly spinsterish—which did not do much for her yet failed to make her appear at all gauche.

I had the impression that I was seeing right into her, just as I had seen inside Monsieur Chantal's feelings only moments before, and that her entire life, her humble, simple life of self-sacrifice, was being exposed to my gaze. But on my lips I felt an urge, a compulsion to question her, to know whether she too had been in love with him and whether or not she too had suffered the enduring, secret, searing anguish that is not seen or known or even guessed at but surfaces at night in dark, lonely bedrooms. I watched her, I saw her heart beat under her smockinged bodice, and I wondered if that gentle, candid face had sighed each night into her damp, absorbent pillow, and sobbed and writhed and squirmed in her hot, feverish bed.

As a child might break an ornament, to see what's inside, I whispered: 'If you'd only seen Monsieur Chantal crying just now, you'd have felt really sorry for him.'

She gave a start: 'What do you mean? Has he been crying?'

'Oh yes! He's been crying all right!'

'Whatever for?'

She seemed to be deeply moved. I replied: 'It was on your account.'

'On my account?'

'Yes. He'd been telling me how much he loved you all those years ago, and about the high price he paid for marrying his wife instead of you . . .'

Her pale face seemed to fall slightly. Her wide, calm eyes closed suddenly, so suddenly that they appeared to have shut for good. She slid from her chair and collapsed onto the floor, slowly, like a dropped scarf.

I shouted: 'Here! Help! Mademoiselle Pearl's been taken ill!'

Madame Chantal and her daughters rushed over and while they were busy fetching water and vinegar and a towel, I took my hat and made off.

I walked away quickly, emotionally pretty shaken and mentally full of remorse and regret. But there were moments too when I felt pleased: I felt I had done something commendable, something that had needed doing. I asked myself: 'Was I wrong? Was I right?' The thing was there in their souls like a bullet in an old wound. Surely they would be happier now? It was too late for the suffering to begin all over again, but not too late for them to remember it fondly.

And perhaps some evening in the not too distant spring, touched by the moonlight falling across the grass at their feet through the branches, they will hold each other in their arms and join hands in memory of all the cruel pain they bore in silence. And perhaps, too, their brief embrace will stir in their blood just a little of the ecstasy which they will never fully know, and prompt in two hearts that were dead but are suddenly alive the instant, divine sense of careless rapture which gives lovers more happiness in a single moment of abandon than other men will ever extract from their whole lives!

Rosalie Prudent

SOMEWHERE in the case before the court there was a puzzle, a mystery which neither the members of the jury, nor the presiding judge, nor even counsel for the prosecution could quite fathom.

Rosalie Prudent, unmarried, a maid in the Varambot household at Mantes, having become pregnant without the knowledge of her employers, had given birth one night in her attic room to a child which she had then killed and buried in the garden.

You have there the usual pattern of cases of baby murders committed by servant girls. But one fact remained unexplained. The search of the accused's room had turned up a complete layette made by the prisoner herself who had sat up night after night over a period of three months cutting it out and sewing it up. The grocer, from whom, with her own wages, she had bought the candles she needed for the lengthy task she had set herself, had been called as a witness. Moreover, it had been established that the local midwife, who had been alerted to her condition, had given her all the information and practical advice she might need in case she was brought to term at a time when help was not available. Furthermore, the midwife had made enquiries at Poissy about finding another position for the accused, who had expected to be dismissed from her post, since neither Monsieur nor Madame Varambot were particularly tolerant in moral matters.

Both husband and wife were in court. They were dull provincial people with private means, and they were extremely angry because this chit of a girl had defiled their home. They would have been quite happy to see her guillotined on the spot, without trial, and they had given bitter evidence against her in such a tone that what they said amounted to accusations.

The accused, a tall, good-looking girl who hailed from

upper Normandy, quite well educated for a person of her class, wept all the time and refused to answer questions. One was left surmising that she had carried out the barbarous deed in a moment of madness and despair, since all the indications were that she fully intended to keep her son and bring him up herself.

The judge again tried to make her speak, to get her to admit the truth, and in the end, after talking to her with great kindness, managed to make her understand that none of the gentlemen who where there to pass judgment on her had any wish to call for the death sentence, but on the contrary even felt rather sorry for her.

So she made up her mind.

He asked: 'Well then. Perhaps you would begin by telling who is the father of the child.' So far she had stubbornly refused to divulge his name.

She answered quickly, and as she did so she looked straight at her employers who only moments before had been saying angry, slanderous things about her.

'It was Monsieur Joseph, Monsieur Varambot's nephew.'

Husband and wife both gave a start and shouted together: 'It's not true! She's lying! It's a disgrace!'

The judge ordered them to be silent and continued: 'Go on, please, and tell us how it happened.'

Suddenly she began talking, and the words gushed out, relieving her pent-up feelings, easing her poor, lonely, battered heart, venting her grief and all her sorrows for the benefit of these sober men whom she had until now regarded as enemies and her inflexible judges.

'Yes, it was Monsieur Joseph Varambot, when he was on leave last year.'

'And what does this Joseph Varambot do?'

'He's a sub-lieutenant in the artillery, sir. Anyway, he come and stayed in the house for two months. Two months last summer. I wasn't thinking of anything particular when he starts staring at me and saying nice things and going on at me morning noon and night. I s'pose I let myself get caught, your honour. He went on about how I was a nice-looking girl and good fun . . . said he liked me. . . . And I liked

him too. . . . That's how these things happen. . . . When
you're all by yourself, without anyone to turn to, like I am,
you listen to what they say. I got nobody in the whole
world, nobody to talk to, not a soul to listen to my troubles.
I got no father, I got no mother nor brothers nor sisters, I
got nobody! So it was exackly like having a brother come
home when he starts chatting to me. Then one evening he
says would I go down by the river with him, to talk, quiet
like. I went all right. I dunno how it happened, couldn't
even say after it did. . . . He put his arm round my
waist. . . . Of course I didn't want to . . . 'course I
didn't . . . I couldn't stop him . . . the air and everything
was so nice that it made me feel like crying . . . the moon
was shining . . . I couldn't . . . . I swear . . . I just couldn't
stop meself . . . I just let him do what he wanted. . . .
Things went on like that for another three weeks, which was
as long as he stayed. I'd have followed him to the ends of the
earth. Then he went away. I didn't know I was having a
baby. I only found out the month following.' She began
sobbing so helplessly that she had to be given time to
compose herself.

Then the judge took up the questioning in the tones of a
priest in the confessional box: 'Come now, please go on.'

She began speaking again: 'When I realized I was going to
have a baby, I told Madame Boudin, the midwife, who is
sitting over there and can vouch for it. And I asked her what
I ought to do in case I was took when she wasn't there. I sat
up every night till one in the morning and got all the baby's
things made bit by bit. Then I started looking for another
position because I knew I would be dismissed. But I wanted
to stay on in the house until the very last minute, to save
money, seeing as how I don't have much and as how I'd be
needing it for the baby . . .'

'So you had no intention of killing it?'

'Oh no, your honour, the very idea!'

'But why, then, did you kill it?'

'It was like this. He came sooner than I bargained for. It
started in the kitchen just as I was finishing my pots.
Monsieur and Madame Varambot were already in bed

asleep. So upstairs I go, and hard work it was too, pulling myself up on the bannister. I lay down on the floor, which was bare boards, so as not to mess up the bed. It went on for about an hour, maybe two, maybe three, I couldn't say, the pains was terrible. And then I pushed as hard as I could. I felt him coming out and I picked him up and hugged him.

'Oh, I was happy as anything. I did all the things Madame Boudin had told me to, every one! After, I lay down him on my bed. And then I had this pain, it was so bad I thought I was going to die. If men knew how bad it gets, they wouldn't be so anxious to go round being the cause of it. I got down on my knees and then lay on the floor on my back. Then the pains started again and carried on for another hour or perhaps two, with me all by myself . . . and then out comes another one, another little baby—that made two, yes two, just like that! I picked him up like the first one and put him onto the bed so that the pair of them was lying side by side. Two! Can you imagine it? Two children! And with me earning twenty francs a month! Can you imagine what that meant, can you? One's all right, you can manage with one if you go without yourself, but not two. It was all too much for me, I suppose. There wasn't anything else I could have done, was there?

'Don't ask me what happened. I thought I'd reached the end of my tether. Hardly knowing what I was doing, I put the pillow over their faces. I couldn't keep two of them. Then I lay down on top of them. I lay there tossing and turning and crying till dawn came up. I seen it through the window. Under the pillow, they was both dead. I tucked them underneath my arm and crept downstairs, went out into the vegetable garden, got the gardener's spade, and buried them in the ground as good and deep as I could, separate and not together so that they couldn't talk about their mother, that is if little dead babies can talk. How should I know?

'But when I got back to bed, I come over so bad that I couldn't get up. The doctor was called and of course he knew at once what was up. And that's the honest truth, your honour. Do what you want with me. I'm ready.'

Half the jury were busily blowing their noses to prevent themselves weeping. Women in the public gallery sobbed.

The judge asked: 'And exactly where did you bury the other infant?'

She said: 'Which one you got?'

'Er . . . the one that was in the artichoke patch.'

'Fair enough. The other's in with the raspberries, just by the well.' And she began to sob uncontrollably and her moans were quite heartbreaking.

The accused, Rosalie Prudent, was acquitted.

Our Spot

Assault with grievous bodily harm resulting in manslaughter.
Such was the charge which landed Léopold Renard,
upholsterer, in the Assize Court.

Gathered round him, the main witnesses: Madame
Flamèche, the dead man's widow, together with Louis
Ladureau, a journeyman cabinet-maker, and Jean Durdent,
a plumber.

At the accused's side, his wife, in black, a short, ugly
woman: mutton dressed as lamb.

And this is how Léopold Renard related how it all
happened.

As God is my judge, it was an accident, and from the word
go it was me that was meant to come off worst. I never
intended it to happen. The facts speak for themselves, your
honour. I'm a decent working man. I've been an upholsterer
in the same street for sixteen years, well known, well liked,
thought well of and respected by all, as the neighbours have
said on oath, even the concierge who's not a woman who'll
spare you a smile every day of the week. I like working. I
like being careful with money, I like decent folk and honest
fun. That's what landed me where I am today, and that's
the size of it. I never intended it to happen, and I don't
think any the worse of meself that it did.

Anyroad, every Sunday now these five years past, meself
and the wife—that's her over there—have been up and off
to Poissy for the day. It gets us out into the fresh air, not to
mention letting us do a spot of fishing, which we like better
than anything. It was Mélie that put me onto it, the cow,
she's madder for it than me, damn her eyes! She's the one
what caused all this to-do, as you'll be able to see for
yourselves from what happened.

Now I'm a big, easy-going sort of chap, but there's not a
penn'orth of spite in me. Not like her! Oh dear me no! She's

nothing to look at, she's no size and there's not an ounce of fat on her, but she's nastier than a weasel. I don't say she's not got her good side, for she has, and very handy it is too for the business. But what a temper! You can ask anybody round about, even the concierge who spoke up for me just now . . . she'll tell you a thing or two about her.

She's forever telling me I'm too soft. 'Nobody would pull the wool over my eyes like this! I wouldn't let anybody walk over me like that!' If I'd listened to her, your honour, I'd have been in at least three fights a month . . .

Madame Renard interrupted him: 'That's right! Tell the whole world. But just you remember: them that laugh last laugh longest!'

He turned and faced her good-naturedly: 'I'm in my rights to say what I like about you. It ain't you that's on trial here.'

Then turning back to the bench:

Now where was I? Oh yes, I was saying that we used to go down Poissy way of a Saturday evening so as we could be out fishing at first light next morning. It got to be such a habit that it became what they call second nature to us. Three years ago this summer, I found this spot, some spot it was an' all, lots of shade, eight foot of water at least and maybe ten, a real pool, with deep places running in right under the bank, a haven for the fish and an anglers' paradise. That spot, your honour, I had every right to think of as being mine, since I was the one that discovered it, like Columbus discovered America. Everybody thereabouts knew about it, unanimous it was. 'That spot', they used to say, 'is Renard's spot.' And nobody would have dreamed of fishing there, not even Monsieur Plumeau who's well known—I hope he won't be offended if I say so—for pinching other people's spots.

Anyroad, knowing as how I could always count on having my spot, I treated it as if it was my very own. As soon as I got there on a Saturday, I'd get into *Delilah*—*Delilah* is my Norwegian skiff, I had her made special at the Fournaise yard, she's light but she's steady. As I was saying, we'd get aboard *Delilah* and set the bait. There's no one like me for baiting, and all me mates know it. If you was to arsk how I prepare it, I couldn't ever tell you. It's got nothing to do with the accident. I couldn't say how, it's my secret. There must be more'n two hundred who have arsked. I been offered no ends of drinks and whitebait dinners and fish-stews to make me talk. You should see how the chub go for it! I can tell you, I've had all sorts tried on me to get me to let them in on it. There's only the wife that knows . . . and she'd not give it away any more'n I would. Isn't that a fact, Mélie?

The Judge interrupted: 'Will you come to the point!'
   The accused went on:

All right! I'm coming to it! Anyroad, that Saturday, 8 July, we'd got the 5.25 down, and before we had our supper, we went off to set the bait, just like we did every Saturday. The weather was set fair. I said to Mélie: 'Hey up, looks as if it'll be a grand day tomorrow.' And she says: 'Red sky at night.' We don't talk a lot when we're together.

When we'd done, we went back and had our supper. I was happy as a sandboy and felt like a drink. And that's what caused the bother, your honour. I said to Mélie: 'Mélie, it's a grand evening. I think I'll try a bottle of nightcap.' It's a nice little wine and we called it that because if you take a drop too much, it stops you sleeping and sits on your head just like a nightcap, if you take my meaning.

So she says: 'Do as you please, but it'll make you feel bad and you won't be able to get up in the morning.' That was true: it was sensible, it was reasonable. I admit it. But I couldn't resist and downed the whole bottle. All this to-do came out of that bottle.

The upshot was I couldn't get to sleep. Heaven help me, at two in the morning I still had that winy old nightcap sitting on my head. Then bang! I drops off dead to the world so that I wouldn't have heard the last trump if the Angel of the Lord hisself had blown it in my earhole.

Any rate, the wife wakes me at six. I jump out of bed and in two ticks it's on with my trousers and jersey. A bit of a lick round the ears and we're climbing aboard *Delilah*. But it's too late! When I got to my spot, there's somebody else there already! Nothing like it ever happened before, your honour, not in three years! I felt just like somebody was robbing me with me just standing and watching them do it. I said: 'Hell and damnation! Damn and blast!' And then the wife starts into me: 'So much for your nightcaps. See what you've gone and done with your boozing! I suppose you're happy now, you great clown!'

I didn't say anything. It was all true, every word.

All the same, I tied up near my spot so as to be handy for any leavings that might be going. And perhaps the other chap wouldn't catch anything and would maybe go away.

He was small and thin, dressed in white trousers, and he had this great big straw hat on his head. He had his missis with him, a great fat lump sitting behind him doing her embroidering.

When she saw us settling in just by my spot, she starts muttering: 'Anybody'd think there wasn't no other places on the river.'

And the wife, who was boiling, replies: 'People that's been brought up right would ask first what the done thing was before going around squatting in places that's reserved!'

I didn't want trouble, so I said: 'Shut up, Mélie. Leave off, will you? Let's just wait and see.'

Anyroad, we'd run *Delilah* in under the willows, we'd got out of her and Mélie and me was fishing away, side by side, just a bit away from the other two.

At this point, your honour, I'm going to have to go into details.

We hadn't been there five minutes when this bloke's line starts bobbing up and down two or three times. And then he pulls one out, a chubb, thick as the top of my leg it was, well p'raps not quite, but pretty near. My heart's going thump, thump, I'm sweating cogs and Mélie's saying: 'Did you see that, you soak, just take a look at that!'

Just then, Monsieur Bru, who's got the grocer's shop at

Poissy, he's a gudgeon man himself, rows by in his boat and
shouts over at me: 'I see somebody's taken your spot,
Monsieur Renard.' And I shout back: 'That's right,
Monsieur Bru, there's some people who got no consideration
and no idea of what's done and what ain't done.'

The little bloke in the white trousers just across from me
didn't look as if he'd heard, nor his great fat lump of a wife,
the cow!

The Judge interrupted him a second time: 'Have a care!
Your remarks are offensive to the widow Flamèche who is
present in court.'

Renard apologized: 'I'm very sorry. I got carried away by
my feelin's.'

Anyroad, a quarter of an hour hadn't gone by when the
bloke in the white trousers lands another chub—and
another almost on top of it, and then another one five
minutes after.

There was tears in my eyes. And then I felt Madame
Renard seething. She went on at me all the time: 'Oh, I
never saw the like! You do realize he's stealing your fish,
don't you? You'll catch nowt. You'll not even get a frog.
Oooh! it makes my hands itch just thinking about it.'

And I kept saying to meself: 'Just hang on till dinner
time. He'll pack up his poaching and go off for his dinner
and I'll get me spot back.' For you see, your honour, I
always have mine on the job every Sunday. We bring our
own dinner with us on the *Delilah*.

And then it strikes twelve! But the swine had a cold
chicken wrapped in newspaper, and while he was chomping
away on it he lands another chub!

Mélie and me have ours, just a snack, hardly anything
really, our hearts wasn't in it.

Then to help it go down, I took a look at the paper. Every
Sunday regular, I read *Gil Blas** sitting in the shade of the
river bank. It's the day Colombine appears—you know,
Colombine, as writes them articles in *Gil Blas*? I used to get
the wife worked up by pretending I knew this Colombine. It

wasn't true, I didn't know her, never clapped eyes on her, not that it matters, anyway she's a very good writer. And, for a woman, she don't half come out with some things! Anyroad, she's all right by me, there's not many a one can touch her.

So I start having the wife on, but straight off she loses her rag something chronic, so I shut up.

Just then, on the other side of the river, our two witnesses showed up: that's them over there, Monsieur Ladureau and Monsieur Durdent. We knew each other by sight.

The bloke had begun fishing again. He was pulling them out so fast that it made me go weak at the knees. And then his missis pipes up: ' 'Ere, Désiré, this ain't half a good spot! We'll have to come back 'ere always!'

I felt a shiver running up and down my spine. And the wife kept saying over and over: 'Call yourself a man! Chicken blood, that's what you got in your veins!'

Then all of a sudden, I tell her: 'Look, I think I'd better be off. I might do something I'd be sorry for.'

And just as if she was dangling a red-hot poker in front of my face, she hissed: 'Call yourself a man! Look at you! Running away and just letting them have our spot. You're no better than that Bazaine!'*

This got right under my guard. But I didn't flinch.

But then this bloke lands a bream like I never saw in the whole of my life. Never.

And the wife starts talking again in a loud voice, but as if she was thinking thoughts, like. You can see from here what tack she was on. She said: 'If you arsks me, I'd say that fish there is a stolen fish, seeing as how it was us that set the bait in our spot. You'd think the least they could do was to pay us back for what we spent on the bait.'

Then the bloke in the white trouser's wife starts too: ' 'Ere, are you referrin' to us?'

'I'm referrin' to people that steal fish and get the benefit of money laid out by other folk.'

'Are you saying we're stealing fish?'

And they set to arguing, and next they're calling each other names. Blimey! Those two didn't half come out with choice items! They was hollering so loud that, for a laugh, the two witnesses there who was on the opposite bank, started calling out: 'Hey! You two over there! Let's have some hush. You'll stop your old men fishing with all that row!'

The fact is that the bloke in the white trousers and me stayed sitting still as tree-stumps. We stopped there, staring into the water, as if we couldn't hear a thing. But oh dearie me, we heard it all right:

'You're a liar!'

'Bloody ole bag!'

'Trollop!'

'Slut!'

And backwards and forwards they went at it. A sailor couldn't have taught them much.

All of a sudden, I hear this noise back of me. I turn round. It was the fat woman going hell for leather for the wife with her sunshade. Thwack! Wollop! Mélie takes a couple of good swipes. But then she loses her rag, and when Mélie loses her rag, she just lashes out. She grabs this fat woman by the hair and bang! bang! there's thumps and clouts like ripe plums falling off a tree.

If it had been just me, I'd have let them get on with it. Men against men, and women against women. Mixed brawling is out, right? But the little bloke in the white trousers shoots up like a jack-in-the-box and starts going for the wife. Now hold on! Just a minute! I'm not having any of that, friend! I land him one with my fist. Then bang! Wollop! I stick him one in the face and another in the gut. Up go his arms and legs and he falls backwards into the river, smack in the middle of our spot.

I'd have fished him out like a shot, honest, your honour, if I'd had a minute to spare. But to cap it all, the fat woman was getting the best of it and was really laying into Mélie. Now I know I shouldn't have gone in to sort it out while the bloke was going down for the third time. But I never thought he'd drown. I just said to meself: 'That'll cool him off!'

So I go up to the women to separate them. And it's me

that cops it: thumps, nails, teeth, the lot. Blimey, a right couple of bitches!

Anyroad, to cut a long story short, it took me a good five minutes, maybe ten, to get them apart. They just wouldn't let go.

I turn round. Nothing to be seen. The water's calm as a millpond. And these blokes on the other bank was shouting: 'Get him out! Get him out!'

It's all right saying that, but I can't swim, much less dive, that's for sure.

In the end, the chap who looks after the weir came with two men with poles. The whole thing lasted a good quarter of an hour. They found him at the bottom of my pool, under eight foot of water—I told you it was that deep, and the bloke in the white trousers was under all of it.

That's how it was and I hereby swear to it. I'm innocent, your honour.

After the witnesses had given evidence confirming his story, the accused was acquitted.

Clochette

HOW strange are those old memories which haunt you and simply cannot be persuaded to go away, try as you might!

This one is old, so old that I cannot comprehend for the life of me why it should have stayed so strong and green in my mind. Since that time, I have witnessed so many sinister, moving, and dreadful things that I am amazed that hardly a day goes by when I do not see the face of old Clochette, exactly as I knew her all those years ago when I was 10 or 12.

Clochette was an old seamstress who came once a week, on a Tuesday, to mend clothes and linen in my parents' house. They lived in one of those country places which are called 'manors' but are really no more than old houses with pointed roofs and four or five farmsteads grouped round them.

The village, a large village, a small town really, was visible a few hundred metres off, nestling round the church which was made of time-blackened red brick.

Every Tuesday old Clochette would arrive between half-past-six and seven in the morning, go straight up to the linen room, and settle down to work.

She was tall and thin and bearded—no, hairy, rather, for she had whiskers all over her face, astounding, unexpected whiskers sprouting in unbelievable bunches and curly tufts which seemed to have been sown by some madman all over her large face and made her look like a policeman in skirts. Hair grew on her nose, in her nose, around her nose, on her chin and over her cheeks, and her eyebrows, excessively thin and long, quite grey, very bushy and bristling, looked for all the world like a pair of moustaches which had been put there by mistake.

She walked with a limp, not an ordinary limp, but a limp which made her rock like a ship at anchor. When she put the full weight of her large, crooked, bony frame on her good leg, she seemed to be gathering herself up to crest some monstrous wave and then, suddenly plummetting as though about to disappear into a deep trough, she would sink into the ground. When she walked, she pitched and rolled and made you think of a ship in a storm. With each step she took, her head, on which she always wore a huge white mob-cap which trailed ribbons down her back, seemed to sweep the horizon, from north to south and south to north.

I adored old Clochette. The moment I got up, I would run up to the linen room where I would find her sewing busily, with her feet on a foot-warmer. When I arrived, she would force me to take the foot-warmer and sit me down on it so that I wouldn't catch cold there in her enormous chill room under the eaves. 'There, dear. The cold draws all the blood from the chest,' she would say.

She used to tell me stories as she darned with fingers which were bent but nimble. Behind her thick-lensed, amplifying glasses—for age had dimmed her sight— her eyes seemed huge, strangely unplumbed and ambiguous.

As far as I can remember from the things she told me, things which stirred me at a time when I had the heart of a child, she had the generous spirit of a woman of no substance. She saw things clearly and simply. She would tell me about what went on in the village, about the cow that had got out of its barn and had been found one morning standing in front of Prosper Malet's mill watching the wooden sails going round, or about the hen's egg that had been discovered in the church belfry and how no one ever knew how the bird that laid it had managed to find its way up there, or about Jean-Jean Pilas's dog which had travelled over twenty miles to retrieve a pair of its master's trousers stolen by a passer-by as they were hanging up to dry outside the door after a walk in the rain. She told me these simple tales in such a way that to my mind they assumed the proportions of unforgettable dramas and grandiose, poetic mysteries. The clever narratives made up by poets which my mother related each evening never had the pungent

quality, the expansiveness, and the power of the old
countrywoman's stories.

One Tuesday, having spent the whole morning listening to
old Clochette, I thought later in the day, after I had been
out gathering hazelnuts with the servant in Hallets' wood
behind the Noirpré farm, that I would go up and see her
again. I remember it as clearly as I do things that happened
yesterday.

As I opened the linen-room door, I saw the old girl
stretched out on the floor by her chair, face down, her arms
spread-eagled, still clutching her needle in one hand and
one of my shirts in the other. One of her legs, doubtless her
good one, in its blue stocking, was caught under her chair.
Her glasses gleamed at the foot of a wall some way away
where they had rolled.

Yelling my head off, I turned and fled. People came
running and a few minutes later I learned that old Clochette
was dead.

I cannot say what deep, dreadful, heart-breaking feelings
gripped my childish heart. I walked slowly downstairs to
the drawing-room and hid in a dark corner, clambering onto
a huge, very old armchair where I got on my knees to cry. I
must have stayed there for some time, for night fell.

Eventually, someone came into the room with a lamp. I
remained out of sight and then overheard my mother and
father talking with the doctor whose voice I recognized.

He had been sent for at once, and he started explaining
how the accident had happened. I did not make much of
what was said. Then he sat down and said yes to a glass of
liqueur and a biscuit.

He went on talking and what he said remains and will
remain engraved in my memory until the day I die! I do believe
I can even reproduce almost exactly the words he used.

Ah! (he said), a sad case. She was my very first patient here.
She broke her leg the day I arrived and I'd just had time to
wash my hands after stepping down from the coach when I
was sent for urgently, for it was a bad break, very bad.

She was 17 and she was a very, very pretty girl. Who'd have believed it? I've never said anything about what happened and apart from myself and one other person who no longer lives in the district, no one ever knew. But now she's dead, there's no need for me to be so discreet.

At the time, a new teacher had just come to live in the village. He was good-looking and as handsomely built as any subaltern. All the girls ran after him but he wouldn't have anything to do with them, not least because he was terrified of old man Grabu, the headmaster, to whom he was answerable and who was not always in the best of tempers.

Hortense was already being employed by Grabu to do his bits of darning for him—the same Hortense who has just passed away upstairs, though after her accident they called her 'hopalong' Clochette. The young teacher noticed her and in all likelihood she was flattered to be picked out by the unattainable heart-breaker. Any rate, she fell for him and he persuaded her to meet him in the schoolhouse loft on one of her sewing days, after dark.

She pretended to go home, but instead of going down the steps when she came out of Grabu's house, she went up them and hid in the hay where she waited for her lover to come. He arrived soon after and was beginning to say sweet nothings to her when the loft door swung open a second time revealing the headmaster who asked: 'What are you doing up there, Sigisbert?'

Fearing that he would be caught, the teacher panicked and foolishly replied: 'I just came up for a bit of a rest in the hay, sir.'

The loft was very high, absolutely enormous, and pitch dark. Sigisbert pushed the terrified girl towards the far end, saying: 'Get over there and hide. I'll get the sack. Go on over there, and hide!'

Hearing whispering, the headmaster went on: 'Do I take it you're not alone?'

'Oh no, sir!'

'Oh yes, sir! I heard you talking.'

'I swear there's no one here, sir!'

'I'm going to see for myself,' the old man said. And

double-locking the door behind him, he retreated down the
stairs to fetch a candle.

At this, the young man—a coward, there are plenty like
him around—lost his head and suddenly becoming furious,
apparently kept saying: 'Go on, hide! He mustn't find you.
I'll never get another job and it'll be your fault. You'll ruin
my career! . . . Go on, hide!'

They heard the key turn in the lock.

Hortense ran over to the gable-end window overlooking
the street, flung it open, and whispered determinedly:
'Come and pick up the pieces when he's gone.'

And she jumped.

Grabu did not find anybody and clambered down again
feel rather puzzled.

A quarter of an hour later, Sigisbert called and told me
what had happened. The girl was still lying at the foot of the
wall for, having fallen two stories, she could not get up. I
went with him to get her. It was pouring with rain and I
took the poor girl back to my place. Her right leg was
broken in three places and the bone had been rammed
through the skin. She did not complain but merely said with
admirable resignation: 'It's a judgement, I got what was
coming to me.'

I called in outside help, sent for the girl's parents, and
spun them a yarn about a runaway carriage which had
knocked her over and left her lying outside my door. My
story was believed, and for a month the police went looking
for the person who had caused the accident.

And that's it, really. But I tell you that girl was a true
heroine, and I rank her with the women who have been
responsible throughout history for carrying out the finest
actions.

She never loved anyone else. She died a virgin. She was a
martyr, a soul of great price, sublime and faithful to the
end! If I did not have the greatest admiration for her, I
should not have told you this story which I would never
have divulged to anyone as long as she was alive, for reasons
which you can appreciate.

The doctor had fallen silent. My mother was crying. Father said a few words which I did not quite catch. Then they left the room.

I stayed kneeling in my armchair and through my sobs I heard a strange sound of heavy footfalls and thuds coming from the stairs.

They were bringing down Clochette's body.

Le Horla

8 MAY.—It has been a splendid day! I spent all morning stretched out on the lawn in front of my house under the huge plane tree which hangs over it and provides both shelter and shade. I love this part of the world, and I like living here because it's where I have my roots, deep, delicate roots which make a man cling to the place where his fathers before him were born and died, keep him loyal to the way people think and the things they eat, to local customs and dishes, and bind him to regional turns of speech, the accents of the farmers, and the smells of the earth and the villages and even of the air itself.

I love this house of mine where I grew up. From my windows I can see the Seine flowing along the length of my garden beyond the road. The great, broad Seine, which goes from Rouen to Le Havre, always full of boats passing by, virtually runs through my property.

Away to the left I can see Rouen, a sprawling city of blue roofs spread out beneath its population of pointed gothic spires. There are too many to count, but fragile or stolid, all are dwarfed by the ironclad steeple of the cathedral. And all are full of bells which ring out in the blue air on fine, clear mornings, and their mellow, far-off, metal-bound tolling reaches me here, a song of brass brought on the breeze, sounding faint or loud as the wind rises or dies away.

This morning was really marvellous!

At about eleven, a long convoy of boats sailed past my gates, towed by a tug the size of a bluebottle which chugged and gasped with the strain and released clouds of thick smoke.

Behind two English schooners with red flags fluttering against the sky, came a magnificent Brazilian three-master, brilliantly white and sparklingly clean and gleaming. For some reason I waved, for just seeing it gave me such pleasure.

12 May.—I have been running a slight temperature these last few days. I'm not feeling up to the mark—or rather I feel a little depressed.

What is the cause of those mysterious influences which convert our happiness into dejection and turn optimism to anguish? It is as though the air, the air we cannot see, were full of unknowable powers with mysterious force-fields which affect us in some way. I can wake up as cheerful as you could wish, with songs in my heart and an urge to sing them. Why? I go for a stroll along the river bank and then, for no reason, after walking no distance at all, I turn back feeling very down, as though something terrible were waiting for me when I got back home. Why? Is it because the touch of a sudden chill on my skin has unsettled my nerves and drawn shadows in my mind? Is it because the clouds have the shape that they have, or is it the colour of the day, the infinitely variable colour of things, which enters my eyes and confuses my thoughts? Who can tell? Everything around us, the things we see and never look at, the things we brush against and ignore, the things we touch but do not pause to feel—everything we encounter and fail to notice influences us, our organs, and via them, the way we feel, and produces effects which are instant, unexpected, and inexplicable.

How fathomless the mystery of the Unseen is! We cannot plumb its depths with our feeble senses—with eyes which cannot see the infinitely small or the infinitely great, nor anything too close or too distant, such as the beings who live on a star or the creatures which live in a drop of water . . . with ears that deceive us by converting vibrations of the air into tones that we can hear, for they are sprites which miraculously change movement into sound, a meta-morphosis which gives birth to harmonies which turn the silent agitation of nature into song . . . with our sense of smell, which is poorer than any dog's . . . with our sense of taste, which is barely capable of detecting the age of a wine!

Ah! If we had other senses which would work other miracles for us, how many more things would we not discover around us!

16 May.—I am unquestionably ill. And I was so well last month! I have a fever, a raging fever—no, it's rather a feverish restlessness which makes me as sick in mind as I am in body. I am constantly aware of a feeling of imminent danger, and I sense some impending disaster or the approach of death, and it all amounts to a presentiment which is quite likely the first sign of some illness which has yet to declare itself, but is already germinating in my blood and in my flesh.

18 May.—I've just been to see my doctor because I was not sleeping. He said my pulse was rapid, my pupils dilated, my nerves on edge, but found no symptoms which gave grounds for concern. He recommended regular showers and told me to take potassium bromide.

25 May.—No change. I am in a very strange state indeed. As evening approaches, an incomprehensible feeling of anxiety comes over me, as though the night ahead held some terrible threat. I dine quickly and then try to read; but I cannot understand the words; I can hardly focus on the letters on the page. So I walk around my drawing-room feeling oppressed by vague, irresistible fears—fear of sleeping and fear of going to bed.

About ten o'clock, I go upstairs to my bedroom. The moment I'm inside, I double-lock and bolt the door; and I feel afraid . . . but of what? . . . I never used to be afraid of anything . . . I open my wardrobes and look under the bed; and I listen . . . I listen for . . . what exactly? Isn't it strange that a minor indisposition—a circulation problem perhaps, a group of inflamed nerve-ends, or a touch of chestiness, some slight disorder of the very imperfect and delicately balanced functioning of the body mechanism— can plunge the happiest of men into despair and change the bravest into cowards? Then I get into bed and wait for sleep as some await their executioner. As I lie there terrified waiting for it to come, my heart pounds and my legs tremble; and under the warm bedclothes, my whole body continues to shake until the moment I fall into sleep as a man falls into a pit of stagnant water to drown. I cannot tell, as I once could, just when perfidious sleep which lurks nearby, waiting and watching me, will pounce on my head, close my eyes, and annihilate me.

I sleep for some time—two or three hours—and then a dream, no, a nightmare takes hold of me. I'm aware that I'm in bed asleep, I feel it, I know it, but I'm also aware of the approach of someone who looks at me, touches me, gets onto the bed, kneels on my chest, takes my neck in both hands, and squeezes and squeezes with all his strength. He wants to strangle me.

I struggle, hampered by that awful weakness which paralyses us when we dream. I try to cry out, but can't; I try to move, but can't; gasping for air, I make appalling efforts to turn over and push away whoever it is who is crushing and choking me—and I can't!

Suddenly I wake up in a panic and soaked in sweat. I light a candle. There's no one there.

Once the crisis, which recurs every night, is past, I can finally sleep, which I do, peacefully, until daybreak.

2 June.—My condition has worsened further. Whatever is the matter with me? The bromide is not doing me any good, nor the showers. Earlier on, to tire my body, though it is already pretty exhausted, I went for a long walk in the forest of Roumare. As I set out, I felt that the fresh, light, mild air full of the scents of grass and leaves was pumping new blood into my veins and putting new energy into me. I followed a wide avenue used by hunters, then turned off towards La Bouille along a narrow path between two armies of tremendously tall trees which created a green, dense, almost impenetrably dark canopy between me and the sky.

Suddenly, a shiver ran down my back—not a shiver of cold but a strange shiver of dread.

I quickened my step, uneasy at being alone in the wood, frightened for no reason, foolishly afraid of the utter solitude. All at once, I had the feeling that I was being followed, that somebody was walking just behind me, very close, close enough to touch me.

I turned round sharply. There was no one there. All I

could see behind me was the wide, straight, towering track which was empty, alarmingly empty; and ahead of me, it also stretched away out of sight, looking exactly the same that way too, and just as terrifying.

I closed my eyes. Why did I do this? And I started turning round and round on one foot, very fast, like a top. I almost fell over; I opened my eyes; the trees were spinning and the ground heaved; I had to sit down. And then I realized I did not know which way I'd come! It was peculiar, most peculiar! Not the faintest idea! Off I set, making towards the right, and eventually was brought back to the broad avenue which had led me into the middle of the forest.

3 June.—Last night was unspeakable. I've decided to go away for a few weeks. A brief holiday will probably put me back on my feet.

2 July.—I'm home again, completely cured—and I had a most delightful time. I went to the Mont Saint-Michel which I'd never seen before.

You get quite a sight if, as I did, you arrive at Avranches towards evening. The town stands on a hill. I was taken to the civic gardens which are situated at the far end of the old town. I gave a gasp of amazement. An enormous bay spread out before me as far as the eye could see between two shorelines which ran away into the distance on either side before disappearing into the mist. And in the middle of this huge sandy bay, under a clear gold sky, a strange hill loomed up dark and pointed among the dunes. The sun had just gone down and there, silhouetted against the still blazing horizon, was the outline of the fantastic rock on whose summit stood a no less fantastic monumental pile.

I was up at dawn and made straight for it. The tide was out, as it had been the previous evening, and I watched the astonishing abbey rise higher and higher above me as I drew nearer. After walking for several hours, I reached the huge stone outcrop on which stands the little town dominated by the enormous church. Climbing the steep, narrow street, I stepped into the most splendid Gothic dwelling-place ever

built for God on this earth, as large as a town, honeycombed
with low rooms crouching under vaulted roofs, and hung
with high galleries supported on slender columns. I entered,
as I said, this gigantic granite gem which is as delicate as
fine lace and bristles with towers and slim bell-turrets inside
which are spirals of steps which lead ever up; and into the
blue sky by day and the dark firmament by night these
pinnacles, linked to each other by finely worked arches,
thrust their bizarre eyries barbed with goblins, devils,
fantastic creatures, and monstrous flowers.

When I was standing on the top, I said to the monk who
was showing me round: 'This must be a splendid place to
live!'

He replied: 'It's often very windy,' and we began to talk
as we watched the tide come in, racing over the sand and
covering it with a breastplate of shining steel.

The monk told me many stories, all old stories associated
with the place, legends, endless legends.

One of them struck me forcibly. The local people who
live on the mount say that at night voices can be heard in the
dunes, accompanied by the bleating of two goats, one loud
and one faint. Unbelievers say it's nothing more than the
screeching of sea-birds which can sometimes sound like
bleating and sometimes like human cries. But fishermen
returning late swear that between the tides they have met an
old shepherd prowling through the dunes near the little
town which has been cast off from the rest of the world.
They have never seen his features which are hidden by his
cloak. He wanders along leading a goat with the face of a
man and a nanny-goat with the face of a woman, both with
coats of long white hair, and both talk all the time, arguing
in a strange language and then suddenly breaking off and
bleating for all they are worth.

I said to the monk: 'Do you believe their story?'

'I don't know,' he murmured.

I went on: 'If other creatures existed on earth besides
ourselves, how is it that we have never got to know about
them after all these centuries? Why have you never seen
them? How come I never have?'

He replied: 'Are we able to see a hundred-thousandth part of what exists? Look, the wind's getting up. Wind is the greatest natural force there is. It blows men off their feet, demolishes buildings, uproots trees, whips the sea into mountains of water, destroys cliffs, and drives great ships onto the rocks: it kills and shrieks and moans and roars. Have you ever seen it? Can you see it? And yet it exists all right.'

His simple logic silenced me. The man may have been wise or he may have been a fool. I couldn't have said which; but I held my tongue. For what he said, I had often thought myself.

3 July.—Slept badly. There is obviously something fever-ridden about this place, for my coachman has gone down with whatever I've got. When I got back yesterday, I noticed that he was unusually pale.

'What's the matter, Jean?' I asked him.

'I can't seem to get me rest, sir. Can't get to sleep at nights and then I'm all wore out all day. It's been the same ever since you went away, sir, like I was 'witched.'

The other servants are fit enough, though. But I'm very afraid that it might get me again.

4 July.—No doubt about it: it's got me all right. My old nightmares have come back. Last night I felt someone crouching on top of me. He had his lips on mine and was sucking the life out of me through my mouth, yes, drawing my life out of me like a leech. Then, having had his fill, he got off me and I awoke feeling so battered, broken, and drained that I was too weak to move. If things go on like this for another few days, I shall certainly leave this place.

5 July.—Have I gone mad? What happened, what I saw last night, is so fantastic that my head spins just thinking about it!

I had locked my door as I do now every evening; I drank half a glass of water and as I did so happened to notice that my carafe of water was full right up to the glass stopper.

Then I got into bed and fell into one of my terrifying deep

sleeps from which I was woken two hours later by an even more horrendous shock.

Picture a sleeping man who is being murdered. He wakes with a knife in his chest, groaning and covered with blood. He cannot breathe, he knows he is dying and does not understand what has happened—and you will have some idea of how I felt.

In the end, when I'd managed to collect my wits, I felt thirsty again. I lit a candle and went over to the table where I kept the carafe. I raised it and tilted my glass: nothing came out. It was empty! It was completely empty! At first I could not make it out. I was gripped by a wave of desperation which was so bleak that I had to sit down—or rather I collapsed onto a chair. Immediately I jumped up in a panic and looked all around me. Then I sat down again with the clear crystal carafe in front of me, paralysed by astonishment and fear. I stared at it, trying to work out what was going on. My hands shook. Had someone drunk the water? Who could it have been? It must have been me. Who else could it have been but me? If so, I have been walking in my sleep and, without knowing it, living a mysterious double life which makes a man suspect that two separate beings exist inside us, or that there are times, when our soul is lulled and torpid, when an unknown, invisible alien takes over our captive body which it obeys as it obeys us, only even more readily.

How can anyone have any idea of the appalling horror I felt? Who could possibly understand the state of mind of a man in full possession of his faculties, wide awake, and with all his wits about him, who can stare in terror into a glass carafe and wonder what has happened to a small quantity of water which has vanished while he was sleeping! I remained there not moving until dawn, not daring to go back to bed.

6 July.—I am going mad. Someone drank all the water in my carafe again last night—or rather, I did!

But was it me? Did I do it? Who else could it be? Who? Oh God, I am going mad. Who will save me?

10 July.—I have just tried some surprising experiments.

I really am mad! And yet . . .

On 6 July, before going to bed, I placed some wine, milk, and water together with bread and some strawberries on my table.

Someone drank—I drank—all the water and a little milk. The wine, bread, and strawberries were left untouched.

On 7 July I repeated the experiment which gave exactly the same results.

On 8 July I omitted the water and the milk. Nothing was touched.

Finally, on 9 July, I just set out milk and water on the table, and took good care to wrap both carafes in white muslin cloths and tie the stoppers down with string. Then I rubbed graphite on my lips, beard, and hands and turned in.

I was overpowered by sleep and then subjected to the same ghastly awakening. I had not stirred and there were no smears on the bedclothes. I rushed across to the table. The cloths around the bottles were absolutely unmarked. I undid the string, shaking with fear. Somebody had drunk all the water and all the milk. Oh God! . . .

I am leaving shortly for Paris.

12 July.—Paris. I must have been panicking these last few days! In all probability, I was the plaything of a fevered imagination—unless I really do walk in my sleep or have been acting under one of those well-documented but nevertheless inexplicable influences called suggestions. Either way, my panic verged on madness, and twenty-four hours in Paris have been enough to put me back on an even keel.

Yesterday, after attending to some business and paying a few calls, which blew the cobwebs out of my head and put new life into me, I ended the evening at the Théâtre Français. There was a play on by Alexandre Dumas *fils*,* a man with a strong, lively mind, who completed the cure. Solitude is obviously dangerous for people with active brains. We need men around us who have ideas and like talking. Leave us alone for any length of time, and we start filling the void with supernatural creatures.

I walked back to my hotel along the boulevards in high fettle. As I made my way through the jostling crowd, I thought, not without an ironical smile, about the terrors and wild conjectures of last week, for I believed, yes, I really believed that an invisible being was living beneath my roof. What weak and easily disturbed brains we have, and how we panic the moment we become aware of some insignificant fact which we cannot explain!

Instead of dropping the matter and saying: 'I do not understand because the cause escapes me', we immediately begin inventing alarming mysteries and occult powers.

14 July.—Bastille Day. I have been out walking through the streets. I enjoyed the fireworks and the flags as much as if I were still a little boy. It is really very silly to expect people to be happy on a set day appointed by order of the government. The general public is a brainless herd which swings between stupid passivity and bloodthirsty rebellion. You tell it: 'Enjoy yourself' and it enjoys itself. Tell it: 'Go and wage war on your neighbour' and it goes off and fights. Tell it: 'Vote for the Emperor' and it votes for the Emperor. The next moment, you say: 'Vote for the Republic' and it votes for the Republic.

Its rulers are just as stupid. But instead of obeying men, they obey principles which cannot be anything else but inane, sterile, and false for the simple reason that they are principles, that is ideas which are thought to be incontrovertible and immutable in a world where no one can be sure of anything, not even light, which is an illusion, or sound, which is another.

16 July.—Yesterday I witnessed a number of things which have seriously disturbed me.

I was dining at the house of my cousin, Madame Sablé, whose husband commands the 76th Light Horse at Limoges. I found myself next to two young women, one of whom was the wife of a medical man, a Doctor Parent, who has a considerable interest in nervous disorders and the unusual phenomena which are currently being generated by experiments in hypnosis and suggestion.*

He told us at some length about the amazing results obtained by English researchers and the doctors of the Nancy school. The facts he produced struck me as being so bizarre that I confessed that they left me completely sceptical.

'We are on the point', he asserted, 'of discovering one of the most important of nature's secrets, that is to say one of nature's most important secrets on this earth, since it is quite clear that there are far more important secrets out there among the stars. Ever since man first learnt to think and began speaking his thoughts and writing them down, he has been aware of a mystery beyond the reach of his crude, imperfect senses, and he has attempted to make good the deficiency of his perceptions through the power of his intellect. As long as his intelligence remained on a rudimentary level, the feeling that he was haunted by invisible phenomena assumed crude, frightening forms. Hence the popular belief in the supernatural and all those legends which tell of wandering spirits, fairies, hobgoblins, and ghosts, and I would go so far as to include the myth of God, for our notions of a journeyman-creator, from whatever religion we derive them, are really the feeblest, the most foolish inventions imaginable, the most unacceptable products of the frightened brains of created life. Nothing could be truer than Voltaire's dictum: "God made man in his own image, but man has surely returned the compliment." '*

'But for a little over a century now, there has been a feeling that something new is happening. Mesmer* and a number of others have set us on a quite unexpected path and we have reached a point, especially in the last four or five years, where we are getting astonishing results.'

My cousin, who was also highly sceptical, smiled. Doctor Parent said: 'Would you like me to try to send you to sleep, madame?'

'Yes, very well.'

She sat in an armchair and he began staring hypnotically into her eyes. For my part, I suddenly felt slightly uneasy: my heart pounded in my chest and there was a tightness in my throat. I saw Madame Sablé's eyes grow heavy, her mouth tense up, and her chest begin to heave. Ten minutes later, she was asleep.

'Go and sit behind her,' said the doctor.

I did as he asked. He put a visiting card in her hands and said: 'This is a mirror. What do you see in it?'

She answered: 'I can see my cousin.'

'What is he doing?'

'Fiddling with his moustache.'

'What's he doing now?'

'Taking a photograph out of his pocket.'

'What is it a photograph of?'

'Himself.'

She was right! And that photograph had only just been delivered to me at my hotel earlier in the evening.

'How does he appear in the photograph?'

'He is standing. He's holding his hat in his hand.'

So she was seeing in the card, which was plain white, everything she would have seen had it been a mirror.

The young women were frightened and said: 'Stop! Do stop! That's enough!'

But the doctor went on: 'You will get up tomorrow at eight o'clock. Then you will go round to your cousin's hotel and beg him to lend you five thousand francs which your husband has asked you to get and will want when he is next home on leave.' Then he woke her up.

As I walked back to my hotel I mulled over the peculiar events of the evening and I was assailed by doubts, not about the absolute, unquestionable good faith of my cousin whom I had always thought of as a sister ever since we were children, but about the possibility that the doctor might be a fraud. Might he not have had a mirror concealed in his hand which he had somehow shown my hypnotized cousin at the same time as the visiting card? Professional conjurors can manage much cleverer things than that.

When I got back to my hotel I went straight to bed.

Then this morning, at about half-past-eight, I was awakened by my man who said: 'Madame Sablé is here, sir. She wishes to speak to you at once.'

I dressed hurriedly and went to see what she wanted.

She sat down looking terribly agitated. She kept staring at the floor and, without lifting her veil, said: 'I have a big favour to ask you.'

'What is it?'

'I find it very difficult to put this into words, but I have no choice. I need, I must have, five thousand francs.'

'You need money? Surely not.'

'Yes, I do. Or rather my husband does. He has asked me to find it for him.'

I was so staggered that I could only mumble some sort of answer. I wondered whether she and Doctor Parent had joined forces to pull my leg, and whether it was not all some straightforward practical joke they had planned in advance and executed extremely well.

But as I stood watching her closely, all my doubts vanished. She shook, was clearly distressed, and obviously found the situation highly embarrassing. I sensed from her voice that she was only just holding back the tears.

I knew that she was extremely well off and I carried on: 'Surely your husband can lay his hands on five thousand francs! Come now, think. Are you absolutely sure he sent you to ask me for the money?'

She hesitated for a few moments as though a great effort were required to ransack her memory, and then she answered: 'Oh yes. . . . Yes. . . . Quite sure.'

'Did he write you a letter?'

She hesitated again as she thought about this. I sensed that the effort of thinking was extremely painful for her. She did not know. All she knew was that she had to borrow five thousand francs from me for her husband. She steeled herself and lied. 'Yes. He wrote to me about it.'

'When was this? You didn't mention anything about it yesterday.'

'I got the letter this morning.'

'Can I see it?'

'No . . . no. . . . There were private things in it . . . it was too personal. . . . I . . . I . . . I burnt it.'

'So your husband has been running up debts?'

She hesitated once more and then murmured: 'I don't know.'

I said sharply: 'The fact is, cousin, I can't put my hands on five thousand francs just at the moment.'

She gave an almost agonized cry: 'Oh please! I beg you! You must find me the money!' She grew quite frantic and clasped her hands together as though she were pleading with me. As she spoke, the tone of her voice changed: she wept and stammered, driven, dominated by the irresistible order which she had been given. 'Oh, I beg you. . . . If you only knew how unhappy I am. . . . I must have the money today.'

I took pity on her. 'You'll have the money soon, I swear.'

'Oh thank you!' she cried. 'Thank you! You are so very kind.'

I went on: 'Do you have any recollection of what happened yesterday at your house?'

'Of course.'

'Do you remember Doctor Parent hypnotizing you?'

'Yes.'

'Well, he ordered you to come here this morning and borrow five thousand francs from me, and you are now merely responding to his suggestion.'

She thought for a few moments and then said: 'But it's my husband who wants the money.'

For a whole hour I tried persuading her, but failed utterly.

When she had gone, I hurried round to the doctor's. He was just about to go out. He listened with a smile and then said: 'Now do you believe?'

'Can't see I have any choice.'

'Let's go and call on your cousin.'

She was already half asleep on a chaise-longue, completely exhausted. The doctor took her pulse and fixed her with his gaze for some considerable time while he pointed one hand to her eyes which slowly closed under the irresistible influence of his magnetic power.

When she was in a trance, he said: 'Your husband does not now need five thousand francs. You will therefore forget you asked your cousin to lend you the money and if he ever mentions the matter, you will not understand him.'

Then he woke her. I took my wallet out of my pocket: 'Here. I've brought the money you asked me for this morning.'

She was so taken aback that I did not have the heart to press the point. Still, I did try to jog her memory, but she strenuously denied everything, seemed to think that I was making fun of her, and in the end very nearly got quite cross.

I am now back at my hotel. I couldn't eat a thing at lunch. The whole business has been deeply disturbing.

19 July.—A lot of people I've talked to about what happened have simply laughed in my face. I don't know what to think. A philosopher would say: Perhaps.

21 July.—Travelled down to Bougival for dinner, then spent the rest of the evening at the sailing-club ball. It's pretty clear that it all depends on places and surroundings. On the island of La Grenouillère, you would be completely mad to believe in the supernatural . . . but would you be so sure standing on top of the Mont Saint-Michel? Or in India? We are horribly open to the influence of our surroundings. I shall be going home next week.

30 July.—I've been back in my house a week. All is well.

2 August.—No change. The weather is magnificent. I spend each day watching the Seine flow by.

4 August.—The servants have been quarrelling. They say someone has been going around at night smashing the wineglasses in the cupboards. My man says it's the cook, who blames the linen-maid, who claims it was the other two. Who is responsible? It would take a clever man to know.

6 August.—This time, I know I'm not mad. I've seen him! I saw him with my own eyes! There's no doubt in my mind now: I saw him! My blood still runs cold. I can still feel the fear in my bones. I saw him!

At about two this afternoon, with the sun blazing down, I was strolling through my rosebeds where the autumn roses are just beginning to show.

I had paused to examine a variety of Battle Giant which bore three magnificent blooms, when I clearly saw the stem of the nearest rose bend, as though an invisible hand had twisted it, and then snap, as though the hand had picked it! The flower ascended, following the trajectory which an arm would have needed to follow as it brought it close to a mouth, and then remained suspended in the clear air, by itself, quite still, a ghastly blotch of red not three feet from where I stood.

I made a frantic grab for it. But there was nothing there; it had disappeared. I immediately felt extremely angry with myself, for sane, serious-minded men such as myself do not have hallucinations like this.

But was it a hallucination? I turned to see if I could locate the stem. It was there, of course, on the rose-tree, freshly broken, between the two other roses which had remained on the branch.

After that, I walked back to the house not knowing what to think. For I am now certain, as certain as I am that night follows day, that lurking somewhere around there is an invisible being which lives on milk and water, is able to touch things, pick them up, and move them around, a being who must therefore be endowed with some sort of material existence undetectable by human senses, and lives with me under my own roof.

7 August.—Had a peaceful night's sleep. He drank the water in the carafe, but did not disturb my sleep.

I wonder if I've gone mad. Walking along the river bank in the bright sunshine a little while ago, I began having doubts about my sanity, not the kind of vague doubts which I have had up to now, but specific, very real doubts. I have seen mad people. I've known some who were intelligent, lucid, even shrewd on all aspects of life except one. They may be talking about any subject clearly, easily, and profoundly when all of a sudden their train of thought founders on the reef of their folly and disintegrates, breaking up and sinking into the alarming, raging ocean fraught with surging waves, fogs, and sudden storms which is known as 'insanity'.

I would certainly believe I was mad, quite mad, if I were not aware, if I were not so absolutely sure of my state of mind, if I were not able to probe and analyse its working with such total lucidity. In short, I am a rational man who happens to see things. It seems likely that some mysterious disturbance has been produced in my brain, one of those disturbances which modern physiologists are currently attempting to describe and define. This disturbance has in all probability created a deep rift in my mind, in the order and logic of my thoughts. Similar phenomena occur in dreams which herd us through the most unlikely fantasmagoria without making us turn a hair because the regulating mechanism and our sense of proportion have been lulled to sleep, while our imagination remains wide awake and working. Might it not be the case that one of the unnoticed keys of my cerebral keyboard has become stuck? Men who have survived accidents lose their capacity for remembering names or verbs or numbers, or just dates. The locations of each part of the thinking process have now been definitively established. So there is nothing particularly surprising if my ability to process the unreality of certain hallucinations happens at the moment to be dormant.

I was thinking along these lines when I reached the water's edge. The sun was bright on the river and made the land roundabout look quite delightful. The spectacle filled me with love for life, for the swallows whose swooping flight I have always found a joy to behold, for the grasses on the bank whose soft sighing is music to my ears.

But little by little, an inexplicable feeling of unease came over me. I had the impression that some force, an occult force, was slowing me down, forcing me to stop, preventing me from going any further, telling me to turn and go back. I had that awful depressing urge to go home which comes on you when you have gone out leaving behind someone you love who is ill and whose condition you somehow sense has suddenly worsened.

So in spite of myself I returned home, quite sure that I would find bad news waiting for me, a letter, perhaps, or a telegram. But there was nothing and I was left feeling more surprised and more anxious than if I had had another fantastic vision.

8 August.—Yesterday evening was horrible. He doesn't show himself any more, but I feel him near me, spying on me, watching, probing, dominating me. He is much more frightening when he keeps himself hidden like this than if he were to give notice of his constant, invisible presence by producing supernatural phenomena.

Even so, I slept.

9 August.—Nothing, but I am afraid.

10 August.—Nothing. What will happen tomorrow?

11 August.—Still nothing. I can no longer remain in this house with these fears and thoughts rooted in my mind. I am going away.

12 August, ten o'clock at night.—All day I have been trying to get away but have not been able to manage it. I was quite determined to carry out a simple, uncomplicated act of free will—leave the house, get into my coach, and head for Rouen. But I couldn't do it. Why not?

13 August.—With certain kinds of illness, the resilience of the physical being seems to be entirely destroyed, all energy is drained, muscles turn weak, and bones become as soft as flesh and flesh as liquid as water. In a strange and very distressing way, this is precisely what I feel in my spiritual being. I have no strength left, no courage, no control over myself, not even the power to mobilize my will. I have lost the ability to will anything: but someone else is doing my willing for me; and I do what he says.

LE HORLA 293

14 August.—I am lost! Someone has taken over my mind and is controlling it! Someone is in command of all my actions, movements, and thoughts. I am nothing inside, merely a spectator enslaved and terrified by everything I do. I decide to go out. I can't. He doesn't want to. So I remain where I am, helpless and shaking, sitting in the chair where he forces me to remain seated. All I want to do is stand up and get up out of the chair, so that I might feel that I am my own master. But I can't! I am rooted to my chair, the chair is rooted to the floor, and no power on earth could ever raise it or me.

Then I have this sudden urge, an overpowering, imperious desire to go all the way down to the bottom of the garden, pick strawberries, and eat them. So I go. I pick strawberries and eat them! God! God! Oh God! Is there a God in heaven? If there is, deliver me, save me, help me! Forgive me! Have pity! Have mercy on me! I suffer agony! torture! and such horror!

15 August.—This is exactly how my poor cousin was possessed and controlled that day when she tried to borrow the five thousand francs. She was acting under the influence of an alien will which had entered into her, like a second soul, another parasitical, overbearing soul. Is the world coming to an end?

What sort of creature is it who has taken control of me? He is invisible, unknowable: is he a roving member of some supernatural race?

So there are such things as creatures who are invisible! Then why, since the beginning of the world, have they never ever shown themselves clearly to others as they are now doing to me? I have never read anything which even remotely resembles what has been going on in my house. If only I could get out of here, go away, escape, and never return, I would be saved—but I cannot do it.

16 August.—I managed to escape today for a couple of hours, like a prisoner who finds that the door of his cell has been left unlocked by accident. I suddenly felt I was free and that he was far away. I ordered the horses to be

harnessed and reached Rouen. What a marvellous sensation it is to be able to say to a man 'Drive to Rouen' and see him obey!

I got him to stop outside the library where I asked to borrow the great treatise by Doctor Hermann Herestauss* on the unknown inhabitants of the ancient and modern worlds.

Then, just as I was about to climb back into my carriage, I tried to say: 'The station!' but I shouted—not said, shouted—so loudly that people passing by turned round: 'Home!' and I collapsed in panic and terror onto the upholstered seats of my carriage. He had found me and taken over again.

17 August.—What a night! What a terrible night! And yet I feel as though I have something to cheer about. I managed to read until one in the morning! Hermann Herestauss, doctor of philosophy and theogony, is the author of a history of the manifestations of all the invisible beings who have ever haunted man or been imagined by men. He describes their origin, their domain, and their powers. But not one of them is anything like the being who haunts me. It is as if men, from the moment they began to think, have always sensed the presence of a new kind of being whom they have feared, stronger than they are, who will one day be their successor in this world; and aware that this superior being is near, but unable to define its nature, they have created in their terror a whole host of occult beings and hazy phantoms which are born of fear.

So having read until one in the morning, I sat by my open window, to cool my head and my thoughts in the gentle breeze which blew out of the darkness.

It was very fine and pleasantly warm. There was a time when I loved such nights.

There was no moon. Against the blackness of the sky the stars sparkled and shimmered. Who lives in those far-off worlds? What forms of life, what kind of living creatures, what sort of animal and plants exist out there? Do the creatures who can think in those distant universes know any more than we do? What can they know that we do not?

What can they see that we have no knowledge of? Some day, will one of them travel through space and invade and conquer our planet just as the Normans once crossed the seas to subjugate weaker peoples?

We humans are weak, defenceless, ignorant, insignificant creatures who cling to a grain of sand which revolves in a drop of water.

Speculating thus in the cool night air, I dozed off.

When I had been asleep for perhaps forty minutes, I opened my eyes without moving, having been awoken by some kind of vague, rather peculiar sensation. At first I couldn't see anything, but all of a sudden I had this feeling that a page of the book I had left open on my table had turned over by itself. No breath of wind had come in from the window. Surprised, I sat and waited. After about four minutes, I saw, I really saw, with my very own eyes, another page rise and then settle back onto the previous one exactly as if a hand had turned it. My reading chair was empty, or at least it looked empty; but I knew that he was there, sitting in my seat, reading. I leaped up angrily, like a wild animal about to turn on its trainer and tear him to pieces, and rushed across the room intending to grab him, strangle him, kill him! . . . But before I could get there, my chair tipped over as if its occupant had got up to avoid me, my table rocked, my lamp fell over and went out, and my window closed as though a burglar I had disturbed had escaped into the night, banging it shut as he went.

So he had run away! He had been afraid, afraid of me!

It means that tomorrow, some other time, one of these days, I will be able to grab him with both hands and smash him to the ground. After all, dogs sometimes bite their masters; don't they go for the throat?

18 August.—I've spent the day thinking. I shall certainly obey him to the letter, follow his whims, do whatever he wants; I shall be humble, meek, abject. He may be stronger than I am. But there'll come a time . . .

19 August.—Now I know everything, everything! I have just read the following in *The World Scientific Review*:

'A rather curious report has just reached us from Rio de Janeiro. An outbreak or rather an epidemic of madness not unlike the contagious collective insanity which attacked the peoples of Europe in the Middle Ages, is currently raging in the province of San-Paulo. People are frantically leaving their homes, deserting their villages, and abandoning their crops, claiming that they are being controlled, possessed, and herded like so many human cattle by beings who are invisible but not intangible, a kind of vampire which feeds on their life-forces while they sleep but also drinks water and milk, though it does not appear to take nourishment of any other kind.

'Professor Don Pedro Henriquez, accompanied by a team of medical experts, has left for San-Paulo province. His purpose is to conduct a field-study of the causes and symptoms of this extraordinary outbreak of hysteria, and to recommend to the Emperor measures which, in his view, will prove most effective in restoring the sanity of the distraught population.'

Of course! Now I remember! I remember that magnificent Brazilian three-master which sailed past my house as it was being towed up the Seine on 8 May last! I thought she was so handsome and sparkling and gay! The thing must have been on board. It had come from over the sea, far away, where its kind originates! And it saw me! It saw my white house too. And it must have leaped ashore off the ship. Oh God!

Now I know, I understand: man's reign on earth is over.

The thing is here, the One so feared by early peoples in their primitive terrors! The One whom anxious priests fought with exorcisms! The One whom sorcerers summoned at dead of night but never did see. The One whom men with second sight, sensing the existence of these elusive masters of the world, clothed in grotesque or pleasant shapes in the form of goblins, ghosts, djinns, fairies, and sprites. Then after these crude inventions, which were a product of the terror-stricken minds of our first ancestors, came clearer-sighted men who detected his presence more clearly. Mesmer realized the truth and in the last ten years medical science has discovered in precise terms the nature of his power long before he came finally to use it himself. Doctors have toyed with the principal weapon in our new Lord's armoury: the power of a mysterious force of will over the enslaved human mind. They called it magnetism, hypnotism, suggestion . . . and other names besides. I have seen them playing with this ghastly force like unsuspecting children. Woe betide us! Mankind is doomed! He is here with us . . . the . . . the . . . what is his name? . . . the . . . I seem to hear him crying his name but I can't quite catch . . . the . . . yes! . . . he's shouting his name . . . I listen but I can't. . . . Say it again! . . . the . . . Horla.* . . . I hear it distinctly now . . . the Horla! He is the Horla! . . . and he has come! . . .

From the beginning, the vulture has eaten the dove; the wolf has eaten the lamb; the lion has devoured the sharp-horned buffalo; man has slain the lion with arrow, sword and gun. But the Horla will use man as we have used the horse and the ox: he will make us his chattel, his slave, and his food by using nothing more than the power of his will. Woe betide us!

Yet sometimes an animal will turn and kill its master! I too would like . . . and I know I can. . . . But first, I shall need to know what he is like, to touch him and see him! Scientists say that the eyes of animals are not the same as ours and they do not see as we do. My eyes cannot see the interloper who holds me in bondage.

Why can't I? Wait a moment, I remember now what the monk told me that day on the Mont Saint-Michel: 'Are we able to see a hundred-thousandth part of what exists? Look, the wind's getting up. Wind is the greatest natural force there is. It blows men off their feet, demolishes buildings, uproots trees, whips the sea into mountains of water, destroys cliffs, and drives great ships onto the rocks: it kills and shrieks and moans and roars. Have you ever seen it? Can you see it? And yet it exists all right.'

Then I thought: my eye is so weak and imperfect that it cannot even see solid objects when they are transparent, like glass! If a sheet of unsilvered glass bars my way, I blunder into it just as a bird that has got into a room hurls itself against the panes of the window. And there are a great many other things too which deceive and mislead the eye. Is it at all surprising, then, if it is unable to perceive a new kind of object through which light passes?

A new kind of being? No reason why not. It had to happen. There's absolutely no reason why we should be the last of creation. Why can't we see him the way we can see all the other creatures who came before us? Because he is more perfect by nature, because his body is made of finer stuff and is more finely wrought than ours which is so weak, badly designed, and clogged by organs which are perpetually overworked and strained like unnecessarily complex springs in a clock. In comparison, our bodies exist like plants and animals, and are inefficiently sustained by air, grass, and flesh, for they are animal machines constantly subject to sickness, crippling disease, and putrefaction, unreliable, badly tuned, primitive, and eccentric, ingeniously botched artefacts which are both crude and temperamental, like the prototype for a being who has the potential to become intelligent and magnificent.

There are not many created species, precious few on the whole earth, and the line runs from oysters to man. Why should not another kind of being emerge once the necessary time has elapsed between the appearance of one species and another?

Why not one more? Why not other types of trees with huge brilliant flowers which fill whole regions with new scents? Why not other elements besides earth, air, fire, and water? There are four of them, just four, and they are the sources on which all life feeds! It's lamentable! Why not forty, four hundred, four thousand? It's all so poor, petty, and miserly! it's all been so grudgingly given, skimped, and clumsily executed. Yet the elephant or the hippopotamus have such grace! and the camel such elegance!

But, you say, what about the butterfly, is it not a flower with wings? I can imagine a butterfly as large as a hundred universes, with wings whose shape, beauty, colour, and movement I couldn't begin to describe. But I can see it: it flits from star to star, reviving and perfuming each one with the harmonious, airy flutter of its flight! . . . And as it passes, planet-dwellers out there in space watch in an ecstasy of delight! . . .

. . . What's got into me? It's him! It's the Horla, haunting me, forcing me to think these crazy things! He has got inside me. He is taking possesion of my soul. I'll kill him!

19 August.*—I shall kill him. I've seen him. Yesterday evening I sat down at my desk and pretended to be completely absorbed in what I was writing. Of course, I knew he'd come prowling around—close, so close that perhaps I'd be able to touch him, even grab hold of him. And what if I managed to? I'd have the strength of desperation; I'd use everything, hands, legs, chest, head, teeth, to strangle and crush and bite and smash him to pieces!

I waited and watched with every sense on full alert.

I had lit both lamps and the eight candles on the mantelpiece, hoping that it would be bright enough for me to see him.

Facing me was my bed, an old oak four-poster; on the right, my fireplace; on the left, my door which I had carefully closed after leaving it open for long enough to attract his attention; at my back was a very tall wardrobe with a full mirror front which I use each morning for shaving and dressing and in which I normally glance at myself from head to foot every time I walk past.

So I was sitting there, pretending to write to allay his suspicions, for he too was watching me. Then all at once I sensed that he was there, reading over my shoulder, almost touching my ear.

I leaped up with my arms out and turned round so quickly that I almost fell over. And then . . . ? It was as bright as day, but I could not see myself in my mirror! . . . It was empty, very bright, bursting with light! But my reflection was not there . . . and I was standing directly in front of it! I could see the tall, clear glass from top to bottom. I stared at it in a panic, not daring to step forward, not daring to move, while all the time I sensed that he was there and that he had gobbled up my reflection. I knew he would escape me yet again.

I was absolutely terrified! And then all at once, in the depths of the mirror, I began to see myself through a mist, a swirling mist, as though I were looking through the ripples of a lake. And I had the impression of water slowly surging from left to right so that my reflection became clearer by the second. It was like the end of an eclipse. Whatever was hiding me did not have any well-defined shape, but a kind of opaque transparency which grew fainter and fainter.

Eventually, I was able to see all of myself, as I do every day when I look in the mirror.

I had seen him! The fear has stayed with me and I am still shaking.

20 August.—How am I to kill him, since I can't get to him? Poison? No; he'd see me putting it in the water. In any case, would the poisons we have be effective against his invisible body? No . . . definitely no. . . . But then how? How?

21 August.—I sent for a locksmith from Rouen and ordered metal shutters for my bedroom, the kind that private houses in Paris sometimes have on the ground floor as a precaution against burglars. I've also got him to make me a door to match. I've as good as said I am a coward, but I don't care!

10 September.—Hotel Continental, Rouen. It's done, done! But is he dead? My mind is still spinning after what I've seen.

Yesterday, after the locksmith had finished installing my shutters and my steel door, I left everything wide open until midnight, even though it was beginning to get cold.

Suddenly I felt that he was there, and I was filled with a wild sense of exultation. I stood up slowly and walked this way and that for some time, to throw him off the scent. Then I took off my boots and casually put on my slippers. Next I closed the metal shutters and, crossing the room unhurriedly, also closed the door which I double-locked. Returning to the window, I padlocked it and put the key in my pocket.

LE HORLA 301

All of a sudden, I sensed that he was circling me nervously, that he was also afraid, and that he was willing
me to let him out. I almost gave in to him, but I didn't.
Then, standing with my back against the door, I opened it a
little way, just wide enough to allow me to back out through
it. And since I am quite tall, my head touched the lintel. I
was convinced he couldn't possibly have got out, so I locked
him in by himself and left him there all alone. I exulted! I
had him! I ran down the stairs, went into my drawing-room
which is directly under my bedroom, took both my lamps,
and emptied all the oil onto the carpet, over the furniture,
over everything. I put a match to it and then got out of the
house fast, double-locking the great front door behind me.

I went and hid at the bottom of the garden in a clump of
laurel bushes. What a time it took! Everything was pitch
black, quiet, and still. Not a breath of wind, not one star,
but mountains of invisible clouds which lay heavy upon me
and crushed me beneath their weight.

I kept watching the house and I waited on. What an
unconscionable time it was taking. I was starting to think
that the fire had gone out by itself or that He had put it out,
when one of the ground-floor windows shattered under the
force of the heat, and a tongue of flame, a great red and
yellow, tall, languid, licking tongue of flame, shot up the
white wall and caressed it as it climbed to the roof. Shafts of
light ran through the trees, over branches and leaves, and
with them came a shudder of fear too. The birds awoke; a
dog began to howl; it felt as though day were about to
break. Almost immediately, another two windows shattered
and I saw that the whole of the ground floor of my house was
a blazing inferno! But then a scream, a horrible, high-
pitched, blood-curdling scream echoed in the night air, and
two attic windows were flung open! I had forgotten all about
the servants! I could see their frenzied faces and their arms
waving wildly . . .

Frantic with horror, I began running towards the village
bellowing: 'Help! Help! Fire! Fire!' As I ran, I met people
who were already on their way and I went back with them to
watch.

By this time the house was nothing but a ghastly, magnificent bonfire, a monstrous blazing heap which lit up the ground all around, a funeral pyre which was even then roasting the bodies of men—but also consuming Him, my prisoner, the New Being, the New Master, the Horla!

Suddenly the whole roof collapsed inwards and a volcano of flames leaped high into the sky. Through all the gutted windows that opened into the furnace, I could see a cauldron of fire, and I thought that he was there, in that blazing inferno, dead . . .

Dead! But perhaps. . . . What if he were not dead? But surely his body . . . ? But if light could pass through his body, was his body not indestructibly immune to the methods used to destroy ours?

What if he were not dead! Perhaps only time has any power over the Invisible, Deadly Lord. Why should he be given a transparent, unknowable body, a body made of spiritual matter, if like us he was going to have to fear pain, injury, infirmity, and premature death?

Premature death! It is the cause of every human fear. After man, the Horla. After man who may die any day, at any hour, at any moment, of accidents of every kind, has come He who will never die before his time, before the appointed hour, before the fixed moment, but only when he reaches the end of his natural life.

No. . . . No. . . . There is not, nor can there be, any doubt: he is not dead. Given that . . . this is so . . . . I shall obviously have no choice but to kill . . . myself.

EXPLANATORY NOTES

3 'Out on the River': first published as En canot in Le Bulletin français of 10 Mar. 1876; reprinted in La Maison Tellier (1881).

an all-consuming, irresistible passion: the river: in his 20s, Maupassant was himself mad about boats: like the hero of this tale, he too rented rooms on the river, went out rowing at night, and owned a heavy skiff. In Mouche (1890) he confessed: 'My great, my only, my all-absorbing passion for ten years of my life, was the Seine.' He remembered those years with great pleasure, and a number of the stories which follow are set on the Seine, around Argenteuil and Bezons, where young Parisian men and their shopgirls spent their Sundays and staider families went for outings. For Maupassant, the river was an exotic place of adventure but also a source of mystery. The river, and water generally, is the moody representative of nature, and he exploits its moods to demonstrate his view that civilization is precarious and that mankind is but a step removed from base animality.

4 a poet: Victor Hugo (1802–85), in Oceano Nox, of which the last five lines are quoted here.

10 'Simon's Dad': first published in La Réforme politique et littéraire, 1 Dec. 1879; reprinted in La Maison Tellier (1881).

19 'Family Life': first published in La Nouvelle Revue, 15 Feb. 1881; reprinted in La Maison Tellier (1881).

48 'A Farm Girl's Story': first published in La Revue politique et littéraire, 26 Mar. 1881; reprinted in La Maison Tellier (1881).

67 'A Day in the Country': first published in La Vie moderne, 2 and 9 April 1881; reprinted in La Maison Tellier (1881).

80 'Marroca': first published in Gil Blas, 2 Mar. 1882; reprinted in Mademoiselle Fifi (1882).

82 dressed . . . like Hassan: a reference to Namouna, an 'oriental poem' by Alfred du Musset (1810–57) which depicts Hassan reclining on a bearskin divan soft as a cat and fresh as a rose. Furthermore, Hassan is 'naked as Eve when first she sinned'.

90 'Country Living': first published in Le Gaulois, 31 Oct. 1882; reprinted in Les Contes de la bécasse (1883).

97 '*Riding Out*': first published in *Le Gaulois*, 14 Jan. 1883; reprinted in *Mademoiselle Fifi* (1882).

105 '*A Railway Story*': first published in *Le Gaulois*, 10 May 1883; reprinted in *Miss Harriet* (1884).

111 '*Old Milon*': first published in *Le Gaulois*, 22 May 1883; reprinted in *Le Père Milon* (1899).

118 '*Our Chum Patience*': first published in *Gil Blas*, 4 Sept. 1883; reprinted in *Toine* (1886).

119 *Le Temps*: founded in 1861, *Le Temps* was a highly respected, serious newspaper of moderate republican tendencies. It ceased publication in 1942.

122 *Paul et Virginie*: Bernardin de Saint Pierre's idyllic novel of virtue, set on the Island of Mauritius, was published in 1787. The presence of these engravings in Patience's house is an expression of Maupassant's contempt for the fraudulent sentimentality of his hypocritical age.

124 '*A Coup d'État*': first published in *Clair de lune* (1884).

the disaster at Sedan: war between France and Germany was declared on 19 July 1870. The French Army, considered to be the most powerful in Europe, was outmanœuvred before being crushingly defeated at Sedan which surrendered on 1 Sept. The French Emperor was taken prisoner the same day. Until June 1871, France continued to be rocked by the defeat, the collapse of the Empire, the peace, the declaration of the Third Republic, and, in May, the Paris Commune. Maupassant was mobilized immediately but never saw real action. Like many Frenchmen, he felt the bitter humiliation deeply and wrote nearly twenty war stories which castigate the incompetence of the army, snipe at the smugness of the comfortable middle classes, and champion the resistance put up by ordinary people such as Old Milon or the prostitutes of *Boule de Suif* or *Bed 29*. The Franco-Prussian war clarified long-standing tensions within French society. It ended the conservatism of Louis-Napoleon's Empire (1852–70) and cut short the fortunes of the Bourbon dynasty, symbolized by the white flag which the Mayor will brandish ironically at Monsieur de Varnetot. It also gave a highly charged political meaning to the cry 'Long live the Nation!', which became an expression of political opposition to the conservative establishment, and a statement of faith in the liberal, democratic, antimilitaristic, and anti-clerical tradition of the French Revolution of 1789.

135 *'The Christening'*: first published in *Le Gaulois*, 14 Jan. 1884; reprinted in *Miss Harriet* (1884).

140 *'Coco'*: first published in *Le Gaulois*, 21 Jan. 1884; reprinted in *Contes du jour et de la nuit* (1885).

145 *'A Coward'*: first published in *Le Gaulois*, 27 Jan. 1884; reprinted in *Contes du jour et de la nuit* (1885).

an ice at Tortoni's: founded early in the century, Tortoni's, on the corner of the rue Taitbout and the Boulevard des Italiens, was, by the 1880s, past its best as one of the city's most elegant cafés and was then known especially as a meeting place for followers of the turf.

151 *Chateauvillard's duelling code*: Maupassant, who was a very physical man, took a keen interest in 'manly' pursuits, and while he never fought a duel himself, he was attracted by combat both on a personal and on a literary level. The Comte de Chateauvillard's *Essai sur le duel* was published in 1836. The Baron de Vaux, who wrote articles for *Gil Blas*, published *Les Tireurs au pistolet* in 1883, with a preface by Maupassant who knew him well. Gastinne-Renette was one of the best-known gunsmiths in Paris, having a shop in the fashionable avenue d'Antin.

153 *'The Patron'*: first published in *Gil Blas*, 5 Feb. 1884; reprinted in *Toine* (1886).

154 *the Café Américain . . . everywhere*: these were the most fashionable and elegant cafés on or around the *boulevards*. The Café Américain was at no. 4, Boulevard des Capucines, and the Napolitain, at no. 1, was, like Tortoni's (see note to p. 145), famous for its ice cream. Bignon was the name of the proprietor of the Café de Foy on the Boulevard des Italiens, where were also situated the Café Riche (no. 16) and the Helder (no. 19) which were popular with journalists and writers. At no. 13, the Café des Anglais was known for the quality of its wines, while the nearby Maison d'Or (usually known as the Maison Dorée because of its gilt balconies) still enjoyed a reputation for its cuisine, and for its fish dishes in particular.

159 *'The Umbrella'*: first published in *Le Gaulois*, 10 Feb. 1884; reprinted in *Les Sœurs Rondoli* (1884).

166 *new Government matches*: in 1875, in the generally protec-
tionist economic climate of the early Third Republic, the
manufacture and sale of matches were made a State mono-
poly. It was widely believed that 'Government matches' were
inferior in quality to the old, imported variety.

168 *'The Necklace'*: first published in *Le Gaulois*, 17 Feb. 1884;
reprinted in *Contes du jour et de la nuit* (1885).

177 *'Strolling'*: first published in *Gil Blas*, 27 May 1884; reprinted
in *Yvette* (1885).

183 *'Bed 29'*: first published in *Gil Blas*, 8 July 1884; reprinted in
Toine (1886).

   why his hair had fallen out: in 1877 Maupassant complained to
Turgenev of a loss of hair which he attributed to a stomach
disorder. To Flaubert, the following year, he wrote several
times that he was losing his hair which, however, subsequently
regrew: in 1889 Blanche Roosevelt, an American admirer,
noted that 'his hair, brown and wavy, is now combed straight
back in the fashion of modern Roman youth'. It is more than
likely that Maupassant's temporary baldness was an early
symptom of the syphilis which eventually drove him insane.
Captain Epivent's baldness is quite likely to have the same
cause, in which case his behaviour towards Irma becomes
even more objectionable.

184 *Bourbaki*: Charles Bourbaki (1816–97) saw distinguished
service in the Crimean War and acquired a reputation as one
of the most daring and capable officers in the French Army.
This is how Captain Epivent sees him in 1868. However,
Bourbaki subsequently became involved in a variety of
reactionary activities and the reader of 1884 is thus encouraged
to see in Epivent's admiration for him a bravado which was
old-fashioned and out of step with the new Republican times.

193 *more Prussians than you ever did*: the theme of 'revenge sex'
was not, of course, new, either in literature or in history.
Bachaumont's *Mémoires secrets* (6 July 1782) mentions a
'Mademoiselle La Forêt, a former courtesan, who claims to
know all there is to know about the various modes of
prostitution as practised by all nations. During the struggle
for Grenada, it was said that the actual taking of the Island
cost Great Britain the lives of fewer soldiers than the much
larger number who died of her infected embraces.'

195 *'The Gamekeeper'*: first published in *Le Gaulois*, 8 Oct. 1884; reprinted in *Yvette* (1885).

203 *'The Little Roque Girl'*: first published in *Gil Blas*, 18–23 Dec. 1885; reprinted in *La Petite Roque* (1886).

225 *Saint Anthony*: the story of the trials of Saint Anthony was well known but had been revived by Flaubert's *La Tentation de Saint-Antoine* (1874). Flaubert, Maupassant's guide and mentor, shows Saint Anthony alone in the desert, reviewing old temptations and assailed by new ones, including intellectual doubt and erotic visions. The allusion makes Renardet's plight dramatically clear.

228 *regulating social relationships*: the *philosophes* of the eighteenth century sought to free mankind from the shackles of religion, and the *Encyclopédie* (1751–72) was intended to be a vast compendium of knowledge angled towards rational enlightenment. Representing applied rather than pure reason, they were regarded as precursors of the scientific positivism of the nineteenth century. Those who regretted the *ancien régime* formed the clerical, pro-establishment, and often monarchical right wing; the supporters of the goals of the Revolution of 1789 tended to be liberals who believed in democracy and the Rights of Man. When set against his generally authoritarian and not very liberal behaviour, Renardet's social views place him squarely in the ranks of the new middle class which throve during the period of the Empire. Maupassant's own view of the eighteenth century was compounded of admiration for Voltaire and the 'philosophic' movement and a hankering after the refined elegance (see *Our Chum Patience*) for which the society of the *ancien régime* was notorious.

239 *'Mademoiselle Pearl'*: first published in *Le Figaro*, 16 Jan. 1886; reprinted in *La Petite Roque* (1886).

to be my queen: in France, *La Fête des Rois*, that is Epiphany or Twelfth Night, is regarded not only as an important religious festival but also an occasion for a more general family celebration which traditionally features a Twelfth-cake. An object—a 'bean'—is placed inside the 'gâteau des rois' and the person lucky enough to find it in his piece of cake elects a 'king' or a 'queen' for the evening and together they order the jollifications which follow.

241 *the Tonkin business*: in the second half of the nineteenth century, France, slow to wake up to the economic and

political advantages of having an overseas empire, sought expansion and influence especially in North Africa and Indo-China. A treaty signed in June 1885 made Annam a French protectorate, but French involvement had dragged on inconclusively, attracted much criticism at home, and caused the fall of Jules Ferry's government in March 1885. Maupassant several times expressed his extreme hostility to the policy of colonial expansion.

256 *'Rosalie Prudent'*: first published in *Gil Blas*, 2 Mar. 1886; reprinted in *La Petite Roque* (1886).

261 *'Our Spot'*: first published in *Gil Blas*, 9 Nov. 1886; reprinted in *Le Horla* (1887).

265 *Gil Blas*: Maupassant cheekily provides a puff for the magazine in which this story was first published. According to Louis Forestier, there were at least two journalists, both men, who used the pseudonym 'Colombine' in *Gil Blas*, but he points out further that same name was also regularly used by any number of staff writers. Renard's assumption that 'Colombine' was a woman only adds, of course, to the joke.

266 *Bazaine*: François-Achille Bazaine (1811–88) was given command of the main French armies in August 1870, a month after the outbreak of the Franco-Prussian war. He suffered a number of severe defeats and withdrew to Metz which was besieged. Bazaine finally surrendered on 27 October and emerged as the national scapegoat. In 1873 he was court-martialled for military inertia and for failing to do his duty: he was condemned to degradation and death, though the sentence was later commuted to twenty years' detention on the Ile Sainte Marguerite, which lies off the French coast near Cannes. He contrived to escape in 1874 and fled to Italy where he died in 1888. The name of Bazaine became synonymous with the military humiliation of France.

269 *'Clochette'*: first published in *Gil Blas*, 21 Dec. 1886; reprinted in *Le Horla* (1887).

275 *'Le Horla'*: first published in *Le Horla* (1887).

283 *Alexandre Dumas fils*: Dumas fils (1824–95) began his career as a prolific novelist, but with the stage version of *La Dame aux camélias* (1852) became one of the most performed playwrights of his century. He specialized in the 'play of ideas' and expressed opinions on a variety of social issues which, after about 1870, became increasingly reactionary.

(Thus, on the 'feminist question', he concluded wearily that 'women should be given the vote: it's the only way of making them harmless'.) Maupassant knew him, shared a number of his opinions, and here pays him an elegant compliment.

285 *hypnosis and suggestion*: though there was a general vogue for hypnotism at the time, Maupassant had, since the early 1880s, been particularly interested in the power of suggestion and in the new analyses of mental illness. He followed the work of Jean-Martin Charcot (1825–93) who studied cases of neurosis and hysteria at the hospital of La Salpêtrière. For a while Freud attended his classes, and Maupassant heard him lecture. Though he was not convinced by Charcot, he used some of his ideas—on hypnotism, for example—in the continuing flow of nightmare and horror stories. The 'English researchers', active especially during the 1840s, were led by James Braid, while the 'Nancy School' was founded in 1866 by Liébeau and directed in Maupassant's day by Bernheim: together they had rehabilitated hypnotism as a respectable form of treatment ('medicine without drugs and operations without incisions') which was further enhanced by Charcot's reputation as one of the world's leading neurologists.

returned the compliment: this comment, from the commonplace book which he called his *Sottisier*, shows Voltaire in the mood which Maupassant most admired: cynical, ironic, and bleak.

Mesmer: Anton Mesmer (1733–1815) developed a theory of 'animal magnetism' based on the idea that the universe is filled with a magnetic fluid which conveys strong astral influences. He constructed a cauldron-like contraption with rods which, when held by patients, transmitted the influence which he intensified by using hypnotic techniques. He settled in Paris in 1778 and quickly acquired a European reputation. In 1785 his work was investigated by a commission of eminent scientists who concluded that 'magnetism without imagination produces nothing'. Mesmer was exposed as a charlatan and the techniques he had pioneered were discredited until interest in them revived in the middle of the nineteenth century.

294 *Herman Herestauss*: the name, like the book, is an invention and, it has been suggested, may be a mixture of two German words, *Her[r]* and *aus*, that is, 'he-who-is-outside', like the Horla himself. See note to p. 297.

310 EXPLANATORY NOTES

297 *the Horla*: a number of ingenious suggestions have been put
forward to explain Maupassant's choice of this word, but it
seems most likely that some combination of *hors* [= out] and
là [= there] is intended to start a train of association leading to
the concept of 'alien' or 'outsider'.

299 *19 August*: this date appears twice in the text, presumably in
error.

APPENDIX

MAUPASSANT AS SEEN BY HIS CRITICS

1. 'Monsieur de Maupassant will never know the pain of regret: the moment he touches a thing, he is quite ready to let it drop. He has never felt, and never will feel, that need for tenderness which torments us all. There are feelings which are quite beyond his scope: he is emotionally impotent' (Georges de Porto-Riche, 1849–1930).

2. 'Ever since hearing the news [of Maupassant's admission to the madhouse], I cannot get out of my head a remark made by Saint-Just: "He who is without friends shall die!" Maupassant never loved anything, not his art, not a flower, nothing! He has been struck down by poetic justice!' (Octave Mirbeau, 1848–1917).

3. 'Monsieur de Maupassant has simply skipped the whole reflective part of his men and women—that reflective part which governs conduct and produces character. . . . The author fixes a hard eye on some spot of human life, usually some dreary, ugly, shabby, sordid one, takes up the particle, and squeezes it either till it grimaces or till it bleeds. Sometimes the grimace is very droll, sometimes the wound is very horrible. . . . Monsieur de Maupassant sees human life as a terribly ugly business relieved by the comical' (Henry James, 1843–1916).

4. 'Monsieur de Maupassant, at least, has never flattered human nature. He has never scrupled to ride roughshod over our optimism and spit on our cherished ideals. And he has always set about it with such honesty and straightforwardness, with a heart that is so simple and staunch, that no one can really find him objectionable. . . . Moreover, he does not go in for ideas: he is neither subtle nor does he provoke. And his talent is so powerful, his touch so sure and so marvellously daring that you might as well just sit back and let him say whatever he has to say' (Anatole France, 1844–1924).

5. 'I believe that Maupassant is one of our greatest born-storytellers. A little lacking in stamina and narrow in range, he is nevertheless an excellent writer, an ingenious deviser of plots, an unequalled master of his craft who always remains at the point where realism meets poetry and who has demonstrated in the most emphatic way that he has a sense of the tragedy of everyday life which, for me, is always a sign that a writer has the novelist's true temperament' (Roger Martin du Gard, 1881–1958).

6. 'Maupassant's literary fortunes constitute a very interesting chapter in the history of literature. He was the most popular of all French writers of his time, after Zola; at the turn of the century, he became a victim of developments which took place in the novel: thereafter, new tastes, partly shaped by the influence of Freud and Proust, gradually turned French readers against an author whom they long held in such high esteem' (Artine Artinian).

7. 'Chekhov, only ten years younger than Maupassant, provides the nearest comparison. They both possessed equally the gift of simplicity and economy, that of cutting to the bone with grace; and they were equally sensitive to trifling details that acquire significance in their proper setting. Yet Chekhov, however discreet, however objective in his style, always noticeably shared in the sufferings of his characters and particularly in their melancholia. He may have been more human, more sympathetic, more poetic than Maupassant; but he was less perfect in his craft' (Paul Ignotus).

8. 'It could be said that if Maupassant never wrote about faithful wives, or devoted or intellectual women, it was because he needed to please his readers who preferred stories about whores. . . . I believe that Maupassant wrote exactly what he wished to write, and that his choice of female characters reflects his own view of women. It would be too easy to deceive ourselves, and quite pointless to do so, by saying that he set his sights too high and asked too much of women not to be disappointed, for why should he not have described his ideal? The plain fact is that Maupassant took a dim view of women. He attributed two roles to her: love and motherhood—and then hardly ever spoke of motherhood' (Lorraine Gaudefroy-Demombynes).

9. 'As a freelance writer, Maupassant could not afford to write just for a literary élite and needed to exploit his talent to live; he wrote in the manner and form he did for the newspapers and periodicals who paid him and for their readers. In so doing, he virtually resuscitated the short story and gave it both a literary form and a new popularity. The fact that his stories and novels are today as exciting, provoking or amusing as they were when they first appeared shows that, while his life is representative of his age, his work belongs to the age of classic literature' (Michael Lerner).